Patti Davis is the daught
She is an actress as well
three novels and an autobiography. She lives in Connecticut.

Bondage

Patti Davis

WARNER BOOKS

A *Warner* Book

First published in the USA
by Simon & Schuster, Inc in 1994
This edition published in Great Britain
by Warner Books in 1994

A CIP catalogue record for this book
is available from the British Library.

ISBN 0 7515 0994 9

Typeset by Hewer Text Composition Services, Edinburgh
Printed and bound in Great Britain by
Clays Ltd, St Ives plc

Warner Books
A Division of
Little, Brown and Company (UK)
Brettenham House
Lancaster Place
London WC2E 7EN

Acknowledgments

THANK YOU to Michael Korda and Chuck Adams for taking such good care of me; Michael for bringing a white owl into my garden, and Chuck for having such a great phone voice. And to Flip Brophy for going beyond agenting and being a friend as well. To Michael Grecco, for getting me through another photo session and for once again making it fun. Thanks to Gail Abarbanel at Rape Treatment Center, Santa Monica Hospital, for being available; Michael White for answering a lot of lawyer questions; Stephanie Locke for answering a lot of bondage questions. I'm also eternally grateful to Molly White and Paul Sand for getting into the story and offering their feedback.

Prologue

SOMETIMES WE turn a corner in our lives and everything changes. A stranger is standing there – in sun or in shadow, it doesn't matter. He is there for us. He moves the pieces on the board when we're not looking, wipes tears from our eyes when we thought we were laughing and places them on our tongue so we'll recognize the taste, wince at the saltiness.

It happens in the most carefully planned lives, the most protected. Lives that have put miles around them, that have been built far out in the wilderness under the naive assumption that no hunters will find them. But lives like that are already an endangered species. In hunting season, they're the first to go.

Sara would eventually see her life this way, and examine the interior parts of herself, testing for reflexes, searching for what was still alive and what had died. Something had died, that much she knew, but by then so much time had gone by.

There are questions that need to be asked at just the right moment, or they might as well not be asked at all – she knew that, too.

There were many questions she should have asked

Belinda, and even more things that she should have shared with her. They were friends – best friends – yet she'd kept quiet, silently cutting some of the strings that are supposed to keep friends together. Now when she thinks about it, she doesn't see strings; she sees lifelines, severed by all the things she didn't say.

Sometimes when it rains, Sara thinks she hears Belinda, coming up behind her – cowboy boots clomping on the wet sidewalk. She turns, but of course it's someone else – another girl with boots beneath her long, gathered skirt, hair frosted with rain, red fingernails holding her raincoat together, mascara smudged a little from the dampness.

It was raining the first time Sara almost told Belinda everything, all that had been going on. She'd almost described how, the night before, she'd been on the floor, her legs spread wide, her skin damp – steaming almost, she thought. She had lifted her head to look down at her thighs, and between, where she was still wet and glistening. Her wrists still remembered the whisper of silk around them, even though Anthony had untied the bonds a while ago. It's the same thing, she'd wanted to tell Belinda. We've both gone through the same thing, even though on the surface it all looks so different.

It's all about surrender. It's about wondering whether fear or trust is leading you, and whether or not it matters. It's about wondering if you were ever younger than this, or if you will ever be older, because there is a circle drawn around one single moment, and time exists outside the circle like a dream you can't remember. It's about lying down with danger and closing your eyes. It's about opening your eyes and seeing him above you, and not being able to imagine it any other way. Was there ever a time when you weren't saying yes to him?

But she'd said nothing. The rain came down between them and Sara watched as Belinda raced down the wet sidewalk.

It's often the people who are the strongest, who have spent years guarding the soft spots of their souls, who willingly approach the stranger as they round the corner. They think he's not there for them. Until they discover that he is. He always was. But by then it's too late. One day, they search their own inner landscapes and find his fingerprints everywhere. And no matter how hard it rains, the fingerprints stay.

The only thing Sara was certain of was that she would never again be as safe, as protected, as she had once believed she was.

One

Sara

IT WAS 1965. Sara was eleven years old. America was losing its innocence – fine, white hopes scattered by a wind no one was prepared for. The storm had begun two years earlier, with a bullet fired from the Book Depository, or from the grassy knoll, depending on which theory you believed. Sara was losing her innocence too, although not quite as quickly as America.

Over the radio, Petula Clark was singing "Downtown." Sonny and Cher were singing "I Got You, Babe." Sara thought Cher was much cooler than Petula Clark – so did her brother, Mark, three years older and Sara's barometer for what cool was all about.

It was the year Martin Luther King marched in Alabama, from Selma to Montgomery, protesting discrimination against blacks. Sara knew this because her parents talked about it; their world was bigger than hers. She knew there were rumblings in the country around her – a war being protested, people losing sons – but the world that was real to her was the San Fernando Valley neighbourhood where her parents had lived for fifteen years. It used to look different, they told her – more space between the houses, more orchards.

"Used to be sorta like the country out here," her father said, usually when he was behind the wheel of their beige Cadillac that had so many miles on it Sara's mother said God must like cars, otherwise this one would be dead. "Damn roads and houses just taking over" was her father's frequent lament. Despite his complaints, some hints of what had been remained. There were still groves of orange and avocado trees in the neighborhood, plenty of room for a child to roam and explore.

Nineteen sixty-five was the year Sara saw what loneliness looked like. She had driven with her family to Palm Springs one weekend to visit her grandparents, she and Mark in the backseat, their parents in front, in the Cadillac that owed its life to the God-of-automobiles. After a long, boring weekend, they drove back late Sunday night, through miles of flat desert, the highway slicing through – a narrow ribbon through miles of nothing. Headlights punctured the dark, and the road seemed to go on forever. To Sara, it became the look of loneliness: a dark highway cutting through vast stretches of flat land.

The image trailed her for years afterward, like the headlights had trailed the darkness on that long drive back to Los Angeles. At times she felt she was the highway and the acreage on either side was her life – dark and monotonous, speeding by outside the window.

It was also the year Sara's education about boys began, in the orange grove behind her house. It was May. The orange trees were blossoming; their perfume left sweet trails along the streets and drifted through windows as families sat down to dinner in the late blue twilight. In spring the days were long enough that there was still time to play outside after dinner – just until the stars pricked pinholes in the sky and mothers stood at back doors, calling for their children.

Her friends had always been boys – specifically, three boys who lived in her neighborhood, and who went to the same school. Sara wasn't interested in girl things like dolls, or tea parties, or playing with her mother's lipstick. She understood boys, or thought she did, and she could hold her own with them. She could hit a baseball as hard, run as fast – usually faster – wrestle, pick up bugs, and throw spitballs. She couldn't, however, pee like a boy; she'd tried that at age five, out in the front yard. She'd seen Mark pee into the bushes, so the front yard seemed perfectly appropriate to her. But her mother dragged her into the house, washed her off, and demanded to know "just what in God's green earth" had gotten into her.

"Boys do it like that," Sara had said.

"Well, you're not a boy."

"Why aren't I?"

"I've been wondering that myself," her mother had answered.

She'd learned a lot about boys from listening to Mark and his friends – not eavesdropping exactly, but hanging around them so often that after a while they just forgot she was there. She looked over their shoulders while they panted over the *Playboy* magazines Mark kept hidden under his bed. She memorized the dialogue that photographs of naked women seemed to inspire in teenage boys.

"Man, I could get it up for her," one of his friends said one day, gazing at a picture of a woman with breasts so large Sara was certain the woman could never sleep on her stomach.

"What does that mean – get it up?" Sara asked. She

tried not to ask too many questions, but sometimes she just had to.

Mark and his two friends giggled. "You know," the boy said, pointing at his crotch. "It has to get up before you can use it."

Later, when she was alone with Mark, he explained it in more detail, which Sara found illuminating but a little irritating. Why did boys get to have bodies that changed like that? Hers never did. Although maybe she just hadn't noticed. She locked herself in the bathroom one day, took off her jeans, sat in front of the mirror, and waited for something to happen. After an hour, when nothing did, she got bored and decided that being a boy had to be a lot more fun.

Sometimes boys' language was completely baffling – not only to her, but apparently to boys, too. She overheard a friend of Mark's saying that he'd tried to "beat off" – like the guys always talked about. He'd gone out to the garage and beat his penis with a stick. The boys who were gathered in Mark's room roared with laughter, and then threw Sara out so they could explain to their poor bruised friend what he'd done wrong. Listening outside the door, Sara thought he'd made an understandable mistake. Why didn't they just say what they meant in the first place?

On a spring evening in 1965, with the sky bending into night, Sara learned that her education in the world of boys was still incomplete. There was much more to learn.

"You're supposed to count to ten!" she yelled, her voice bouncing between the trees and the soft, brown soil. Jerome, Tommy, and Lane were chasing her, and it was a game she usually won; her legs were longer and she was twice as fast. She probably didn't even need the ten-count lead, but they gave it to her anyway because that was the rule someone had decided upon. Except on this evening, the count of five was followed by the sound of running feet. Sara ran faster, her breath scraping through her throat as she darted around trees, avoiding a few fallen oranges that were rotting on the ground. They were getting closer; she could hear them panting now. But she was sure she'd win again, even though they seemed to be getting faster every week. She was almost to the edge of the grove – the lights of houses were blinking up ahead of her – when she tripped over a tree root. Before she could get up, they were on her.

"What are you doing? Get off – goddamn it!" she shouted as the three boys piled on top of her.

She managed to turn over on her back and start to flail at them with her arms, but Tommy pinned her arms down and Lane sat on her legs. A shudder passed through her as she realized this wasn't a game anymore . . . but she wasn't sure what it was. Above her, the sky was turning a deep blue; any minute, she would be able to see the stars. The smell of orange blossoms was thick in her head.

"Okay, Jerome, you gotta do it now!" Lane shouted, still at her legs, holding them now by her ankles.

"Goddamn it! Get off!" Sara screamed again, her throat feeling dry and cracked.

But she knew they wouldn't stop – they had a plan. Jerome – it was perfect that their plan had him at its center. Jerome was smaller than the other two boys; he wore thick glasses and did whatever Tommy and Lane told him to do. And he was following their orders now, moving toward Sara, toward her legs – everything suddenly going into slow motion. A breeze rattled the leaves above her and she could feel Lane's fingers digging into her ankles as Jerome unzipped his pants and fell to his knees.

"You little bastard," Sara hissed, "you'll never be able to do it."

Jerome's hands, trembling and damp, tugged at her underpants, and then he was trying to push into her. But he was soft and obviously nervous.

"Come on, Jerome – do it – stick it in her," Tommy shouted, his fingernails scratching Sara's wrists.

"You little wimp," she said, through clenched jaws. "You'll never do it – you can't."

Jerome's breath was fast and warm and smelled like licorice. Sara knew she was winning – he'd never do it. He was still trying to stuff himself into her, his hands fumbling between her legs, but he was scared now. His face was next to her breasts and Sara lifted her head and spit at him; she watched it hit his glasses and roll down. Behind the spit trail, his eyes were wide and frozen, like an animal staring down the barrel of a gun.

"Come on, come on," Lane said. "What's the matter with you, Jerome – do it!"

"He can't, you asshole!" Sara shouted back. "Can you, Jerome?"

She started laughing then, because she knew it wasn't going to happen – hard, angry, relieved laughter that made tears spring from her eyes.

Shocked at this outburst, Lane and Tommy loosened their hold on her. Jerome stood up, his pants bunched up around his ankles, his penis soft and sad against his thigh – giving him away, announcing his failure. His face crumpled and tears streamed down into his mouth; he pulled up his pants and ran away through the orchard.

"Go home and cry to your mother, you little baby!" Sara shouted after him.

She slid her underpants back onto her hips and stood

up, damp soil clinging to her back. Tommy and Lane looked frightened, frozen in the path of this new rage that was coming at them like a truck with the brakes gone.

"What about you two? Are you afraid you couldn't do it either? Is that why you made Jerome try it? You couldn't, you wimps!" Sara shoved Lane backward; her hand hit his chest with a slapping sound.

"Chickenshits!" She turned and walked away, leaving the two boys among the orange trees, with night feathering around them. Somewhere past the shadows, mothers were standing under porch lights, calling to their children.

Sara's mother was standing at the sink washing string beans.

"Better get to your homework," she said to the sound of the back door opening and closing. Sara tried to make the sound seem ordinary, not angry or hurried. She didn't want her mother to turn around.

"I'm going to do it now," she said casually. She realized, as she moved through the kitchen, that her mother often addressed her with her back turned. She was always leaning over the sink or bending over a bed she was making. Sara knew her mother's back; it had thickened over the years, changed shape. It curved now between her shoulder blades. "Dowager's hump" her mother called it, as though this were an inevitable symptom of age.

When Sara thought of her father, she thought of his hands – rough, callused, the fingernails always a little ragged. He installed air conditioners and heaters in people's homes and was always crawling underneath houses or up in attics. At this point in his life, his hands looked strong but tired.

Sara loved her parents, but she couldn't really talk to them. Instead she'd run to Mark, who always seemed to know how to smooth whatever edges were cutting her at the moment. But first she had to get past his bedroom door, and the poster of Muhammad Ali, gloved fists raised. "Don't come in, or else" was the message it imparted. Sara knew it didn't really apply to her, but she was respectful of it anyway.

On this evening, Mark's door was ajar and he heard her footsteps in the hall.

"Hey, come in here." His voice snagged her before she could disappear into the bathroom.

Sara walked into his room and shut the door behind her. She didn't sit down because she would have left a dark smudge of dirt on whatever she touched.

"What the hell happened to you?" Mark said.

"They tried to make Jerome . . . do it to me."

"Do what?"

"You know. *It*."

Mark sat down on the bed, his brown eyes fixed on her. He ran one hand through his dark hair while his other hand tensed, curled into a fist against his thigh.

"Who?" he said, his voice tight.

"Lane and Tommy. He didn't do it, though. I mean, he tried, but he couldn't."

Mark stood up and came over to her; he wrapped his arms around her and pulled her against him. She could smell Old Spice – it was a recent thing, this addition of aftershave, and she was still getting used to it. She didn't fully understand these things, but she knew that Mark was special. She saw how college girls in convertibles slowed down and stared at him sometimes, ignoring or perhaps enchanted by his youth.

"Go get cleaned up," he said to Sara. "We'll talk about it tomorrow. And this is just between us, okay?"

"Yeah – okay."

Clouds moved in the next day; a spring storm was gathering. Mark and Sara went to the orchard in the evening, the thick air sticking to them, the perfume from the trees rolling past them in waves.

"Maybe they won't come," Sara said.

"Then we'll go find them."

She looked at her brother's arms folded across his chest and thought of how many times they had folded around her and made her feel safe. Mark was always there to protect her from the world – to lift it off her when she was in danger of being crushed. Atlas coming to the rescue whenever the sky started to fall.

She heard their voices at the same moment Mark did – Tommy and Lane – Jerome's voice wasn't part of the sound, but he might be there, trailing silently behind.

Mark's arms dropped to his side when they came into view – two skinny boys, ten years old and trying to be older. Sara almost started laughing again.

"Hey, boys," Mark called out. Seeing him, they stopped, a small cloud of dust rising up where their feet hit a wall of fear and couldn't move forward.

Mark walked over to them, Sara close behind. "Okay – whose idea was that yesterday?" he asked.

"Lane's," Tommy blurted out.

"You fink," Lane said and then, turning to Mark,

putting on an I-don't-care face, added, "so what? She didn't get hurt."

"I don't really think that's the point," Mark said, moving a little closer. "Do you think that's the point, Sara?"

"No."

In one quick lunge, Mark grabbed Lane's arms and pinned them behind his back. Lane's face started to change then; his mouth quivered and his forehead squeezed in on itself and grew smaller.

"You can do whatever you want to him, Sara," Mark told her, his eyes staring hard at her.

"What do you mean?" She wanted guidance, instructions.

"Just what I said."

She looked at Lane, who was twisting vainly against Mark's strong grip, and her hand made the decision for her. It closed into a fist, almost involuntarily, and she walked over to Lane, stood less than an arm's length away, and swung at his face. She felt the bone of his nose crack under her knuckles, saw blood on her hand when she pulled it back. His mouth opened to scream, but only breath came out at first.

When the scream finally came, it ripped through the thick gray air, ragged and full of pain. Sara felt it in her bones. And then everything around them moved. Tommy turned and ran back through the trees, Mark let go of Lane, who slumped to the ground, holding his nose, trying to stop the red stream that was gushing from it, and the sky shivered and let go a wash of rain that trickled across the blood on Sara's knuckles.

It was dark when they got back from the orange grove. Sara went into her room and closed the door so she could stare at her hand in private. Her knuckles were bruised, a faint smudge of blue spreading out under the skin, and there was still a smear of blood on one finger. She knew her hand would always remember the feel of Lane's nose cracking under its force; the rain hadn't washed that away, and neither would time. She wasn't sure she liked the feeling.

The rain had become a steady downpour by then. Sara opened the window and stood in front of it, facing the dark, letting drops bounce off the sill onto her shirt. Like Scarlett O'Hara resolving never to be hungry again, she resolved never again to be fooled by boys. She would get to know them so well that nothing they did would take her by surprise. She obviously had some things to learn. For one thing, she had assumed that these boys were too old to cry; this was because she assumed that men didn't cry. That men *couldn't* cry. She thought boys reached a certain age and went through some sort of metamorphosis in which they lost the capacity for tears – their tear ducts just dried up, or fell out like baby teeth. She wasn't sure *how* wrong she was about this – maybe she'd just gotten the time frame wrong. She'd never seen Mark cry; certainly her father seemed incapable of tears – she'd have to ask Mark about it.

She also believed that men didn't dream – she'd have to check on that one, too, because she could be wrong again. She'd reached this conclusion one day when she told her father about a dream she'd had. In it, she was walking along a beach at night; moonlight was silvering the waves, and it was so bright she could see her shadow on the sand. Jesus was walking toward her, and it seemed perfectly natural that he should be there. They sat down together on the sand, stared out at the ocean, and talked. Sara told him about how, just that afternoon, she'd made ten baskets in a row while she was practicing out in the driveway. She'd challenged herself by moving a little farther from the hoop with each shot. Then she told him about the rabbit she saw at the pet store, and how badly she wanted it. Jesus didn't really say much; he just listened, which didn't surprise her either. She'd always figured that he would be a good listener. They got up and walked away from each other before the moon had sailed across the sky.

When she finished telling her father about this dream, she looked at him expectantly, proud of herself for having shared such an exquisite secret with him. He gave her a crinkled look and said, "Well, that's sure a strange one." It was his only comment. Her conclusion – because it was the least painful one she could come up with – was that men didn't dream, so of course he couldn't understand. But now she wasn't so sure. Maybe her father's sleep was filled with things he didn't want to talk about. Maybe it was just that girls shared their dreams and men pretended not to have any.

At school the next day, Lane sat behind Sara in class, his eyes ringed with bruises like a sad raccoon, and a white bandage dividing his face in half. Sara knew he hadn't told anyone what happened, because then he'd have to answer for what he'd done to her.

"We're even, okay?" Sara whispered to him in the hall.

Lane nodded, looking at her through the dark swelling around his eyes, and she knew she had won. These are the rules, she was telling him. An eye for an eye – so to speak.

Two days later, Sara lost her voice. It went suddenly, in the middle of the night. She started coughing, couldn't stop, and when her mother came in to check on her, she tried to speak and couldn't. Her vocal cords could only produce a whisper. The doctor told her she had to rest her voice and her father bought her a small notepad on a string to hang around her neck, with a pencil attached by another string. She didn't really use the notepad, except at the dinner table – notes like "pass the peas," or "don't take the last ear of corn, Mark."

She sank into her voiceless world, aware that her other senses picked up the slack, became heightened. She heard more, saw more – learned more, which was really what she wanted. It was the closest she could come to being invisible, which she'd always thought would be an exciting adventure, at least for a day or two. Because if she were invisible, she'd be the best spy around.

There are junctures in one's life when a shift happens; something penetrates deeply and things are changed forever. Time shifts gears – speeds up or slows down – according to its own whim. Morning slants through the window at a different angle, and night feels thicker, strangely quiet. Childhood noises no longer interfere. The man under the bed has turned silent, his breath no longer pushes against the darkness, and cars passing on the highway no longer sound like the ocean.

Sara would always look back on the spring of her twelfth year as one of those times. Years later, the smell of orange blossoms would still trigger memories – of her arms and legs pinned, her throat dry and frightened; or of her hand drawing back and whistling forward, the bone of Lane's nose cracking like a toothpick under her knuckles.

And she would remember the feel of her vocal cords refusing to come together the way they should, refusing to produce a voice. It gave her distance, the sense of hanging back at the sidelines, so silent that people forgot she was there. But she was there – watching, listening, taking it all in, learning how never to be fooled again. In time her voice would come back, but the ability to stand apart – observing, spying – would never leave her.

Sara began hanging around with Mark and his friend Bill, getting to know cars and the language of boys. Her parents would raise their eyebrows when she came home with grease smudges on her clothes, but Claire and Roger Norton were too demure to ask too many questions. They believed in gentle coaxing, not interrogations – although Sara could feel her mother's eyes trailing her through the house, wondering why her only daughter was acting more and more like a boy.

"You're going out with Mark again?" her mother would ask.

"Yeah – he doesn't mind."

"Maybe you could invite some of the girls from your class over."

"I'd rather be with Mark and his friends," Sara would answer, knowing she was confusing her mother, and probably worrying her.

It wasn't until Sara was fourteen that her mother gave up her coaxing. But there was a final push before she surrendered. It had to do with Sara's long, stringy hair and her wardrobe of ripped jeans and T-shirts handed down to her by Mark.

"I have an idea," her mother said one Saturday morning. "You can go to the hairdresser with me and I'll treat you to a permanent."

"I'd rather have a temporary," Sara answered, just to prove that these things were only words to her.

"Well, I thought maybe we could go shopping, too – get you some, uh . . . nicer clothes."

Sara looked down at her knee poking through the tear in her jeans. "I like these clothes. They're comfortable."

Finally, her mother gave up. Sara overheard her one night talking in a low voice to her father.

"I never thought my only daughter would grow up to be a grease monkey," Claire Norton said in the soft glow of the late night kitchen, the low-watt counter light melting across the linoleum.

"Now, Claire, she's not grown up yet," her father answered. He had on his blue bathrobe and leather slippers that scraped on the floor as he spoke. "She's just trying to keep up with Mark. She'll get over it. Just leave her alone."

"But she never does anything that other girls do. She only wants to fix cars and hang around garages. I don't want her to grow up and work in a gas station or something."

"You don't get it," Sara thought from her hiding place in the living room. It was a conversation not meant for her ears, but that was the best kind to listen to.

By just quietly hanging around, Sara knew that she was being tutored in the subject of boys, and that she knew a lot more than other girls. Take cars, for example, she thought. They think cars are just for transportation, or backseat sex. Well, I know what they really represent.

If she could understand cars, she would understand boys. They are an encyclopedia of the male sex. It wasn't necessarily that Sara knew how to break down a carburetor and put it back together, or take an engine apart;

it was the significance of the engine that she understood. It meant power, motion, noise. To the boys who sat around playing the radio too loud as they tinkered with auto parts, it was the image of sex – their sex – and the power their imaginations told them it had. Understand engines and you understand how a boy feels about his penis, she thought. How could going to shopping malls possibly compare to this kind of education?

Sports was the other area that Sara infiltrated – a spy in the house of sports. She would sit in the living room with Mark and his friends, eating peanuts and drinking Coke, while teams battled each other inside the television. It didn't matter if it was football, basketball, or baseball; Sara wasn't there as a student of the players. She was a student of the watchers who wanted to be players, and thought they were. It was a study in scores, in winners and losers, in tackling, strategy, and faking out your opponent.

Okay, she thought, I get it. It was just a matter of mapping out the game ahead of time, with all its possible variations. Diagraming the plays. And, of course, being faster than the other guy – which she fully intended to be for the rest of her life.

Two

Sara

ONE EVENT that Sara expected to be a life-changing experience wasn't. She was seventeen when she lost her virginity, and she'd been preparing for it for years – listening carefully to Mark's detailed descriptions, rolling around in bed at night with her pillow, trying out the positions Mark had described. She found that her knee was a good thing to practice kisses on, and even though her pillow hardly resembled a boy, she would try it out between her legs, or underneath her. Sara thought that when it actually happened, it would be one of those rockets-in-the-sky kind of things. The earth beneath her feet would feel different and she would suddenly look different. Not in an obvious way, of course – it would be a subtle change. But it would be noticeable. Friends would stop, look puzzled, and say things like, "Did you change your hair or something? Lose weight?"

She felt it moving closer, as though destiny was tracking her down. She was sure of it the afternoon she and Mark went down to the Santa Monica Pier and she visited a gypsy who looked into a crystal ball, laid out some Tarot cards, and told Sara her life was about to change. She paid the gypsy fifteen dollars and walked out of the dark booth into the bright sun where Mark was waiting for her.

"So what did she say?" he asked, as gulls swooped past them and waves hit the pilings below. The breeze tasted like salt spray and smelled like popcorn.

"She said my life's going to change."

"How?"

"She didn't say. Specifics probably cost more. I guess I'll have to think of some way to change it so I won't feel like I wasted fifteen bucks."

But Sara believed the gypsy, and she felt that she knew what the change would be. At night, she practiced more diligently, using her fingers to probe as deeply into herself as her fingers would go. She used two fingers because she figured they more closely approximated the circumference of a penis, although she was pretty sure a penis was bigger still. The one piece of information she could never get from Mark or any of his friends was what the average size of a penis was. To hear them talk, each guy sounded like his was so big he had to fold it up just to get his pants on. Sara knew they were exaggerating, but still, two fingers was probably underestimating the actual size.

Then, just before school let out for the summer, she realized who it was going to be. Nathan. She had to be right – they were both outsiders, not part of the mainstream school crowd. Sara wasn't well liked by girls because she preferred hanging around with boys, but the boys her age didn't really like her because she had them figured out. She was too smart, too athletic, and seemed to not give a damn what anyone thought. She usually ate her lunch alone, reading a current issue of *Road & Track* or a worn copy of Camus's *The Stranger*. Nathan ate lunch alone too, reading Charles Dickens.

Nathan always sat behind her in history class; she could feel his eyes on the back of her head, sliding down her spine. He was pale and slender, with hair that was trying to be blond if only it were exposed to enough sunlight. Nathan looked as if he had been forced to take piano lessons while the other kids played outside. He walked with a strange tilting motion, as though the ground beneath his feet was tipping back and forth.

Sara knew she was considering him, although she wasn't entirely sure why. She chalked it up to destiny and forged ahead. At a party a classmate threw while his parents were out of town, she saw Nathan sitting on the couch drinking a beer, politely turning his face away from the couple next to him who had melted into each other. Sara saw the gypsy's prediction unfolding before her. She went over and kneeled down beside the couch.

"Hi, Nathan – can I have a sip of your beer?"

"Sure." He handed it to her, green eyes following the movement of her head as she tilted it back and let the beer run down her throat.

Sara nodded toward the couple next to him. "They should probably go upstairs before they embarrass themselves, huh?"

"Yeah." He laughed uncomfortably.

"Or we should."

"We should?"

Sara stood up and held out her hand. "Come on."

The Rolling Stones were singing "Satisfaction" as they walked up the stairs. She hoped that's what it would be.

"I had no idea you liked me," Nathan said, when they had locked themselves in one of the guest bedrooms.

The problem was, Sara wasn't sure she did. The idea of taking him upstairs had just come to her – like a vision, she thought – a voice from beyond that said, "Do it now, with him, tonight." But maybe she was supposed to feel more, be excited or nervous; her calmness was a little frightening. Guilt tapped her on the shoulder, slid its fingers around her throat; to free herself from its hold, she pulled Nathan down onto the bed and kissed him. His kisses in response were eager and wet, like a puppy starved for affection, and she felt sweat gathering at the base of his neck. She moved her hands down to his shoulders, but they were getting damp too. She thought they should probably get it over with before one of them drowned, but she knew he was waiting for her to give him permission

She wedged her hand between their bodies, tugged at his belt, at the buttons on his jeans. His hands answered, pulling up her skirt and scraping her underpants off her hips. She slid her hands between his jeans and his skin, and pushed down until he was naked enough. One of her hands found his penis and wrapped around it – it was definitely bigger than the two fingers she'd been practicing with, which meant this was probably going to hurt. But she had thought there would be more.

"What are you doing?" Nathan asked, pulling his body away from her. She realized that her fingers were circling and exploring every part of his penis.

"Nothing," she said, pulling him back down. She couldn't tell him she was measuring.

She stood back mentally for a moment, observing, steeling herself against the pain she knew would be coming. She listened to Nathan's C-sharp breathing and thought it wasn't fair that girls had to suffer pain the first time and boys didn't. That was probably proof right there that God is a man.

While Sara was gritting her teeth, Nathan was breathing

faster, at an even higher pitch, and saying, "Oh God," which made perfect sense, since God was clearly on his side. She could have endured the prayers, and sharp stab of pain, but the sound he made when he came was like fingernails on a blackboard. He whined – a thin, sad sound, the kind that sends people scurrying to windows to see if a cat's been injured.

"Are you okay?" Nathan asked afterward, which she expected, since she knew all boys asked this, particularly after the first time. God gave girls the pain, and then boys wanted to hear that it hadn't hurt that much.

"Uh-huh. Are you?"

"Yes – oh, yes. It was – incredible."

Sara thumped back down the stairs into the noise and chaos of the party. The guilt was back, had gained weight, was pressing her down. She was sure her footsteps were shaking the foundation of the house. She'd really done it now – gotten herself into something that wasn't going to be easy to get out of. She got another beer and walked outside to the swimming pool. She'd wanted something dramatic; she'd wanted her fifteen-dollar investment in the gypsy to turn into a windfall – a life-changing experience worth millions. Okay, something had changed – she'd lost her virginity – but it didn't feel like anything special. And now Nathan thought she was going to wear his class ring, or his sweater, or some emblem of possession. She stared down at the dark water in the swimming pool. The strange thing was, he looked completely different to her once he got excited; suddenly she hadn't wanted to be there at all. Was it always going to be like that? Princes would disrobe and turn into frogs? This was going to make sex difficult . . . and she'd had such high expectations for it.

Once she was back in the living room, Nathan kept watching her with an expression that made her think he was composing poems in his head. Finally, she called Mark and asked him to come pick her up.

"Depending on how you look at it," she said when she got into Mark's '64 Mustang, with its rebuilt engine, "either the gypsy lied, or losing one's virginity isn't as exciting a life change as I had expected."

Mark stared at her, yellow street lights illuminating the inside of the car. "You're disappointed? Angry? What?"

"I just feel . . . horrible. I think I'm about to hurt someone's feelings. Or else I already have and he just doesn't know it yet."

Nathan began calling her so often Sara considered asking her parents if they would change their phone number. And he always seemed to be whining, as if his voice had gotten stuck in the middle of an orgasm.

"Nathan's on the phone!" Mark would call up the stairs in a singsong voice

"I'm not here!" Sara would shout back.

"Too late – I already said you were."

"You son-of-a-bitch!"

"Sara, watch your language." Their mother's voice would suddenly materialize, as mothers voices have a tendency to do the minute any profanity is uttered.

"Mark, he's driving me crazy," Sara said after more than a week of phone calls.

They were sitting on the roof, which was the only place they could go around the house and be assured that their mother's long-distance hearing wouldn't tune into the radio waves of their conversation. It was a warm summer night. The breeze was thick and heavy, and a half-moon, full-starred sky curved above them. Somewhere, Orion strode through the heavens.

"So, tell him you just wanted to get laid and he shouldn't read so much into it," Mark suggested.

"What a typically masculine perspective."

"It's the only perspective I have to offer."

"Are you really that cold to girls?" Sara asked. "Do you go to bed with them and then tell them it didn't mean anything?"

"Confidentially?"

"Absolutely."

"No – but I tell the other guys I do."

Sara laughed. "Is this like notches on a gun?"

"Something like that – yeah."

So she had another chapter to add to her constantly changing manual on male behavior patterns. Secrets – not only from girls, but from other guys – all for the sake of image. All for the sake of games.

By the age of thirty-five, Sara could point to very few life-changing experiences, although she was constantly on the lookout. It was one of her problems with relationships – high expectations. With each one, at the start anyway, she thought that perhaps the seas would part this time, the mountains would move a few inches. But it was always the same pattern – dinners grew less interesting and more silent, sex that began with marathon sessions in every conceivable position, aided by massage oil and soft commands, would become hopelessly abbreviated. The massage oil would stay under the bed where it had rolled weeks before, and the whole thing didn't last long enough for anyone to change positions.

She'd succeeded in her goal of figuring out men, so no one ever got the better of her. She never fell for the ploys that other girls did. Like her friend Belinda Perry, who fell much too easily. Sara would try to warn her, but Belinda would always say something like, "No, you don't understand. He's different. He's really sincere." Of course, whoever the "he" was wasn't sincere at all. As far as Sara was concerned, no man was.

Belinda reminded Sara sometimes of a porcelain doll. She was slight, with skin that looked as if it had matured in the English countryside. Her hair, in its natural state, was blond, but its natural state had been dyed so many different colors, it was only a memory. She had the kind of features – small and delicately chiseled – that made even the shortest haircut look feminine.

Belinda's latest heartbreak had come at the hands of a Hollywood producer who was married to, and supposedly separated from, a moderately successful actress. He told Belinda he was just about to file for divorce, after having gone through several separations and attempts at reconciliation.

"But now I'm sure. Emotionally, I'm out of the marriage. It's just the paperwork that's left," he told Belinda, who then told Sara over the phone the morning after their first date, which had consisted of nothing more than cold pizza at his house.

"Oh, please," Sara said. "Tell him to get back to you after the divorce is final. This is a disaster waiting to happen."

"But he told me that he really wanted to be honest with

me. He told me all about his marriage, and the one before, too. He said he didn't want there to be any surprises."

"Yeah? Well, I bet his wife might be a little surprised, since she isn't his ex-wife yet. What else *would* he tell you, Belinda? That he'll say anything he thinks will work so he can fuck you a few times?"

Sara turned out to be pretty much on the mark about that one. The entire relationship consisted of a few evenings of lovemaking, no sleeping together because he "just couldn't handle it," no dinner dates or movies, and as few phone calls as he could get away with. His last call to Belinda was over his car phone, and it was to tell her that he had suddenly realized he wasn't "emotionally out of his marriage after all." So he couldn't see her anymore.

Belinda showed up at Sara's house in tears after that one, and Sara was faced with the task of comforting her and educating her at the same time.

"Do you know why he never took you out?" Sara asked, as Belinda worked her way through a box of Kleenex. "He was scared someone would gossip about it and his wife would get pissed off at him. That's how low this shmuck's consciousness is. He was scared to go out in public with you."

Things like that didn't happen to Sara. She would have known the guy was a liar from the start, and the "why don't you come up to my house for pizza" bit would never have worked. She never hit the lows that Belinda did – the depressions that made tears spring up whenever something like "Bridge Over Troubled Water" came on the car radio. The problem was, Sara never got the highs either. She had begun to think that by making sure no man could take advantage of her heart she was also making sure no one could get to it at all.

Her fantasies were different. When she was alone in her bed at night, her imagination could lead her to orgasms that no man had brought her to – no real man, that is. There were certainly men in her fantasies; women too, although in reality Sara wasn't particularly drawn to the idea of making love to a woman. But that was the beauty of fantasies – there were no restrictions, no guidelines. Just whatever could get her there.

And the whole scene could change if she wanted it to. Blackout, new characters, a new setting. Two women and a man could change to two men and a woman – whatever felt good at the moment. But usually, it was two women and a man, and Sara could become any one of them – even the man. In the night-time world of her imagination, it seemed perfectly natural to have a cock, to feel it pushing deeper into a woman, feel her getting wetter around it, tightening her muscles to squeeze everything out of it. But then Sara could be the woman – either one of the women, actually. The one on her back, with her thighs open to the man and her mouth open to the woman who was straddling her face. She knew the woman's taste – the thick sweetness of her – she wanted it, was hungry for it, reached for it with her tongue. She could hear the woman above her, telling her to put her tongue in deeper, to fuck her with it.

In reality, Sara never thought about acting these things out. They were fantasies, nothing more.

Sometimes, of course, she would come closer to reality. There would be only two – herself and a man, and she didn't change back and forth between bodies like some errant spirit who could inhabit whomever she pleased but was only herself. She was more ravenous with this dream figure, and he with her, than in any lovemaking she'd actually experienced. She would hear his voice whispering to her how much he wanted her; she'd feel his hands playing with her breasts, his mouth moving down, teasing her nipples with his teeth. She would whisper back that she loved him, that she couldn't get enough of him.

She had actually never told a man she loved him. Once she thought she loved someone, but it passed. And she rarely whispered anything during sex that didn't have to do with genitals.

The orgasms she brought herself to in her fantasies were deeper, more intense than any she'd had with a real man. A low moan would fill the room and she would realize that it was hers – her voice, her ecstasy, and sometimes afterward, her tears. Because she wanted it to be real. She wanted to get so lost in a real, flesh-and-blood man that her moans would travel through the darkness and linger in the room. But it was only her dream-people, her fantasy figures, that could do that to her. And none of them had faces.

Maybe that fact made it easier – the facelessness of each player. There was no name, no eyes to fall into, no half smile to mystify or seduce, no shadowed expression hinting of some past lover – the steam heat of sex on a cold winter morning, some reminiscence of a hotel room in Paris or an afternoon in Central Park. Sex, in Sara's fantasy world, was an anonymous flame with no identity and no history. Being consumed by it wasn't dangerous at all.

But then, sometimes there was sadness and she told no one about that, neither Mark nor Belinda. It would steal through the window at dawn, leak in with the first gray light, and always it would find her awake. Her dreams would still be damp between her legs, sometimes held there by her hand, unwilling to let go. Her eyelids would be heavy but open, and the sadness would go right for her heart. It knew her, it gave shape and weight to her loneliness, to the feeling that maybe no one – no one real anyway – would ever be able to scale the walls, cross the moat, carry her out of the castle, and spend nights instructing her body in all the ways it could be driven crazy. Maybe nothing real was ever like that . . . that was the message of this dark visitor who only stayed until the sun rose full in the sky. Maybe the real world, with all its unkindness, all its betrayals, didn't leave room for that kind of abandon.

It had surprised everyone when Sara became a costume designer for films. Her parents boasted constantly that their son was a lawyer, but their daughter's choice to dress actors, design their wardrobes, brought blank, confused expressions.

"The people can't dress themselves?" her mother asked.

"That's not the way it works," Sara explained. "You can't let everyone just follow their own fashion tastes."

Her father added, "Claire, just be glad she's not going to be a mechanic."

Sara's efforts to get Mark to understand came close to a confession. "It's illusion, fantasy – that's what I like about it. I'm helping to create a make-believe world." Which was as close as she could come to admitting her addiction to fantasies.

Belinda had been the hairdresser on Sara's first television movie, and from that point on they had been friends. They managed to work on other productions together, but even when they didn't, several phone conversations a day was the norm. Sara thought, if she were ever to let anyone really know her, it would be Belinda. But so far, that hadn't happened. She still had a secret life, played out in her imagination, and no one had been allowed to enter that world.

Three

Belinda

BELINDA COULDN'T stop thinking about how suddenly life can change. The day had started out so perfectly. She and Sara went out to brunch on Montana Avenue in Santa Monica and then walked the length of the street, going into almost every store. They weren't shopping for anything in particular and found very little that they could afford even if they had wanted something, but they acted as though they had all the money in the world.

In one antique store, the man who worked there started flirting with Sara. He wasn't bad- looking, actually – in his thirties, lean, and over six feet tall.

"Want to go to a basketball game with me tonight?" he asked. "I've got Clippers tickets."

"Nope," Sara said.

"Oh – sorry. Have you got a boyfriend? Is he bigger than me?"

"I don't know," Sara shot back. "How big are you?"

They left the store laughing at Sara's remark, although the embarrassed man was sure they were laughing at him.

Ever since they became friends, Belinda had wished she could be more like Sara when dealing with men –

confident, flip, definitely not an easy mark. Sara radiated an attitude of "I don't need you." And it worked. If Belinda could just master that. Once, a man told Belinda that she was "easily seducible" – just before he seduced her, proving his point.

After all the window shopping, they didn't get back to Sara's house until late afternoon. Their feet ached from walking, they had worn themselves out laughing, and Belinda found herself wishing again that she could be more like Sara.

Sara gave in to that kind of happiness as if she felt entitled to it. Belinda, on the other hand, regarded laughter as part of a barter system – it paid for the times when there was nothing to laugh about. And those times seemed always to be hovering nearby. She might be joking with Sara, laughing, but she could still hear the tribal drums in the distance beating out a battle warning. Belinda still held her breath when she drove past graveyards. She knew too much about them. Sara would probably stop and walk right in just to look at the trees and read the tombstones.

Later they sat together in the garden of Sara's rented house. March had brought the jasmine vines into full flower, and in the moonlight, they looked like a wall of snowflakes. On this evening there was no breeze, as there usually was, to stir the vine, so the sweetness just sat there, motionless and heady. Belinda was curled up beside Sara on the oak chaise longue that Sara had spent too much money on a few summers ago, when she wanted desperately to relax out in the garden in the evenings. Belinda knew her face was probably even paler in the moonlight;

she could sense the lack of blood beneath the surface of her skin. It was as though her heart were tired. She slid closer to Sara and rested her head on Sara's lap; they knew each other well enough that this wasn't unusual. And besides, Belinda knew that Sara's mind was following the trail of her thoughts.

At that moment, Belinda's thoughts had turned again to the blood in the toilet bowl that would have been a baby if it had just been able to hang on for seven more months and grow the way it was supposed to. Sara stroked Belinda's forehead, her face tilted up to the stars and the glow of city lights that washed out the heavens and made it impossible to see how many stars there really were.

"It might be for the best, Belinda," she said carefully. "I don't know if you'd given single motherhood enough thought."

"I did, though. I was really sure." Belinda's voice was thin; it fluttered as one of the jasmine blossoms would have if only there had been some wind.

She'd felt it a second before it happened – felt it let go – just like that. One minute it was a life growing inside her and the next it was red and flowing out. As though it had changed its mind.

Sara had been supportive of whatever Belinda wanted to do, but she wasn't happy about the prospect of Belinda raising a child on her own. They both knew that. Especially since the father was the producer whose marriage was some kind of emotionally charged revolving door and whose idea of a romantic evening was cold pizza and a detailed account of his marriages. From the start, Sara had said she would never work on any of his shows no matter how badly she needed a job. So when Belinda said she was pregnant and was going to have the baby, all Sara could reply was, "You're kidding," although she knew Belinda wasn't.

Belinda closed her eyes against the moonlight, imagining it as silver pressing on her lids. She thought how perfect it was that the night was windless; there was something solemn and reverent about the air's refusal to move.

Her plans had been so simple – maybe too simple – but laid out in the darkness on the nights she couldn't sleep, they didn't seem out of reach. She could take the baby with her on some films, depending on the director and the producer and the mood on the set. Because it would just be the two of them – her and the baby. She'd left three messages for this man who ended relationships over his car phone; he'd never returned her calls.

"So, that's it," Belinda told Sara. "I tried to tell him I was going to have his child. He didn't call me back. So I don't think I have any obligation to let him even visit us, do you?"

"No, absolutely not. And think of it this way. You'll be saving your child from the pain of knowing his father's a jerk." Sara had at least found one thing to be happy about in this situation.

"You said 'his,' " Belinda pointed out. "Maybe it will be a boy – with his eyes. I think I first fell in love with his eyes."

"Jesus, Belinda, the man would leave his mother standing in the middle of the freeway if he had other things on his agenda. It's too bad he wasn't wearing sunglasses – maybe you would never have fallen for him."

Belinda did feel a certain sense of delight, imagining her former lover hearing rumors that there was a son he had never met. A son whose mother taught him about the ocean and the songs of birds, heard his first words, and cradled him during thunderstorms. A son he might have known if only he'd had the consideration to return his phone messages. She'd liked the justice of it . . . but now it was all irrelevant.

When it happened, Sara and Belinda stood there for a while, neither one wanting to flush the toilet. They knew that once they did, the burial would be over. Clean water would fill the bowl and the rest would be a memory. Finally, Sara put her hand on the handle, looked at Belinda, who nodded and whispered, "Good-bye," and then it was over.

She turned her face a little so her cheek was against Sara's leg, and the moon poured into her ear. She imagined it as pale whispers. She hadn't told Sara that a few days earlier, she was driving down to the beach to take a walk and she thought she saw him jogging along the side of the road – the father of her child who might never know he was. Her breath caught, but then she decided she was wrong. It was just someone who looked like him. The hair color was wrong; the man running had less gray. But then, as Belinda glanced back at him again in her rearview mirror, she wasn't sure. She made a U-turn, doubled back, and then realized it *was* him. How could she have thought she was in love with this man when she couldn't even remember his hair color?

Sara shifted her legs and looked down at Belinda. Silver light was striped across them – dividing them, connecting them. "I have a really nice bottle of burgundy inside. I think we should open it," she said, lifting Belinda's head.

"Yeah – I guess I don't have a reason not to drink anymore."

The bottle was half gone before they spoke again.

Belinda felt the wine thickening her blood, flushing her cheeks.

"Since we're a little high," Sara said, "I want to make a request regarding your choice of men in the future."

" I'm listening."

"Do you think you could try to choose men who are a little farther up the evolutionary ladder? I mean, let's face it, metaphorically speaking, some of your lovers have had webbed feet and no thumbs."

Laughter was the last thing Belinda expected on this evening, but suddenly she and Sara were leaning against each other, barely able to breathe they were laughing so hard. And somehow, Belinda felt that the soul who'd visited her would approve of laughter as an ending for its brief stay.

Four

Sara

THERE WAS a late rainstorm in April. For two days, Sara watched puddles turn into tiny lakes in her yard; she watched clouds collide in the sky, rumble away from each other, and then crash again, as if in some celestial war game. She sat by the fire and read, cleaned out her closets, and let the sound of rain make her drowsy and slow.

In the mornings, the light was dull and gray; she turned on lamps and drank her coffee by the window, with rain pelting the glass. She hadn't worked in a month. It was one of those spells when there weren't even any offers, and she knew how seductive these days were. They drifted by, her time was her own, and with the rain she could pull her world in around her. A soft world, lit by lamplight, with a chorus of rain outside, and occasionally a distant clap of thunder. There was no one there to interrupt her solitude, and she knew she was in danger of becoming too much of a recluse.

So when the clouds finally moved east and the world outside sparkled, she was ready to get out of the house and readily accepted Belinda's invitation to go to a party with her.

"Why is this party at an art gallery?" she asked as she climbed into Belinda's VW bug.

"I don't know. I think something's being unveiled – a painting or something."

"So this is a party with a reason?"

"Yeah, but our reason is just that it's a party." Belinda said, checking her hair in the rearview mirror. This week it was white-blond and slightly spiked. Being a hairdresser gave her ample opportunity to experiment on herself, so it always depended on a roll of the dice who would arrive at Sara's house when they went out together – a brunette, a blonde, a redhead, or some mutation that God never intended.

Sara pulled down the visor and looked at herself in the mirror, at her shoulder-length brown hair with too many split ends. She was like the Cowardly Lion when it came to hairstyles – mention a change and she cringed. Belinda had given up.

The gallery was already crowded and noisy when they arrived. Rod Stewart was singing through the speakers.

"Do you know anyone here?" Sara asked as they pushed their way through to the bar.

"I haven't figured that out yet – I'm still looking."

They got in line at the bar, and Sara recognized the man ahead of her. He was one of the more controversial film directors of the day. He always seemed to be doing battle with the ratings board, or defending himself against the religious right. He'd become as big a celebrity as the actors who starred in his films.

"Do you know who that is?" Belinda whispered.

"Yeah – Anthony Cole. So?"

He turned around and smiled at Sara, as though he sensed he was being talked about.

"He's gorgeous." Belinda said.

"He's okay." Sara said, although she knew that Belinda was much more on target. He was tall, his hair was a deep brown, and long enough to make her think about sending her hands in to rummage through it. His jawline had that chiseled, square shape that says, "I'm very honest – elect me to something," and the wire-rim glasses made him look as if he could just as easily be majoring in literature at Harvard as presiding over film sets and directing actors.

One glass of wine later, Belinda was engrossed in conversation with some friends she'd run into, and Anthony Cole came up behind Sara. She felt him before he said anything, and turned around a second before she should have.

"Hi – I'm Anthony Cole."

She shook the hand he offered. "Sara Norton. Nice to meet you."

"Want another drink?" he asked.

"Sure – okay."

They walked back to the bar, Sara wondering how much control she'd be sacrificing if she had another drink. Even men with square jaws can play games. What she noticed about him was that he walked through the crowd as if his eyes were collecting everything in the path of his vision, but from a slight distance, as though none of it really mattered. He looked at Sara the same way; his eyes backed up a little, assessing, measuring, pulling away to take in the whole picture, as though she were a painting on the wall and he was evaluating it: Will this go in my living room? Will it clash or blend?

"So you came with your girlfriend?" Anthony asked after they got their drinks and moved away from the bar, back into the crush of people.

"Uh-huh." Her eyes narrowed, asking him how long he'd been watching her.

"I noticed the two of you when you walked in," he said, in response to her silent question.

He asked her about her work, and talked about the next film he was doing. Industry talk, but Sara kept feeling that wasn't really what they were talking about. She had lost track of time; she had no idea how long they'd been standing there, or whether there was anyone else still at the party. She demanded that her mind come back to earth and pay attention.

"So it looks like you're here alone," she said after a long pause. "When I've seen pictures of you, or read about you, you've always been half of a couple."

"We're not so much of a couple anymore. It's been sort of an adjustment, but actually I've been enjoying going out alone, spending time alone. You do that a lot, don't you?"

"How do you know that?" Sara asked, although she felt he probably knew even more than that about her. There was something about the way he looked at her that made her feel she was standing naked on a stage with only him in the audience, only his eyes traveling over her, opening her, exploring her most secret places.

"I bet you loved these last few days with the rain," he continued. "It's a great excuse to just stay by yourself in your own world."

"Jesus, how can you know these things about me? Where did you come from – inside my head?"

Anthony leaned closer, his mouth next to her ear. "Maybe I came from your fantasies."

Sara felt the wine evaporate in her stomach. She backed up a step and stared at him, unable to leave his eyes and knowing they wouldn't let her up. "You're scaring me," she said softly.

He put his hand on her shoulder and squeezed just hard enough that she could feel a pulse – his or her own, she wasn't sure. "It doesn't have to be scary," he said. "Sometimes people just connect."

"I need another glass of wine." Maybe more alcohol would make them disconnect, since this connection thing was getting way too frightening.

But three glasses of wine was over her limit – she knew that. She felt the alcohol race through her bloodstream and kick at her brain cells with steel-tipped boots.

She'd spent years figuring out men's games and suddenly, with Anthony, she felt as though she'd been raised by wolves and just yesterday had been plopped into the middle of civilization, zipped into a black minidress, and sent to a party. Hadn't Mark warned her? The problem with games is that, eventually, no matter how good you are, you meet someone who is better. Or who knows a different game that you never learned. Or who plays by different rules. Or who just disregards the rules and makes it up as he goes along. And then you're lost in the middle of a jungle you've never been in before, down on your hands and knees, looking for a trail of bread crumbs.

A man came up and began talking to Anthony. Sara would have drifted away, but he kept his hand on her arm. So she let her head drift off, since her body couldn't. She tried to watch Anthony as though she hadn't met him, as if he were across the room from her. But she was incapable of putting distance between them. He had some sort of mysterious power; she felt it wind around her, like silk ropes brushing her skin, circling her limbs. Her right hand involuntarily grasped her left wrist, as though it knew what the future held. Something inside her was changing, like continents shifting to make room for a new ocean . . . and she'd never been more frightened in her life.

Just before midnight, Belinda caught her eye.

"I think my friend is ready to go," Sara told Anthony.

"Why don't you let me drive you home?"

"Well, I don't know," she teased. "What kind of car do you have?"

"Mercedes 280 SE – it's a classic. Is that acceptable?" Anthony smiled down at her.

"Yeah – better than a VW bug."

Later, as they drove down Hollywood Boulevard, back toward the ocean and Sara's tiny house, which she hoped was clean, she said, "I knew this would be your car. I play this game where I try to figure out what kind of car someone has. I'm right most of the time. Now, if I could just get myself into the car that I'm perfect for . . ."

"What kind of car do you have?" Anthony asked, turning down the stereo and rolling up the window so only a thin stream of wind blew across them. The air still smelled like rain.

"A Volvo. But I'd like to have a four-wheel drive. Black with big tires. That's really what I see myself in – a macho car. Sort of the automotive version of penis envy."

Anthony's laughter washed over her; she liked where it came from – somewhere deep in his chest, somewhere that sounded like he meant it.

Jesus, she thought, my defenses are really down. But maybe there isn't any game being played here. Trust your instincts, she told herself. That's what most people say. Or is it just psychics and transchannelers who say that? People who go on cable TV and turn into fourteenth-century Tibetan monks who somehow learned the English language on their way through time?

Her front door was stuck. It had been getting stuck for a couple of weeks, but after the rain it got worse. The house had settled, or the door had risen – one of those mysterious construction ailments that never failed to bring out Sara's latent tendencies toward procrastination.

"Shit." She leaned her weight into the door and pulled up on the knob, which usually worked. But nothing worked the same after three glasses of wine.

Anthony was standing behind her; she could feel his chest breathing into her back. "Here," he said, reaching around her, pulling up on the knob and turning the key. The door opened, and as it did, he leaned down and kissed her neck. They got through the door, turned around, and let their mouths find each other. Acutely aware of the dark space of the house, Sara reached behind her to turn on a lamp, and in the process knocked a ceramic rabbit to the floor. She could tell it was the rabbit, and that he'd probably been decapitated.

"What was that?" Anthony asked, pulling back from their interrupted kiss.

"Nothing – I mean, I was trying to turn on the lamp and – it's okay – just part of my collection of ceramic wildlife."

"Why were you turning on the lamp?" His voice was velvety as it slipped through the shadows. One of those dangerous man-voices that you hear with every part of your body except your ears.

"I didn't think we knew each other well enough to be doing this in the dark," she said.

"Sure we do." He was pulling her into him again.

"Wait – wait a minute," Sara said, backing up from his arms and his mouth and the voice that was crawling between her legs. She walked across the living room to turn on a lamp – the dimmest one in the house. But before she got to it, she turned back and looked at him, and for the briefest moment, she saw him as a shadow.

"We have to talk." she said, as soft light fell on the floor. She motioned him to the couch. "We have to have the conversation. You know, condoms, AIDS tests, sexual history, Social Security number, next of kin."

"We can probably condense all that," Anthony told her, taking out his wallet and sliding a laminated card out. He handed it to her and leaned back on the cushions.

"What's this?" She looked at it and started laughing. It was a certificate saying that Anthony Cole had been tested and was HIV negative. "They give out certificates for this? Like a driver's license for sex? This person is allowed to fuck without a condom, but he has to wear corrective lenses?"

"It's from a very reputable medical clinic," he said defensively.

"Well, I'm sure it is. I just . . . I didn't know they had these things. I mean, it's sort of – I don't know – funny, I guess."

He reached over and slipped his hand around the back of her neck. His mouth was more insistent this time, taking her breath and replacing it with his. "Where's your bedroom?"

"Back there – down the hall."

When she looked at his eyes they were full of secrets, and it was the secrets that pulled her through the dark house into the bedroom.

"Light a candle," he said, and she didn't even wonder how he knew about the candle and matches on the nightstand behind them.

Candlelight fringed the dark as her dress was slipped over her head – black bra tossed into the corner, Anthony's hands sliding down her hips until no clothes covered her. She shivered a little; a window was open somewhere.

"Undress me," he said, and her hands obeyed, but her eyes couldn't leave his face.

How they moved to the bed she would never be able to remember. Suddenly they were there, his weight on her, her mouth hard against his shoulder. She looked at their reflection in the mirrored closet doors, watched him slide into her, watched her legs clench around him. She was so wet she felt the sheet beneath her getting damp. He pushed into her so deep it hurt, but the pain was from resisting him, from the fear of what was on the other side of the ache.

"Open up to me," he said, looking down at her, with all those secrets still in his eyes. "Let me in."

And then he was – pushing past the barrier of pain that she'd held on to to protect her from the chance of any man getting to where it really mattered. Because what was on the other side was trembling and soft and crying out to Anthony now as the candle burned down, and a nightbird sang outside, and a car drove by on its way to somewhere.

"Do you like having my cock this deep in you?" he asked her, his hands holding her head still. "No one's ever been in you this deep, have they?"

"No." Her voice sounded foreign to her – tiny and young, as if it belonged to someone who had been locked away for a very long time.

His hands tightened on her head. "Look at me while I'm coming inside you."

And she did, bleeding his eyes of everything she could get from them. But then something changed. The eyes she was looking at suddenly belonged to no one. Anthony was gone; he'd abandoned her there, left his body against her and his cock inside her, but the rest of him had headed for the highway.

Sara buried her head against his neck. She was shaky and wet and confused, and her legs didn't want to let go of him, although they didn't know who they were holding anymore.

After a few minutes, Anthony said, "I'm going to walk out in your garden for a minute – cool off."

His footsteps were a strange echo in a house that usually held only Sara's sounds. She heard the kitchen door open, knew he was out in the garden. But he could have been in another city. She turned on her side so she could see her body in the mirror, put her hand between her legs and let his semen spill over her fingers. And then she put her fingers in her mouth, wondering if she would still remember his taste tomorrow.

When she walked outside, she saw him standing under the trees; above him, stars blinked through the leaves and the glow of street lights spilling over the fence outlined his body. Sara felt the light and the cold night air defining her own nakedness as she walked over to him.

In that moment, she realized what had happened. They weren't alone. There were ghosts hanging from the branches, peering over the fence, floating between them as she pressed her body to his and circled him with her arms. His hands touched the small of her back, but ghosts held his wrists. She could hear their whispers but couldn't make out their words. They were telling stories that had nothing to do with her. They were his ghosts, and they had come into her bedroom to claim him.

"Do you want to leave?" Sara whispered into his neck, into the smell of sex that rose up from their bodies.

"Why do you say that?" Anthony asked.

"Because you already have."

"What do you mean?"

"I saw you leave," she told him. "You were there, inside me, looking down at me, and then it was like you turned and ran. Something took you away – something that had nothing to do with me. Your body was there, but you were gone."

He tightened his arms around her, and she felt ghosts flutter away reluctantly. "I'm here. I don't want to leave."

But she was afraid to look at his eyes to see if he had really returned.

Sometime during the night, she thought she was wound around him, breathing him in. But her eyes opened and the bed beside her was empty. He appeared then at the bedside.

"I dreamed you were next to me," she said in a thick, sleepy voice. "And I woke up and you weren't. But now you're here."

"I just went to the bathroom," he whispered, lying down, his body tight against hers.

"How did you get into my dreams already?"

Anthony brushed her hair back from the side of her face – a curtain brushed back from sleep. "Do you trust me, Sara?"

"Yes." She didn't know why, but that was the only answer.

"Do you trust me enough to do things with me you've never done before?" he asked.

"Yes."

Her dreams climbed onto the sound of his voice and rode it into sleep.

The next morning, she watched him drive away in the glare of sunlight and she thought, "Maybe this is how it happens. You meet someone and it's like you already know him. And the only possible answer is yes."

"Are you out of your fucking mind?" Belinda said when Sara called her, a cup of coffee and two aspirins in front of her. "You just met him. I'm not saying you shouldn't have slept with him, but how could you not use anything?"

"It's okay, really. He had this card – this certificate saying he'd been tested and he was okay. Besides, this wasn't just fucking. It meant something."

"And using a condom would have changed the meaning? What do you mean – a certificate?"

"This card. You carry it around in your wallet, or at least he does," Sara said. "I mean, I don't think you could get that kind of thing forged."

"No, there's probably not a black market for that yet. It'll take a few more years to get that together," Belinda replied.

"Belinda, I'm trusting my intuition, okay? It felt right."

"Don't you remember what you told me once about things feeling right? You said that leaves a wide margin for error."

Two weeks later, Anthony picked her up for dinner in a limousine. "I thought I'd take you out in style," he said.

"Oh, and I just assumed your car was in the shop." She was trying to be cool, but she was impressed.

He was taking her to dinner in Beverly Hills, and Sara had borrowed a dress from Belinda, an ankle-length black Betsey Johnson so fitted that she couldn't wear underwear beneath it.

Anthony pushed a button and the partition in the limo went up, cutting off the driver's view of them. "Come here." he said, and pulled her onto his lap. Her knees pressed in against his hips, and down onto the leather seat. She thought of her legs as a vise, holding him captive. Her hands messed up his hair and her mouth wouldn't let him speak, until he pulled back enough to say, "Touch me, Sara."

She unzipped his pants, knowing even before she got there that he would be hard. It only took the grip of her hand to make him harder. "I like it that you get hard so quickly," she whispered, as she lifted her body up and put him inside her. She could have come right then, and could have taken him with her – easily – one of those desperate fucks that can't wait. But she wanted to wait. She lifted herself up again and released him.

"Sara – "

"Ssh. I don't want you to come yet. I don't want you to come until I tell you. Let me tease you tonight, okay? Let me play with you. I want you to hold back for me."

He didn't answer; his mouth was half-open and his eyes watched her as she covered him up, zipped his pants again. She thought she felt him tremble.

She knew her face was flushed when they walked into the restaurant; she felt like she had a fever, and she wanted it to last. It did, until their food arrived and Anthony's expression changed. He turned serious, leaned forward on his elbows and studied her for an uncomfortably long moment.

"Sara, I want to be honest with you."

The fever left and her throat turned cold. "You mean you haven't been?"

There was something disquieting in his tone – like a storm warning or a small-craft advisory.

"Well, I don't think I've been dishonest, but I haven't told you everything. The woman I was involved with – it is over for me emotionally – but we still see each other."

"And sleep together?"

"We have, yes. It *will* be over, but for now . . ."

"Don't you think the honest thing would have been to tell me right up front? Like before we made love?"

"Sara, don't get self-righteous with me," Anthony said. "You went to bed with me the first night we met. You weren't entitled to my whole life story."

"Oh, I see. The truth only comes out after – what? Two dates? Two weeks? You know, men like you should wear signs around their necks – 'I'm an asshole. Don't trust me. I just want to get laid.' It'll be more honest and better for your karma."

Anthony's face softened, which made her more suspicious. "I didn't just want to get laid. I want to be with you, Sara. But I don't want to keep anything from you."

His eyes were telling her more than that, though. They were drinking in her anger, warming to it, getting off on it. She wondered for a quick second if he was testing her, making up a story that would anger her so that he could sit back and watch. But it was too strange for her to believe – or too frightening. She looked away from him and exhaled so violently that she almost blew out the candle.

"I trusted you." she said, her voice stiff and unforgiving. "I trusted that whatever I needed to know about you, you would tell me before we had our clothes off. And this definitely falls under the heading of things I needed to know. You son-of-a-bitch. Is there anything else? A few wives scattered across the country maybe? A few dozen kids?"

He reached across the table and took her hand. "Sara, stop it – you're just angry."

The feeling nudged her again that she was auditioning for something and getting the part.

"Angry?" she said. "No, this is not really anger yet. This is nursery-school anger. I can go all the way to a Ph.D."

But she was on shaky ground. The night they met, she had disregarded the first rule of any game: never assume your opponent isn't playing one. She took the deepest breath she could and forced herself past her anger to a calmer place.

"Well now that I'm adequately informed," she said evenly, "this is what I propose. We'll date, have sex, but no unprotected sex because I don't trust you anymore. And if you add to your stable of women, maybe you'd be good enough to let me know." Liar, something in her brain screamed.

"So we're going to have an arrangement? That's pretty cold, isn't it?"

"Is it? Maybe you thought men had a monopoly on arrangements."

When they walked out of the restaurant and into the parking lot to the waiting limo. Sara wished she had her own car there. Or more accurately, the car of her dreams – a four-wheel drive with oversized tires. She'd get in, gun the engine, and drive off in a car that said "Don't fuck with me. I own the road."

But maybe it wouldn't make that much difference. She had the nagging sense that, whatever road she turned down, it would lead back to Anthony. She pictured dark ribbons of highway and white lines, but if she followed them long enough, all she could come to was him. Her legs would be clenched around him, his breath would be in her ear, and she would still be saying yes when he asked if she trusted him.

Five

Sara

SARA DIDN'T even let him walk her to the door. She was back in the comfort zone of anger, and she knew how to play this one out. She said goodnight, got out of the limo, and slammed the door behind her. But she glanced at Anthony's face just before she got out, and his eyes were enjoying her fury. It was one of the ways he had her – the amusement that kept her off guard, kept her curious and coming back for more.

She paced around her dark living room for nearly an hour, trying to force him away, to will him out of her mind. What she wanted was to get to the place where she couldn't quite remember his face or the sound of his voice. She'd done it so many times with so many men, she couldn't believe it was this difficult now. She'd gotten it down to a formula – sending a man down a long road in her mind, over some hills, into the next county, so that within a matter of minutes she'd be saying, "What color were his eyes?" or "What was that way he had of smiling that looked so sweet?" And then, when she couldn't remember, she'd know she was free. But with Anthony, she couldn't remember the formula. Every way she turned, he was right in front of her. And it *mattered* that some of his time was being spent with someone else. She imagined smelling another woman's scent on him, tasting something that she knew wasn't of him. And she didn't know if she could stand it.

It was the third time Sara had woken up and glanced at the clock. Now it read four-thirteen. It wasn't that she was anxious for dawn to come, it was that sleep kept bringing uneasy, ragged dreams. She couldn't remember the actual dreams, but the feeling of nervousness lingered, gnawing at her, boring holes in her bones.

She closed her eyes again, hoping for at least another hour of sleep, no matter how restless it might be. Two hours later, night lifted and gray light brushed across her face. She sat up in bed and reached for the phone. Midway into dialing Anthony's number, she wondered what she was doing, but she didn't stop.

"Yeah?" His voice was sleepy enough that she couldn't be sure, but something told her he knew who was calling even before she said, "It's me."

"Hi, Sara." She tried to read his voice, pick up signals from it. But there was too much sleepiness in it and not enough sleep on her end to judge anything.

"Can I come over there for a few minutes?" she said. "You don't need to get up. Just unlock the door."

His "Okay" gave her nothing more than the word itself. No encouragement, no warning.

Anthony's house was closer to the ocean than hers. The air got saltier, wetter – the kind of air that leaves a damp film on everything. Children are told not to leave their bikes outside because they'll rust, pianos go out of tune, and cars are never quite shiny enough. Another storm was coming; California hadn't decided it was ready for spring, and it was still playing winter games.

When she got to the front door, a pigeon perched on the roof stared down at her.

"I know," she whispered to the bird's unblinking eyes. "I'm completely out of my mind."

She tiptoed into the house and looked around more carefully than she had the first time he had taken her there. She hadn't stayed over at his house yet. He'd driven her up there one afternoon and given her a tour almost as if he didn't want her to become too familiar with his home environment. In the early stillness, with storm clouds rolling past the windows, she had more of a chance to take it all in. The house was pure man – Indian rugs and cowboy art, leather sofas and thick wood tables. A house that made no apology for winning the West and running off with the artifacts. It smelled like he'd lit a fire the night before. She wondered if, while she was pacing her living room, he was sitting on the stone hearth with a glass of whiskey. She walked softly up the stairs into his bedroom. Anthony was lying on his back, his eyes half open, looking at her.

"Take off your clothes," he said, and he watched her as she took off her sweatshirt and jeans. His eyes made her skin tingle and her nipples harden, and she was vaguely aware that the light in the room had darkened and rain was hitting the roof. There was an echo somewhere of the sky doing something, but she was locked in again to a world that began and ended with his vision of her.

She slid into bed beside him, felt how warm his skin was next to hers. Morning chill against a night of sleep.

"Why can't I get away from you?" she said. "You're everywhere. It's like you're watching me even when you're not there."

"Do you want to get away from me?" Anthony asked, taking her hand and sliding it down his chest, over his stomach, to his cock that was already hard.

"Yes." Her hand closed around him. "No . . . I don't know. You're still seeing someone else. That should be my exit cue."

"I don't end relationships abruptly," he said. "But that's not what's confusing you, or making you angry. You've built such a pretty cage around yourself, but you know I'm not fooled by it. Inside is just a lonely person huddled in a corner, trying to convince herself that her life is okay the way it is. That's what scares you, Sara – that I see you so clearly."

She felt her mouth tremble and tears spring into her eyes; she buried her face in his chest. "Goddamn you. I don't cry in front of people. I just don't. How did you get me to do this? How do you get me to be so vulnerable in front of you?" Her fist hit his shoulder, but he didn't flinch.

"You don't get it, do you?" Anthony asked. "But you're starting to. I haven't gotten you to do anything. You rounded a corner in your life and I was there, and the language you thought you knew didn't work anymore. We're in a different country now, the weather is different, the landscape is foreign, and the only choice is to surrender to it."

"But you're not surrendering – you're controlling me."

"That's the part you don't get. It's the same thing. I'll surrender to you. I'll get on my knees and do whatever you want me to do."

He rolled her off him, stood up and reached for her legs,

sliding them around to the edge of the bed. He lifted her by her arms so she was sitting with her feet on the floor. Kneeling down in front of her, he pushed her thighs apart and before his face disappeared between her legs, he looked at her and the brightness of his eyes made her blink. She felt his tongue playing with her – teasing her, drawing on her, and then parting her lips and plunging into her. Sara's breath drew in sharply and she started to fall back on the bed, but his hands grabbed the small of her back and stopped her. He lifted his head and she could see the wetness around his mouth. Her wetness – that would always give away how much she wanted him.

"Don't lie back. Stay there and watch," he said. And then his tongue was inside her again, his fingers playing with her, her breath coming faster, and her hands clutching his head.

At some point, her eyes couldn't stay open any longer. She needed darkness to let the sensations tumble into each other, sharpen and tear and burn through her until it felt like something deep inside was splitting open. In the only part of her mind that was still able to function, she knew nothing would ever be the same. She was in the wilderness, and there was no trail and no way home.

Anthony pushed her back on the bed, swung her legs around so her spine was pressed into the coolness of the sheet, and lay down on top of her. She opened her legs and waited for him to enter her, but he didn't. He pressed against her, propped up on his elbows, his eyes locked on hers.

"Tell me what you want."

"Fuck me," she whispered. Her voice was hoarse and trapped in her throat. Her legs were locked around his hips and she was trying to maneuver him into her.

She was about to learn something – that what once seemed like madness can change when someone says yes. With that one word, it no longer looks like madness.

"Wait," Anthony said, lifting his body off her. "I want to get something."

Sara watched his back as he walked toward the bathroom – the muscles that moved as his arm reached for the door handle. It was one of those moments when the artistry of the human body can't be ignored. Whatever God was responsible for this creation must have had a sculptor's eye.

Anthony returned with the silk sash from his bathrobe, climbed onto the bed, and knelt beside her. She let him lift her arms up above her head so that her fingers were touching the oak slats of the headboard. There was no resistance, and only the faintest murmur of fear inside her.

"Do you trust me, Sara?"

"Yes."

Dark green silk was sliding across the lighter green veins of her wrist. "But I want you to trust yourself," Anthony said. "I want you to know how it feels to just lie there and receive and not do anything."

It was an easy surrender. She was already imprisoned. The green sash binding her wrists to the headboard was just decoration.

When Anthony kissed her, her arms started to reach for him, but the silk held them. He was right – the idea of not participating, not doing anything, was foreign to her. His hair fell across her eyes, she breathed in the shampoo smell, and gave up trying to see or reach for him. She closed her eyes as he moved down her body, his mouth taking hold of her breasts, the skin over her ribs. All she could control was her legs; she spread them wider – an open invitation – keeping her eyes closed even when Anthony was over her again, his breath on her face. Even when she felt him enter her, she let all the sensations run together in the dark. She remained sightless, her wrists bound, and her legs too shaky to remember that they were unbound. His mouth was on hers when he came; she felt his voice scrape her tongue and knew her own cries were slipping down his throat.

Sara didn't know how much time had passed – how long she'd been lying there or when the silk had been untied from her wrists. Time had stopped, or speeded up, or done something mysterious to detach itself from her awareness. She was drifting, trying to remember how to move her limbs. It was raining harder outside – that was all she was certain of.

Suddenly, a warm towel was wiping her forehead, her breasts, between her legs. She opened her eyes on Anthony's face, studied how his concentration on the task of washing her had gathered in his forehead.

"Is it still morning?" she asked him.

"Uh-huh. It's almost ten."

"The film business is great – you're either on the road at five a.m. or still in bed at noon."

"Actually, I have a couple of weeks off," Anthony said. "We could drive up the coast tomorrow."

"What about your other girlfriend? Are you sure you wouldn't rather take her?"

"Stop it, Sara. She's no longer my girlfriend, but she is someone I still see once in a while. That won't go on forever, though – you know that."

Sara sat up and pulled a pillow into her lap. Suddenly, she didn't want to be quite that naked. "How am I supposed to know that?"

"If you trusted me more, you would."

It kept coming back to that. Trust – the one thing she had spent her life running from.

It was as though Anthony had always been in her life – she just hadn't noticed him. She had brushed past him in some of the rooms of her house, smelled his scent, felt him in the shadows, but she'd thought nothing of it. Her eyes had been on the door, her mind on other things. Then one day he locked the door, made her stand in front of him and stare at what his eyes had been seeing all along.

He stripped her down to a place in her soul where there was no place left to hide. Naked, she shivered before him even though it wasn't cold, cried even though she wasn't sad. She stood as both child and woman, with history and innocence battling for power. What had once felt like a safe, controlled life was at risk. She sniffed danger on every wind that blew past her. Yet she couldn't leave.

Because the more he surrendered to her, the more he got down on his knees, the more control he had over her. That was why they were the same thing – surrender and control. Because she still feared surrender, she had no control.

A thief steals but often leaves something behind – a fingerprint, a scent of cologne, an object moved an inch from where it always sat. Anthony was the thief in Sara's life. But a good thief is subtle. It takes time to discover what he's stolen and what he's left behind. She sensed things were disappearing from her life, but she wasn't even sure what they were, or if they'd ever had any value. And she would come to a dead stop sometimes, certain that something was different. That the sun hit the floor at a different angle or bounced off something that wasn't there before. But what? Things had been rearranged, or their appearance had been altered in some way. She could never identify exactly what it was, but she knew he had everything to do with it.

It was almost lunchtime when Sara and Anthony walked into the Malibu restaurant with its picture-window view of the ocean, its hanging plants and potted ficus trees. A back-to-nature, forget-about-the-smog kind of place. They had probably missed breakfast hour; they'd taken too long in the shower, washing each other, letting water rain down on them as they stood there kissing, pressing into each other and toying with the logistics of making love in the shower.

They were seated at a table near the window, with the surf crashing on the other side of the glass, and were handed lunch menus. Something made Sara look across the restaurant to the opposite wall and her eyes went straight to a woman she recognized as Anthony's ex-girlfriend or not-quite-ex. Helen Wilder, an actress who turned up periodically in movies of the week and guest roles on television series. Sara remembered the photos she'd seen of Helen and Anthony – arms linked, going into premieres or trendy restaurants. Something was different now, though. Helen's hair was blond, not red as it had been, and her breasts had been done with implants several sizes too big for her frame.

"Someone you know is over there," Sara said to Anthony, who was studying the menu. She nodded toward Helen's table, and Anthony looked over; his eyes – it seemed to Sara – pulled Helen's up and turned them in his direction. He waved and smiled, and that was the cue. She was on her way over to their table.

Sara watched her cross the restaurant and thought, "I should dislike this woman. I should be jealous of her." She looked at Helen's faded jeans, fashionably ripped at both knees, her white T-shirt that had probably fit her better before she got her breasts done, straight blond hair framing a high-cheekboned face. But she saw more than that. She saw beneath the surface, to the places Anthony had been, to the areas of Helen's soul he had staked out. Sara couldn't dislike her – they had too much in common.

"Sara, this is China," Anthony said.

"China?" Sara asked.

"I changed my name," Helen/China explained, her eyes studying Sara.

"How are you?" Anthony asked her.

There was a moment before she answered. A moment when some silent communication passed between them, one of those wordless dialogues that lovers get so good at after a while. Sara felt exiled; for those few seconds, she was on an island, looking back at the mainland.

"I've been fine," China said finally. "Good to see you." She turned wide blue eyes on Sara. "Nice to have met you." And then she turned and walked away.

Sara watched Anthony's face, scrutinizing it, but he gave nothing away. "So is that the effect you have on women?" she asked. "They get their tits done and rename themselves after Third World countries?"

"Very funny, Sara. She chose to transform herself. I had nothing to do with it."

But Sara knew better. He treated women like kingdoms. There were tunnels behind Helen's eyes where Anthony still lived and ruled. They were cluttered with memories – of nights when her body couldn't get enough of him, when all she could say was yes. Of mornings when sunlight played across his skin and she waited for him to wake up and tell her she hadn't dreamed the night. This is what happens when he leaves, Helen's eyes had told Sara. You feel lost, like you're speaking the wrong language, you have the wrong currency, and no map of the country exists. Wilderness can be a prison, too, her sad smile had said. You wander there, your eyes seeing only the harshness, only the wide miles that hold you. There are strange sounds in the night and the sun moves too heavily through the days. There is no blessing of familiarity.

No wonder she changed her name, Sara thought. She needed some kind of geographical landmark.

Six

Belinda

IT WAS the one thing Belinda had kept from Sara, and probably always would. At least that's what she thought.

She was sitting on a wooden bench at the park just off Beverly Glen, watching children climb on the jungle gym. Younger children were being pushed on swings by maids who cooed in Spanish and ensured that the children would grow up bilingual. A mile away, up a steep street, was the Playboy mansion where good girls went to be bad.

That's what Belinda's father had called her when she was sixteen – a bad girl – but she really wasn't. She hadn't intended to get pregnant; it had just happened. Carelessness, too much passion, and far too little knowledge about the timing of her body's cycles.

She and Nicholas had made love a total of three times, getting a little more adept each time. The first two times were in the backseat of Nicholas's Mustang; the third time was in the cemetery, under a full moon, next to a tombstone marked "Here Lies Burton Pikes, 1917–1928." Whether it happened on that night or not Belinda would never know, but she believed that was when she got pregnant.

Poor Burton – dead at eleven – a soul not ready to leave the earth. Belinda imagined his ghost hovering around the grave site, could almost feel the air stir as he slid past her. He was still railing against his untimely death, against the dying of the light that had come before he'd even gotten to know what the light was all about. And then came his salvation: Two sweaty teenagers playing Russian roulette with sperms and eggs, too shy to take off all their clothes, illuminated by the moon, just daring a soul to take advantage of their innocence. That was Burton's cue for his return journey to an earthly realm that he missed terribly. At least, that's how Belinda saw it.

She would have kept the baby, named it Burton if it was a boy, even though she didn't particularly like the name.

Sitting in the park eighteen years later, watching children who might look the way her child would have if she'd only gotten to know him, she remembered the night she told her parents.

They were in the living room with the worn olive green carpet and the leaf-print wallpaper. It made her think of a faded forest.

"Daddy," she began, because it had more to do with him than with her mother. Her father was her lord, she his princess, and the house was his domain. "I know I'm only sixteen, and I don't know if I want to marry Nicholas, but . . . I'm pregnant, and I want to have the baby. I know I'm young, but I can get a job. I can handle it, really, I might need some help at first. . . ." The words were a rush of sound, propelled by her fear, her knowledge that her father was on the throne, it was his kingdom, and her meager wishes were meaningless if he deemed them so. He wielded the scepter, and right about then she could feel it poised over her head. Guillotine psychology.

"How could you do this?" he asked. "What could have made you turn into this kind of girl?"

"What kind of girl is that?" Belinda asked feebly.

"A bad one." Her father glanced at her mother, whose expression had not changed. Maybe just a sadness in her eyes. "You are not going to be a teenage mother," her father continued.

"But – "

"No. You'll have the baby, all right. There will be no abortion discussed in this family. But we're going to arrange for adoption – right away."

Belinda looked at her mother, diminutive and quiet, curls of graying hair framing a face that had learned, over the years, to show nothing. Her expression had settled into blandness; her smile – when it appeared – was fragile, uncertain, and her eyes had a tiredness to them. They just didn't want to watch anymore.

When Belinda remembered the birth, she recalled a white stream of noise and pain. The child who had been floating inside her was being ripped from her. Calm voices were telling her to push and her own screams answered them; she didn't even recognize her own voice after a while. But part of her wanted to hold on because she knew that when it was over, it would really be over. Her father had left no room for negotiating, not even room for tears or pleading. His word was law, and no amount of crying would change that. The baby had been taken away at birth; the milk in Belinda's breasts would dry up.

But before it did, while she was still heavy and wearing the nursing bra that had required a special trip to

Thrifty's, she and Nicholas went back to the cemetery.

It was moonless this time; the black night seemed to cling to them. And Belinda knew that Burton's ghost was gone. She could feel its absence in the stillness of the air around his grave.

"Let's sit on top of the grave," she told Nicholas. Because she sensed a loneliness there now – bones crumbling in the earth, and no spirit winging by to tell them they weren't forgotten.

She leaned against the tombstone, and Nicholas sat in front of her, facing her. He bent forward and kissed her – a soft, blond kiss that had grown up in the months they'd been together.

"I'm so sorry, Belinda – about everything."

"Sh . . ."

Years later she still wondered about it. Maybe it was the pain in her breasts, the tenderness, the aching that was so distracting, that made her pull Nicholas's head down. At first he thought she meant he should kiss her neck, but as he nuzzled the skin below her ear, she pushed him down further, frantically unbuttoning her blouse with the other hand. He unhooked the back of her bra, pushed it up, and his mouth understood what she wanted; it closed around one of her nipples, drawing hard on it until she could feel the milk being pulled out. The nerve paths throughout her body came alive and she turned sleepy, as though closing her eyes would be enough to transport her into dreams. But she didn't want to close her eyes. Nicholas's head was at her breast, like her baby's never would be. Milk was flowing from her into his mouth – white like the moon that hadn't come out for them on this night. There was nothing to illuminate but two sad children who had grown up too fast and would never parent the child they'd conceived.

Would never even know that child – whisked away and placed into the arms of some other woman who had age, a husband, financial security, and no milk in her breasts. Better that they were left in darkness; moonlight would have seemed cruel.

"I want to taste it," Belinda whispered, her hand slipping under Nicholas's chin and tilting his face up. His mouth released her nipple for an instant and then he moved to her other breast. Her nerves tingled again as the milk started flowing. He pulled away and pressed his mouth to hers, filling it with warm sweet liquid that tasted like no milk she could remember.

She looked at Nicholas's face, lit only by the faint yellow sheen of a faraway street lamp, and she wondered if their child had his eyes, his mouth. She only knew it was a boy; they hadn't given her a chance to study his features – whisked away, while she was still wiping tears out of her eyes.

She thought of making love to Nicholas, his lips wet with her milk. But she was still too sore inside.

"This is our pact," Belinda told him. "We're drinking this milk like a Communion service, to ask forgiveness for not taking our baby and running away with him. And to promise each other that we'll never forget him – ever. Promise."

"I promise," Nicholas whispered, bowing his head to take more milk from her breast and funnel it from his mouth into hers.

Belinda had kept her promise, although she hadn't spoken to Nicholas in years and had no idea if he'd kept his. She sat in parks and watched children. Her son was eighteen now; he might be asking for a car, was probably getting into trouble constantly, at least by somebody's standards. He wouldn't still come to a children's park. But Belinda sat there because time had stopped for her. In her heart, he was still tiny, and she wanted to see what he would have looked like. She wanted a vision of all the years she missed. Occasionally, a child caught her eye and she thought, "Him – that child. There's a resemblance there, I'm sure of it."

It made no sense, really – her weekly visits to various parks around the city. It was a fantasy, and fantasies don't have to make sense. They just have to soothe the rough parts of reality.

Belinda had been trying to deal with reality – specifically, the rough parts of hers. She'd taken advantage of California's standing offer: Whatever your problem is, whatever you think it is, there's a support group or a seminar with your name on it. And Belinda had managed to put her name on a lot of them. Sara had shown little patience with this tendency, but then she never really knew about those forces driving Belinda. She didn't know about the hours Belinda spent in parks, watching children, imagining what it would have been like if her son hadn't been taken from her.

"Belinda, I think you've become a self-help junkie," Sara once said – lightly, the way people do when they're more serious than they'd like to admit. "I know you're searching for something, but it's like you're trying to feed yourself intravenously, and you keep missing the vein. In one month, I've watched you go from a group for co-dependent people, to a meditation group, to Alcoholics Anonymous, and you hardly even drink."

Belinda didn't say anything – except, "Well, I like to try different things." Which was the same as not saying anything.

Because her search had nothing to do with veins, or food. It had to do with the hole in a corner of her soul, where nothing ever came to fill it. It was dark, cold, and Belinda couldn't stop visiting it. Her memories pulled her there, back to the fire that exploded in her at the actual moment of birth, and the way she immediately began aching for the child – her child – as though, if she couldn't hold him against her, something inside her would die. They took him away, and something did.

What she was searching for was a miracle, a laying on of hands – something that would take away the ache and bring the dead part of her soul back to life. She couldn't tell Sara about this, or anyone probably – it sounded insane even to her.

She couldn't bring herself to talk about how once, on an airplane flight, a baby's persistent crying two rows back made her breasts ache, made them respond suddenly to the child's tears as though they were full of milk again. The memory was stored in her body, in her tissues, and maybe it would never leave her. Things seemed to bring it to life – a baby's tears or the sight of a tiny hand reaching for a larger one. Once, on a busy sidewalk, she heard a child's quick steps behind her, running in her direction. She turned, her arms just ready to open and catch the child before she remembered that this was someone else's little boy, laughing in that wide-open way that children do, as he ran away from his mother.

Belinda wondered who had chased her son when he was small and still enchanted with escape games. Did the woman who posed as his mother laugh and for that moment become a child again herself, or did she fail to appreciate his playfulness?

It was always small moments that seemed to bring up the greatest pain. They could happen on any sidewalk or in any café in any city. They always caught her unprepared – Belinda knew this by now – and they always aimed for her heart.

Once she heard about a girl who committed suicide by stabbing herself in the heart, over and over with a kitchen knife. The story stayed with her, because she wondered if that girl had been hunted down by the same kind of hurt – the desperation of wanting to feed, to nourish another life. There was supposed to be a mouth there, reaching for her breast, but instead there was nothing. No one. Only the dark air of nights alone pressing down on her, needing nothing from her. And in the end, only the plunge of cold steel would stop it and bring her peace. For weeks, Belinda thought about that girl, and sometimes she still did. Of all the ways to die, she chose to tear away at her heart, her hand clutching the knife and stabbing with a strength she probably didn't know she had. Aiming straight for her heart because that's where the pain was.

The sun was starting to sink and the light turned a deep orange because of the smog. Belinda wrapped her sweater around her and got up to leave, thinking, The planet may be choking to death, but it'll go out with a hell of a sunset. She glanced back at a blond boy, maybe seven or eight, hanging from the monkey bars. At least for today, she'd decide that's what her son looked like once upon a time, ten years ago.

If Belinda had a treasure chest, there would be only one thing in it – one secret. Her son, wherever he was, whoever he'd become. If she unlocked the chest, let anyone else look – even Sara – something would change, she believed that completely. It would rust, tarnish, look different to her. It was the only thing in her life that still looked shiny, and no matter what, she would keep it that way.

Seven

Sara

THE TIDE was coming in. Sara could feel it, could almost taste it, even though Anthony's taste was still in her mouth. The saltiness of his come – not that much different from the ocean, really, she thought.

They had walked down Zuma Beach, onto the private section of Trancas, past large, wealthy houses, to a cave accessible only at low tide. The cave was encrusted with mussels and damp with the smell of the sea. With their sweatshirts spread out as a blanket, they made love tentatively at first, unaccustomed to being so naked in the open air, miles of ocean on the other side of the rocks and a stretch of sand that anyone could walk along and discover them wound around each other, Sara's legs circling Anthony's hips.

But the gentleness didn't last long. As their breath came faster and their lovemaking became more intense, they stopped caring that someone might stroll down the beach and find them. Sara heard her voice bouncing off the rocks, repeating Anthony's name again and again. It seemed she was always either saying his name or saying yes – language lifelines pulling her through uncharted waters.

Anthony pulled out of her and slid up her body toward her face; he opened his legs over her, straddling her. His come, when it filled her throat, could have been one of the waves crashing outside; everything seemed to be in rhythm. The crash of a wave, the explosion of him in her mouth, in her throat, in parts of her being that had never been willing to receive anyone before.

Lying there afterward, she imagined the ocean coming in, trapping them there. It might – she didn't know how much time had gone by. The spray each time a wave broke was thicker. Maybe it wouldn't matter if the ocean drowned her; part of her was drowning anyway – had been for weeks. Whenever she opened her mouth to say yes to him, something always rushed in and seized her breath – the sea air, the wind, his body.

"We should go," Anthony said, sitting up to find his clothes. "The tide's coming in." She reached over and touched his cock, soft now, satisfied, resting against his leg. She liked it this way too – soft, vulnerable. She still said yes to it, but in a different way.

The sea inched closer – a wall of water just outside the rocks, ready to sweep her away. Or was it his eyes – the look he was giving her that made her feel as if she were being scraped across the sand, closer to the undertow?

"Come on – before the waves get us," Anthony said.

He picked up her sweatshirt, shook the sand off it, and put it over her head, guiding her arms into the sleeves. He lifted her hair up and smoothed it back from her face. Maybe it was these moments, not the dangerous ones, that held her prisoner. The times when he became both parent and lover, and she felt herself grow smaller, in need of his protection, more vulnerable than she'd ever felt, even as a child.

When they were walking back up the beach, Sara said,

"I keep feeling like you're putting this spell on me. It's so uncomfortable sometimes."

"You could leave," Anthony said, staring past her at the waves. "If it's really that uncomfortable, why would you want to stay? Have you asked yourself that?"

"Only a few hundred times a day."

"And?"

"You're addictive. Although I might have found a way to ease myself away from you. I've been offered a movie and I might take it. It shoots in Florida, so I'd have a chance to wean myself from you. I might not even have time to think about you – you know, twelve-hour days, wardrobe problems with the actors that stretch things out to fourteen-hour days."

Anthony didn't say anything for a minute; his eyes studied the sand. "That's too bad," he said finally. "I was going to ask you to meet me in Paris."

"Paris?"

"That's the first location for the movie I'm doing. We'll be there for at least a couple of weeks, staying on the Left Bank. It'd be great to be with you in Paris, but if you have a job . . ."

"I'll think about it," Sara said, although she knew she was making up her mind already.

"I think I'm going to do it," she told Belinda on the phone that night. "I may be crazy to pass on this job, but Paris . . ."

"You have to be impractical sometimes. How often does a chance like this come up? Go for it. I would." Belinda the romantic.

Sara's agent was less enthusiastic. "You're saying no to the first feature film you've been offered in ages? What the hell is the matter with you?" she screamed.

Sara pulled the receiver away from her ear. "Miriam, I hate it when you yell. Your New York accent comes back and you sound like a cab driver. I'm going to Paris. I've been invited."

"Oh – invited – this does not sound work-related. Who is he?"

"Anthony Cole."

"Excuse me? In that case, why isn't this work-related? He's directing a film over there. Why doesn't he get you on it, doing the wardrobe?"

"Oh, that would look good, wouldn't it?" Sara said.

"Happens all the time. But let me tell you something else. I think you must have taken leave of your senses getting involved with someone like him. The guy goes through women like Henry VIII went through wives. I thought you were smarter than this."

"There's that New York cynicism again."

"No – not cynicism," Miriam answered. "Just common sense, which seems to be eluding you. Guys like him don't change. And you can see them coming a mile away. They have warning labels on them – 'Hazardous to your health! Do not take internally!' So what's come over you that this is attractive to you?"

"Miriam . . . I can handle it . . . I think."

There was an exasperated sigh on the other end of the phone. "Look, I know I'm just your agent, but I do care about you. And men like Anthony Cole feed on women who think they can handle it. To prove that you're not handling it, you're turning down work."

"We'll talk about it when I get back from Paris," Sara said.

She knew she was painting a picture in her mind of Paris and Anthony, and things that she wanted to come true. It was a different experience of fantasy than any she'd had before. It wasn't about some faceless, shadowy dream figure; this one was flesh and blood and had a grip on her that left bruises.

She was aware of the ways in which she was softening. Going to Paris was part of that – a romantic excursion with her lover. Except her lover had calluses on his hands from tearing away at people's defenses, and now he was tearing away at hers. That knowledge was the rebel part of her that refused to soften.

When she went over to Mark's apartment to say good-bye to him, he gave her a puzzled look and said, "Why do I feel compelled to ask you if you're in love? Maybe it's the fact that you said no to a job to rush off to Paris with Anthony? This is a bit out of character for you."

"There are moments when I think I'm in love," Sara told him, "and moments when I just think I'm temporarily insane."

Mark laughed and hugged her. "You know, I think love only works if you're willing to go all the way with it."

"Yeah, well, that's my dilemma. This is how it looks to me – no matter how close I am with Anthony, or how intimate, I still keep a gun in the drawer of the bedside table. It's not loaded, but it's there. I can't seem to come to this completely unarmed."

"I'm starting to see how Paris fits in," Mark said. "You can't transport weapons across international borders, right?"

"I guess so," Sara admitted. "As usual, you figured it out before I did."

Belinda drove her to the airport and waited with her until the flight was called.

"Have the most beautiful, romantic time of your life," she said to Sara as passengers filed past them. Then she stepped back and held Sara by the shoulders. "That is what you want, isn't it? Why am I suddenly confused?"

"Because it is confusing. I haven't been in my right mind since I met him."

"Paris makes you want to become a painter," Sara wrote to Belinda two days after she arrived. "It's something about the light. I've been told that it's the moisture in the air or something in the atmosphere here that makes the light different than in any other city. I understand now why artists have always gravitated to Paris. The clouds have been rolling in each afternoon, rain falls for a little while, and then the sky changes again." She wrote nothing to Belinda about Anthony.

Anthony and most of the actors were staying at the Lutetia, a hotel on the Left Bank. Much of the movie was being filmed in a refurbished castle about thirty minutes outside Paris, and on most days Anthony left the hotel just after dawn.

The film was a modern-day romance that had little to distinguish it from premodern romances, except that the actors wore Guess? jeans and Armani jackets. Rich young man falls for poor younger girl who doesn't know how to coordinate an outfit to save her life, has no idea which fork to use, or why there are so many of them at a single place setting. Her father is a grocer or something, and the rich young man's parents freak out and threaten to cut him off, leave him penniless and out of the will if he dares to stay with her. Will love survive? And who really cares anyway, because it's been done so many times, any ending will do. Although Sara, reading the script one night in the bathtub where the warm water and the predictability of the story were lulling her to sleep, thought the only thing that could save it would be a surprise ending, like the grocer's daughter shooting everyone except her boyfriend's father and then running off with the old man so she could live a life of wealth, go to Berlitz and learn Spanish so she could order the maids around, and read Emily Post to learn about the layout of silverware. Anthony had decided to try a safe, noncontroversial film.

"What do you think of it?" Anthony had asked her that night, waking her up seconds before she slipped under the water.

"Oh . . . it's, uh, very sweet," Sara told him. She knew that the location was probably what sold the story to everyone, since most people wouldn't mind shooting in the French countryside. But she didn't bother to get into that with him.

Since Sara didn't want to spend every day hanging around the set, she walked through the streets of Paris, listening to the music of a language she only barely understood. She struggled to remember her high school French, bravely asked directions whenever she got lost, which happened at least once a day, and laughed with strangers at her language mistakes, which were numerous. She sat at cafés and fed tiny birds pieces of bread, and went jogging in the Luxembourg Gardens near the hotel.

She liked the pattern she'd fallen into – having her days to herself and sharing the nights with Anthony. Except the nights felt strange to her. He felt strange. Sex was starting to feel like an old habit – cerebral almost. Sara told herself it was because he was working so hard; she told herself that, but with no conviction behind it. Still, there was a sense of safety about it. If he was distant, he couldn't leave her shaky and wanting more, but he couldn't damage her either. Damage was always a possibility.

It was evening and she'd just gotten back to the hotel. She was sitting out on the balcony, wishing that she hadn't gone out to the set that day. In the week that she'd been in Paris, she'd only visited the set twice and hadn't stayed long. Until today. All afternoon, as she watched Anthony direct the actors, talk to the crew, and walk around the set as though it was his private empire, she felt something tightening in her stomach. One of those unnamed premonitions that eludes definition but refuses to go away.

The sky was darkening. Sara could see the Eiffel Tower from her balcony – lit up against the night sky. And above the buildings across the street, a yellow moon floated like a bright balloon in black water. Her hotel room was lit by candles, and something about the romance of the whole setting made her feel foolish. Perhaps she was a fool, standing there in the soft Paris night looking down at every taxi that stopped in front of the hotel, waiting for Anthony to come back.

She played back portions of the day in her head – the moments when her stomach screamed at her, when her blood chilled in her veins. The moments she tried to tell herself she was imagining things. Anthony wasn't really flirting with the lead actress – right in front of Sara – he was just directing her, being supportive and nurturing, the way any good director is. But then why did Sara feel as if she were drowning? As if the air wouldn't hold out much longer?

The actress was in her twenties, with chin-length blond hair that was cut in no particular style. There was something in the girl's casual attitude about herself that was so confident it was unnerving. She had a slender, boyish body, wore no bra, did nothing to her hair but run a brush through it, and even when she was filming wore a minimum of makeup. It was as though she knew her beauty needed nothing done to it. Sara started to feel painted and overdone; the little bit of mascara on her eyelashes seemed to gain weight and pull on her lids. She chewed off her lipstick, trying to strip down, claw her way to some shred of self-confidence that had to be there still – it had been there once – before Anthony. But she only sank deeper, dangerous waters rising over her head.

"Allison," Anthony had called out after one of her scenes. "Let me talk to you for a minute." He walked over, put his arm around her shoulders, and led her away from the set. Something about the way he stood facing her, his hands on her upper arms, something about his face bending down to hers . . . Sara wanted to run, but she couldn't tear herself away. She couldn't stop watching them; it felt forbidden, as though she were peeking through someone's bedroom window. Then her own hands curled in, her fingers started to bend, as though she were the one holding onto Allison's shoulders. She could smell Allison's hair, feel the brush of her breath on her own skin. For a moment, she became Anthony; she was wearing his skin, feeling what he was feeling.

Sara leaned her arms on the balcony as the moon sailed past her and taxis stopped to unload passengers, none of them Anthony. She knew she had just realized something important. "I'm turning into him," she thought. She remembered the day before – Sunday – when they were sitting outside at the Café Flore in Saint-Germain-des-Prés, and Sara had looked at a girl walking by as Anthony would have looked at her. She'd stared at the girl's thighs, at the way she walked, at her mouth, but it wasn't her own eyes she was seeing through. She imagined the girl naked, her legs spread wide, but it wasn't her own imagination – it was Anthony's. And then she glanced at Anthony, and he wasn't watching the girl, he was watching Sara. He knew. He knew he had conquered her, superimposed his thoughts onto hers.

She knew before the white taxi made its U-turn to pull up outside the hotel that Anthony would get out. She leaned farther over the balcony to watch as the door opened and his familiar shape stood by the curb. Then Allison got out after him. Sara hadn't anticipated this part of the scene, although it made sense – they were both staying at the Lutetia. It was almost nine-thirty. He'd told her he needed to go over some scenes with Allison; his eyes had watched her for a reaction. But Sara knew enough at this point to not react. That was two and a half hours ago. She wondered if she would smell Allison on him. She wouldn't ask any questions, no matter what, mostly because he wanted her to. It was a game of small victories. It was a game of being quick enough to step back from the edge before she fell into the alligator pit.

The moon had moved on and wasn't staring at her anymore when she heard Anthony's key in the door. Yet she continued to stare at the sky.

"I asked the concierge to order a bottle of wine for us from room service," he said as he walked in the room and tossed his jacket on the bed.

She could hear the sound of glasses clinking together down the hallway. "Two glasses or three?" she asked, and wanted to bite her tongue as soon as she had said it. She still hadn't moved toward the French doors that led out to the balcony. Something wouldn't let her move closer to him.

"I ordered two glasses," he said calmly. "Why? Did you have other ideas?"

She hated him right then. But she also wanted him – and that made her hate him more.

"You didn't tell me you'd be this late," she said, digging herself in deeper. Shit, she thought, I'm really being a bitch.

"Sara, I'm in the middle of directing a film. I'm not here on vacation. I didn't tell you that I'd be spending every evening with you, did I? I mean, have I misled you in any way?"

She could have kissed the waiter for walking in right then, because there was never any winning response to Anthony's cool, logical, go-fuck-yourself-if-you-don't-like-it statements.

It seemed to take forever for the waiter to uncork the wine, pour out just enough for Anthony to taste it and give his approval, and for both glasses to be filled. She still hadn't moved, although she desperately wanted to sit down. Her knees felt weak. Are sea legs when your legs feel steady, or when they're still wobbly? She couldn't remember. Whichever it was, the floor felt watery and treacherous.

"Are you angry with me?" Anthony asked, walking over to her and handing her a glass of wine.

"Do I have a reason to be?"

"Not from my perspective. But then, we see things differently, don't we?"

She moved past him and sat down on the edge of the bed. "Maybe you're the one who's angry at me, Anthony. You have such creative ways of fucking with my head."

He sat down next to her, his thigh pressing against hers, his hand reaching for her wineglass, putting both it and his own on the floor, breathing against her throat. "Is that what I'm fucking with, Sara?"

It wasn't even a question, really, not anymore. It had been asked and answered when they first met.

Sara had the vague feeling that something had moved her out of the way and taken over her body; she was tempted to look behind her. But instead she gripped the back of Anthony's neck and pulled him to her so that there was no room between them. Their mouths were fused, her tongue pushed against his, and she drew his breath into her lungs. She pushed him back on the bed and started stripping off his clothes, so roughly that some of the buttons on his shirt tore off. She didn't recognize her own hands; they were strong, fierce hands – not the ones she had woken up with that morning. She peeled off her own clothes and straddled him.

"I'm going to fuck you as hard as you've ever fucked me," Sara said in a low voice, lifting herself up to put him inside her and then coming down hard on him – wanting to hurt him. Wanting to frighten him. She looked down between her legs where he had disappeared inside her. A man once told her that there was an element of fear in fucking a woman – castration fears. "You see yourself disappear inside her," he said, "and some small, ancient voice says you may never come out whole again."

Sara was wishing for a ripple of fear across Anthony's face.

"You hate me sometimes, don't you?" she said. "You

hate it that you like me. You get so angry at me for that, you want to hurt me, right? That's why you try to make me jealous and insecure." She was fucking him so hard she was out of breath, and starting to feel raw inside. But the pain only made her want him more; she pushed her legs farther apart and came down on him even harder than before.

"Are you trying to hurt me?" Anthony said. "Are you trying to be mean to me?"

"Yes. Just like you're mean to me sometimes. Did you think you were the only one capable of it?" Sara didn't know whose voice was coming out of her; just like her hands, it wasn't her own. He'd talked of surrender, but she felt like she'd been conquered.

Anthony smiled up at her, but it was a tentative smile. Not fear yet, but close. Sara was controlling the night now, but he wasn't going to give up easily. His hands were gripping her hips and he tried to steady his breathing.

"I haven't been mean to you," he said. His voice was hoarse, trapped in his throat. "If I wanted to be mean to you, I'd fuck another woman right in front of you. And I'd tie your hands to the headboard so you couldn't touch yourself. I'd make you watch while I bent her over – I'd take her from behind, just the way you like it. And you'd get turned on watching it, and you'd hate it that it turned you on. And you wouldn't even be able to masturbate because your hands would be tied."

He pushed Sara off him and rolled on top of her, still inside her. He pulled her arms above her head and pinned them down with his hands. "How hard do you want it, Sara? How mean do you want me to be?"

"Your anger doesn't scare me. You can't hurt me." Except he was hurting her. She wondered if she was so raw inside that she was bleeding. It didn't matter because she wanted more. The more he pushed into her, the tighter her legs held him. "If I wanted to be mean to you," she told him, her teeth clenched and sweat running down her neck, "when you untied me, I wouldn't fuck you. I'd fuck the girl. I'd ignore you just like you ignored me today."

Anthony laughed. "You don't know me very well. That wouldn't be mean – I'd love to watch you with another woman."

"But I'd tie you up, so you couldn't touch yourself, and I'd go down on her right in front of you, put my tongue inside her until you were going crazy."

He stopped moving and stared down at her. Sara realized the balance of power had just shifted, but she didn't yet know how. There was an instant of fear – a breath-holding wedge of time that seemed both quick and endless – before Anthony deserted her body and rolled away from her. Night roared in between her legs. He picked up the phone and punched in four numbers. Another room.

"Allison," he said into the receiver. "Why don't you come down to 509?"

Sara knew what her defeat was – surprise. Allison had probably been waiting by the phone. Anthony went past Sara, picked up his wineglass, and drained it. They didn't meet each other's eyes. She knew this much: that the story had already been written; all that was left was the acting out.

Allison showed up in a matter of minutes, in a white T-shirt and faded jeans. No one said anything, except Anthony, who said, "Hi, how are you?" Sara rolled over on her stomach, wetness leaking out of her onto the bedspread. She forced her eyes to meet Allison's, to lie about the fear that was hiding behind them. The waters were getting more deadly, roiling over her head, and she was headed for the falls where she would almost certainly be annihilated on the rocks. Unless Anthony went over first. The night wasn't finished yet.

Sara watched as Allison stripped her T-shirt off her perfect twenty-two-year-old breasts. Her face looked playful and expectant. This was just another game to her, Sara thought. There was the shadow of a bruise on her lower lip – the kind Anthony had left on Sara's lip more than once. So this had been a whole night of games for Allison.

Anthony was sitting behind Sara on the bed, and she couldn't resist turning and glancing at him. There was nothing in his eyes, no expression; they were flat. She remembered a conversation she and Belinda had had once about some guy who revealed himself as being seriously into leaving emotional carnage behind him. She couldn't even recall now whose guy it was – hers or Belinda's. He must have been Belinda's, she decided, sliding down a little on the bed as Allison undressed in front of her. Because it was Belinda who talked about his eyes. "Eyes like a shark's," she'd said. "You know the look? That numbed, killer look that's a few galaxies removed from any kind of human emotion?" So now it was Paris, a couple of years later, Anthony was the shark, and Sara's blood was in the water.

She got off the bed and walked over to Allison, feeling Anthony's muscles moving her limbs, his heart pumping her blood, his eyes behind her own. It wasn't that she and Anthony had exchanged places; it was that they had melted together, overlapped, become one place. One game. A paint-by-numbers game. Except he was paint and painter, and she was just the numbers. What chance did a jumble of numbers have against an artist with his expertise?

She slid her hands down Allison's back, pressed their bodies together. Such a strange sensation, feeling the softness of a woman's breasts against her own, the smoothness of her stomach, the absence of a cock, the curve of Allison's hips matching her own, moving into her. She forced her tongue into Allison's mouth, found by memory the pale bruise on her lower lip, and she sucked on it, trying to make it darker, branding her more than Anthony had. Allison plunged her hand between Sara's legs, knowing just how to make her shudder. It's such a small movement of the fingers – men never seem to learn that. But Sara didn't want to give in to it yet – soon, inevitably, but not yet.

She pushed Allison away and turned around to Anthony. He was stretched out on the bed, watching them. He was hard and his hand was resting on his thigh. This is where I win, Sara thought.

She went into the bathroom, got the sash from the white terry-cloth bathrobe, and came back into the bedroom. Except for the curtain billowing in the night breeze, hers was the only movement in the room. Allison was frozen in place, her hands limp at her sides, the bruise swelling on her lip. Sara knew the young actress had never done anything like this before either. We're both under the same spell, she thought.

Anthony didn't resist when she grabbed his wrists and pulled him around so he was lengthwise on the bed. She looped the terry-cloth sash around each wrist and tied the ends to the bed post.

"I don't want you touching yourself," she told him. "You're not going to get off until I say you can."

Allison parted her legs a little as Sara walked back over to her. She turned her so that she could watch Anthony in the mirror – make eye contact with his mirror image – then she dropped down on her knees and pushed Allison's legs farther apart. It wasn't unfamiliar, the way she thought it would be. Maybe because it wasn't her tongue, circling and probing, making the girl moan and sway a little on her feet. It was Anthony's; his shadow had fallen across her soul again, melted her will into his. Allison's taste was so different from Anthony's – sweeter, more delicate – that was the only surprise. She'd gotten so used to his saltiness. She sank into Allison, her head anchored by hands much younger than her own, while her hands held onto Allison's hips. Sara closed her eyes; all she needed was her mouth. But when Allison began moaning louder and breathing harder, Sara pulled back enough that she could look at Anthony in the mirror. He was twisting uncomfortably, and something was leaking into his eyes. She couldn't tell if it was fear or anger.

She went faster with Allison, wanting to be finished with her. She knew she should take more time, but her concentration wasn't on being a good lover; her concentration was on Anthony, twisting against his bound wrists, filling up the mirror with confusion.

As soon as Sara rose from her knees and began walking to Anthony, Allison seemed to fade into the distance. Sara stood over Anthony. The candles were burning down; their light quivered on the walls.

"Have I given you enough misery?" she asked in a low voice. "Do you want it to end now?"

"No."

His answer didn't sound like defiance; it left her wondering who was winning at that moment. She felt as though she was in control, but of what, she wasn't sure. "Do you want me to punish you some more?" Sara said.

"Yes." His eyes weren't looking at her. They were fixed on the ceiling.

"Because you deserve to be punished?" she asked. "Do you deserve to be hurt, Anthony?"

He nodded.

She stepped back and slapped his cock, not hard enough to hurt him badly, but hard enough that he drew in a sharp breath.

"You've hurt me, Anthony." She wondered again whose voice was coming out of her. "You like hurting me sometimes, don't you?"

He said yes – softly, almost reluctantly. But Sara had a vague feeling that he wasn't talking to her. He had retreated into some other world. He bent his knee up – a reflex action to shield himself – but she pushed it down and slapped him again. His eyes met hers for a second. Just a flicker, but enough for her to wonder who he was.

She pulled her arm back to swing at him. She wanted to hit him harder than before. "I want to hurt you," she said, more to herself than to him. Reclaiming herself, separating from him.

Her arm dropped to her side and she stared down at Anthony. His face looked soft and young, but something violent fluttered around the edges. She wanted to make him cry, she wanted to make him crumble in front of her. She was so angry at him, she wanted to get pleasure from his pain. But she also wanted to lie down next to him, cradle his head, and keep him safe from pain. She stood motionless, too many things colliding inside her. She hated him, but she kept falling in love with him; her rage was white-hot, but she wanted to make love to him with so much tenderness that the world would turn a different color.

She had forgotten that they weren't alone until she was reminded by Allison's footsteps crossing the floor. Allison came up behind her, leaned into her, and slid her hands over Sara's breasts.

But the change in Anthony's face splintered the moment and made Sara break free of the circle of Allison's arms. Tears were streaming from Anthony's eyes; something was breaking inside him, but Sara didn't know what it was.

"You have to leave now, Allison," she said, picking up the girl's clothes from the floor and handing them to her. "I'm sorry," she added, although she really didn't think she was.

Allison was too stunned by the suddenness of the dismissal to do anything but obey. She dressed quickly and left the room – a silent soldier exiled from the battlefield.

Sara untied Anthony's wrists and used the terry-cloth sash to wipe the tears that had gathered beneath his eyes. "Talk to me," she said softly. She lay down beside him and he turned on his side, curling up against her like a child.

"It just all came back to me," he said.

"What? What came back to you?"

"My mother walking past the door and seeing what was going on . . . and not stopping it. Maybe it was something about Allison moving up behind you . . . I don't know." He was talking in the dull monotone that people use when the pain of a memory numbs them.

Sara shifted around so she could face him. She put her hand on his cheek, catching his tears as they fell. "What did she see, Anthony?"

"My father standing over me." Anthony's voice was a

flat line; his eyes were half closed. "My father was a minister, and every morning he'd make me get down on my knees and pray in front of him. He'd stand over me naked, and as I prayed, he'd get an erection. He never touched me, he never touched himself. I used to close my eyes and try to forget that he was towering over me with a hard-on. But one morning I opened my eyes and I saw my mother walk past the doorway. She looked in and saw what was going on. But she just kept walking. No one ever talked about it. To this day, neither of them has ever talked about it."

"How old were you? How long did this go on?" Sara asked, a little afraid of the answer.

"I was about seven when it started. It went on until I was twelve."

He cried quietly against her, and Sara knew that silence was the only appropriate response to what he'd just told her. She wrapped her arms around him like a cloak, as if winter had just blown in and she had to protect him. She only barely noticed that the candles had burned down. For a moment, when she tried to bring the image of his face into her mind – the face that was buried in her breasts – she couldn't do it. It was as though, for those few seconds, Anthony had been erased from her mind. A computer error, a power failure, a mental black hole. All she could see was a seven-year-old boy kneeling in prayer, his eyes shut tight.

Later that night, Sara awoke and went into the bathroom. Anthony was still lying on his side, curled up like a child, but his breathing was steady. Sleep had carried him into calmer seas. She closed the bathroom door softly before turning on the light so as not to wake him. When she looked in the mirror, she saw a bruise on her lower lip – the same as Allison's, the same as she had seen on herself after the times that Anthony had devoured her mouth with his kisses. But when she looked closer, it wasn't there. For a second, though . . . Maybe I just imagined it, she thought. Or maybe it was always there, just under the surface, and when the light hit her in a certain way or her eyesight was unusually sharp, it would show up, reminding her that she was different now. Anthony had left his mark on her – like ink on wood, it had seeped in and would never wash off.

Eight

Sara

IT WAS the quiet side of dawn; the light in the room was pale, colorless. A time of uncertainty. Sara felt Anthony get up, heard his slow, sleepy footsteps travel across the floor, followed by the creak of the bathroom door. In the Lutetia, because it was an old hotel, the toilet was separate from the rest of the bathroom. The water closet, Anthony called it, preferring to be properly European. Still not fully awake, Sara got out of bed and followed the sound of water streaming into the bowl.

If Anthony was surprised when she walked in and slipped behind him, he didn't show it. Or maybe she was too tired to notice his reaction. Maybe they were both too tired – sleepwalking through the gray morning. Pressed against his back, Sara reached around his waist and put her hands over his, holding him as if she were holding part of her own body, as if it were the most natural thing in the world for her to stand over the toilet bowl. She turned her face so her cheek was against his shoulder blade.

"Why do I keep feeling like I'm becoming you?" she whispered, as his hands slipped out from under hers and it was only her holding him. "I even think I know what it would be like to pee like this. I'm starting to forget who I was before I met you."

Anthony bent forward a little and pushed the button on top of the toilet; the sound of flushing woke her up for a moment. But then Anthony took her hand, led her back to bed, and she slid again into dreams.

It even seemed like a dream a little later when she opened her eyes halfway as Anthony kissed her goodbye and left to go to the set. She would try later to remember if he'd said anything, but all of it seemed out of focus. At nine-thirty, when she was on the phone to Belinda, who was watching daylight fade in a different time zone, Sara wondered if she had imagined everything. The past twenty-four hours . . . maybe she'd been kidnapped by a very long hallucination.

She didn't tell Belinda about Allison, although she did talk about Anthony's efforts to make her jealous by flirting with other women. She didn't tell her the story about Anthony's father and the seven-year-old boy who got up off his knees only to find that a part of his soul had been nailed to the floor. She didn't tell her about tying Anthony's wrists to the headboard, and the anger, the slaps, the desire to hurt him, the desire to hurt herself. She told Belinda about Anthony's eyes, how they would go dead, and she would taste fear in the back of her throat. She told her about feeling sometimes as if she was turning into him.

"It sounds more like you're turning into me," Belinda said. "He's starting to sound like the kind of guy who's been my downfall – a control freak who enjoys hurting your heart just to keep things interesting – just to see if you'll fight back."

"Yeah, that is sort of your taste, isn't it? A Sagittarius with a big cock and a mean streak."

"My Achilles' heel," Belinda agreed. "But I'm working on it. Now you can see why I go to so many seminars and lectures. I'm looking for a recovery program that will get me off of men like that."

Sara felt her own sarcasm collide with the memory of holding Anthony as he cried. Her skin remembered his tears; maybe they had seeped in and her blood was saltier this morning. But she kept that part of the story from Belinda, too. Secrets were piling up between them.

There was a knock on the door and Sara told Belinda to hang on. She expected to see the maid standing there, vacuum cleaner in hand, ready to inhale all traces of the night before. But it was the concierge who handed her a phone message.

"Emergency call," he said, and hurried off.

"Your mother," the message read. "Call her at the hospital. Mark has been in an accident." The phone number for the hospital was written at the bottom.

There was the awful slowing down of time as she told Belinda she had to hang up and call her mother – something had happened to Mark. The long-distance number clicking across seas and continents seemed to take forever. There was the fear that felt like hot irons searing her. She could feel her cheeks reddening, her body temperature rising; sunlight coming through the French doors was scoring her eyes. Years passed after the switchboard operator at the hospital answered and said she'd connect her to the room.

"I told him that car made me nervous," Claire Norton said almost immediately after she heard Sara's voice. "I just had a feeling about it. Just because he's a lawyer, he doesn't have to have a flashy car. They all like to drive those tiny sports . . . things."

" Porsche," Sara said. "Mother, what happened?"

"He was going too fast around a curve on Sunset." Sara could tell her mother's emotions were almost at the breaking point. "He hit a pole. His leg is broken and he has some cuts on his face – one deep one."

"But he'll be all right?" Sara asked. "His leg will heal okay?"

"Yes, he's sleeping now."

Sara smiled at the memory that rushed in on her. When they were children, no matter what was wrong with them, if they were sleeping, it was considered an encouraging sign.

"He'll probably have a scar on his face," her mother added. "On his cheek."

She's beyond tears, Sara thought – she's cried them all and is wondering why she feels like a dry well. Sara's tears hadn't started yet. They were building up inside her; the onslaught would begin soon. "I'm taking a plane back today," she said. "When he wakes up, tell Mark I love him. And tell him not to go out dancing until I get there."

The airline was understanding, but the only seat she could get on the two o'clock flight direct to L.A. was in first class, so she took it, making a mental note that her credit card was now used to its limit. She tossed clothes into her suitcase without folding them, and realized after she zipped it shut that she had to call Anthony on the set and tell him. The thought of him seemed distant to her now – a vague image of someone she had known. The only face in her mind now was Mark's. She remembered when he first bought his Porsche – black with gray interior. He drove her up the Coast Highway into Malibu and talked about his dream of becoming a partner in the law firm where he'd been for two and a half years.

"You better become a partner," she teased. "You have to pay off this car."

Just past the Malibu Pier, they had pulled over to watch surfers gliding down waves – small figures against a steep blue background.

"I always wanted to learn how to surf," Sara said.

"Yeah? Gotta watch out for sharks, though." She remembered how Mark had winked at her when he said it.

"Sharks don't scare me," she told him. "Guys in Porsches scare me. The way they make those quick lane changes."

Was that what happened? Had he changed lanes too fast? Or did he not change when he should have? Her mind sped down a long road, took the curves, tried to change what had already happened, erase the sound of impact, of breaking glass.

She'd been sitting on the bed beside her packed suitcase for almost twenty minutes, daydreaming. I have to call Anthony, she reminded herself.

It took almost five minutes for him to come to the phone, even though she'd said it was an emergency. When she told him what had happened, and that she'd be flying back to Los Angeles that afternoon, he answered her in a voice that sounded removed and a little cold.

"Call me when you get there," Anthony told her. "Let me know how he is."

One brief thought snuck through Sara's sadness and fear and stung her as she hung up the phone. She wondered if Allison would be sleeping on Sara's side of the bed that night.

The plane flew through endless daylight, leaving night somewhere behind, in another land. Each time she dozed off, Sara saw Mark's face floating in front of her, always out of reach, at the other end of the sky. She would stretch out her arm, trying to touch him, but he would dissolve, like a mirage when you move closer. It would be early evening when they landed; she calculated how much time it would take to drop her suitcases off at home and drive to the hospital.

The air in Los Angeles was soft and cool and reassuring. It's a city that has a way of welcoming home its natives, Sara thought as she drove to the hospital with all the windows down in the car, glad that she was home, far from Paris and Anthony, telling herself over and over – like a mantra – that Mark was going to be all right. Despite the confusion of time zones and altitudes, and the strange, floating feeling they produce, Sara's mind felt totally focused.

It was almost seven when she walked into his hospital room. Mark was sitting up in bed, eating and watching television. The fact that no one else was there was a good sign; it meant that Claire and Roger Norton felt secure enough in their son's recovery to go home for the night.

"Hey you," Sara said gently, kissing the cheek that didn't have a bandage on it. "I told you Porsche drivers are dangerous."

"No, it's not us. It's the roads that are dangerous." Mark smiled at her, but his eyes hesitated. "You didn't have to come back," he said. "But I'm glad you did."

Sara sat down on the bed. The cast on his left leg was all

the way up to his hip. "You holding up okay?" she asked.

"Yeah, I guess. I keep dreaming about it, though – every time I doze off, I go back to that curve. You know what's strange? I can't remember any sound. It was like the whole world went still. I didn't know – right afterward – how badly I was hurt. My face was bloody and I was in shock, I guess, and I thought, this could be it, I could die."

Sara knew this was the part he hadn't told their parents. How can you talk to your parents about dying, she thought, about the cold wash of terror that comes when you think death might be close? There's a point where talk like that becomes their domain, and you just don't want to trespass. Roger Norton stared out the window a lot these days, mostly at the sky. He walked more slowly and talked often about the slippage of time, when he wasn't talking about their old Cadillac, which he obviously still missed. Claire Norton worried over him, made sure he ate his breakfast, cooked whatever he wanted, and mused about their funeral arrangements. Sara and Mark hadn't talked about it, but she knew they were both feeling the same things. Both of them kept their own personal fears to themselves; neither of them would suggest that fate is unpredictable and that death can blow through anyone's window.

"How did it happen?" Sara asked her brother, focusing her eyes on the right side of his face, avoiding the bandage because she didn't want to imagine what was underneath it.

"I was going too fast – a common ailment of Porsche drivers. I spun out on the curve. See, you were wrong about the quick lane changes. Speed is a bigger problem. I *should* have changed lanes. I might not be in the hospital, and I might still have a car."

That was when Sara's tears came. "Yeah," she said. "I probably should have changed lanes, too. Like a month ago. Jesus, Mark – this isn't supposed to happen to you. You're my big brother, my protector. You're not supposed to get hurt – ever."

She let herself collapse against him, cry against his chest, against the hospital gown that had an antiseptic smell to it.

"Sara, I'm okay," Mark told her, stroking her hair.

"I know. It's just . . . everything."

"Everything, huh. Like Anthony?"

"Yes, partly. Well . . . mostly. But you getting hurt like this . . ." She'd forgotten momentarily how to finish a sentence. Her tears kept cutting her off.

"Hey – " Mark took Sara's face between his hands and stared at her. "I thought you could handle any guy. I didn't think anyone could get the better of you."

"Well, I thought you could handle any car and take any curve. Maybe that's it, huh? We never have as much control as we think we do."

Mark didn't say anything. He let Sara's head rest against his chest again. She could hear her brother's heartbeat in her ear, and she said a silent prayer of thanks that it hadn't been silenced in the explosion of glass and metal.

"You know," Mark said, "I earn my living by trying to take control of situations – the cases people bring me, the courtroom sparring – it's all about control. And I'm good at it. And you've been good at controlling relationships – always making sure you had the upper hand and the last word. The danger is, we get too confident and then something has to happen to restore the balance. We crash, or we slip and fall down a rabbit hole where everything's the wrong size and nothing makes sense. The way I look at it, when I crashed into that pole, I really crashed into myself."

"And me?" Sara said. "Did I fall into myself?"

"I don't know. You're the one down the rabbit hole. You tell me."

"Well, I'm either turning into someone I don't know, or I'm meeting previously unknown parts of myself."

Mark pushed her hair back from her forehead. "I can't tell you what to do about him," he said softly.

"I know. But I can tell *you* what to do – get a bigger car and slow down." She stood up to go. "You should get some sleep. Maybe you'll have better dreams tonight. I'll see you tomorrow."

"You still haven't told me about the rabbit hole."

"I will – as soon as I figure out how I got there."

Sara walked down the hospital corridor, feeling disconnected, heavy with jet lag. The fluorescent lights hurt her eyes. A couple of the doors were ajar, and like a driver downshifting to look at a roadside accident, she slowed down and glanced into one of the rooms where a nurse was bending over a patient's arm, giving an injection. She heard the sound of soft, mumbled words coming from the bed.

She was aware she was intruding – there was probably an unwritten hospital rule that visitors have to keep their eyes straight ahead – but she couldn't help herself. It was a glimpse into other people's suffering and it made her feel better about her own, about Mark's, about their parents' fear. That's probably everyone's motivation for that kind of voyeurism, she thought – it shows how things could be worse.

There was one more open door as she moved down the hall toward the elevator. The room was dark except for a low-watt bulb beside the bed. There was a drawn curtain in the center of the room; beyond it, someone else's pain was hidden from her. But what she saw, just inside the doorway, made her blink a few times, wondering if her jet lag was worse than she had thought. Was it causing her to hallucinate?

An American Indian was sitting at the bedside of a man who Sara guessed was in his thirties. Blood was leaking through the bandage around the man's head and bottles dangled above him, dripping liquids into his veins. The Indian turned and looked at her.

"Come in," he said calmly, as if he'd been waiting for her.

She told herself that curiosity was pulling her into the room, or maybe it was her exhaustion that felt like a hypnotic drug. But she had the vague sense that he was pulling her in – with some kind of energy she couldn't identify.

He had long hair, anchored with a thin leather headband, an eagle feather dangling from it, and beaded and turquoise jewelry around his neck and wrists. Sara guessed he was in his late fifties, maybe even sixty; his hair was streaked with gray and his face was deeply lined.

"Pull that chair up," he said in a soft voice – almost in a whisper.

She moved the chair over and sat down beside him. His eyes were so dark they were almost black. And they had stories in them, she could see that. But then, hers probably did too and she wasn't at all sure she wanted anyone to decipher them.

"You shouldn't be so reckless with your soul. You're letting too many fingerprints get on it," he said, staring hard at her, deciphering things whether she liked it or not.

"Actually, it's my body that has too many fingerprints on it, but that's another story."

She broke away from his stare, which was starting to make her squirm, and looked at the bandaged man in the bed. His breathing was slow and labored. She half expected to turn her eyes back to the Indian and find him gone – an apparition, a phantom from another world who just dropped by to give her a message. But he was still there, watching her as though he'd known her for years. She knew that if he were just some guy in a suit from C & R Clothiers, she'd have been on the elevator five minutes ago. She could hear herself telling Mark the next day, "No, he was a real Indian, I swear."

"Who is he?" Sara asked, tilting her head toward the bed.

"My son. He had a motorcycle accident."

"Will he be okay?"

"He won't be the same," he said softly. His voice made her think of wind.

"What's your name?" she asked after a moment.

"Loqui." He zeroed in on her again. "You ever hear of walk-ins?"

"Only as they apply to closets."

"You make jokes when you're nervous, don't you? What's your name?"

"Sara. And yes, I do. Some people bite their nails, I make jokes."

"A walk-in is a spirit that hasn't been able to move on, that's still tied to the earth, still has things it wants to accomplish here. In order to do that, it has to inhabit someone who is physically here. It has to walk into a body – someone who for whatever reason can't defend themselves against that kind of invasion."

"If you're telling me that some spirit has moved in on me, I'd say it's probably a toss-up between H. G. Wells and Sylvia Plath."

He stared hard at her. A serious stare, one that said, stop fucking around.

"Okay," Sara said, "I'll try to refrain from making jokes. So why are you telling me this? You think I've been infiltrated?"

"No, but I think you've been around a walk-in. Maybe someone who pushes you, then pulls you, who changes quickly, mysteriously? Someone who confuses you?"

"What makes you think that?"

"Because you look confused," Loqui said.

Sara laughed a little. "Oh, I get it – this is about logic, not mysticism, right?"

"Mysticism is always about logic to a certain degree. You have the same look in your eyes that my son had in his for a long time. I tried to warn him about some of the people he was hanging around with. Not just because I'm his father, and not just because of the motorcycle and the drinking. It was more than that. A darkness was creeping in, and he was sinking – I could see it. And the fingerprints on his soul – there were too many, like I told you. The world is never a safe place. You have to protect yourself even against things you can't see."

Behind Loqui's voice, Sara thought she heard other sounds, faint and distant – the sweep of wind across flat, empty land, the call of an owl, the beating of a drum. History was at her heels, turning her into Achilles. He was the Native American; she was the Impostor, descended from thieves who slaughtered for the right to use the name.

"How can I protect myself?" Sara asked.

"You already know the answers. You just have to remember. I have to go now – I need to be alone and pray. My son will not live through the night."

"The doctors told you that?" Sara said.

"No. They don't know. But I do."

He shook her hand good-bye. It was a hand she didn't want to let go of. As she walked out, she looked back and almost expected the shadows to fold around him and swallow him. But he stayed – in the uncomfortable hospital chair, eyes closed in prayer.

Sara wasn't even sure anymore if she was tired. She wasn't sure of very much. It was one of those "Toto, are we still on planet Earth?" feelings. She wandered in the general direction of her car, not really wanting to go home and be alone with just the sound of her own footsteps. She passed a pay phone, stopped, and decided to wait for the man huddled in the fluorescent-lit cubicle to finish his call. Belinda lived near UCLA; she might be home and save Sara from the fate of walking through an empty house, colliding with herself.

Slices of life are played out at pay phones. She'd used enough of them, she'd seen just about everything – men lying to their wives as their date stands outside, trying to look nonchalant; tears, anger, the desperation of calling for a job or an apartment. The man in the booth was so bent in on himself, he was hard to read. One arm was draped over the top of the phone, the other was wrapped across his stomach, and he was sort of doubled over, as if he were feeling the onset of appendicitis. Sara guessed: mid-thirties, maybe a stockbroker or a real estate agent, and either someone he knows is in the hospital or he's just been told to slow down before his heart explodes. Probably smokes, chews gum, and drinks coffee all at the same time. He hung up the phone abruptly, burst out of the phone booth, and said "Sorry" to Sara as he rushed past. For what, she didn't know; maybe he thought she'd been waiting there for an hour.

"Belinda, it's me."

"You're here?"

"I'm at UCLA. I just saw Mark and he's doing okay. But I didn't feel like going home. I guess I just feel kind of lonely. Can I come over?"

"Come over," Belinda said. "Stay the night. I don't want you to be alone."

Belinda lived in a guest house on a tree-shaded street just east of Westwood Village. A large yard separated her house from the main one, and a narrow pebbled path led to her door. Anyone entering Belinda's house passed into a magical world of crystals, old lace, and Maxfield Parrish prints. She had antique shawls draped over tables, crystals hanging in front of windows so that at various times of the day prismatic light danced across the walls and floor. Incense was almost always burning, and at night the house was lit more by candles than lamps. Sara knew, from being on a couple of location shoots with Belinda, that she did something similar to hotel rooms – bought flowers, draped shawls and lace over the chairs – made them more like home.

Belinda opened the door before Sara had a chance to knock. The crunching of footsteps on the path alerted her to visitors. Framed in the doorway, with gold light behind her, she looked young and fragile. Her hair was still bleached white-blond, but it wasn't moussed and gelled and spiked. It was soft and boyish, falling over her forehead. She was wearing an ivory-colored antique slip, and the smell of incense hovered around her, poured out of the open door.

"You okay?" she said when she and Sara hugged.

"Yeah – just sort of strung out, you know. There's been a lot of drama lately."

They didn't talk much, as if they both understood that, for a while at least, wandering around the house, looking at a new dress Belinda had bought, fixing toast and tea, was enough to take the edge off a bad night. Belinda's house was small and the living-room couch wasn't long enough to sleep on. It was just understood that they would both sleep in the bed. They didn't really start talking until they were under the covers and Belinda had blown out the jasmine-scented candle that had been the only light illuminating the room.

"I should leave him, but I don't think I can," Sara said, her voice threading into the dark.

"Anthony?"

"Uh-huh. My life feels like it's coming apart at the seams."

"I know that feeling," Belinda said, propping herself up on her elbow. Sara could smell the coconut body lotion she always used. "You know, it seems so unfair," Belinda continued. "Why are the men who are so seductive, so sexy, and so magnetic, usually the heart pirates? And the real nerdy ones are the sensitive, caring souls who would never fuck you over."

"Would never fuck you at all," Sara added.

"Exactly. Or if they do, it's over in two minutes and the guy's so small you can't really tell if he's come or not."

"You gotta check out their feet, Belinda. You know, big feet, big dick?"

"The other night, I was out to dinner with a girl who was my assistant on the last film. The waiter brought over a bottle of wine and said that it had been sent over to us by an admirer. So I looked around the restaurant and found the dorkiest guy in the place and said, 'Him?' The waiter said, 'Yeah, how'd you know?' I mean, it always happens, right? It couldn't possibly have been the guy with the great tan who looked like the Aramis ad."

Sara rolled over on her side and squished the pillow under her head. "Belinda, do you think there was some cosmic plot way back at the beginning of time? Where God said, 'Okay, here's the deal. The guys with small penises and no aptitude for lovemaking, the guys who drool when they kiss and come too fast, will have the redeeming qualities of integrity, sensitivity, and just general niceness. And in the other column, I'll put the guys with big dicks, who give great head, know how to make women scream, give them multiple orgasms every night. Of course, they'll be the schmucks of the earth and will leave a trail of shattered hearts behind them. But, hey, you can't have everything.' I guess the real question is, do you think God was having a bad day when He created men?"

"Maybe," Belinda said. "It's really the only logical explanation." She lay back on the pillow, took a deep breath, and let it out slowly. "Who came up with that theory about the size of a man's penis being irrelevant, anyway?"

"Some guy with a small one."

"No woman I know has ever said that. I mean, you can't even tell if he's inside you. And then you feel so guilty because you don't want to hurt him – after all, he can't help it – but it's like, you really don't know. Is he inside or outside? It seems kind of rude to ask."

"Too big isn't good either, though," Sara said. "I started seeing this guy when I got out of college. The first time we went to bed, and I realized how big he was, I thought, 'Jesus, I don't think I can handle this.' I swear, he was so big I didn't know what to do with it. So I just hugged it."

"See, the problem is that the guys with perfect dicks are usually the dangerous ones. They kind of fuck you into this trance and when you come out of it you look down and say, 'Holy shit, what happened to my heart? It looks like scorched earth.' "

"Yeah, so what's the solution?" Sara asked. "Find a guy with small feet and invest in a vibrator?"

Belinda laughed and then fell silent. After a minute or two she rolled on her side and propped herself up on her elbow again. "You know what? I'm really sorry if Anthony is causing you pain, but at least now I feel you can understand what I go through. I always felt you were kind of above it, you know? Like this kind of thing could never happen to you."

"I thought that, too," Sara said. "I guess I'm being humbled." She could feel the silk of Belinda's slip against her thigh. She reached up and hugged her. "I love you a lot."

"I love you, too," Belinda told her, and lay back on her pillow. "Good night."

"Good night."

Sara stared at the ceiling, listening to Belinda's breathing beside her. Why had it been so easy to have sex with Allison – someone she didn't know and might never see again? Yet with Belinda, whom she loved and would probably risk her life for, sex had never even been a consideration. What did Erica Jong call it? The zipless fuck? Maybe anonymity is where the greatest freedom is. Maybe boundaries are set up with the people you know and have relationships with – the people who might still be there a year from now. But with the stranger in the hotel room, the stranger in a foreign city, nothing is reined in – you go at it like the wind's at your back and you have a passport to anywhere.

Sara slid her hand across the sheet and found Belinda's hand. Their fingers locked and held on, but Sara wasn't sure if Belinda was awake; maybe her hand involuntarily responded to her friend's closeness, even in sleep. She was lying on her back and Sara was trying to see a flutter of her eyelids – some sign that she was awake. But the room was too dark. Her other hand moved through the shadows and came to rest on Belinda's collarbone. She let her fingers travel where they wanted – along the length of bone to the shoulder, into the crease between her arm and her breast where the skin was softer.

Belinda turned onto her side then, her body giving in, surrendering against Sara's. But still the only sound was their breathing. Sara buried her face in Belinda's neck, pressed her mouth against the pulse. Their legs were intertwined; the silk of Belinda's slip was the only thing between them. It slid across Sara's skin, with the warmth of flesh just beneath it. It was when she started to slide it up, over Belinda's hips, and her arm pushed the two of them more tightly together, when there was no longer any silk between them and Belinda was wet against her thigh, moving against her, that something inside Sara backed up and said no. She shifted her leg back a little and Belinda hesitated, some of the fever draining out of her.

"I can't do this with someone I love," Sara whispered,

and then moved her mouth over Belinda's, kissing her before pulling away.

Maybe the kiss was to stop any words from falling out of Belinda's mouth. Maybe it was a way of saying "I'm sorry" or "Please understand." Or maybe it was the only thing that made sense right then. Sara wasn't sure. But no words did fall out of Belinda's mouth; she rolled over, back to her side of a bed that suddenly seemed much wider. And Sara squeezed her eyes shut against the darkness, thinking that it wasn't dark enough.

The dream that took over her eventual sleep was so real that for weeks to come, Sara could remember it vividly. In it, she was sitting outside the mouth of a small cave. Inside there was a huge fire, burning so hot that Sara had to move back from the entrance – the heat was singeing her. Yet inside the cave, apparently immune to the fire, sat Anthony, looking perfectly relaxed and comfortable. A few yards from Sara, leaning against a tree, was Belinda, who was yelling at Anthony, calling him a bastard, a motherfucker, screaming that she hated him. Anthony turned and glanced at Sara, brushed a burning ember from his hair, and that was when Sara noticed Allison sitting beside him in the cave, also unaffected by the flames and the heat. Sara wondered why she couldn't do that, why she found the heat so intense she couldn't even get close to the entrance. She watched as Allison leaned over and kissed Anthony, and he encircled her with his arms. Sara's voice rose to match Belinda's.

"Get off my property!" she screamed at Anthony. "Go fuck the blonde somewhere else!"

Allison and Anthony crawled out of the cave, brushed cinders off themselves, and walked into the woods. The only sounds came from inside the cave and from the woods – flames slapping against the rock and a gasp of wind through the trees that had swallowed Allison and Anthony.

Nine

Sara

THE NEXT morning, Sara and Belinda didn't talk about what had happened between them. Sara told her about her dream. They picked oranges off the tree in the backyard and made juice, fixed toast and coffee, and read their horoscopes aloud from the morning paper.

"What are you doing tonight?" Belinda asked, sitting down at the kitchen table across from Sara and mixing butter and brown sugar together with a fork until it was brown goo, which she then spread on her toast.

"What are you doing to your toast? is a more relevant question," Sara said.

"I like it this way. I used to do it with white sugar when I was a kid, but I switched to brown so it would be healthier."

"Belinda, that's like someone bragging that they used to smoke Marlboros, but they switched to Carltons for the health of their lungs. Sugar is sugar and smoke is smoke. Anyway, I don't have plans tonight. I'm going to visit Mark this morning and I'll probably go out to my parents' house later."

Belinda moved her chair back from the table. "I'd really like you to come to a lecture with me," she said.

"Do I dare ask what it is? People whose mothers didn't breast-feed them?"

"See, you always do this," Belinda said, tossing her toast onto the plate. "Whenever there's something you don't want to hear about, you get sarcastic and make fun of it."

"Someone else just commented on that," Sara mumbled under her breath.

"What?"

"Nothing. Okay, I promise I'll be open-minded. No more jokes. What's the lecture on?"

"He's a spiritual guide – his name's Philippe," Belinda said.

"Oh yeah, I've heard of him. What's his last name, anyway?"

"Just Philippe. He lectures on conquering your spiritual enemies by defending your soul. He says other people will steal it unless you guard it and defend it."

"What kind of armaments are we talking about here?" Sara had a feeling that when Loqui cautioned her about protecting herself, he wasn't thinking quite so militaristically.

"The will," Belinda told her, leaning forward as if she were sharing a well-guarded secret. "Philippe says your will has to become like iron. He even has us do physical exercises to strengthen our willpower." She had a slightly enraptured look on her face, a too-familiar expression that always made Sara nervous. Belinda didn't have the best judgment when it came to getting enraptured.

"Okay, I'll come with you. But if these exercises are in the walking-on-burning-coals category, I'm out of there."

"No, they're not like that. Meet me back here at six."

Sara started to think back over the things she'd heard

about Philippe. He seemed to be carving out a spiritual path for an increasingly large number of followers, based solely on his own interpretation of the Cosmos, the Bible, and whatever else fell into the pot. There were numerous stories about him. Supposedly, he had done healings, performed miracles, but refused to demonstrate these gifts publicly, saying he didn't want to be a circus act. But all of these stories were related through others; Philippe himself never commented on anything to the press. He shunned the media, letting his followers build up his celebrity status. The aura of mystery that surrounded him was either a reflection of who he really was, Sara thought, or the best public relations strategy she'd seen in years.

Sara arrived at the hospital a little after ten. As she got off the elevator, she thought she smelled her mother's perfume. Chanel No. 5. It had been Claire Norton's scent for all of Sara's life. To reach Mark's room, she had to pass the room Loqui had been in last night. Maybe he'd be in there, maybe his son would be awake and she could tell him she'd met his father and they had talked for a while. She knocked softly on the door and after a few seconds of silence, opened it slowly. The bed was empty, remade with fresh sheets and square corners.

"He won't live through the night," Loqui had told her.

"Were you looking for someone?" A woman's voice came from behind her. Sara turned. A nurse was standing in the hallway holding a tray with little paper cups full of pills on it.

"The man who was in this room," Sara said. "What happened?"

"I'm sorry – are you a friend of his? Or of the family?"

"No. I mean – I just met his father last night. I was going to visit, and – is he – did he die?"

"I'm sorry . . . yes. Late last night," the nurse said, and then turned away.

Nurses make such a soft, white sound when they walk away, Sara thought – as if they don't want to leave too much of a memory behind.

Sara knew she would never see Loqui again. She leaned against the wall in the hallway and closed her eyes, trying to imagine where Loqui might be right then, trying to place him in some setting that made sense. But she couldn't imagine him in Los Angeles, or in any city, for that matter. All that came to mind was snow, as if he could only exist as part of winter, with bare black branches etching the sky above him. It was only in that landscape that Loqui's face came to her. She could even hear his footsteps crunching through the snow, echoing in the frozen white air.

There was a time when Sara could only imagine Mark in a white world with shavings of snow on the shoulders of his overcoat. When he was at Columbia Law School, his letters to her were so vivid in their descriptions of breath-clouds hanging in the air and snow piled against buildings that she couldn't picture him walking through any other season. When he came home that summer and she saw him coming up the brick path at their parents' house, with sunlight blazing around him, she almost didn't recognize him.

"Are you okay?"

The voice came from outside her daydream. Sara opened her eyes and saw a young man in a white doctor's jacket standing in front of her.

"Yeah. I was just resting my eyes . . . catching my breath. Something like that. I'm here to see my brother."

She moved toward Mark's door, in case there was some regulation about loitering in hospital corridors. Maybe the guy thought she was there to steal stethoscopes or get signatures on a petition. She wanted to make it clear that she was a legitimate visitor, there on hospital business.

". . . it won't be any trouble, you can have your old room," her mother was saying to Mark when Sara walked in.

"His old room? You mean the one that hasn't changed at all since he went away to college twenty years ago?" Sara said, kissing her mother on the cheek. "In fact, I'll bet we could probably dig up your old Lone Ranger bed sheets."

Sara hugged Mark, holding on to him longer than she had intended. He was the one person in her life whom she felt she could always run to, no matter what. His arms would always open to take her in.

"Where's Dad?"

"He didn't feel like coming." Claire Norton's face shifted expressions, turned darker, the way faces do when some sadness bubbles to the surface.

"Is he okay?" Sara asked. "Is he sick?"

"No, dear, it's not like that. He just got very upset being in the hospital, and seeing Mark. . . ."

"He was here the first night," Mark added.

But Sara knew what it was. Her father was getting to the point in his life when hospitals looked like omens. Lives shouldn't end in places like this, is probably what he was thinking. He probably held it together long enough to be assured that Mark would be all right, then his own fears caught up with him.

Sara looked at her mother touching Mark's forehead as

though he were a child again and she needed to determine if she should keep him home from school. She was wearing navy blue slacks, a white blouse, and flat, unstylish shoes with the backs scrunched down from her habit of slipping her feet halfway out whenever she sat down. Something about the shoes made Sara sad. They were a marker of her mother's age, a sign that she just couldn't be bothered putting on real shoes before going out of the house; she was leaving that kind of vanity to younger women. What do you do when you see these changes in your parents? Sara wondered. Remember to look in the mirror tonight and ask yourself where the years went, she thought, briefly acknowledging her guilt at being a less-than-attentive child to her parents.

"So it's all settled," Claire Norton said to Mark. "You'll get well at home, where I can take care of you."

"For a little while, Mother," Mark answered. "Just until I can get around better."

"It's all settled, then." She stood up and tucked her purse under her arm. "Come by later," she said to Sara. "Visit your father."

"I will. 'Bye, Mother."

Sara sat on the bed and crossed her legs Indian-style; it was the way she used to sit on Mark's bed when they were younger and were having one of their serious discussions about life.

"You're making her very happy, you know," she told him. "She gets to be a mother again."

"I know. How could I turn her down? So? What's going on with you? I can see all these little storm clouds swirling around your head."

"That obvious, huh?" The bandage on Mark's face had been changed to a smaller one, easier for Sara to look at.

She took a deep breath and exhaled slowly. "I feel like I don't know who I am anymore. I even think my face is changing – like from the inside out. You know what I mean?"

"I think it's called an identity crisis."

"Yeah, aptly named. I don't know what's happening to me, Mark. I'm doing things that are totally against my nature. At least I think they are."

"Such as?" he asked.

"I stayed with Belinda last night and I almost made love with her – I mean, we started to and then we stopped. I'm not sure what confuses me the most, that it began or that we stopped."

One of the things Sara loved about Mark was that nothing ever shocked him. He was one of those people she could say anything to with no fear about what his reaction might be.

"I'm not so sure you should be confused about it," he said after thinking for a few seconds. "The two of you have been friends for a long time. People search for ways to express their love. Maybe at that moment, it seemed like sex was the way to do it. Maybe your feelings for her were overwhelming, you felt really close to her and wanted to be closer. It could be as uncomplicated as that, you know."

"But it was loving her that stopped me . . . I think. Shit, I'm so confused. I hate this – I'm used to having things figured out."

Mark narrowed his eyes and didn't move them from Sara's face. "Is there something you're not telling me? Some part of this story you're leaving out?"

"This is why you're a good lawyer, isn't it?" Sara said.

"Uh-huh. It's that instinct thing. So? You going to give me the missing link?"

Sara wanted to look away from her brother, but she didn't let herself. "I had sex with this woman – girl, actually – I mean, she was younger than me – in Paris. With Anthony."

Mark blinked his eyes slowly a couple of times. "You mean the three of you together?"

"Not exactly. Anthony just watched. It was all he could do. I tied him up."

Mark started laughing; his face was getting red and his eyes were watering. "Did you untie him before you left for L.A.?" He put his hand up to his bandaged cheek. "Ow. What's that joke about it only hurting when you laugh?" But he couldn't stop.

"Why is this funny?" Sara asked, but she was starting to laugh too, with no idea why.

"I don't know. From what you've told me, we might be talking karmic retribution here."

They were both laughing uncontrollably and Sara was afraid the nurse would come in and sedate Mark just to shut him up. "Sh – they're going to kick me out for disturbing the peace," she said between fits of laughter.

"Okay, okay." Mark took some deep breaths and got himself under control. "Serious question. Did you like it with this girl?"

"I don't know. It doesn't even seem real now. It was like a dream – a very angry dream. Anthony can do that to me. He has some kind of power over me."

"You know what I think?" Mark said.

"Tell me."

"You're not going to like it."

"Yeah, well that seems to be par for the course these days."

Mark smiled. "I think Anthony might be the best thing that ever happened to you."

"Excuse me?"

"You remember the day we went back to the orchard and you hit Lane?" Mark asked her.

"Of course I remember. I broke his nose."

"Well, I watched you that day. And afterward. I thought that even though there was a part of you that was horrified at smashing someone's face in, there was also a part of you that liked taking charge and winning. And over the years, I've seen you refine that technique – not by bloodying your knuckles, but by letting men bloody theirs trying to get through the fortress you've put around you."

He stopped talking and the silence between them felt fragile and motionless, as if neither of them were breathing.

"Go on," Sara said softly.

"You'd go for men who seemed kind of dangerous, then you'd manage to turn them into sniveling little boys."

"Like Lane."

"Exactly. Without the bloody nose, of course, but metaphorically . . . you were back in the orchard with your dukes up. I don't know if you've ever really left the orchard. It makes sense that you'd eventually meet your match. The only guy who almost made you soften – almost made you let someone in – was that guy in your senior year of college. The one with gray eyes."

"Daniel. The transplanted New Yorker who thought California was better headquarters for revolutionizing America."

"As soon as you saw that he could get through your armor," Mark said, "you dumped him. And as I remember, you were pretty fucking cold about it."

"So I needed to be taken down a few notches and that's

Anthony's role in my life – is that what you're saying, O Wise Sage?"

"Basically, yes. He's dangerous enough to keep you interested, and you can't get control of him, which is even more interesting. So, something's gotta give. You're going to learn some things from this one, baby sister. Things about yourself. Better be prepared."

"I hate it when you tell me what I need to hear," Sara said, as she gingerly unfolded her leg, which had fallen asleep while they were talking. "Just for your information, though, I haven't been entirely consistent in my choice of men. Daniel didn't attract me because he was dangerous. He attracted me because he was an amazing person. And along with that, he had this thing with his eyes – no matter what he was talking about, his eyes looked like sex. It was incredible. Without a sound track, you'd swear he either just made love, was about to, or was deep in the throes of some erotic fantasy."

"Okay, I stand corrected on that one small, slightly irrelevant point. Come here and hug me so I know you're not pissed off at me," Mark said.

Sara slid up on the bed and nestled against him, wishing she were younger than she was and could still believe that her brother would protect her from anything the world threw at her.

She walked out of the hospital into the city's thick smog and syrupy air. Even the trees along the sidewalk looked as though they were expiring from heat exhaustion. It was one of those days that turn entire families into serial killers, Sara thought.

But part of her was back on the Berkeley campus in October, all those years ago, standing beside Daniel, staring into dark gray eyes that made her think of the sea after a storm. He was out to save the world – from nuclear proliferation, environmental disaster, and the male-macho obsession with missiles. Sara was there merely to get a liberal arts degree. In the presence of such a crusader, she really had felt herself softening; Mark had been right. It was Jericho time – walls were tumbling down, and it scared the hell out of her. In Daniel's presence, she felt herself becoming defenseless; she was in awe of his commitment, and when she listened to him, it was as though fissures were opening up in her, letting strange sensations in. It was his eyes that held her, but it was also that his whole face was sort of stormy – dark, strong lines and black hair that he tied back most of the time but that other times blew across his face and made him look like an Indian brave out to defend the prairie against the scourge of the white man. Actually, Daniel was Italian, but with his hair down . . . Sara's imagination jumped into overdrive whenever she was with him, which was another thing that scared her.

And when they made love, she felt herself flowing into him, as if they were under water and tides were pushing them together with a strength greater than their own. She felt lost, out of her element – and definitely out of control. She started to insist on always being on top during sex, but she still felt moons and tides were at her back, pushing her closer, when she had never in her life wanted to be that close to anyone, even a man with drop-dead looks, Gandhi's spirit, and De Niro's accent. Mark was right about her coldness, too. She just jumped ship without giving Daniel a lifeboat. She didn't even give him the "we'll still be friends" bit – the expected consolation prize at the end of any relationship. It was more like: "I can't handle this. I'm outa here. Don't call, because I'll hang up and I won't call back." He did call, she did hang up, and when he left messages she never called back. She felt guilty at the time, but not guilty enough to stop acting like a spoiled, inconsiderate brat.

The heat pressed down on her, rose up from the cement and made her feet feel like glue. She wished she had the power to transform the sky – make black clouds gather and crack open. She wanted rain to change the color and mood of a day she didn't like. She wanted it to churn in gutters, make streets impassable, drive everyone indoors. Everyone except her, of course. She'd stand out in the storm until she was drenched. Until she felt the rain had washed her clean.

Her house looked dustier in daylight than it had the night before; her unpacked suitcases were in the middle of the floor and the message light on the phone machine was blinking. She stood in the doorway for a minute, wondering what to do first – play back her messages, unpack, or attack the room with the Dustbuster. The phone machine won.

"*Ma chérie*," Anthony's recorded voice said, in a bad French accent. "I wanted to check on you and see how you are. I hope your brother is okay. It's around five here – eight a.m. your time, which makes me wonder where you are. I'm at the hotel. I'll be waiting to hear from you."

She felt irritated – at the arrogant tone of his voice, at the atrocious French accent.

"He oughta leave the accents to actors. He's a director. Suddenly he's trying to be Gérard Depardieu," Sara mumbled as she erased his message, feeling some kind of power at being able to send his voice into phone-message oblivion. But mostly she was irritated that the sound of his voice made her want to take off her clothes, climb into bed, and make out with her pillow.

She took a shower, rehearsed an I-don't-care tone of voice ("Hi, Anthony, I'm returning your call . . .") that bounced off the tiles and hardly sounded convincing. She took her time getting dressed and drying her hair, as if somehow Anthony would know that she wasn't rushing to call him back. When she finally sat down on the bed to call, it was after nine in Paris. They rang his room and the line was busy. Sara said she'd hold for a couple of minutes, but after almost five, she hung up. Whatever power she'd thought she had drained out of her fingertips when she put the receiver down; he could weaken her without even getting on the line. Just a busy signal could do it. She imagined his phone off the hook, Allison on top of him. Or maybe someone else – some French chick with a pouty mouth and no cellulite anywhere on her body.

Sara hated it that she was getting angry. She hated it that she cared. She took a deep breath and called again. Still busy.

"Fuck you," she said as she slammed the phone down.

She sat on the bed and listened to the silence of the house. And then she looked down at her hands. Seeing them, it seemed, for the first time. Were they really her hands? The skin was coarse, the veins were prominent, the skin over her knuckles was loose. Oh God, she was getting older. She had no children and her history of relationships read like a wargames manual. There was a pile of clothes in the corner and a stack of books by the window that she hadn't gotten around to putting away. But no one was there to see her disorganization – to add his own to it or to inspire her to clean things up. There are women who don't even know what it's like to live alone, without a man. Sara knew a few like that – women who had never lived in a house as silent as hers, never wondered who would come if they called out late at night. These women knew someone would respond. Sara had wondered occasionally, on sleepless nights, if anyone would hear her if she screamed, if anyone would find her if . . . She tried to put roadblocks up along her imagination's more morbid detours. Usually, she was only marginally successful.

Sometimes solitude feels like a dungeon, she thought. You hear chains rattling and you know they're yours. Alexander Graham Bell probably invented the phone at a time like that – sitting alone in his room, smoking a pipe, feeling himself getting closer to the falls, the black slide of depression. He probably thought, "If only I could reach someone easily. A letter takes too long and carrier pigeons are hardly dependable." Because it's at those moments when the phone becomes more than a convenience. It becomes a lifeline. People with a stomach full of sleeping pills and doubts tiptoeing in reach for it before they die. They call to say good-bye, or please save me, but actually, it's the same message. The phone becomes the vehicle for saying please save me from myself, and please hurry.

Sara knew she had to call someone. But who? That's when you know it's bad: when the phone itself and the act of connecting becomes more important than the person you're calling. When you can't even decide who to call. When it doesn't even matter. Anyone will do – any voice, any living presence on the other end of the line. Those are the only times when that silly jingle "Reach out and touch someone" makes sense. They don't tell you whom you should touch. They don't say reach out and touch your mother or your sister or your best friend. Just someone. Anyone.

For some reason, Sara thought of calling her agent. But Miriam was probably still annoyed at her for blowing off that film job and going to Paris. Besides, it was Saturday; she'd have to call her at home, and Miriam was a single mother with a fourteen-year-old son. She was even crankier at home than she was at the office.

The hospital switchboard put her through to Mark's room in a matter of seconds.

"Hello?"

"Mark, I'm scared. What if I end up as one of those weird old ladies who wear their bathrobes till noon and spend their nights watching 'Wheel of Fortune' and eating Stouffer's Lean Cuisine on one of those little fold-out TV tables?"

"Sara, did something happen between the time you left here and the time you got home? Where did this come from?"

"My head," Sara told him. "It came from my head."

"That's what I was afraid of."

"I just had this vision of myself thirty years from now, all alone, with back issues of *National Geographic* and *The Enquirer* piled up on the floor and fifty-five cats running around, and weeds all around the house because the gardener thought I was crazy and wouldn't come back. And the only time I get out is on Tuesdays when the old person's shuttle bus comes to get me – "

"Sara – "

"What?"

"What are you talking about?"

Sara thought for a minute, looked down at her hands, which actually didn't look too bad after all, except she needed a manicure. "I don't really know," she said. "I just got this depressing picture of the rest of my life and got hysterical."

"*National Geographic* and *The Enquirer*?" Mark asked.

"It could happen. Diversity, you know?"

"I have a suggestion for you, Sara," Mark said.

"What? Put Thorazine in my morning coffee?"

"No. Go out and see Mother and Dad like you planned, get out of the house, and stop waiting for Anthony to call."

"Actually, he did call when I was at the hospital," Sara said. "I've been waiting for him to get off the phone so I could return his call."

"Stop waiting for him to get off the phone. I told you you'd learn some lessons from this. I didn't say you had to become obsessed."

"That's the problem – I am," Sara said softly. "But you're right – I'll say hello to your old room for you, tell it you'll be back soon and maybe I can even scrounge up those Lone Ranger sheets."

There were always smells around the house Sara grew up in that sent her tumbling back into childhood – for a moment at least. Usually there was the smell of orange blossoms. There weren't as many trees as there used to be, but there were enough to perfume the air.

Roger Norton was sitting by the living room window, staring out at a landscape that wasn't too much of a landscape anymore. Just a lot of asphalt and houses, with a few trees here and there. But as Sara pulled a chair over beside him and sat down, she suspected that his mind's eye was seeing something different – changing the view outside the window, softening it with memories.

"Hi, Dad," she said quietly, not wanting to startle him.

His eyes smiled a little; they were more gray than they used to be, as if the blue had given up and let a softer color move in. "Remember that old car we used to have?" he said. "The Cadillac?"

"Yeah. The car that wouldn't die."

"Best car I ever had. I miss that car sometimes." He looked at Sara and blinked a few times, bringing her into focus.

"I saw Mark today, Dad. He's doing much better. He's going to leave the hospital and stay here for a few days – Mother probably told you. Just until he gets stronger."

"I know," her father said. And now his eyes were riveted on her. "That hospital scared me. When you get to my age, you start to get glimpses of the end of your life and you see real clear how you don't want it to end. There are some places you just don't want to be in when you close your eyes for the last time."

"Dad, you're going to be around for a long time," Sara told him, and took his hand. But that wasn't true and they both knew it. Time was catching up to him, conquering him.

He turned back to the window and Sara sat quietly. For nearly an hour she sat with him, holding his hand, saying nothing. It just mattered that she was there – his eyes had told her that.

She spent the rest of the afternoon helping her mother get Mark's room ready.

"Remember when I used to wake you kids up – from naps or in the morning?" Claire Norton said at one point, while she was busy smoothing out wrinkles from the bedspread. "Remember what I used to tell you?"

"Uh-huh. You told us you had to look and see if there were stars in our eyes. Because then you'd know whether we'd slept and gone to dreamland."

Her mother got a sweet, distant look on her face. "You always get stars in your eyes in dreamland," she said. "It's funny – Mark always liked to hear about that more than you did."

"I was afraid to dream," Sara said in a soft voice.

"What, dear?"

"Nothing. Just mumbling to myself."

Belinda had that enraptured look on her face again as she maneuvered her VW in and out of traffic, telling Sara too many times that she didn't want to miss one word of Philippe's lecture.

"Where are we going?" Sara asked. "Where does this amazing event take place?"

"In the ballroom of the Holiday Inn."

"I didn't know Holiday Inns had ballrooms. Somehow it seems incongruous."

"Stop it, Sara. All hotels have ballrooms," Belinda said.

Although not all hotel ballrooms are filled with the smell of incense, Sara thought as they entered the place, and have people swaying with eyes half closed to Helen Reddy's "You and Me Against the World".

"Belinda," Sara whispered as they stood in line, waiting to pay their twenty dollars so they could walk into the incense cloud, "if this is a Greatest Hits CD and 'I Am Woman' plays next, I'm outa here."

Which actually seemed like a distinct possibility, since there were far fewer men milling around than women. And all the women seemed to have the same enraptured look that Belinda was wearing. Mass hypnosis. Or else very strong incense. After they paid their money, the woman standing at the doorway hugged each of them and said, "Welcome. I'm so glad you're here."

"Belinda," Sara whispered insistently.

"What?"

"Is this one of those things where you have to hug everyone? I hate strangers touching me."

"Sara, you have to open up more. That's one of the reasons I thought this would be really good for you."

They found seats and two more people came up and hugged Belinda. Sara sat silently, staring at her lap hoping that they would assume she was meditating and leave her alone. It was hard to tell when the shaking inside her began. It started in her stomach and spread to her other organs. She thought that maybe she'd had too much coffee, but she hadn't had any since that morning. And then, while she was wondering about it, the entire room fell quiet. Sara turned around to look behind her, and a wiry, dark-haired man was walking down the center aisle; people were parting for him like the Red Sea. As he got closer to the row where she and Belinda were sitting, Sara's shaking got worse. And as he passed them and moved farther away, the shaking diminished. But it left, in its wake, a sense of terror, something icy and glacial that was beyond the range of rational thought.

"Who is this guy?" Sara said to Belinda, although she wasn't really sure she was directing the question at Belinda. It probably should have been directed at the heavens, like in some Greek tragedy – please, God, who is this? Because something's happening here, Sara thought, and it doesn't feel right.

"It's Philippe," Belinda whispered back. "I told you."

"I know. That's not what I meant."

Belinda gave her a puzzled look and then turned back to stare at Philippe, who was poised in front of the microphone. As Sara raised her head and looked toward the front of the room, she realized that this small, wiry man with slicked-back hair and an expensive suit was sending some kind of energy into the crowd, and even if there had been a thousand people there, they never could have overpowered whatever was coming from him.

Ten

Belinda

AT WHAT point does another person slip into the cracks of your psyche? Belinda wondered. Is there a precise moment? How can someone set up residence in the tunnels of your soul, in those private spaces you've spent years locking everyone out of? Can it happen at the first meeting? Or only after they've sized you up, mapped out the entry points? Or only after you've handed them the keys?

These thoughts occurred to Belinda as she sat in the Holiday Inn ballroom, but not for the first time. Philippe had gotten in there – that much she knew. She kept bumping into him in her mind; at every turn of her thoughts she saw him standing there, arms outstretched, beckoning her. There was something calm about him, yet something unsettling, frenzied. She felt as if she were playing at the edge of a hurricane, and she wasn't sure if Philippe was the calm eye or the wind.

She'd avoided telling Sara that she'd met with him privately. It had happened the fifth time she came to one of his lectures. A staff member came over to her and whispered, "Philippe would like to see you afterward." And so she waited, the dutiful disciple, as he shook the hands of those who lined up to get a sliver of personal attention from him. When the ballroom was nearly empty, he walked over to where Belinda was sitting – he moved like a piece of silk, barely disturbing the air currents – and said, "Let's go in the cocktail lounge and talk."

She was glad the lights in the bar were dim. She could feel heat blooming in her cheeks, turning them bright red. She wanted to order something strong, a drink that would numb her nerves and render them comatose. Something like a tequila shooter with a beer chaser. But Philippe was staring at her, his hands folded serenely in front of him, waiting for her to reveal something about herself by whatever drink she ordered. At least that's what she was afraid of. Bad girls order things like tequila with beer chasers – girls who have spent way too much time in bars and probably even have a favorite brand of tequila.

"Perrier with lime," she told the waiter.

"I'll have the same," Philippe said.

He stared at her a while longer – needles slipping under her skin, looking for a vein.

"I've been watching you in the audience while I've been speaking," he said finally. "And I thought it was time we talked."

"Time?"

"Isn't that what you've wanted? I know you, Belinda – something about you feels familiar to me. Once in a while someone comes along like that, and I'm moved to give them some extra attention." He leaned closer to her, flirting with the shadows. But it was she who felt herself moving closer, even though her body was frozen in place. "I can see the pain of your life in your eyes, in your whole demeanor," he continued, his gaze coiling around her, squeezing strength from her.

She tried to get control of herself by going through a mental checklist of what she was noticing about him. His cheekbones – they were high and angular; they made him look exotic, especially with his dark eyes. And she noticed the signs of age in his face – the bags that were starting to form under his eyes, although not symmetrically. His left eye looked older than his right. She noticed the thickness of his whiskers – he probably had to shave twice a day – and the tiny vein in his forehead that seemed to pulse constantly. She couldn't decide whether or not he was good-looking. Her brain just stayed busy, clicking off what her eyes were seeing. Mental calisthenics, mental weight training. Isn't this what prisoners do to hold on to their sanity?

"Are you ready to change your life, Belinda?" Philippe asked.

Belinda nodded, struck mute momentarily by the power he apparently had to see right into her. How many times had she prayed for her life to change and wept because it hadn't and because she hated its sameness?

"We'll have to do some emotional surgery," he told her, a smile playing at the corners of his mouth. "It's not without pain, but I think you can handle it. I think you're ready for it."

She nodded again, and an image came into her mind of those people who do psychic surgery – reaching into someone's body and pulling out handfuls of slimy, bloody stuff that doesn't look as if it belongs in a human body.

At some point in the conversation, Philippe touched her cheek and she had the oddest feeling that his body temperature was lower than it should be. His fingers felt cold, bloodless, and – even more odd – she thought the tips of his fingers were unnaturally smooth, as though he'd filed away his fingerprints. He could break in anywhere, steal anything, and never leave a clue.

She met with him again at his office one afternoon. It seemed to her that no sunlight came through the windows of his private office, even though the drapes were open and the day outside was blazing. She thought about it later and the whole memory seemed shadowy and dim. Of course she did have her eyes closed for much of the time.

"We have to go back to the moment in your life when everything fell apart," he said as he stood up from behind his desk and moved over to her. He motioned for her to follow him to the couch, but once she was there he didn't sit beside her, as she had thought he would. Instead he sat in the armchair, and she felt suddenly abandoned, cut adrift.

"There was a single moment, wasn't there," he continued, "when your faith shattered and you knew you'd never be the same again?"

"Yes," Belinda answered, and suddenly she felt herself there again, in the hospital, and her baby was being carried out the door. Forever.

"You have to trust me, Belinda, and take me back with you. Otherwise I can't help you." His voice promised relief. Peace.

So she did. She took him back to the awful hollowness of it all – the feeling that her body was this empty cave, a repository for nothing except dead silence. She told him of the stillness that fell over the room when the door closed and the baby was gone, his face a memory that would always bleed inside her. And she remembered the air moving slowly between her legs, still spread wide. She'd given her child all that room to come into the world, and then he was gone and she was still lying there, her thighs refusing to close, refusing to acknowledge the child's disappearance.

"Don't leave," Philippe was saying, beside her now, his voice in her ear. "You have to explore everything about that experience. Don't run away from it."

"I'm afraid," Belinda said. Her voice cut her throat like razor blades.

"I know. That's why I'm with you."

There had been voices in her room that day that she had been too numb to hear, but she heard them now, years later, in Philippe's office. The doctor had said, "She'll get over it. In a few months she won't even remember." As if youth carried with it a built-in capacity for amnesia.

It was a painful trip through memory for Belinda. She felt as though she were clawing desperately for the surface of a lake, fighting for air. She didn't want to be in that room anymore, but Philippe kept pushing her down, telling her she couldn't run away from it. Somehow she knew she would break the surface only when he decided it was time.

When he finally let her up, when she returned from the memory and opened her eyes, Philippe's office still seemed strangely dim, yet she had a vague sense that some immutable change had occurred. Philippe was a part of her past now; she'd invited him along, taken him back with her. So from now on, whenever her mind went back to that room, to the blood on the sheets, and the child whose crying she didn't even have time to memorize, Philippe would be there too. They were fused together, guide and willing follower, in a shadowy wedge of history that used to belong only to Belinda. She wondered that day if twins felt like that. Do their ribs rise and fall with the same rhythm? Do their dreams swim in the same dark waters and then burst into the light at the same instant?

Belinda glanced at Sara, trying to determine how she felt about Philippe. It was obvious that she was listening intently to his lecture, but her face gave away nothing in the way of reaction. Belinda wanted her devotion to Philippe to be all right with Sara; she wanted Sara's seal of approval. She didn't know how to give herself that kind of reinforcement.

"If you follow me, I will show you the way to heaven," Philippe was saying. "No matter what the world tells you."

Belinda knew she would follow him through life.

She remembered another meeting with Philippe – one that she'd hoped would be private, but didn't turn out to be. An assistant from Philippe's office called Belinda in the morning and asked if she could come to the office at five o'clock.

"Yes," she said quickly, fearing that the invitation would be snatched away if she hesitated for even a second.

She had a job interview at four, for a low-budget film – not the most prestigious offer, but she couldn't afford to be choosy. She considered canceling the interview, but she knew she couldn't be that irresponsible. Inwardly, though, Philippe was her top priority; he took precedence over everything, even a possible job.

She arrived at his office a few minutes past five. In Century City, the sun was sliding down the sides of buildings, setting in hundreds of windows. Philippe's office was on the fourteenth floor, and Belinda brushed her hair in the elevator, found lip gloss in her purse and replaced what she'd chewed off during her job interview. It was a bad habit – one that always surfaced when she was being evaluated, when any part of her future was being knocked back and forth like a ping-pong ball.

There was no one at the desk in his outer office, and the door to his inner sanctum was ajar. She pictured him in there, waiting for her, glancing at the gold clock on his desk. But as she approached the door, something unexpected drifted out – the sound of several voices. Belinda was embarrassed at the disappointment she felt. She'd just assumed they would be alone.

Four people were in his office and Philippe was sitting behind his desk. It looked like an elite classroom – a group of top honor students called in to confer with the professor.

"Belinda, come in. We were waiting for you," Philippe said.

He didn't get up but motioned her to come in and join the others. She recognized the faces from his lectures.

"I don't know whom you know here," he told her. "From left to right – Astrid, Michelle, Kenneth, and Dionne. Unfortunately, Dionne's husband was going to be here but decided not to." He gave Dionne – a frail, timid-looking woman – a serious look. "We'll have to discuss that, won't we?"

"Yes," Dionne answered, her shoulders bending forward – a child who had been chastised.

"Yes," Philippe repeated. "We have to be careful in life who we form alliances with."

He was making Belinda nervous. She felt something had been snatched away from her – his approval, his personal attention. But the more nervous she felt, the more she wanted his approval.

"I called you all here for a very serious reason," Philippe continued. "And you were not chosen at random. I need to know where my support lies. I need to know that I can count on you – as disciples, if you will – because, I promise you, things are going to get dark. Astrid and Michelle have been with me for a while, and they've heard me discuss this before – how things get very dark before the light comes. We are coming into that time. And if any of you don't believe that I am on this earth to help bring the light, I want you to leave now." He paused dramatically, letting his eyes travel slowly around the room. No one moved. "Fine," he said, and closed his eyes for a second, as if summoning up an inner voice. "We are coming into a bad time in this world – in fact, it's already here. There are those who will perish and those who will survive. The chosen will survive. But to be one of the chosen means to have a price on your head because there are dark forces that will try to conquer you."

"Are you talking about actual danger?" Michelle asked.

"Don't interrupt," Philippe said, and his tone was a slash of ice. "We've talked about your cowardice before, Michelle. If you're not prepared to outgrow it, you know where the door is."

No one looked at Michelle, and Belinda knew they were all feeling the same thing. If it came down to it, they would abandon her or anyone else to get a smile and a nod of recognition from Philippe. Michelle might as well be an old Eskimo, left to die in the snow, with no one even glancing back.

"I'm sorry," she said.

"That's better," Philippe told her. His voice had changed seasons. It was warm now, soothing, inviting her back to the fold.

"In the Bible," he continued, "Revelations talks about a call for the endurance and faith of the saints. I want you to understand that, along the path we have chosen, there will be much to endure. People will persecute us for our beliefs and for our faith. Some in our midst may turn against us. There are those who will choose the way of Judas. But I would remind you of these words also in Revelations." He reached across the desk for a Bible and opened it to a marked page. " 'But as for the cowardly,' " he read, his voice rising as if he were aiming it at the clouds, " 'the faithless, the polluted, as for murderers, fornicators, sorcerers, idolaters, and all liars, their lot shall be in the lake that burns with fire and brimstone, which is the second death.' "

He closed the Bible and put it down, pausing long enough to make everyone in the room squirm. And then he said, "I am offering you renewed life if you will have faith in my leadership. You must be willing to endure hardship for me, put your hands in the fire if necessary. Otherwise, I can't fulfill my mission on this earth." His voice broke a little and Belinda thought he was going to cry. "I was put on this earth to lead. But I need your help. I need you to support me and fortify me with your faith. The Bible tells us that Armageddon will come – I'm telling you it's here. Not everyone will survive. But there will be a chosen few, and my reason for being on this earth at this time is to lead those chosen few through the flames."

It was dark when Belinda left his office that evening. She walked out with the others, but no one had much to say.

I've been chosen, was the refrain that kept running through her mind. I'm in the inner circle, one of the trusted few, one of his disciples. Surely, she thought, this is the end to all the sadness in my life. Peace of mind must be the reward for this allegiance. Her past would fall away, all her sins would turn to dust, and she would be reborn into the happy person she'd always wanted to be.

The lights in the ballroom were being dimmed. It was always done at the end of the lecture. Belinda wanted to look at Sara, get some reading of her reaction, but her eyes were unable to leave Philippe. She was waiting for some kind of communication, for his eyes to brush across hers – a signal that he'd noticed her in the audience. It had happened before, and when it did, Belinda felt as if she were being waltzed around a crowded dance floor, the lights spinning, the people just a blur of faces. She was infused with the dizzy, euphoric feeling that the rest of the world had fallen away. That was all she wanted – just one dance.

But instead, Philippe bowed his head to lead the audience in a meditation.

"Years ago, Pilgrims followed their leaders across the Atlantic into the unknown," he said, in a voice so filled with warmth and passion that it could melt the tundra. "They had to be fearless. That's what I'm asking you to be. Follow me where I lead you, even though it may look dark and dangerous and you want to turn back. You were sent to me for a reason. And I promise you that, in the end, your dreams will be realized. Now, I want us to go into the silence and contemplate this, until I tell you to open your eyes."

There was the sound of breathing, a few muffled sobs, and the hum of the ventilation system. But the silence was louder. And after about five minutes, he said softly, "All right, you may open your eyes now."

Philippe walked down the center aisle and Belinda had the impression that the room was waking up from a deep sleep. People were unfolding, stretching and bending toward him as if they were new green shoots and he was the sun. She waited for Sara to say something, braced herself for some kind of derisive comment, but Sara had a vague look on her face. They walked out of the ballroom silently, into a night that felt like autumn.

"So what do you think?" Belinda said finally, as she unlocked the car.

"I'm not sure. I guess he's interesting. I could do without the hugging stuff and people waving incense sticks in my face. It's like some kind of Biblical ceremony, only they ran out of palm leaves."

"You don't think he deserves that kind of devotion?" Belinda knew it was a question to which she desperately wanted an answer, but maybe not from Sara.

"I don't know," Sara said, staring straight ahead at the road. "It's probably not for me to judge."

Eleven

Sara

THAT NIGHT, Sara walked out of the ballroom feeling as though fingers were around her throat, making it hard for her to find her voice, harder still to figure out whose fingers, and whether or not they were strangling her or caressing her. Something had happened in there, something unnerving, something that Philippe had orchestrated. His lecture was at once baffling, seductive, and threatening. Sara saw how he used the weight of the Bible and all its darkest predictions to make his listeners huddle together behind him, trusting that he would lead them into the light. She had the impression that in Philippe's mind, he and God were arranging a holy war together and dividing the human race into opposing armies. The militaristic angle was disturbing to her, but she could also see the appeal of it. If reaching enlightenment could be plotted out and strategized like a battle plan, then how hard could it be?

She'd actually meant it when she told Belinda it wasn't for her to judge Philippe. She was too confused to judge anything. If he'd done nothing else, he'd at least invaded her thoughts and tossed them around until there was only chaos in her head.

When they got back to Belinda's house, Sara lingered awkwardly at the car. She wanted to go inside, but she was afraid to.

"Well, listen – thanks for asking me along." She scraped the toe of her shoe along a crack in the sidewalk. "I'm pretty tired, so I'm going to go home."

"Okay," Belinda said.

They stood there like two teenagers on a first date, caught in that awful moment of wondering how to say goodnight. We're friends, Sara told herself – we can still touch each other like friends, even though last night we touched as lovers.

Tentatively, she hugged Belinda, and then it came rushing back to her. She thought of lying beside her friend, of sliding across the mattress and opening Belinda's thighs with her own. But she couldn't look at the whole image – just jigsaw pieces of it. She saw their mouths, hungry and afraid, but then her thoughts panicked and ran away.

Belinda was letting Sara hug her, letting heat collect between them, and maybe it was that which made another image move into Sara's mind. She imagined herself blindfolded, unbuttoning Belinda's shirt and peeling off her own, standing half naked in the night while the street lamp hummed above them and cars drove past. It was the blindfold that made her willing to explore the scenario, even though it was something that would probably never occur. The blindfold would take away all responsibility. Being sightless would make her innocent. Her emotions wouldn't be blinking warning lights at her; they'd be somewhere else, on the next street, waiting for her to regain her sight.

Belinda pushed her away gently; their hug was lasting too long. Sara could feel her nervousness. "I'll talk to you tomorrow," Belinda said. "Get some sleep, and let me know if Anthony calls."

Sara got in her car and started the engine. Anthony . . . she'd almost said, "Who?" She pulled his face into her mind, reacquainting herself with him. But she didn't really want to. Anthony felt like a rough edge in her life, and she wanted to escape into something softer – someone softer. It was what she'd wanted with Belinda the night before, but the depth of her love had stopped her. She didn't even know how to begin analyzing that one, she just knew it was true. She thought of Paris, the feel of Allison's mouth – she wanted to be with a woman. Don't ask why, Sara told herself – the answer might scare you. She drove into Hollywood and pulled up to a lesbian bar that an actress friend had told her about.

The light inside was soft and red; as soon as she walked in, Sara felt like she had entered a different world – something warm and womblike, where anything was permissible. A world of women where men had no say. Dance music was playing – Paula Abdul, Sara thought, although she wasn't sure – and a tall black woman in a halter top and tights was dancing with herself just inside the doorway. The room was already crowded with women, and more women were walking in.

It took only a few minutes before it seemed perfectly normal to Sara to see female couples at the bar, manicured hands caressing pale shoulders, lipsticked mouths rummaging through long hair to whisper into ears.

Two girls were tending bar. Sara caught the eye of the one with a lion's mane of blond hair and a spangled, low-cut top. "Vodka on the rocks," she said. It was a drink she hadn't tasted in years, but obviously tradition was out the window on this night.

A girl with short, dark hair was talking to two women and kept glancing at Sara; she could feel the girl's eyes heat up the side of her face every time they turned in her direction. She didn't have to look over to know when the girl was moving closer.

"Hi, I'm Pamela."

"Sara. Hi."

"You're drinking all alone."

There was something so clear and matter-of-fact about the approach that Sara didn't flinch, didn't even avert her eyes. It was an unusual reaction for her, and suddenly she realized what was different: Whenever a man hit on her, her spine stiffened and her anger rushed to the front lines, ready to attack. But she felt none of that with this woman. Everything inside her stayed relaxed.

"I'm waiting for someone," Sara said. And although technically that wasn't true, it wasn't exactly a lie either. She *was* waiting for someone; she just wasn't sure who.

A few other women were dancing near the doorway with each other or by themselves; it didn't seem to matter. Pamela drifted off in that direction, and Sara had the idea that some of the women in the place were schoolteachers – straitlaced and proper during the day, teaching Chaucer and the American Revolution, but waiting anxiously for night, when they could grab their girlfriends and dive into this softly lit world where they could be themselves.

The girl must have come in while Sara was talking to Pamela, because when she looked around the bar again, her eyes immediately went to her. She had long, straight hair, spiked on top, and dyed a deep red. She was wearing a black leather motorcycle jacket over a white tank top and jeans. Sara found herself staring, without embarrassment, at a mouth that looked like Belinda's and eyes that had her same teasing look as well. Belinda always complained about her eyes. "People get the wrong impression," she told Sara once. "I look at a guy and he always thinks I want to seduce him."

"Well, don't you?" Sara said.

"On some occasions, yeah. But my eyes have that look all the time, even when I think the guy's a worm."

"Overabundance of fuck-me hormones" was Sara's diagnosis. "They rise up and come out of your eyes."

So now Sara was looking into this stranger's eyes, and wondering if she always had that look, too, or if it meant something special. She knew which she wanted it to be, she knew then what she'd come here for. So did the girl, who began walking behind the barstools toward Sara. For some reason, it seemed to take a long time for her to cross the floor. Then she was next to her, leaning against the bar, wedged between Sara and the girl sitting on the next stool, the scent of Ralph Lauren perfume moving in with her.

The hand she extended to Sara had long red fingernails, but the one resting on the bar had nails cut so short that the red polish looked like drops of blood. One vampire hand and one for the victim, was how Sara thought of it.

"I'm Lacey," she said.

"Sara. Nice to meet you." She glanced away just long enough to take a sip of her drink. "You look like my girlfriend Belinda. The two of you could be sisters."

"Yeah? So where is she? You two get in a fight?"

"Oh – she's not a girlfriend like that," Sara explained nervously. "She's just my friend."

Lacey smiled. "But you'd like her to be more, right?"

"I don't know."

Lacey watched her, taking her in with a stranger's eyes,

smiling at her with Belinda's mouth. "I do. You've never been to a place like this before, have you?"

Sara took a large swallow of her drink. "No. Does it show that much?"

"What do you think?"

"Why do I feel like I'm about to be audited?"

Lacey laughed. It wasn't Belinda's laugh – it was freer, had more colors in it. "It's not like that. You're allowed to stay. We don't require entrance exams here. So what's the story, Sara? You have this girlfriend, and who else? A man?"

"Yes . . . a man." Sara got the bartender's attention and ordered another drink. "A man who scares me sometimes. Things with him have a way of getting intense."

"So dump him and take up with your girlfriend," Lacey said.

"That idea scares me more. I love her, but I don't think I can be her lover. I feel like I'd turn into one of those balloons that drifts up into the sky and disappears forever."

She'd been staring into her drink. She looked up at Lacey, half expecting to see a puzzled frown on her face. But Lacey didn't seem puzzled at all. Maybe she was accustomed to barstool confessions from strangers.

"Why are you here, Sara?" she asked.

"I wanted to see what it was like."

"A lesbian bar?"

"Everything."

"Are you sure?" Lacey said.

Sara hesitated. Was she sure? If it was curiosity, why hadn't Allison satisfied that? Or Belinda? Even though she and Belinda stopped – didn't really make love – the memory was still warm on her skin. But this is different, she told herself Anthony isn't commanding me, and love has nothing to do with it. Anthony is across the seas and love is across town.

"Yeah, I'm sure," she said.

Lacey smiled. The vampire hand reached for her, long nails scraping against Sara's palm. They got up and moved through the crowd of women to the door.

The night was warm, lit by neon and a half-moon. As they rounded the corner and walked toward the alley, Lacey let go of Sara's hand and put her arm around her waist. The smell of garbage and stale beer waited for them in the alley. Sara blinked against the asphalt dark as they walked between trash cans; the street noise seemed distant now. A cat clattered across one of the cans, stopping a moment to give them a sharp yellow stare before running away. Midway down the alley, Lacey angled Sara over to the brick exterior of a building and turned her so that her back was pressed against the wall.

"You don't have to know what you want," she whispered, her mouth brushing Sara's. "I know."

Sara felt her whole body soften as Lacey moved against her, kissing her, circling Sara's tongue with her own. With Allison, Sara had been in control, positioning the girl, silently commanding her to do a dance both of them were unfamiliar with. Sara had taken charge, choreographed everything. Now, it was reversed. She was pliant, obedient, answering the movements of Lacey's body, but initiating nothing. Long fingernails dented the nape of her neck while the other hand unzipped her jeans and slid inside, knowing exactly where it was going.

"You always go without underwear?" Lacey said, her voice gravelly now, falling into Sara's ear.

"No. Usually I wear them. Just tonight I didn't . . . for some reason."

"Uh-huh." Lacey's tongue silenced Sara and her fingers slipped inside her. Her thumb massaged her with more skill than most men ever master, making Sara moan and pull her breath in through clenched teeth so she wouldn't scream and attract attention from whoever might be passing by the alley. She wanted to cry out a name, but she was scared of whose name it would be. Lacey's eyes watched her; Belinda's mouth moved down over her throat to her breasts. Her teeth took Sara's nipple with just enough pressure to put her on the tightrope between pain and ecstasy. She sank down onto her knees, pushing Sara's jeans off her hips and burying her face, mouth closed – as if she were breathing her in, memorizing the animal scent of her.

Sara remembered being on her knees in front of Allison, and knowing with perfect certainty that in that position, she had all the power. But she didn't want power now, she was content to stand on her feet and be the prisoner. She dug her fingers into Lacey's head; she wanted more, she wanted to be invaded, devoured, drained of whatever strength was still allowing her legs to support her. She wanted to be weakened to the point of collapse. She wasn't scared – she was blindfolded by the dark, stale-beer alley and this stranger whose last name she didn't know and probably never would. She was lost in the anonymity of it all. She wasn't even Sara. She was just one of those night people who fuck in alleys and in the morning put on different clothes.

Lacey looked up at her. "Don't fight it, Sara. Let me make you come."

Sara squeezed her eyes shut, softly at first, then tighter as Lacey's tongue worked on her, telling her it knew what she needed. Her hands held onto Sara's knees, as if she sensed that they were getting weaker. She slowed down just long enough to make Sara feel she'd lose her mind, and then her mouth moved faster again, in total command of its prisoner, until it drank in everything Sara gave. The rest of Sara's body trembled against the bricks and she bit into her lower lip so hard she could swear she tasted blood.

Lacey stayed on her knees for a few minutes, face hidden between Sara's legs, not ready yet to release her prisoner. When she rose, she pulled Sara's jeans up and zipped them, concealing the evidence. Her mouthprint would always be there, even after the lipstick had washed off.

"You want to go back inside?" she said, her face close to Sara's.

"No. I think I'll go home." Her throat felt gritty, like particles of asphalt had found their way into her mouth.

"I didn't really think you'd want to stick around," Lacey said.

Sara couldn't read the meaning beneath her words. Was there disappointment there or was she just stating a fact? That's the thing about strangers, she realized – their words have all these possible meanings crawling underneath them. You wonder about it for a moment, and then get into your car and drive away, figuring it was probably none of your business anyway.

Twelve

Sara

SARA WALKED into her house with an armload of groceries, left her keys in the door, and headed straight for the phone machine. She couldn't stand it that she'd become a slave to it, but she'd left a message for Anthony at the hotel and was waiting for his call – something she'd always sworn she would never do for any man. She'd called him late at night – her night, his morning – so he had probably left for the set already. She'd called him with traces of Lacey's lipstick still on the inside of her thighs. She was actually relieved that he wasn't there; they hadn't spoken since she'd been home and already she didn't trust herself in conversation with him. It had only been a few days, but it seemed longer.

Her phone machine had recorded three messages. She put the bag of groceries on the floor, knew how badly she wanted one of them to be from Anthony, and hit Playback.

"Nice to get your message, Sara," his voice said, with a slight hint of reprimand in it. "It's about nine in the evening here. I'm at the hotel if you want to call – I would love to hear from you. I have been thinking of you often."

Sara turned off the machine; she'd get to the other two messages later.

"He sounds like a Hallmark card with an attitude problem," she said aloud.

While she put her groceries away; she rehearsed several possible conversations in her mind.

He answered the phone with "Yes?" making her wonder whom exactly he was expecting at the other end.

"It's Sara."

"How are you?" he said, revealing no emotion. His talent for acting cool and detached was infuriating.

"I'm okay," Sara said. "Mark is getting better. His leg's broken, so he's going to stay at our parents' house for a little while – and be waited on."

"Uh-huh. Well, I'm glad it wasn't too serious. And what about you? What else have you been up to?"

"Actually, I've been trying to get my mind off you," Sara said.

She knew what she was trying to do – she was trying to elicit some kind of reaction in him – anything, actually. She hated it when the needle stayed stuck at cool. She didn't care which direction it went, as long as it moved.

"Really?" he said. The needle wasn't moving. "And how have you been going about that?"

"By going to a gay bar and picking up the second woman I talked to." Jesus, did I just say that? she thought. She knew she wanted a reaction from him, but this could be overkill.

"Did you have sex with her?" Anthony asked.

Sara realized that all she'd done was get him intrigued. Frankenstein was watching his creation go to the head of the class. "Yes, I did," she answered, too deep in it now to back out.

"Hmm. Well, I'll look forward to hearing about it when I see you. I shouldn't be in Paris too much longer – maybe a week."

"Anthony, don't you care that I was with someone else?"

There was a long pause – too long. "I don't like it when you try to make me jealous, Sara," he said, his tone polished and smooth. "It's a game that's really beneath you, don't you think?"

When she hung up with him, she wondered how exactly he was able to do this – turn a conversation upside down so it ended with her doubting herself, feeling disempowered and weak.

Her other messages were from Belinda and an old friend, Charlene, who had gotten married and disappeared from everyone's life. It was probably not a good sign that she was calling and saying she desperately needed to talk to Sara. Belinda sounded less desperate, but Sara called her back first.

"I decided I'm going to have a dinner party on Saturday night, for Philippe," Belinda said, with a giddiness that was always unsettling. "I think six people, since that's all I can really fit at my table – "

"Belinda, are you sure this is a good idea?" Sara asked.

"Yes – absolutely! What do you mean, is it a good idea? Philippe can come. He has a late-afternoon class with his advanced students and then he'll come over."

"What do you mean, class? What kind of class?"

"Remember, I told you – he has these exercises that help you get in touch with your power?" Belinda said. "He didn't do them the other night, but – "

"Oh yeah, I remember. So it's just your basic walking-on-coals aerobics class."

"Sara, can you believe it?" Belinda gushed, clearly on a roll, or a high, or something other than stark reality. "I'm going to have this great master in my house – right at my dinner table. And I'm going to seat you right next to him."

"Oh God," Sara groaned. "A seating chart. Look, I hate to be the voice of reason here, but don't you think 'master' is a slight exaggeration? It's not like Mozart is coming for dinner. The guy gives lectures, people come, wave incense around, and repeat his more memorable utterances. Let's not elevate him to something he's not."

"You know I hate it when you get cynical. Could you do me a favor? Saturday night, check your cynicism at the door."

"Gee, I'm glad to know that you're going to make arrangements for that. What a good idea. People can check their coats and their cynicism at the same time."

Belinda sighed, the deep, resigned sound of someone coming a little closer to earth. "I have to hang up now. I have to plan the menu."

"Okay, Julia Child – see you Saturday."

Maybe everything would be all right between them, Sara thought as she put away her groceries. Maybe she could forget that she had seen Belinda in Lacey's face, wished Belinda's tongue into Lacey's mouth. Maybe it was just a momentary hallucination – one of those dark-alley, chilled-vodka mirages. And maybe what almost happened between her and Belinda was just a moment when strange wires got crossed and normal currents were interrupted. It was a theory, anyway; that's what theories are for sometimes – mental medicine to alleviate the symptoms while scientists look for a cure.

As a result of returning the other phone call, the one from her old friend Charlene, Sara agreed to go to Beverly

Hills for coffee. She was grateful for the distraction from her own problems with Anthony, and she was also concerned by how upset Charlene seemed.

They met at an outdoor café. Sara got there first and watched Charlene walk toward her between the tables, displaying the same sense of style she'd always had. She was the classic Ann Taylor woman – understated, tailored, and perfectly accessorized.

"I'm getting divorced," she said, in her Texas oil-money voice – a cowgirl twang with debutante breeding.

She talked about the legal costs of her divorce, but Sara had the impression that she was deliberately talking around the real problem.

"So that's why you're so upset?" Sara asked. "Because of the money?"

Charlene shook her head and smoothed back her dark hair, which was already smoothed back. She lit a cigarette and blew a long stream of smoke past Sara. "I just couldn't do it anymore," she said. "I mean, I played along for nearly a year but, honey, there comes a point . . . You don't know what I'm talking about, do you?"

"I haven't a clue, Charlene. You've been talking around it."

"Games is what I'm talking about. Honey, he had me in black spiked-heel boots spanking him with whips."

Sara almost choked on her cappuccino. "God, Charlene, I didn't think that was your style. What else were you wearing?"

"Nothing. Well, a leather bra sometimes."

"No strand of pearls or Cartier watch?"

"Sara – "

"Hey, I'm just trying to get the picture here."

Charlene stubbed out her cigarette and lit another one.

"The son-of-a-bitch is trying to get my money now, after everything I did for him. I suppose it was sort of fun at first. But you know what? It can get scary. I didn't know where it would stop. And I started to think we'd never be able to just make love again – you know, straight, with no games or toys. Like, what about when I want to just cuddle and be romantic? I thought that was going to be lost forever. The weird thing is, though, I still have all our toys in a box in my closet – I just can't seem to throw them out."

Sara finished the rest of her cappuccino. "What kind of toys are we talking about?" she asked, wondering if she really wanted to know.

"Oh, you know, dildos, cock rings, whips – stuff like that."

"Dildos?" Sara said. "You didn't say anything about using dildos."

"Honey, that conversation requires something stronger than coffee."

"Charlene, do you think it always gets out of hand – I mean, games like that? Does it always get scary eventually?"

"I'm not really the most objective person about this. I only know it did for me." Charlene narrowed her eyes and looked at Sara. "Are you asking this for a specific reason? Like a personal reason?"

Sara shrugged. "I don't know."

But she did know, and so did Charlene, who'd been there and back and wasn't about to press Sara for information she wasn't ready to give. Sara was still caught up in the allure of danger; she wasn't ready to be warned away from it.

Sara was the second person to arrive at Belinda's on Saturday night. Belinda introduced the man sitting on the couch as Kenneth.

"I have to go back to the kitchen," she said. "So you two are on your own for now."

Under her cooking apron, Belinda had on a purple velvet peasant skirt and a loose black velvet top. She looked like a gypsy from a D. H. Lawrence novel. Except for the blond spiked hair, which no one had thought of in those times. There was an open bottle of Chardonnay and glasses on the coffee table. Sara noticed, as she poured herself some wine, that Kenneth was drinking Coke.

"So, Kenneth – are you a follower of Philippe's?" She wasn't sure what the correct terminology was: Follower? Student? Disciple? Desperate person in search of a guru?

"Oh yes. I've been studying with him for two years now. He's changed my life. I do some office work for him occasionally, too."

"Uh-huh."

Kenneth looked like a guy she'd love to have as a neighbor. The kind who could wire up anything – the stereo, the VCR, one of those alarms that sounds like a dog barking, Christmas lights. He probably had a pair of wire cutters in his pocket, or at least in the glove compartment of his car.

"So, what do you do, Kenneth? I mean, aside from office work for Philippe?"

"I'm in electronics."

Of course. Before she could ask him how to program the timer on her VCR, the door opened and Philippe walked in, followed by two women. Kenneth jumped up, almost spilling his Coke. The two women seemed to know Kenneth; smiles and hellos bounced between them. But Philippe took center stage, hugged Kenneth, and said, "How did your week go? Any problems?"

"A few. But it was all right. I did the mantras you taught me."

Philippe released him, turned to Sara and said, "Astrologically, this week didn't look good for Kenneth."

"Really?" Sara said. "You told him that he was going to have a bad week?"

"We must be prepared in life," Philippe answered.

Sara remembered trembling when Philippe had passed her at the lecture. She checked herself – no shaking, but there was an odd feeling yawning in her. Something dark and empty, like one of those black holes in space where stars and spaceships are lost forever.

"So how many car accidents did you get into this week, Kenneth?" she said, snapping herself away from Philippe's gaze.

Just then, Belinda came out of the kitchen. "Philippe, hello – I didn't hear you come in." Which was, of course, impossible, since her house was as big as a thumbtack and Philippe's voice could resonate across the Rockies.

Philippe hugged Belinda and said, "You know Astrid and Michelle."

The two women, who hadn't moved an inch since entering the room, nodded shyly and said hello.

Belinda's face was flushed, her smile relentless. "Well, sit down everyone. Dinner will be ready in a few minutes."

Philippe sat on the couch – noisily, since he was wearing one of those nylon warm-up suits that swish and scrape every time the person moves. Astrid and Michelle were both wearing velour sweat clothes – the kind of sweat clothes people who don't sweat always buy. So this is what people wear to walk on coals, Sara thought. She sat across from Philippe and stared at his blue-and-yellow nylon thing, wondering what ever possessed someone to design clothes from that fabric. Did some guy have too much to drink one night and get what he thought was a brilliant idea: I know, I'll design clothes out of kites! They'll be colorful and the wind will catch them and make them billow out in weird places. And people were actually buying them, turning this clothes-out-of-kites thing into an industry. There was a man in Sara's neighborhood who jogged in one; the fabric made so much noise, he'd woken her up on several occasions.

Belinda came back, put a bottle of Pellegrino on the coffee table, and disappeared again. Sara noticed how her eyes clicked across Philippe's – just a blip on the screen, almost unnoticeable, but Sara was playing air traffic controller and nothing got by her.

"So, Sara," Philippe began, leaning forward a little, fixing dark eyes on her and tossing a hand grenade into her nerves. She found it difficult to look at him, but her eyes kept wanting to.

"How'd you know my name?" she asked defensively.

"Belinda has talked about you. She said you're best friends. And she told me you'd be here tonight. How did you like the lecture? I saw you in the audience."

"It was interesting." She hoped he wasn't going to quiz her, and searched her mind for whatever Cliffs Notes might be jotted there – just in case.

"I think it was one of your most inspired lectures," Astrid said.

Both Astrid and Michelle had that polished, half-starved Beverly Hills look about them that never failed to make Sara uncomfortable. They were the kind of women who needed an hour to fix themselves up before they could go to the market, who went to only the best restaurants, but never to eat, just to be seen. Women who seemed to have no fluids left in their bodies – life and all its little bits of sadness had vacuumed them out, left them dry and brittle as twigs. The Embalmed Elite.

When Belinda announced that dinner was ready, the two women didn't even stand up until Philippe had risen, didn't move toward the dining room until his steps had led the way.

Over dinner, Sara found herself fascinated by the two of them. Except for the fact that Michelle was blond and Astrid was brunette, they were hard to tell apart. Those underfed, overliposuctioned bodies, perfectly manicured hands, lined lips that never smiled, and eyes that flickered with judgments . . . and that layer of sadness just below the skin, more stubborn than cellulite.

Belinda had transformed her dining room with candles, crystal wineglasses, and china that Sara had never seen before. Probably some heirloom stuff that had been in boxes for years, she thought.

"Belinda tells me you have a boyfriend who is abroad right now," Philippe said, helping himself to the pasta and passing the bowl to Sara.

"Well, he's in France," Sara said. "That part's true. I don't know if he's my boyfriend, though."

"I'll share with you what I tell all the women who rely on my advice. The most dangerous thing a woman can do is take a man's semen into her. She absorbs all his energy, and much of his history that way." Philippe apparently saw nothing odd about discussing semen over dinner.

The pasta had made its way to Michelle who added, "You told me that when I was – "

"Shut up," Philippe snapped.

Sara realized that his eyes and his concentration were still on her; he obviously tolerated no intrusions.

"Okay," Michelle said quickly, the docile pet sitting on command.

Sara ignored Philippe and stared at Michelle, who, with carefully averted eyes, reached across the table for the salad. As her sleeve slid back on her arm, Sara noticed a large patch of skin grafting – the telltale remains of a burn.

Philippe was following her gaze. "People come to me when they're tired of living on the tattered edge they've gotten accustomed to," he said quietly, in a voice too close to her ear. It nibbled at the black hole inside her, widening it.

"Wow, did you just make that up?" Sara asked, fighting back valiantly against his dark invasion. "Or was that in some Hermann Hesse book?"

He didn't answer, and Belinda seized the moment. "Philippe had an accident when he was a child, and God spoke to him."

That began a lengthy description of his childhood head injury, which had apparently prompted God to stride in with a megaphone and lay out the rest of his life for him. Philippe's voice tumbled out into the candlelight, and it was hard to tell which was more hypnotic. It was obvious to Sara that everyone there had heard this before, but none of them dared act as if they had.

At one point, Kenneth explained that the mathematical probability of such a thing occurring was so infinitesimal that Philippe had to consider himself a truly rare specimen.

"I'll bet you have a picture of Stephen Hawking up in your bedroom," Sara said to Kenneth, making sense to no one but herself.

"Actually, I have a picture of Buddy Holly," he said, making sense to no one but himself. Although it did explain the black-framed glasses.

Sara took her goodnight cue from Philippe and his flock, and headed for the door as part of the group. She knew Belinda would have liked her to stay, but she was afraid they'd get into an argument about Philippe's divinity. Was it real, was it Memorex, or was it one of the best hoaxes to hit L.A. in years?

It didn't escape Sara's notice that he got into a black BMW. Not a good sign. She never trusted men in BMWs. They just had a certain aura of disloyalty about them.

She drove home in her trustworthy Volvo, imagining what it would be like to pull up to her house and know that Anthony was inside. To walk into a scene of domestic security: "Hi, hon, how was the dinner party?" Because their relationship was so solid, so trusting, so . . . evolved . . . that he had work to do that evening and just couldn't go with her, and that was fine. But he wanted to know everything about the dinner, and even though he'd been working, he'd missed her, thought about her, turned down the bed, and changed the alarm to eight a.m. instead of seven.

What would it feel like, she thought, as she drove through dark streets, going back to a house that might as well be dark because, even though she left lights on, a house shows it when there's actual life inside, versus when there's just lighted silence waiting for the sole inhabitant to return.

The fantasy took shape in her head – Anthony working at the desk, making notes in the margins of a script, hearing her car, her key in the door, waiting there for her. And how would she feel, she wondered, coming into the house, into the warmth of the heater, of his body, his smell, the blanket of his voice as it wrapped around her?

But she always chose men who were genetically incapable of being the I'll-light-the-fire-open-the-wine-and-wait-for-you-to-get-here type.

She chose men who were like lighthouses – stoic and solitary, standing at the edge of a raging sea. She could rely on them in heavy fog, or treacherous storms, to guide her toward shore. But if she wanted more than a bond of basic survival, I'll-be-there-in-a-crisis, she'd get, "Hey, I'm a lighthouse. I'm out here on my own and I help out occasionally. You want more than that? Try the Coast Guard."

These fantasies can be so dangerous, Sara decided, as she unlocked her front door and walked into the cold and the quiet of a house that had been waiting for her. They can seem so real. You hear the words, see the whole scene unfold, and then disappointment leans on you and drops its weight. Like a drug high – you fantasize, get the rush, smile like an idiot for an hour or so, and then the crash comes. The Reality Crash. The reality of no one waiting for you at home, or of opening your eyes after the fireworks of orgasm and finding just an alley and a stranger getting up off her knees, brushing the dust off her jeans. Lacey didn't even resemble Belinda anymore after it was all over.

Someone ought to invent a reality hiatus, Sara thought,

turning on the heater and standing next to it, too cold to do anything else. One month out of the year – no reality allowed. Only fantasies.

So, if I had that month and could have whatever I wanted, she wondered, what would it be? Maybe this should be treated like homework – something to be pondered, outlined, and organized into paragraphs. She went to the desk and rummaged around until she found a yellow pad and a pen, and sat down at the dining-room table to do her assignment.

Once, when Sara was about thirteen, she had found her mother sitting at the dining-room table, a cold cup of coffee beside her, hunched over several pieces of pale blue stationery, writing furiously.

"Who are you writing to?" Sara had asked her.

"God," her mother answered, without looking up.

"What?"

"If there's something I need to discuss, and I can't talk to your father about it, I write a letter to God."

"And then what do you do with it?" Sara said, intrigued in spite of herself. "Mail it to 'God, P.O. Box Heaven?' "

"I usually just burn it," Claire Norton told her, with no trace of self-consciousness.

The heater was finally starting to warm the house, so Sara took off her jacket, stared at the blank yellow paper in front of her, and wrote:

Dear God,

What I really want is to be able to love someone without being scared. And to let them love me without hauling out the bricks and mortar and sandbags so they can't get in. And to fall for some brave man who knows that he doesn't have to be scared either. Just once in my life, I want to experience uncontrollable, white-hot love, the kind that sends you over the moon, over the cliff, that lets you bounce around in the stars with no fear, because you've got those wings on your back that make you invincible. And what does fear have to do with love anyway?

Love like that must be possible, otherwise where did the people who wrote all those fairy tales get their ideas? They couldn't have just fashioned from thin air those stories about sleeping princesses magically awakened by a kiss, and princes who scaled castle walls, drop-kicked monsters, and fought their way across hostile kingdoms, all in the name of Love. It must have existed somewhere, at some point in Man's checkered history, or it couldn't have found its way into Man's checkered consciousness.

So, God, just once before I die, or before I'm too old to enjoy it, or before my breasts sag and I start saying those old-woman things like, "I don't think too much about sex anymore" – just once, I want to turn my back on all my little fear-demons, give them the finger, and gallop away on the back of some courageous man's white horse. Symbolically, of course, because a Range-Rover or a Mercedes would be much better suited to L.A.'s freeways.

Sara read the letter over, knew that it would be filed in one of the bottom drawers of her Psyche – and hopefully in God's top drawer – and then she threw it in the fireplace.

As she struck a match, she thought, this isn't the first time I've set this wish on fire and watched it burn. But it's still alive. I'll call it my Phoenix wish – out of the ashes, out of the flames – singed, but not forgotten.

As if in answer, an air current lifted the charred, crackling piece of paper and held it up in the fireplace, suspended above the ashes on invisible wings. And then it disappeared.

Thirteen

Sara

IT WAS lunchtime. Sara had noticed, over the years, that her parents' household seemed to come alive at mealtimes. The rest of the day, a languid, tired feeling drifted through the rooms. As she walked up the path toward the kitchen door, she could hear her mother inside, putting pots on the stove, opening drawers. The back door creaked these days, and the potato vine that bordered it had given up flowering.

There were moments when the light fell a certain way, that made memories rush in. Sara could almost hear Mark singing along with his 45s of Dion, the comforting sound of her mother talking on the phone to one of her friends. She could even see herself, twelve years old, wearing ripped cutoffs and Mark's old T-shirt, telling her father everything she knew about V-8 engines.

Claire Norton had on her gray cardigan that had stretched and unraveled at the elbows. Sara thought back for a second to a time when it was new – a long time ago, a lifetime ago, when her mother would never have appeared in the kitchen with pink curlers in her hair and the floppy blue terry-cloth slippers she was wearing now.

"Hi, Ma – how's it going?" Sara said, coming up behind her and kissing the back of her neck. A pink curler hit her in the nose. "Got a hot date tonight?"

"Oh my Lord, no," her mother said, giggling almost girlishly. "I washed my hair this morning. I'm fixing your father a fried egg for lunch. Do you want one?"

Oil sizzled in the cast iron frying pan and Sara noticed her mother's hand shaking as she lifted an egg out of the carton.

"No, thanks. Sounds rather unappetizing, actually. Fried eggs for lunch?"

"It's what he likes these days. Last week it was peanut butter and mayonnaise sandwiches."

Sara remembered her father sitting in the kitchen with pizza and a beer – twenty years ago – and she wanted to cry. She pushed back the sadness and headed for the swinging door that led to the dining room. "Where's Mark – upstairs?"

"Yes. I just brought him his lunch."

Mark was sitting up in bed, covers kicked off, a towel over his lap for modesty since his T-shirt didn't conceal much, and a briefcase full of papers open beside him.

"Want me to sign your cast?" Sara said.

"Hey, little sister. Actually, what I'd like you to do is eat this peanut-butter-and-jelly sandwich so Mother won't get upset."

"Just be glad you got jelly instead of mayonnaise."

Sara slid his briefcase over and sat on the bed. The bandage was gone from Mark's face, and she could see the scar for the first time. It was dark red but not as large as she'd expected it to be. "You know, I sort of like it," she said, pointing to his cheek. "It makes you look like someone who shouldn't be messed with. It gives your face a Charles Bronson quality."

"Charles Bronson has a scar?"

"No, but he has the kind of face that makes you think he has one. Of course, we'd have to do some work on the rest of the picture here. I mean, you're lying in your childhood bed, with the Snoopy nightlight over there and Archie and Veronica comic books on the shelves next to the accordion you played for all of one month. And has Mother been bringing you milk in your old Popeye mug? This kind of thing could do real damage to the whole Charles Bronson, scar-on-the-face image. Maybe you could compensate by just keeping the limp you'll probably have when they take the cast off. That way, with a scar and a limp, you'll win all your cases. People will be scared to go up against you. They'll figure if you don't break their knees, you probably have someone on staff whose job it is –" She paused because of the way Mark was looking at her. "What? You make me nervous when you stare at me like that."

"Yeah? Well, you make me exasperated when you go into these verbal excursions instead of just getting to what you really want to talk about. I always know, when you start doing a stand-up routine, that there's something going on and if I wait long enough, you might get around to it."

She stared back at Mark and watched his features blur as her eyes clouded over with tears. "I can't seem to stop crying these days," she said softly. "If I'm not actually crying, I'm fighting the urge."

Mark reached over and squeezed the back of her neck. "Here's a novel idea. Why don't you just go ahead and cry? Stop fighting it? You've been fighting all your life. Aren't you tired of it by now?"

"I went to a gay bar the other night, Mark. I picked the

one girl in the place who looked like Belinda, went out in the alley with her, and let her go down on me."

"Yeah?"

"God damn it, how can you be so casual about something like that? I was having sex with a woman in an alley and I don't even know why!"

"You don't? Are you sure?" He squeezed her arm.

"What is this, a quiz or something?" Sara said, pushing Mark's hand away. "I'm confiding in you and you're playing game show host."

"I think the ice queen is finally melting," Mark said gently.

"Excuse me?"

"Sara, you've been queen of your own little frozen kingdom for a long time now. It's practically become your world. Now that it's starting to melt, you don't know what to do. Which way to turn. Who to let in. So you're experimenting, and it's okay to do that. Don't you see? While the rest of us were learning how to be discerning about who to open our hearts to, you were writing manuals on how to build a better ice wall around you. You just have some catching up to do, that's all. And you're doing it. But it doesn't mean you're doing anything wrong – I tried to tell you that before. Consider it an adventure. You're on a quest – like in some Greek myth – the quest is to learn what it feels like to be touched, what it feels like to have someone else wandering around in your kingdom. You're auditioning people – gender is irrelevant."

"But what if I stay confused?"

"Why do you even think of it as confusion? Why don't you think of it as being open-minded? Flexible? Some word that won't make you nervous."

Sara looked around the room. On the wall were ribbons and trophies from high school sports events, and a photograph of Mark in his football uniform. He had the same look in his eyes then as he did at this moment – a look that said: *Relax. It's probably something that can be easily explained.*

"Listen, I need you to do something for me," Mark said.

"What?"

"Take this sandwich and flush it down the toilet so Mother won't get her feelings hurt. And try to find me some fruit or something – without her knowing what you're up to."

Sara came back ten minutes later with a bowl of grapes and a carton of chocolate ripple ice cream.

"Let's find something really trashy on TV," she said. "Remember how we used to do that on Saturday afternoons? We'd find those stupid old horror films – the ones with monsters you felt sorry for and innocent ingenues who were such a pain in the ass you couldn't wait for them to die?"

"And Mother would yell at us to go outside while it was still sunny."

Sara started laughing. "Remember when you took the small TV and put it in the driveway, and ran an extension cord into the garage?"

"She was really pissed off."

"But we were outside while it was still sunny – watching TV."

They found an afternoon soap opera that kept them amused for all of fifteen minutes and then switched around until they landed on an old episode of "The Honeymooners." Claire Norton passed by the room, paused, and smiled at her children who were, for that afternoon, her children once again. She would sleep better that night, knowing that once in a while her illusions could come to life.

As Sara was leaving her parents' house later that day, she stopped for a moment at the foot of the stairs, listening to the silence. The sounds of what had once been there – teenagers screaming, stereos blasting, a phone that (her father always complained) rang too much – had deserted the premises. She knew that, whenever she and Mark returned, they tried to stir up memories, just to make themselves feel better. A beam of late-afternoon sun slanted across the carpet and everything seemed so still Sara was almost afraid to breathe. Her mother was taking a nap, her father was dozing in front of the television. That's what happens when the years pile up – a house gets quiet as bones. And the broken places start to show. Some of the upstairs windows were stuck, the clothes dryer buzzed when it shouldn't, Roger Norton fell asleep every couple of hours, and Claire Norton complained of arthritis in her hands. Even Mark had his broken places. Not just the obvious ones – his broken leg, the scar on his face – but the deeper ones the ones Sara knew about, but wasn't supposed to mention. His last girlfriend had cheated on him and then walked; that was eight months ago, and he was still alone, hiding the damage behind his old-soul eyes.

But eventually they'd all be like this house – in need of repair and tired of hiding it. The thing was, Sara felt she was in need of repair now as well. Too many broken places, all starting to show.

She walked out of the house, and down the front walk to her car, trying not to look at the lawn that needed mowing, and the chipped paint on the fence that used to be shiny white. It felt as though there were a cold wind at her back, warning her not to turn around – she wouldn't like what she saw. Just keep walking and don't look back, it told her, that's what you've been doing all your life.

Sara was sleeping so soundly that when the phone rang it sounded like a fire alarm. She gasped and sat up in bed. Okay . . . phone . . . I have to answer it. But first I have to catch my breath. Which took two more rings to accomplish, and nothing is more nerve-jangling than a phone ringing in the middle of the night.

"Hello?" she was finally able to say.

"Hi – it's me."

"Anthony?" She listened for the background noise of a long-distance connection and heard nothing. "Where are you?"

"I'm home. I got in earlier this evening. Are you in bed?"

"Well, yeah – it's almost one o'clock."

"I know what time it is, Sara. That wasn't the question." He was doing it again – lulling her with his voice. It was burrowing between her legs, aching inside her, while her ears had to be reminded to listen. "This is what I want you to do," he continued. "Get up and unlock your door, go back to bed, take off whatever you're wearing and wait for me. I'll be right there."

Sara opened her mouth to speak, maybe to protest, but nothing came out. She heard Anthony's breathing on the other end, calm and steady.

"Sara?" he said.

"Yes – I'm here. Okay, I'll do it."

"I'll see you soon."

She got up and walked slowly through the living room, thinking how much she hated words like "soon" when they came out of male mouths. With a woman, it's usually clear what things mean; soon means soon, later means soon with some leeway. With men, vague words like that could mean an hour, a few hours, or next Wednesday. But she unlocked the door and walked back to the bedroom, shivering a little as the night air brushed her skin. She was already naked – why didn't he know that? She never slept in anything – had he forgotten that already? Or maybe he'd given those instructions so often, to so many women over the years, that they always came out the same.

She lay in bed with the covers pulled up to her chin, trying not to think about the unlocked door, the risk she was taking. Anyone could just walk in. She decided that if Anthony didn't get there in a half hour, she'd lock the door again. But in the meantime, how did she want him to find her? Should she feign sleep to see how he'd wake her up? Should the covers be off or on? She pushed the blankets down so that only the sheet was over her . . . no, that would look too deliberate. Okay, sheet down too, as though she'd just happened to kick everything off. She spread her hair out across the pillow, angled her legs so her body would look more curved, which it definitely wasn't. But after a few minutes, she gave up. She couldn't take it; she must look as though she were auditioning for a *Penthouse* centerfold. She rolled over on her stomach – no, boring and not very seductive. The next experiment was lying on her side, the covers just up to her waist, hair tossed behind her, one arm delicately covering her breast.

Maybe. It was conceivable that someone could sleep this way. It would have to do, because while she was in the middle of contemplating it, the front door opened, shut softly, and the dead bolt clicked into place. Footsteps, which she hoped were Anthony's, came toward the bedroom. She was fluttering at the edge of danger again. What if some intruder had been cruising the neighborhood and hit the jackpot – her unlocked door? And walked in to find a naked woman posing like Marilyn Monroe at a photo shoot? But Anthony's hand slid up her spine.

"I missed you," he whispered, so softly she trembled. His voice was like a vapor trail in the night sky; her hands opened, trying to catch it.

Sara rolled over and wrapped her arms around his chest, going straight for his heartbeat, pressing her face against his muscles. It seemed like months since she'd touched a man's body.

"I missed you, too," she said. Because right then it seemed she had, although the truth was not quite so generous. A car drove past the house and headlights illuminated Anthony's body for a moment as he stood up to unbutton his shirt. Sara sat halfway up and undid his jeans; she pushed them down, held onto his thighs, and took him in her mouth.

"Wait," he said. "Not yet. Light a candle, okay?"

She rolled over, fumbled around on the night table for matches and heard him behind her, walking out of the room. Candlelight destroyed one corner of the darkness, and Sara backed up on the bed, out of the light's range, feeling safer in the shadows. He came back naked, with the terry-cloth tie from her robe in his hands. So it was to be a replay. She made a mental note to buy a silk robe for just such occasions. Bondage lingerie.

"Lie on your back," he said, kneeling beside her on the bed. Sometimes his body looked so beautiful it took her breath away. He took off his glasses and put them on the nightstand.

He pushed her over a few inches so that half her body glowed orange with reflected candlelight and half was left in the dark. Without waiting for him to tell her, Sara lifted her arms above her head and gripped the rails of the brass headboard. Anthony tied one end of the sash around one wrist, looped it around the railing, knotted it, and did the same with the other wrist.

"I need something else – for your feet," he said.

"Top right drawer of my dresser – I have scarves in there." She could feel her heart beating faster; fear crawled through her muscles.

There was something about what was happening that made her want to laugh, but just as quickly her eyes ached with the pressure of tears. He used black chiffon to tie one ankle to the footboard. Then he took her other ankle in his hands and opened her legs so wide that nothing was hidden from him. Dark blue silk took that leg prisoner.

"Black and blue," Sara whispered, almost to herself. "Like bruises."

"I won't bruise you," Anthony told her, leaning over and kissing her mouth softly.

"You already have."

As she said it, she realized she wasn't sure what she meant. Did she mean the bruise he frequently left on her lip? Or was she talking about something else – some deeper part? But she couldn't wonder about things like that now because he was on top of her, scraping his cock between her legs – teasing her, sensing her urgency, yet refusing her. A sound came out of her throat – something low and unfamiliar. She arched her neck, trying to capture the sound, and she thought of how wolves and dogs show submission to another of their species. They lie back, legs open, throat stretched to expose the jugular. Infinite trust, or infinite surrender, or maybe the intoxication of being that close to danger. Teeth sinking into the soft vein is always a possibility. She looked up at Anthony sitting on top of her. He could do anything to her, she realized, and terror started tying knots in her stomach. But instead of retreating from the feeling, she crawled inside it, suddenly alert to something she hadn't been willing to see before. There is a power in submission, in choosing to be that helpless, that exposed. It's saying, "I know more about you than you know about yourself. I know you're not going to hurt me, even though you may flirt with the idea. You won't do it. I know your limitations. That's the power I have over you. I don't really need to trust you; all I need is to know you. And I do."

She stared up at Anthony, at the candlelight reflected in his eyes, and felt a calmness come over her. She couldn't move, but still she was the one controlling things.

He was moving up on her body, knees under her arms, his hands cupping her breasts, squeezing them together, sliding his cock between them.

"Do you want me to fuck you like this, Sara?" he said, squeezing her breasts even harder, making them ache with just the right amount of pain – a sweet pain.

She didn't answer. Not with words anyway. But her eyes said, "I'm not going to tell you what to do. My role is just to lie here and let you think you're in control."

He abandoned her breasts, leaving a drop of moisture behind, a small spot on her skin – warm at first, then cold as it dried. Her eyes closed as he pushed into her mouth, so deep her throat clenched. She had no hands to use, to stop him from choking her, and suddenly she thought he might. What if she was wrong about him? What if she didn't really know his limitations? But then he pulled back, tracing her lips with the tip of his cock.

That was when she allowed her eyes to open. And when they did, he pulled back further, as if she'd caught him at something, looked at him when he didn't want to be seen. He held himself just out of reach of her mouth. She glanced quickly at his face but then let her eyes travel more slowly down his body. It was how she knew him best. She knew his body's tastes, its movements, its marks. There was a small chicken-pox scar on his back – almost unnoticeable, but she'd found it. Her hands could go to it even in the dark. She knew his cock, had watched it change color as it got hard and filled with blood; her tongue had explored it completely, even probing the tiny hole, just deep enough to make him shudder.

"What are you thinking about?" Anthony asked her.

"Your cock – how much I like it."

He laughed softly, traced her lips again.

She didn't want to look at his face. His body was her lover – she knew its limits even in the danger zones. But his eyes reminded her that he could still be a stranger.

He was in her mouth again, pushing into her throat; instinctively she knew he was trying to scare her. She turned her head to the side sharply, scraping him with her teeth. He gasped and pulled back, but in an instant he had his face composed to mask whatever pain she'd inflicted. He started moving down her body, and she almost told him how badly she wanted him inside her – almost begged him – but she knew she'd get what she wanted only if she said nothing.

He kept moving down until he was standing at the foot of the bed, and then he began untying her ankles.

"What are you doing?" Sara asked, surprised. She'd gotten used to being his hostage; the idea of being released was suddenly frightening.

He didn't say anything. He finished loosening her bonds, yet her legs didn't move; they were still bound by the memory of the restraints. Anthony pushed her legs together, moved up to her hands and untied them as well.

"What are you doing?" she asked again.

"Setting you free." His half-smile made her nervous.

He was still hard. She could take him in her hands; she could wrap her legs around him. She could do anything – her body was free now – but still she could do nothing. He rolled her over on her stomach, and she was like a limp doll in his hands; then he knelt beside her.

"You hurt me, Sara. You scraped me with your teeth. That wasn't very nice. I'm going to have to punish you for that."

He gripped her waist with his hands and lifted her so that her knees bent and scraped across the sheet – kneeling for him. He pushed her knees apart just a little, and the first blow of his hand set off a chain reaction in her nerves that registered as pain for only a second, and then became something else. She felt herself getting wetter, rocking backward on her knees, toward him – silently asking for more. The second and third blows traveled more quickly along her nerve paths, all the way into her womb – like sparks, like fire along a string of explosives.

But there was something else, too – a sense of security in being punished for doing something wrong. There was a childlike simplicity to it, an unshakable logic. It was how she had seen the world when she was very young: a misdeed leads to punishment. It's only when she grew older that she realized justice is selective and often arbitrary. But on her knees, with Anthony spanking her, she was back in the safety zone where things made sense and life seemed predictable.

She heard herself gasp when he stopped. Her skin burned and tingled where his hand had landed, but the feeling of abandonment when he stopped was still more painful. She turned her face to glance behind her. He was leaning into her now, his thighs against her.

Then he was inside. But so gently she felt like she wanted to cry. He was pushing into her, but not forcefully; walls were giving way deep inside, cracking and melting. Like ice. My ice kingdom, she thought, her head bent and a tear dropping onto the sheet. The ice kingdom Mark talked about is inside me, and Anthony's getting past the walls, breaching glaciers, leaving tracks in the snow, and changing the temperature the farther in he goes. What happens when it thaws? What if there's nothing beneath the ice? What if it's barren, with no colors, no tiny shoots of life, like spring after a long winter?

Anthony's hands were over her breasts; her heartbeat was in his palm. He pulled Sara up so her back was pressed against his chest – against his heartbeat – and she couldn't tell where hers stopped and his began.

"I love you," she thought he said between breaths. The words were buried in the quickening of his breath as he came – synchronizing her rhythm to his, taking her with him. Maybe she was wrong and he'd said something else – or nothing at all. She let the moment float away – no response.

Anthony relaxed his body and they both slid down on the bed. His hands were still under her, his heartbeat still pounding against her back. It was so quiet; no cars passed outside, no wind rustled the trees. Somewhere a bird sang, an early riser, letting them know dawn was on its way. For a few minutes they slept, until Anthony's mouth covered Sara's ear.

"I have to go," he said. "We're starting to shoot here in two days and I have a lot of work to do."

"Uh-huh." Sara lifted her body just enough to signal him to get off her. "Do you want to take a shower?"

"No – I'd better go."

She rolled over on her back and watched him get dressed. The candle had burned down, but there was a fringe of gray light around the edge of the curtains. His movements were slow and faintly lit. When he was dressed, he sat down beside her on the bed and pushed her hair back from her forehead.

"I'll call you later. Will you be around?"

"Yeah. I'm suddenly envious that you're working. I think I better call my agent and act anxious so she doesn't think I've gone into early retirement."

"Is your money holding out okay?" Anthony asked.

"So far, but I will have to work soon."

He picked up his glasses from the night table and put them on. Sara remembered how, the first time she saw him, she thought his glasses gave him that just-out-of-Harvard look. He kissed her good-bye; his good-bye kisses were always tame and safe – thanks-for-the-nice-time kisses.

When he left, Sara got up, found her robe and put the tie back where it belonged. She wrapped the robe tightly around her, turned on the heater, and sat down on the floor next to the vent. Suddenly her house felt like the wrong side of town – unfamiliar and dangerously quiet.

She felt the way she had as a child, staring out the window of her father's Cadillac at miles of dark desert, learning what loneliness looked like. The Cadillac was gone, and the child had grown up, but the loneliness still had her number.

She sat there until the heat penetrated her skin and muscles, until she could feel it in her bones, and then she went in to take a shower. Her body in the mirror looked different to her – softer, more female, less angular. In the shower, Sara closed her eyes and let the warm water run over her. When she opened them and looked down, blood had mixed with the water and was spiraling down the drain. She must have started her period while Anthony was making love to her. She squeezed her deepest muscles and watched as more blood streamed out. She hadn't given any thought to using birth control. Belinda was the fertile one. Sara had never been pregnant and had wondered sometimes if she ever would be. Usually she just didn't think about it very much, but the blood made her sad this time – a watery red stream disappearing into the sewers. Maybe it was too cold inside her for a child to grow. All that ice.

It was just before six. Sara pulled on a sweater, jeans, and cowboy boots, grabbed her keys and walked out of the house. A neighbor jogged past and said good morning; the elderly woman from across the street was walking her elderly Doberman. The sky was somewhere behind a lens of gray clouds that diffused the sun and made the morning simmer with a soft orange light. "God-light" is what Sara used to call it when she was younger, because she thought that, if God were a color, the color would have to be something rapturous and otherworldly. So she walked through her neighborhood in this God-light, trying to feel as if she belonged . . . except she felt more like a shadow trapped on the wrong side of dawn. She felt anyone passing by would see that she was in trouble – a person with glaciers inside. She glanced behind her on the sidewalk, half expecting to see a trail of blood and ice.

She could still feel Anthony inside her, but it was Belinda's face that crowded into her mind, pushing everything else out. Sara missed her – with one of those aches that seemed almost physical. Her hand reached up to touch her chest, as if the pain were located there. She sensed that she was losing Belinda and she didn't know how she could survive that.

Sara turned around and walked quickly back to her house. I'll call her, she decided, even if I wake her up. This is important. I have to tell her everything – about Anthony, about the girl in the bar. Everything.

Belinda's voice was raspy and dull when she answered the phone, but something about it didn't sound sleepy.

"Belinda, it's me. I know I probably woke you but . . . did I wake you?"

"No."

Maybe that was the moment that something turned over in Sara's stomach. She would try to remember later when exactly that happened, replaying everything in her mind.

"Belinda, what's wrong? Are you sick?"

"I don't know – maybe. I never thought he . . ." Her voice trailed off.

"He who?" Sara heard the urgency in her own voice, thought she should probably try to remain calm, but she couldn't. "Tell me what happened. Are you hurt? Belinda, talk to me!"

"He raped me." For that one sentence, Belinda pulled

herself together, pushed her voice through her throat, and forced herself to enunciate the words. Sara knew how much effort it had taken.

"Stay there, Belinda. Don't do anything. And don't take a shower."

She didn't need to ask who he was – she already knew.

Fourteen

Sara

SARA KNEW her voice sounded almost hysterical when she called her parents' house and told her mother she needed to speak to Mark.

"I know he's asleep," she said, before Claire Norton had a chance to squeeze a word in. "It's an emergency, Mother – I have to talk to him."

"What happened? What's wrong?"

Sara followed the leap her mother's thoughts had made: an accident, another of my children hurt or in trouble.

"No, I'm fine – it's not me. Something happened to Belinda. Mother, I don't have time to explain now – please."

After what seemed like forever, Mark was on the phone, his voice thick with sleep. "What happened to Belinda?"

"She got raped. Where do I take her?"

"Oh God . . . okay, let me think. Not UCLA. Take her to Santa Monica Hospital. They have a Rape Treatment Center, and it's close – is she home?"

"Yeah. I'm going over there now," Sara said.

"Go to Emergency when you get there. And call me later."

A cold rain had started to fall. "Perfect," Sara said to the steering wheel. "Now it's going to take me longer to get there." But actually, she got to Belinda's house in record time despite the rain – a Volvo racing through West L.A. streets, doing a great imitation of a New York cab.

As she ran down the path toward Belinda's door, the sound she heard leaking from the house made her stop suddenly. Philippe's voice. "What the fuck?" she said under her breath. She knew he'd raped Belinda – she knew it had to be him. But was he in there? She began walking toward the door slowly; then she realized what she was hearing. Belinda was playing a tape of one of his lectures. Sara caught some of the key phrases – "God's warriors" . . . "shielding yourself from other people's energy" . . . "building up your power so you're like a fortress." His usual Norman Schwarzkopf approach to spiritual dominance.

The door was slightly ajar. Belinda was sitting in the middle of the floor in her pink bathrobe, head bowed, listening to Philippe's voice.

"Belinda?" Sara almost felt like she was disturbing a meditation.

When Belinda looked up, Sara saw a face she barely recognized. A large blue bruise was spreading out beneath one eye, her lower lip was swollen and cut. Her face was flushed and streaked with tears. Sara dropped down on the floor beside her and put her arms around shoulders that seemed thinner than they had just days earlier. In fact, Belinda's whole body looked bent, defeated.

"It was Philippe, wasn't it?"

Belinda nodded, dropping her eyes again.

"Why are you listening to this? How can you bear to

hear his voice?" Sara reached over and turned off the tape, grateful for the silence and the reassuring sound of rain on the roof.

Belinda's eyes, when they looked up again and focused on Sara, were so wide and uncomprehending, Sara wasn't sure if they reflected shock or an innocence so pure, so fragile, it never should have survived this long.

"Belinda," Sara said, holding her friend's damaged face in her hands, "he raped you. He beat you up. He's probably done it to other women."

"But why?" Belinda asked. Her eyes widened even more. "I must have done something to make him angry. He was helping me – he's so wise, Sara, and God talked to him when he was a child and told him he had a mission in life to help people, and – "

"Belinda, stop it. Listen to me – you didn't do anything wrong. He's a fraud. He was a wise-ass kid from the Bronx who decided he wanted to be French, changed his name, and figured out how to prey on other people's vulnerabilities. All you did was make a mistake in trusting him. And I'm sure you're not the first. Come on, honey, let's go wash your face and get some clothes on you. I'm going to take you to the hospital."

"Why?"

"Because you've been raped. Come on, let's stand up, okay?"

Sara helped her up, holding her around the waist. When Belinda's robe fell open, Sara could see there were no other bruises, at least not on the front of her body. She was shivering.

"I'm cold."

"I know," Sara said. "Where's the sash to your robe?"

"On the bed."

"Okay. Let's get it and then wash your face off." Sara led her toward the bedroom; Belinda's steps were slow and small, almost shuffling.

The sash was looped and knotted around one of the bedposts, and Sara suddenly got the whole picture – he'd tied her up, made it impossible for her to fight him off. Looped the sash only once. He'd bound her wrists together as he might a prisoner's.

Sara retrieved the sash as quickly as she could, pulled Belinda's robe together, and tied it around her waist. "How long ago did it happen?" she asked.

"A few hours ago. He came earlier – we were talking for a long time." She sounded numb. "I think the sky was getting light. I'm not sure, though."

As Sara took Belinda into the bathroom, the thought occurred to her that they might both have been tied up at the same time – one of them moaning for more, while, across town, the other was sobbing in terror. She pictured Anthony binding her with chiffon scarves, but for a moment, faces got confused and he looked like Philippe. Were their movements synchronized, with the same sun coming up outside? The possibility of that made her want to cry. She had called Belinda to tell her everything that had happened, but now, as she stood in the bathroom, wiping the blood and tears off Belinda's face with a warm washcloth, she knew she couldn't. She might never be able to tell her about the silk around her wrists, about sinking into the helplessness of it and not wanting to stop. Fear for her had been a game – something she and Anthony had used to heat things up, to keep things off balance and dramatic.

For Belinda, fear had been the shadowy figure hiding in the closet, waiting for the right moment to come out and claim her as its victim. And what a victim she'd been. She was crying again now, the tears running down her face faster than Sara could wipe them off.

"I don't feel well," she said, almost choking on the words. "I think I'm going to be sick."

"Okay – it's okay – I'll help you."

Sara turned Belinda around so she could kneel in front of the toilet, and held her head while she vomited. If only it were that simple, Sara thought. If only her system could rid itself of the whole experience by just throwing up.

When they stood up, Sara put toothpaste on the toothbrush and handed it to Belinda as if she were a child getting ready for bed. Her thoughts frantically reached for some innocent analogy. She could see that Belinda was drifting farther away, retreating.

"Belinda, I think we should hurry. I'm going to get some clothes out for you."

She dressed her quickly in a skirt and sweater she grabbed out of the closet. "Here, we'll put this sweater on – I know it's one of your favorites." She hoped that the sound of her voice would lure Belinda back; that at least she could keep her from retreating further.

In the car on the way to the hospital, Sara turned on the radio, but Belinda didn't seem to be hearing anything. Her eyes were glassy, staring at the windshield, watching the rain, but not really seeing it. The weather had to be brighter in the world she'd fled to.

They walked into an Emergency Room where the waiting list was already too long. A man with what Sara guessed was a knife wound in his shoulder was bleeding his way through a bath towel, a middle-aged woman was sitting with her knees scrunched up, moaning loudly, and a teenage boy was standing against the wall, cradling his broken arm with a stoicism John Wayne would have admired.

"What happened?" the nurse behind the desk asked, glancing at Belinda's swollen face.

"She was raped," Sara answered, softly but emphatically. "We need to see someone from the Rape Treatment Center."

"You will, but it might be a wait. Unless you've already filed a police report, I'll need insurance information."

Sara had brought Belinda's wallet with them; she found the insurance card and handed it over, with the absurd feeling that she was vying for a table at a restaurant.

"How long until she can see someone?" she asked.

"I really don't know. We'll call you."

"Uh-huh. Well, we'd like the nonsmoking section." Sara wasn't bothering to hide her irritation.

"What?"

"Nothing. It's just – I mean, you'd think when someone has been raped, they wouldn't be put on a waiting list. They should be given immediate attention."

The nurse stared at her with an expression that made it clear how many times a day she dealt with impatience. "The man over there probably feels the same way about people with knife wounds," she said.

Sara led Belinda over to some empty chairs, as far away from the others as she could – which seems to be the common pattern in places like emergency waiting rooms. No one wants to be distracted from their own suffering, although today Sara wished for something that might distract Belinda; she was slipping away too easily, like a stream flowing backward, returning to some lake hidden deep in the mountains. Sara was tempted to put a mirror in front of her lips to see if her breath would still cloud the glass. A terrifying calm had taken over her face, a calm that reminded Sara of death.

Then, as if picking up on Sara's fear, Belinda turned toward her and said in a raspy, thin voice, "Philippe says there's no such thing as magic, and miracles are just illusions for weak people to cling to. He says you have to learn from life's suffering."

Sara was too stunned to speak. The question taking shape in her mind was "Do you know who raped you?"

But it wasn't that Belinda didn't know – it was that she needed to take this in stages. First, she had to accept that she'd been raped, then she had to accept that it was Philippe. Let me be blind for a while, was what she was really saying. But Sara was afraid there would be a price for that blindness.

She reached over, took Belinda's hand, and held on to it tightly. Come back to the world, she tried to communicate. I know it's painful, but just do it. She knew the turn Belinda's thoughts had taken. There was only confusion in which a dark, hooded rider had assaulted her, raped her, and ridden off without ever showing his face. What would happen when the clouds over her memory cleared and she realized that more cruel than the rape was the fact that he didn't even bother to conceal his face? She wished Belinda would scream, or moan like the woman doubled over in front of them, who, while eliciting sympathy, was also driving everyone mad. But at least she was doing something. Sara wanted Belinda to wake up, focus her eyes, her brain, her memory, and most of all her rage. She was afraid Belinda was going to slip away forever – die without a fight. Part of her seemed already dead.

Sara walked up to the desk. "Look, I know you have other patients in here but I think my friend is in shock. She needs to see someone right away."

"In shock?" the nurse repeated coolly. "Are you a doctor?"

"No, I'm not. But it's pretty fucking obvious. She's been raped, for God's sake! I don't need attitude from you."

She'd said the word "raped" a little louder than she intended, and even without turning around, she knew everyone in the waiting room had heard. She glared at the nurse a moment longer, not exactly sure how to follow her own act, and then went back to her chair.

Twenty more minutes passed before a nurse came out and called Belinda's name.

In the examining room, a doctor and a woman in a wool skirt and blazer were waiting for them. Sara felt as if all her senses were in overdrive; she was noticing and cataloging everything – the woman's bitten-down fingernails, the doctor's reluctance to meet Belinda's eyes, the faint hum of the lights and the hospital smells of disinfectant and rubbing alcohol.

"Hi, I'm Nicole," the woman said, directing herself to Belinda, who still moved in a trancelike state.

"I'm Sara," Sara said to Nicole. "I'm Belinda's friend."

Nicole came closer to Belinda. "Why don't we sit down here for a minute and talk."

Belinda allowed herself to be led to a chair and sat down like an obedient child awaiting some kind of reprimand.

"Do you want to tell me what happened?" Nicole asked her. "Were you raped by someone you know?"

Sara wanted to answer for her, but she knew she had to keep quiet. After a few seconds, Belinda nodded slowly.

"Someone you were dating?" Nicole asked gently.

There was something in her eyes that made Sara think this woman could track Belinda, follow her footprints, and bring her back. Maybe she identified with her; maybe that's why she was a rape counselor.

"He's my teacher," Belinda said in a scratchy voice. Sara noticed the present tense and cringed. "My spiritual teacher," Belinda added.

"Can you tell me more?"

"Philippe."

Even the doctor reacted to that announcement. Sara heard his intake of breath – sharp and quick. Of course, she thought – Philippe is famous, one of those first-name-only celebrities everyone has heard of. Nicole glanced at Sara, who looked back at her with an expression that said, "And I'll bet you thought he was Mr. Clean Jeans, didn't you?"

"Belinda," Nicole said, "the doctor is going to examine you and I'd like you to let us take evidence, in case you decide to report this to the police. You can do that today, or you can think it over. But at least we'll have the evidence. Now, I have to ask you a few more questions to help the doctor. Was there oral copulation?"

Belinda looked blank, as if the words didn't register, but then she said, "No," emphatically enough that it sounded believable.

"Did he ejaculate?" Nicole asked.

A mute nod was the answer.

In her mind, Sara put Philippe in front of her, knocked him to the ground and screamed, "What about your warning to women to not let a man come in them, you motherfucker? Everyone else's come is bad, but yours is okay, huh?" Then she mentally kicked him and left him lying there . . . . It made her feel better for a minute.

Nicole stood up and Belinda, as if pulled by a string, rose too. "I know this won't be easy for you," Nicole said, "but we need you to undress and put on the gown, just like a regular doctor's visit. The doctor is going to do a pelvic exam and take a sample of fluids from your vagina. Do we have your permission to keep this as evidence?"

Belinda had pulled off her sweater and was staring down at her body – as if she were reacquainting herself with it. "Okay," she answered. Sara had the feeling that she hadn't really heard the question, but it didn't matter – she'd given the right answer.

The doctor told her everything he was going to do before he did it. Nicole stood by her head, occasionally telling her to relax, everything would be okay.

But to Sara, it seemed Belinda was too relaxed. She lay motionless, her body limp, seemingly numb – or else afraid to move, afraid to stir up pain. Sara remembered what she'd once heard about shrapnel wounds. Even after the large pieces of metal are removed, tiny slivers remain. Elusive and irretrievable, they remain lodged in the body, and years later the person may turn a certain way, make a slight movement, and experience the pain once more – reviving long forgotten memories. Maybe it would be like that for Belinda. Years down the line, the smallest movement would dislodge a splinter and return her to this white room, the search for injuries and evidence, and the taste of blood on her lip.

Sara left the room while Belinda was getting dressed; she had started to feel lightheaded and short of breath. Standing in the hallway she could hear, through the door, Nicole talking to Belinda about a pregnancy test, an AIDS test, getting further counseling. If Belinda responded, Sara couldn't hear her.

The rain had stopped, but clouds still towered in the sky – soft gray mountains hiding the sun.

"What time is it?" Belinda asked as Sara reached across and fastened the seat belt around her.

"Almost two o'clock." Jesus, over half the day was gone. Wasn't it just dawn a few minutes ago?

They drove to Belinda's house without speaking. Maybe she needed to be left in silence, Sara reasoned. Maybe silence was a balm, a healing herb that would work its magic if given a chance.

When they unlocked Belinda's door and walked inside, Sara noticed a faint smell of cologne hanging in the air. A man's cologne. She hadn't noticed it before, although it must have been there.

"How about if I light some incense?" she said, without explaining why.

"Okay." Belinda was just standing there looking around, the same way she'd looked at her body. Maybe everything seemed unfamiliar to her now.

It took some searching through the cluttered living room to find the sixties artifacts that Belinda hadn't outgrown – incense, matches, and a brass incense burner. When she finally found everything and lit two jasmine sticks, Sara realized that Belinda had drifted off into the bedroom.

She expected to find her sitting on the bed, or lying down, or getting ready to take a shower. She did not expect to come through the doorway and trip over her discarded clothes; she did not expect to see Belinda naked, kneeling down beside the bed, her head bent forward and resting on her folded hands.

"What are you doing?" Sara asked, trying to smooth out her voice into something casual and unconcerned.

"Praying."

Sara knelt down beside her. "What are you praying for?"

"To understand why this happened."

"Belinda, you don't need God to tell you that. I can tell you. It happened because Philippe is a sick bastard and he has to be stopped before he does this to someone else."

Belinda looked at her and for the first time that day her eyes seemed to focus – a blind person regaining her sight. The cut on her lip was opening again; blood was seeping out. It wouldn't stay closed – it kept insisting on being an open wound.

"Your lip's opening up again. Let's find something to put on it."

She helped Belinda stand and took her into the bathroom. As she was reaching for a washcloth, she noticed blood on Belinda's feet and, behind them, smudges on the floor.

"Belinda – "

"I guess I started my period."

"Okay. I'm going to fill up the bathtub for you. A bath will feel good, won't it?"

As the bathroom filled with steam, Sara felt her own blood seeping out of her womb, her cycle interwoven with Belinda's in some mysterious timing – the pull of moons, the inner tides of bodies following ancient rhythms. There had been other occasions when they both got their periods at the same time. They had smiled about it, not needing to say too much. It was one of those unique bonds between women that make men feel left out in the cold. But this time, Sara couldn't smile about it. The blood on Belinda's feet made her think of nail holes.

Sara bathed Belinda, helped her into a nightshirt, and put her to bed.

"I'll stay out here in the living room," she said. "I won't leave you alone, okay?"

"Okay."

Sara looked back at Belinda. She looks so woeful and innocent, Sara thought, like a little girl who has fallen down roller-skating and skinned her face.

No, Sara reminded herself, she fell down trusting the wrong person, and the wounds go deeper than her skin.

Sara called to check her phone machine – two messages from Anthony asking where she was. It was strange how distant he could seem to her at times, like someone she used to know but didn't anymore. And then at other times, she felt he was embedded in her bones. She couldn't call him back now – not from Belinda's house. And there was a part of her that liked keeping him in the distance; it helped her to forget how easily she could feel like his hostage.

The rain began again, lightly at first, like a soft veil brushing across the roof, then bearing down harder. Within minutes, it was steady and loud, making Sara feel it was closing her in. She was trapped now, in a small, dry world with wild wet weather outside. Locked in with Belinda – someone she loved. But how did she love her? This friend, this almost-lover, this soul-twin, this stranger.

She hadn't intended to doze off, but when she opened her eyes again, hours had passed and the house was getting dark. Outside it was still raining. Sara lay on the sofa, listening to the sounds outside, dreaming of distances and things she'd forgotten. Somewhere past the rain, stars were tossing light around; other stars were probably falling. Her mother used to say that every time a soul dies, a star falls. But a soul can't die, can it? Sara reasoned. Maybe just pieces of it – because of days like this, because of people like Philippe who have figured out how to pillage the souls of even the most innocent. A piece of Belinda's soul must have died, Sara thought, like a chunk taken out of a star. But maybe the effect wouldn't be that dramatic; her light would just be refracted – not dimmer, just different.

Sara tiptoed into the bedroom and looked at Belinda sleeping; she felt like a mother checking on her child. She was going to stay the night, on the couch, close enough to hear if Belinda woke up. She would have liked to lie next to her, hold her, protect her from nightmares, but she knew she couldn't. She had to leave some distance between them.

Fifteen

Belinda

WHENEVER BELINDA inhaled, she smelled him – his skin, the scent of Neutrogena shampoo (it seemed at the time such an intimate thing to know about him), and his cologne. She knew Sara caught the smell of cologne, too – that's why she had lit the incense. There were even moments when Belinda drew in her breath and thought she smelled his semen. She knew it should make her ill, but it didn't.

The day was soft and rainy – a day that reminded her of England. That's where Belinda would have liked to be – England, with a low, wet sky over her and mist licking her face. The first time she went there she'd been eighteen. It was a summer trip, marking the transition between high school and college. She remembered that as the plane descended and green land rose up around her, she had thought that she had been there before – in another life, which was how she frequently explained such feelings.

Just thinking about England, and how it rolled out like a soft green carpet made her feel better now.

"Close your eyes and think of England, dear." Didn't she and Sara joke about that sometimes? The admonition

Victorian women used to give their daughters, in an era when only men were supposed to enjoy sex? That's what I'm doing now, Belinda thought – closing my eyes and thinking of England, but not for the right reasons. No, it was to escape the memory of rape.

Rape. It was one of those words she couldn't remember learning. It was just there, as though she'd always known it. It was a word one saw in newspapers, a statistics-are-up kind of word that didn't take shape or carry any weight until she got close to it. Then, once she did, it kept getting heavier and larger, like a snowball rolling downhill, gathering up everything along its path.

Before she left that morning, Sara had scrubbed Woolite into the bloodstains on the carpet. She'd tried to think of reasons to stay, but Belinda insisted that she go. Finally, she said, "Okay, I guess you need to be alone." That had been hours ago.

So now Belinda watched raindrops trickle down the windowpanes. They reminded her of tears and she wondered if she'd ever be able to cry again. Everything inside her felt parched. A desert landscape – old, dried-up bones and bits of broken glass.

Sara had told her she should file a police report; if she didn't, there might be other women. Maybe there already had been. But what about the moment when he had reached over and touched her face and she'd wanted more? She almost saw, in those quick seconds, fantasies forming, like comic-strip balloons over her head. Would someone say that she must have wanted it, so it couldn't really be called rape? Would he say it?

For the first time she allowed herself to replay the events of that previous day. He'd phoned just as she was getting out of the shower. Dripping wet, she was going to let the machine pick up, but something told her to answer it herself. She grabbed a towel, threw it around her, and ran into the bedroom. And the strangest thing happened – just as her hand was about to lift up the receiver, her breath came up short, as if her lungs had suddenly shrunk in size. She sucked air in desperately, forcing it down, but her voice must have sounded odd when she said hello.

Philippe's voice, on the other hand, was like melted chocolate – not syrupy exactly, but thick and dark, and very sweet.

"For some reason, you've been on my mind all day," he said. "I have some free time this evening. Maybe I could come see you and we could talk!"

"Yes, of course," Belinda said, fumbling with the words. The sun was going down outside her bedroom window – a slow burn through the trees – that wintry, orange light that makes people put down what they're doing and stare.

"I can be there in about an hour," he told her. "See you then."

She was very much aware of how jittery she became as she raced around the house, straightening up rooms that were basically always in a state of mild disorder. Quickly, she brushed her hair and put on eye makeup, and then looked in her closet for something to wear. She chose the loose antique velvet dress she'd just bought a week ago. It was the color of pine, so soft she loved the feel of it against her skin. Even the backside of the fabric was soft, like a whisper across bare flesh. She slipped it over her head without putting on underwear. But now that one gesture – that one omission – haunted her. Was it more than the feel of the velvet? More than the fact that she was hurrying so? Was it blatantly sexual? An invitation of sorts?

She knew, as she raced around the house, lighting candles, flicking on lamps, picking up stray shoes, that Philippe seemed almost mythical to her. Part of her couldn't imagine him driving up in a car. He should just land, appear mysteriously, descend from the clouds. Why was he coming to see her alone? Not as part of a group, like when he'd come for dinner or had called her to his office. This time, he'd singled her out. She kept taking deep breaths, trying to banish the nervousness that was knotted inside her. It was true that she was in awe of him, that she believed there was something otherworldly about him. It was sort of like Jesus Christ phoning up to say he was dropping by for tea. But she recognized another sensation; was she frightened of him also? It might be awe, but it felt like fear; it inhabited the same part of her stomach – the part that no amount of deep breathing could get to.

She walked outside to clear her head, to calm herself, to look up and thank the heavens for this unexpected visit on a night when she had nothing planned except watching syndicated reruns of "Married with Children." The night sky had a few clouds in it – a storm was moving in – but between them, handfuls of stars glittered. It was a night that seemed enormous, as though the sky had stretched, expanded, sprouted more stars.

When she heard his car pull up, she went into the house and stood in the living room until he knocked on the door. And then she gave it a few more seconds before walking over and opening it. I'm not the least bit anxious, her inner monologue went – oh, has an hour gone by?

His hair looked just washed – tied back, but with a few renegade strands brushing his forehead. It was shiny black, reflecting the porch light. He was wearing a white

T-shirt and a black Armani suit; from working with Sara, Belinda could pick out designers at a glance.

"How are you, Belinda!" Philippe asked, stepping into the house. He always had a way with that question of making her feel no answer would be acceptable. Before even speaking, she would feel like a liar.

"I'm fine," she answered, expecting him to counter with, "No, you're not," or something to that effect.

But he didn't. "You look beautiful," he said instead.

"Thank you." She closed the door and stood awkwardly for a moment, all rules of etiquette escaping her. "Uh – can I get you something to drink? Juice? Mineral water? I can make some tea."

"Water would be fine," he said, seating himself in a corner of the couch, angling himself as though posing for a fashion ad for the suit he was wearing. "Your house is such a reflection of you," he called out while she was in the kitchen squeezing lime wedges into glasses of Pellegrino.

"In what way!" Belinda asked when she came back into the living room and sat a demure distance from him.

"It's very warm and sensual, but with a sense of humor."

"My house has a sense of humor!"

"Definitely. You have Maxfield Parrish prints over there and in the dining room, scenes from *Winnie the Pooh.*"

Belinda felt her face flush. She wished she weren't prone to blushing. "Well, I collect all sorts of things. I'm a swap-meet junkie, and I guess a part of me never grew up."

"It's a charming quality." He looked at her probingly, a now-we're-going-to-get-down-to-it look. "I've never met anyone quite like you, Belinda," he said, pausing to take a sip of water. "The first time I saw you sitting in the audience, I knew there was something unique about you. And something familiar as well. It's as if I've known you before. I find myself picking up on your thoughts, sometimes your fears. You're very afraid to let people know you, aren't you? Afraid that if they do, they'll leave you, abandon you. So you make them think they've gotten to know you, but you have walls that they're not even aware of."

"Well, I think everyone does that to a certain extent, don't you? I mean, we all have insecurities, and – "

"We were talking about you," he said firmly. "Isn't that what you do? Am I right about that!"

"Yes." The word floated out like a feather in the warmly lit room. "I guess I think that I have a better chance at a relationship if the other person doesn't know all the shadowy places in me – all the dark spots."

"All the bruises!"

"Uh-huh," Belinda admitted.

"Hmm." Philippe sipped his water, and seemed to drift off, reflecting on something distant and puzzling. "Eventually, though," he said, his eyes once again putting her in a choke hold, "we meet someone who we know we have to trust. Someone who isn't fooled by us, who sees right through. It's as though that person is our connection."

"Connection to what!" Belinda asked. She tucked her bare feet underneath her, hiding them beneath the deep green velvet.

"To a part of ourselves. It is true that we all have those places we're reluctant to expose, for fear of being ostracized. That's why we're sent people who can confront us with our own fears. I'm no different, really – I have those same tendencies. That's what I'm trying to tell you – when I first saw you, I felt the tug of all those shadowy places that I hadn't wanted to share with anyone. I knew you had been sent to me for that purpose."

"What kind of places!" There was something surreal about this. Philippe confiding in her? Turning the tables and being the vulnerable one? The one with his hand tilted so all the cards were visible?

But that's what he did.

He leaned back further into the couch, took a long breath, and let it out slowly – the way people do when they're about to tell a story long buried. It's as if that one drawn-out breath is the gateway; once through it, the story can unfold.

"I have a wife," he began. "Well, a wife in the technical sense – we haven't even seen each other in almost seven years now. I had a whole different life at one point, Belinda, a different name too, which is why no one has managed to unearth this part of my history as yet. But there are times when I feel myself looking over my shoulder. The life I had was slowly killing me. It looked proper and well put together on the surface – a house in a nice neighborhood, color-coordinated rooms and all of the pretty trappings that were so important to my wife. Then she was stricken with multiple sclerosis – such a sinister disease, you know. It starts off with such small vague symptoms, people are inclined to ignore them, but all the while it's tightening its noose around them. When we finally separated, she was so weak she could hardly walk without assistance. But her disease was not the reason I left – I want you to understand that."

Belinda nodded. How could she refuse him her unconditional understanding? He was opening up the locked vaults of his life, letting her peek inside. How could she refuse him anything? She pictured him wandering restlessly through Laura Ashley rooms, copies of *House Beautiful* on little white wicker end tables. Wandering, knowing he had to leave, knowing his wife would think her disease was the reason. How do you tell an ill person, no, it's not the disease, it's you, it's us, it's everything but the disease.

"I simply couldn't live the life she wanted. I was meant to serve people as I'm serving them now. And lead them – I always knew I was meant to lead. I send her money, but we rarely speak. If I divorced her, it would be made public – I'm sure you can see that – and I would be judged very harshly. Divorcing a woman who was stricken with such a cruel disease . . ."

"Where does she live?" Belinda asked.

"I can't tell you that," he answered tersely. "The specifics aren't important. What I'm sharing with you now is – the fact that I have fugitive parts of my life, too – things I'm forced to hide and run away from, things I can't talk about. But there is such an enormous relief in finding someone who you know will keep your secrets safe, and not judge you. You know, there are so many who are anxious to judge me – I suppose it's always that way when one chooses to move out in front and show people the way."

A single tear had escaped his eye; absently, he brushed it from his cheek. There was something soft about him, like a charcoal drawing in which the artist has smudged the edges, blurred the lines. His eyes were gleaming as if more tears were gathering there. Belinda put her hand over his, a gesture that said "I understand – I understand the weight of a history you can't share with anyone. The weight is almost crushing sometimes."

Was that when it happened? When the air or the earth

or something enormous shifted? She couldn't remember now. The rain was coming down harder, washing out her memory like a bad stretch of road. She closed her eyes, diving into the deluge for clues, for anything that might help her understand what happened. Her hand over his – she remembered that – and that was when he reached for her. But there was nothing savage in the way he did it; that came later. His palm brushed her cheek, slid over her ear to the back of her neck, and the world stopped and held its breath for a moment. No, wait, not the world – just her, too surprised to breathe, not certain what to do. Sara was right: to Belinda, Philippe was almost divine, untouchable. Yet here he was, touching her like a normal man. She didn't want him to be normal, but she wanted his touch – it wasn't that she didn't. The flutter of fear, though, was unmistakable.

"What you and I represent to each other is connection," Philippe said in that dark voice. "We own each other's secrets now, we're linked in ways that we aren't with anyone else."

He was moving in, his breath like steam on her skin. She wondered briefly if she kissed him whether they would ascend to heaven together. His hand was gripping the back of her neck harder and his other hand was sliding velvet up her thigh. A few more inches and he'd know more secrets – nothing underneath. Was this what she wanted? She tried to slow her mind down, take stock, make a choice – there was a choice, right? But it was not only her mind that was spinning; the room was, too – candle flames and lamplight whirling like carnival lights.

"Philippe, I don't know –" she started to say, but the sentence lurched and stalled.

"Yes, you do. You've known all along," he answered.

She hadn't known, but she did now. That was the moment she realized she was staring into a stranger's eyes. His eyes had sharpened into knife blades, steely and frightening and coming right at her. Nothing about him seemed familiar. The cocoon had ruptured and out had come, not a butterfly, but some mutation. It was a different game then – no more talking, no more gentle confidence of tears. His mouth was over hers, but hard, like a clamp, robbing her breath. His fingers bruised the back of her neck, his other hand was between her thighs, and suddenly he was on top of her, weighing more than she would have expected. The air was being pushed out of her body, sucked out of her mouth. At least that's what she thought. And everything was slowing down – a tape slowing down, a drunken dance.

"Stop," she managed to say with what little breath she had left.

He moved his mouth off of hers, but only barely – just enough so he could speak.

"Are you arguing with me, Belinda?" he said. "Disobeying me? You said you would follow me."

"But –"

"Didn't you?" His voice rose, hurting her ears. "Didn't I tell you that the way wouldn't always be easy? That you had to do whatever I wanted? Didn't you say you would?"

She nodded. It was all she could do – her voice was gone.

"Traitors are punished, Belinda – you should know that."

He pulled back quickly and slammed his hand into her face – part slap, part slug. Her lip opened and blood washed over her teeth. She swallowed it, concentrated on the saltiness, the slippery feel of it – anything to focus her mind inward, away from what was happening. He had touched her face lightly before – just moments before, it seemed – like a lover. Was that what she was being punished for? Her thoughts? They'd been so fleeting, but maybe he knew. For just that second, she'd forgotten to be his disciple; she'd blushed like a lover, and he'd never touch her that lightly again.

He pulled her dress roughly over her head. For an instant, she was safe, hidden in a dark, pine-colored world, her eyes covered by velvet. If only time could have stopped then. Blood and tears filled her throat, but when he pulled her up off the couch, holding her by both wrists, the suddenness of the movement made it all come up – a watery red fluid bubbled out of her mouth and ran down her chin.

Still holding her wrists, he pulled her into the bedroom. "You will never disobey me again," he said, his grip tightening.

When had he taken off his jacket? After he'd pushed himself on top of her? Belinda couldn't figure out time anymore. There was no longer anything linear like the movement of seconds into minutes. It was all a jumble – fast one minute, nauseatingly slow the next.

Her bathrobe, where she had tossed it on the bed – she saw it, wanted it, wanted to be bundled in it and put back to bed, like after a bad dream. She wanted this to be a bad dream. But the sash around her wrists was too real, and his face wasn't a face from dreams. Philippe – her mind raced away from the syllables of his name.

"Shut up!" he said.

But she didn't know she was making noise. Maybe she was crying – salt in her throat – must be tears. She tried to stop making whatever sound she wasn't aware of, listened instead for something outside. Wind – she could hear wind scraping against the house. A storm was coming – by morning, the news had said. But the wind stopped when his hand hit her face again, landing below her eye. Or maybe the wind didn't stop; it was just that all her senses froze in that second. She couldn't see, hear, or feel.

Her mind came to the rescue, the way minds do when the terror is too much. It shut down – not completely – but enough that only some images were processed, some sounds heard, a portion of the pain felt – the rest to be held in trust. But the whole experience was finally catching up to her. It might bury her like an avalanche if she let it. It had been getting worse. The rape kept clawing at her, screaming in the deepest recesses of her psyche. She'd seen it following her, tracking her through the days. It was the shadow that always vanished when she turned to face it. She wanted to give it another name, but she couldn't.

Maybe, eventually, it would just become part of her story, her legacy, and – if luck held out – her wisdom. But that was in the future, if there was such a thing at all. For now, she had to return again and again to those few hours until every detail fell in place, until there was nothing else buried that could jump out and surprise her.

She was more frightened than she'd ever been in her life. It was like being caught in a freeze-frame of someone else's movie. Except she knew it was hers. Her mind broke up, splintered, and chronicled these things:

The sound of his zipper. Light bouncing off a crystal perfume bottle on her dresser. A siren somewhere in the distance. His weight coming down on her again as he crashed into her body – inside, where it's supposed to feel good, but suddenly she couldn't remember when it had ever not hurt. The pain was being forced deeper. Her stomach ached; it was heading for her heart. Hands pulled her hair, but it was only a vague sensation, she couldn't really feel it. She thought of her body being divided in two – you can hurt half of me, but this is where it stops.

And it worked. Her tears ended, her heart was safe, he could only rape half of her. Legs and half a torso, that's all he could have.

And the final image – the one that still lingered on the fringes of her mind, whether awake or sleeping: As he climbed off her, pulled up his pants, and undid the ties from her wrists, he paused for a second, looked down at her and smiled – an icy, cruel smile that drained the remainder of her strength, turned her muscles to water, and made it impossible for her to move from the bed even after he'd walked out the door and the sound of his car had faded away.

The rain was coming down so hard, no drops trickled along the glass; it was just a single sheet of water. Maybe it'll rain for forty days and nights, Belinda thought, but someone else can build the Ark – I'm too tired. She went into the kitchen, stepping gingerly around the wet spots on the carpet that were still faintly pink. She filled the teakettle with water. Some of Philippe's tapes were on the kitchen counter. She had been listening to his lectures so much there were probably tapes scattered all over the house, in every room.

She looked at them the way she imagined a widow would look at her dead husband's clothes – what to do with them? Charity? A garage sale? And there was a reluctance to touch them. Tapes with titles like "God's

Warriors" and "Building Up Your Spiritual Defenses." Only now did the military theme strike her as being somewhat nonspiritual in nature.

The teakettle was whistling; steam filled the kitchen. She turned the flame down slowly, listening to the tone change as the heat diminished. It was as if she'd been away from the world for a long time and had re-entered with a child's curiosity about the most banal things – the whistling kettle, the droplets of steam hanging in the air, the way the windows had fogged up.

And then there was the thing she didn't want to think about – the question of whether or not to file a police report. Whenever she did think of it, she saw the smile he had turned on her just before he walked out of her house – the one that had drained her of blood as surely as a vampire's bite. Somehow the question of reporting the rape was linked to that jagged smile. At least, when she thought of one thing, the image of the other followed.

Minutes must have passed; the teakettle was no longer whistling and the rain sounded different. She'd forgotten about drinking a cup of tea; another thought had moved in. She remembered Nicole handing her a business card. Sara had taken it and put it in Belinda's wallet. Wallet . . . dining-room table . . . where she usually tossed her keys. It was there, which was somewhat amazing, considering nothing was ever easy to find in her house. Belinda stared at the card for what seemed like a long time. Rape Treatment Center – was there really any way to "treat" a rape? Or did the word just make people feel better – like aspirin for a headache? Somewhere beneath the aspirin-mask, the headache still lurks. And somewhere, beneath everything, she would always be a rape victim. He'd raped more than her body – that was what enraged her the most.

He raped a dream that was in its infancy. She'd actually thought that maybe God wasn't angry at her after all, that she wasn't some hopeless sinner condemned to eternal damnation. She had started to believe that her father was wrong, that the world would be all right, life would be good, and she could stand up straight and claim her right to happiness. Wasn't that what Philippe had said?

She had been hitchhiking on a desolate back road and he had picked her up, pointed to the mountain top and said, "There – that's where I'll take you. Up there, where the sun is shining." He'd pulled her through the garden gate, but instead of opening into an enchanted kingdom, it was the gate to hell. Now she was standing in rubble, with that horrible smile of his reflecting off the clouds. It told her future, and it was worse than her past.

"Nicole!" Belinda said to the voice that answered the phone. Belinda's own voice sounded odd and unfamiliar to her; she couldn't remember when she last spoke.

"Yes, this is Nicole."

"This is Belinda – you were with me in the hospital when –"

"Yes, Belinda, how are you doing!" Something in Nicole's tone made Belinda feel better. She remembered her, sounded pleased to hear from her.

"I, uh – I want to file a police report."

Belinda was driving herself back to the hospital. Nicole said a police officer would come to the Treatment Center. She could have called Sara to take her and probably should have, but she needed to do this by herself. It was still raining – steady, hard rain with rivers churning along the sides of the road. The sound of the tires rolling through water was like a lullaby. On the seat beside her was her green velvet dress. "Bring the clothes you were wearing," Nicole told her. "For evidence." It was crumpled into a ball like the bad memory it had become. She knew she'd never wear it again.

"This is Detective Boyd," Nicole said when Belinda was shown into her office. Dark blue suit, the pale blue rug – her mind started splitting off in silly directions – color combinations, the detective's blue eyes set in a ruddy face, his red hair standing out against all the blue in the room. He looked as if he should be sitting in an Irish pub. She reined in her thoughts, tried to focus. This was it – this was the moment when everything was going to blow wide open. Philippe raped me, I'd just like the whole fucking world to know about it. She glanced at the door, considered leaving, but stayed.

Wordlessly, Belinda handed him the velvet dress.

"This is what you had on?" he said, not coldly, but matter-of-factly. It's his job, Belinda thought, a Jack Webb just-the-facts-ma'am job.

"For a while it's what I had on, until he took it off me."

Boyd uncrumpled the dress and studied it. Belinda noticed the rip along the side. She hadn't heard it tear. Maybe she was listening to the wind at that moment.

"What about underwear!" he asked.

"I wasn't wearing any."

He glanced up at her before writing something down. Not a good sign – she knew that. Bad girls go without underwear. She couldn't move her eyes from him; she was afraid, sure even, that standing in the corner behind Nicole's chair was her father's ghost, nodding and mumbling, "I told you so."

"You're going to have to try and tell us what happened as well as you can remember it," Nicole said, and the detective nodded, apparently grateful for the assistance.

Belinda heard herself reciting the events as if she were in an audience, listening to someone else. Boyd made her go through it twice, interrupting occasionally to ask questions. But the things she left out were, to her, the most glaring. It was those omissions that she'd dwell on long afterward. She didn't tell them about Philippe's confession, about his ill wife and his well-buried history. She kept his secret for him – an odd collusion, considering that he had raped her. But she did it without blinking.

"He was telling me how persecuted he is," she said, splitting the truth in two and choosing only half of it. "How people are constantly judging him. I felt sorry for him – that's why I put my hand on his. I wasn't . . . you know, coming on to him or anything." She thought she was telling the truth. At the moment, it was as close as she could come.

"When did he start hitting you!" Boyd asked.

"During . . . in the middle of everything, I guess." She thought of Philippe's eyes. They told her she deserved it, and there was a part of her that wondered if he was right. But she didn't say anything about that to Boyd.

And she didn't tell him about the slim moment, at the beginning, when her heart sped up at the prospect of him kissing her. But the most glaring thing to her was her own coldness – the dry, tearless monotone with which she recounted the story. That's what made her feel like it was someone else speaking. Maybe Philippe was right – concealed in semen are the seeds of a man's character. Take it into you and you've absorbed something essential about him. Was that what he'd done to her? Did he turn her, in some way, into his twin, give her the ice from his veins?

Belinda drove home through wet streets; the rain had backed off to a mist. The road ahead was shiny and she imagined that it was ice – that she'd hit an icy patch on the road commonly referred to as her life. And somewhere up ahead the road was dry, and wider, with gentler curves and fewer hazards. She might have been able to convince herself of that before. But not anymore. It wasn't that she couldn't look out, into the future. It was that, when she did, it all looked like one long winter, and all the roads had ice on them.

Sixteen

Sara

Sara was helping Mark get resettled in his apartment. The experiment of recuperating under parental care had lasted less than a week, proving the axiom "you can't go home again" has more than a few threads of wisdom in it.

What Sara really needed to do was sleep. She'd barely closed her eyes the night before at Belinda's, scrunched uncomfortably on the couch and fighting back the image of Philippe binding Belinda's wrists to the headboard, probably getting turned on by her fear. But as much as she needed sleep, she knew, if she tried to close her eyes, they'd pop open again.

Mark's apartment was on the second floor of an older, elegant building in Beverly Hills. It had peg-and-groove floors, high ceilings, and bay windows that overlooked a shady backyard. The stairs were difficult for him, given his present condition, but he managed, refusing to let Sara help him. He did, however, let her put away his things, make him some tea, and straighten up so he wouldn't be tripping over books and manila folders.

"I feel bad about leaving the house," he told Sara, hobbling around the living room on crutches, his leg still in the cast that Sara had decorated with quotes from Rimbaud and Dorothy Parker. "But I got tired of flushing food down the toilet. I know Mother was doing her best, but really, I needed some proper nourishment. Cream cheese and jelly sandwiches weren't cutting it, and I didn't even know Jell-O was still on the market. Which food group would Jell-O be in, do you think?"

"The mothers-on-a-budget group. Mark, will you sit down? I can straighten up better without you pacing – or limping as the case may be."

"I'm restless," Mark said. "I'm tired of sitting and I'm very tired of lying in bed."

"Maybe we could find you a really slow ten K race to enter. They probably have one for people on crutches. I mean, why not? This is L.A., right? Why let a broken leg interrupt your fitness routine?"

It was at that point, midway into Sara's ruminations on marathons for the temporarily disabled, that the television, which had been background noise until then, grabbed her attention. Philippe's image filled the screen. He was being pulled along by police, and reporters were mobbing him; in the midst of this chaos, he was looking straight ahead, making eye contact with no one. "A young woman, Belinda Perry, has filed formal charges accusing the New Age religious leader of rape," the newswoman was saying, fighting to be heard. Sara and Mark watched the broadcast without comment; both of them were too shocked to speak.

"Jesus," Sara said when they'd moved on to the weather report. "She must have done it after I left there this morning. She didn't even mention she was considering –" she didn't finish the sentence. She was suddenly hurt that Belinda hadn't told her, or called, or asked her to go along for moral support. She felt selfish and immature for thinking of herself right then, but there it was – that sinking feeling of having been left out.

"Mark, I have to go over to Belinda's." She got her purse and her coat.

"Will you be okay?"

"Sure. But do you want me to go with you?"

"I don't think so," Sara said. "I don't know what's going on with her. I'm afraid if I call, she'll tell me not to come, so I'm just going to go."

As she went down the stairs, her footsteps echoing in the narrow passageway, she wondered if she was excluding Mark the same way she thought Belinda had excluded her. But it was only a passing concern, crowded out by the image of Philippe and the media frenzy surrounding him. This is nothing, Sara thought, pulling into the evening traffic on Wilshire Boulevard – it's going to get much worse and Belinda will be at ground zero.

The scene outside Belinda's house was a portent of things to come. News vans lined one side of the street, reporters milled around on the sidewalk. Sara found a parking space three houses away, put on her raincoat even though it was no longer raining, and started walking back toward Belinda's. She recognized the owner of the property – a woman in her sixties who had rented her guest house to Belinda for the past five years – standing in front of a camera with a microphone in her face. ". . . such a thing happening just yards away . . . " was the only phrase Sara could pick up. Usually, this was a woman who padded around in hair curlers and a housecoat. Not tonight.

Break out the jewelry and the silk shirt, Sara thought, almost laughing at the absurdity of it – there's been a rape in the neighborhood and the press is here.

As Sara tried to move through the crowd, she was noticed by one reporter, and then it was a chain reaction. They started swarming around her. "Do you know Ms. Perry?" "Are you a friend?" "Can you just talk to us for a minute?" The questions were thrown out like fishing lines. As hard as she tried, she was not making any progress; they'd formed a human wall around her.

"Get the hell out of my way!" she shouted, which resulted in a narrow corridor opening up, enabling her to cross the property line and enter safe territory.

Belinda's door was locked. Sara knocked and said, "Belinda, open up. It's me."

"Come in," her voice said. It came from the direction of the couch.

"I can't – it's locked."

Belinda came to the door and Sara was both encouraged and worried by her appearance. On the surface, she looked better – more alert, less pale, but there was something in her eyes that seemed strange, almost indifferent. She was wearing the faded denim overalls she used for gardening and a long-sleeved cotton shirt; her feet were bare and her hair needed washing.

"I forgot I locked it," she said.

Sara followed Belinda into the house, relocking the door behind them. Belinda sat down on the couch, stared at the floor, and picked at a frayed seam on her overalls.

"How did they find out where I live?" she asked.

"Honey, these people solved Watergate. Finding out someone's address is hardly a challenge."

"Is he in jail?"

"Yes – but I would imagine he'll be out on bail by tomorrow if not before," Sara said, sitting down beside Belinda and sliding a dog-eared *Vogue* magazine out of the way.

"I'm sorry I didn't tell you I was going to report it," Belinda said, addressing the question Sara hadn't asked. "I decided sometime this morning, and then I just did it – kind of abruptly, I guess."

"It's okay. I'm glad you exposed him. But I worry about how all this is going to affect you. It's just the beginning, you know."

"Yeah . . . I know. I didn't watch the news. I was afraid to see his face." Belinda looked so young in her Tom Sawyer overalls.

"I don't blame you," Sara said.

Belinda turned sideways on the couch and stretched out her legs so her feet rested in Sara's lap. The intimacy, the familiarity of it made Sara's throat tighten and her eyes sting with tears she hadn't expected. She'd thought, after that one night, that one brief interlude of their bodies coiled together, that Belinda was now frightened of her – of them – of what almost happened and might again. But maybe the rape had blown through her life like a hurricane, leveling the memory of every event that had once seemed important. Sara massaged Belinda's feet, pressing her fingers into the arches and watching Belinda's face relax as she kneaded out the tension. The landscape of her life had changed overnight; there are no how to books on the kind of rebuilding she was going to have to do.

They stayed like that for a while, Belinda stretched out, eyes half closed, her feet in Sara's lap. Sara felt her own eyes closing. Too much had happened in the past forty-eight hours. She needed sleep badly.

"Belinda, I better go. And you should try to get some sleep too." She lifted Belinda's feet off her lap.

"Okay, I'll try. I get scared of what I might dream. But I'll try."

Only two reporters were left outside on the street when Sara started walking to her car. Die-hards, probably tabloid reporters – they always seem to keep long hours. She glanced at them – a you-really-don't-want-to-fuck-with-me look. And they got the message.

As she was walking down the street, the sound of a car coming up behind made her move to the side of the road and wait for it to pass. Its headlights captured her, flamed in her eyes and only as it was passing did she notice that it was a black BMW. Philippe's car – it couldn't be, though. He was in jail. Even with his connections and his money, she doubted he could get out this quickly. But a black BMW, moving slowly down Belinda's street, on this particular night? Coincidence couldn't be ruled out, Sara cautioned herself, although coincidence was not a concept she had much faith in. She squinted, trying to see who was inside, and she thought, as the taillights faded into tiny red dots, that she saw a woman behind the wheel.

Suddenly cold, Sara unlocked her car, started the ignition, and turned the heater on full blast, shivering as she waited for it to warm up. She felt queasy and scared; she had no confidence in the future, no sense that things were going to get better. Maybe eventually, but first they were going to get worse. Belinda would have to testify against Philippe, and no one was going to put a blue dot in front of her face when they showed her on television. Her cover was already blown. And Sara knew that there would be hordes of people who would treat

Belinda like the criminal – the madwoman bent on crucifying their savior. Images of the Salem witch trials came to her – who ever said it couldn't happen again? Every century has its own version.

One thing was certain: Belinda and Philippe were linked now and probably always would be. Their names would be spoken in the same sentence by people who knew neither of them; even years down the line – by law students studying rape cases, perhaps, or by news junkies researching famous people embroiled in scandals. The rape would always be like a wedding ring on Belinda's finger. Philippe had put it there, and made her a citizen of a land where no divorce was possible.

Sara was fighting to stay awake on the drive home. Once inside her house, she frantically turned on lights, like a child afraid of the dark. Her phone machine said that four messages had been recorded, but when she hit the play button, the first two were hang-ups. Then her agent's voice exploded out of the machine.

"Sara, it's Miriam. What the hell is going on with you? I left a message for you last week. You never called back so I figured maybe you were still globe-trotting with the Lothario of the Directors Guild. I actually had a job for you. Remember? Work? Then I turn on the news tonight and there you are yelling at reporters outside your friend's house, doing everything but giving them the finger. If you want to become famous, maybe you should give some attention to your career instead of biting the heads off people who are probably in a lower tax bracket than you. You want to call me back, please? I'm at home – you have the number."

Sara slumped down in a chair. She'd forgotten about calling Miriam back – it seemed like months ago now. And she definitely needed work. Then Anthony's voice materialized in the room. He apparently had not seen the news.

"Sara, where are you? I called twice earlier – I thought you'd be there. I should be home all night if you want to call me."

She looked in the refrigerator for something to eat, finding nothing but some wilted carrots and apple juice with yesterday's date on it. Okay, she thought, I have to be responsible here. I'm not going to have an agent anymore if I don't get back to work soon.

Miriam answered on the third ring.

"Hi, it's Sara."

"Sara who?"

"I'm sorry, really. I've just been . . . well, a lot has been happening, and things have been very unpredictable. I do remember getting your message, I meant to call back, and —"

"Okay, okay," Miriam interrupted. "I feel you're going to tell me your dog ate your homework in a minute. So, you want to work or what? There's a movie of the week shooting in L.A. soon – probably be a four- or five-week shoot, and they haven't settled on a costume designer yet. I'm not going to pitch you, though, if you're going to bail out on me. I have my own reputation to think of."

"No, I won't bail – I promise. I do need to go back to work." Sara could hear rap music playing in the background. "Miriam, are you changing your musical tastes? I always thought of you as an Elton John sort of person."

"Funny, Sara. It's my son. He's working on blowing out his eardrums and driving me insane, all at the same time. I'll let you know tomorrow what I find out about the movie. It's not too big a cast, and one of the stars is an orangutan."

"Wait a minute, wait a minute – I have to dress an orangutan?"

"God, I don't think so. Well, if you do I'm sure you'll figure out how to do it."

"Uh-huh," Sara said. "Very carefully, right?"

After hanging up, she sat holding the phone in her lap, wondering whether she really wanted to call Anthony. It was always like this – pulling his face back into her mind; it disappeared so easily sometimes. Out of sight, out of mind – which must mean that she didn't really love him. Because doesn't love mean that person is always with you, even if not physically? Don't people in love hold on to each other's presence, undeterred by distance or by whatever circumstances come along and muscle their way in? Or maybe that was just what she imagined and the reality of love wasn't like that at all.

The phone rang, snapping her out of her thoughts.

"Hi, you're home," Anthony said.

"Uh-huh. I just got in and got your message. I was going to call."

"Where've you been?" he asked. There seemed to be something studied about his voice. This was not a casual question, but Sara was too exhausted to analyze it.

"With my brother for a while and then . . . you didn't watch the news tonight, I guess."

There was a pause before Anthony said, "Why? I'd know where you were if I'd watched the news?"

"Well, actually – yes. My friend Belinda was raped – by Philippe – you know who I'm talking about?"

"That New Age guy," Anthony said.

"She filed charges and all hell broke loose. I went over to her house and had to fight my way through reporters who were camped out there."

"So did you leave any of them alive?"

"Unfortunately, yes," Sara said. "Repentant, but alive."

"Do you want me to come over?" he asked. It definitely was not a casual question.

"No. I want to go to sleep – alone." She could have explained more, asked him to understand, but her eyes ached, she didn't want to talk anymore, and she couldn't decipher her feelings.

Philippe got out on bail the next day and held a press conference outside the jail – or what began as a press conference. It turned into some kind of religious event, with dozens of his followers chanting and crying and hugging each other, and of course the cameras captured all of it. That night, as Sara watched it, she thought that if there had been water nearby, his disciples would probably have started baptizing each other. The strangest moment was when Philippe told his flock to be silent and pray for Belinda, who had gone far astray and was in need of heavenly assistance.

"Give me a fucking break," Sara said to the television, and then went into the kitchen and opened a bottle of wine, half tempted to drink the whole thing, but she'd only had one hangover in her life and she wanted to keep it that way. She tried calling Belinda, let the phone ring about a dozen times, and then hung up. Sara was sure she'd unplugged the phone and the sadness of it all hit her – each in her separate house, one drinking alone and the other too afraid to answer the phone.

The phone calls started a few days later – late at night, when Sara was inevitably in the middle of some disjointed dream. It was a woman's voice – one that sounded oddly familiar, in some vague way that Sara couldn't identify.

"Tell your friend she's in league with the devil" went the first call, at two forty-five in the morning. The message was delivered in a crisp, efficient manner, and then the caller hung up.

Over the next week, there were two more calls, also in the middle of the night, with the same anonymous voice cutting through the still, predawn hour.

"Your friend is crucifying Christ," the voice said on the second call.

The third message was the angriest. "She's the one who'll be made to suffer for her lies and her blasphemy."

"Why don't you turn off your phone at night, and your machine?" Mark asked when she told him about the calls. She hadn't dared mention them to Belinda.

"I'm afraid to. What if there's an emergency? What if Belinda tried to call? What if you fell down and rebroke your leg? I know you're probably doing wind-sprints in your living room."

"Well, I don't know what else to tell you," Mark said. "You could get a loud whistle and try to deafen whoever is on the other end."

That Saturday, after several nights of interrupted sleep, Sara managed to drag Belinda out of her house to go shopping. It was a business shopping excursion for Sara; she'd been hired for the television movie Miriam had told her about. The story was not a very original one, but was mildly entertaining, Sara thought. Two animal trainers who managed to turn their orangutan into something akin to a Rhodes scholar (at least by animal standards) get involved with a devious young woman – a circus groupie of sorts, who flirts with one and seduces the other. The story was an Amy Fisher meets Siegfried and Roy kind of thing, with a few added twists.

Fortunately, Sara was not required to dress the orangutan. He was appearing *au naturel*, although she had been asked to supply some extra boxes of Huggies – the only thing he ever wore, but only off-camera. Apparently, orangutans don't take well to toilet training.

It was a pretty easy job, actually. The clothes she needed were just the average, off-the-rack-at-the-mall kind – as good an excuse as any to head for the Beverly Center. She and Belinda were on the escalator when Belinda's eyes widened and she looked like she was about to jump over the railing.

"What? What is it?" Sara asked, looking around.

"Just behind us – Astrid and Michelle."

Sara turned and saw them, several steps above, looking down on them – perfect hair and lacquered faces. They were more dressed up than they had been the night they came to Belinda's house. Astrid was wearing a straight black skirt, a dark gray cashmere sweater, and black Manolo Blahnik shoes. Michelle wasn't quite as impressive, but she was doing okay – maroon slacks and a matching turtleneck.

Belinda put her sunglasses on as they got off the elevator; there was still a bruise under her eye, although she'd concealed it with makeup.

"Let's walk fast," Sara whispered, although it was unnecessary. Belinda was acting like a horse out of the starting gate. But they weren't fast enough.

"How are you, Belinda?" came a voice from behind them.

Sara was the first to stop – not out of politeness, but because she knew, in that instant, who had been calling her late at night. Astrid was smiling, her lips flawlessly lined and lipsticked, her expression a study in neutrality. It had probably taken years for her face to mold itself into such an impenetrable mask.

"Hi," Belinda said warily.

"We've certainly been hearing a lot about you lately."

It was her – Sara was sure of it. She hadn't even bothered to disguise her voice on the phone.

"I guess you won't be coming to the lectures anymore," Michelle said, glancing quickly at Astrid.

"You know what?" Sara cut in. "We're in a hurry. Nice to see you again. Great shoes, Astrid. Have a nice day." And with that, she took hold of Belinda's arm, wheeled her around, and left Astrid and Michelle standing there with shoppers brushing past them.

"Belinda, I have to tell you something," Sara said, when they were at a safe distance. She pulled her into a shoe store. "I've been getting anonymous phone calls late at night – about you. You know, things like why doesn't she back off. Now I know who's making them."

"Which one? Astrid or Michelle?" Belinda's reaction was calm – too calm, Sara thought.

"Astrid. Ms. Manolo Blahnik shoes."

The cut on Belinda's lip was still faintly visible beneath her lipstick. She chewed on it and took off her sunglasses. "When I get calls," she said "they just say 'bitch' or

'Judas' and then hang up. It's a man's voice, though. I don't recognize it."

"Why didn't you tell me?" Sara said.

"You didn't tell me, either – about the calls you were getting. Until now, I mean."

So there it was – further evidence of the barriers between them – small silences and occasional secrets.

"Has anything else happened that you haven't told me about?" Sara asked.

Belinda rummaged around in her purse and pulled out a folded piece of paper. She handed it to Sara without meeting her eyes. Sara unfolded it and found herself looking at a print of Christ on the Cross. But the picture had been altered. The body was of Jesus, hands and feet impaled, blood seeping from the gash along his rib cage. But the head was Philippe's. She stared hard and held the paper up to the light. Someone must have taken a picture from an art book or magazine, cut out Jesus' head, substituted a photograph of Philippe, and Xeroxed the finished product.

Sara looked around at the people passing by them, suddenly afraid that Astrid and Michelle were nearby. Nothing seemed coincidental anymore; she felt watched, followed, transformed into a George Orwell character, running away from eyes that watched her through walls, from Big Brother who could be waiting around any corner.

"Why are you carrying this with you?" she asked Belinda, still holding the picture in both hands.

"I don't know. Do you think I'm doing the right thing, Sara? Going ahead with this, I mean? The trial and everything – I just don't know sometimes." It would be the only time she'd ever ask this.

Sara gripped Belinda's arm. "Yes, absolutely. Are you really having doubts?"

"I have doubts about everything," Belinda answered in a soft voice. "Come on – let's spend the producer's money. That's what we're here for, right?"

Life changes us, Sara thought later, driving home after dropping Belinda off. That's its function, that's what it's supposed to do. We start out blank and accumulate rings, like those inside the trunks of trees. We grow taller, heavier, with odd bends and gnarled, defiant spots where the outer layers have been damaged and have grown back.

Sara had once had a literature teacher in college who, in the middle of the semester, lost her husband in a night-time burglary of their home. He hadn't anticipated a bullet whistling through the dark, splattering his life all over the living room where, just a month earlier, they had hosted a Christmas party for students of nineteenth-century lit. When her teacher finally returned to the classroom after a couple of weeks, Sara went up to her tentatively and offered her condolences. The woman said, "Life comes at you like a runaway train sometimes. It's as if you're blinded by the lights and you have only an instant to make a choice – jump out of the way or get run down. An instant just isn't enough."

But what about the times when there is no choice? Sara wondered. Maybe by the time Philippe was sitting in Belinda's house, her choices were a thing of the past. But if Belinda didn't see it that way, she would always wonder, always be tempted to punish herself. Gates were closing inside her – Sara could see that; too often now, talking to her felt like yelling across distance. And Sara understood that kind of retreat well enough to be frightened by it.

Seventeen

Sara

THERE WAS a chain of storms off the California coast, so Los Angeles settled into a pattern of a few sunny days followed by a few rainy ones. After monitoring the weather predictions, the producers had altered the shooting schedule of their made-for-TV movie – now retitled *Love Perils*. (Sara was much more fond of the original title: *Primal Love*.) Outdoor location shots were grouped, following one after the other, while indoor setups were held for rainy days. The cause of all this bad weather, supposedly, was the quixotic El Niño, which caused the oceans to be warmer and rain clouds to hover insistently along the coast. An earth out of balance, Sara thought. How appropriate.

Some of the shooting took place on one of the Santa Monica beaches. In one scene the girl and the married animal trainer were supposed to stroll along the shore and discuss what to do with his wife, who probably should have died, but who, of course, didn't. Walking along with them was the orangutan, which struck Sara as completely absurd, because if dogs aren't allowed on the beaches how could anyone get away with walking an orangutan along the sand? Logically, you'd think someone would notice and say something. They even had extras sitting on the beach eating potato chips and talking, and the director never said, "Okay people, there's a large primate walking along the shore. I want to see some reactions here." So of course, everyone acted like it was nothing out of the ordinary – just another day in L.A.

The real animal trainer was a man named Randy – a blond, California surfer type in his early thirties, with the kind of tan that infuriates New Yorkers, and a gentle, nurturing way of working with the orangutan which had all the women on the set weak-kneed. If he was that gentle with a two-hundred-pound orangutan, they reasoned, just think how he'd be with a woman.

The first time Sara met Randy, he was brushing the orangutan's red hair – long, soft strokes with a hairbrush along the animal's head and arms. He stopped, offered his free hand and said, "Hi, I'm Randy. This is my friend, partner, child, and chief breadwinner – Hannibal. Hannibal, shake the lady's hand." And a large, black-fingered hand took Sara's hand gently – like a shy prince, she thought.

"I'm Sara. I'm the costume designer. Hannibal, huh? As in Lecter?"

"No, as in the Carthaginian general. Fought against Rome? The Second Punic War? You know."

"Yeah, right. Of course," Sara said, hoping she sounded convincing. "Were you a history major or something?"

"No – anthropology. History was my minor."

Okay, Sara thought, he's cute, he's smart, he's obviously educated. But he doesn't make me turn cartwheels the way he does every other woman on this set.

Her mind was on too many other things, she decided.

Anthony was redefining her, remapping her – changing boundaries and throwing out the old government. She felt like Russia, with an uncertain identity, teetering on the edge of chaos, a stranger to her own history. Anthony was taking away her history – erasing it, she thought – and writing new chapters in her life.

A few times when she had come home late and tired from the set, he'd brought food over to her house, a bottle of wine, had insisted on running a bath for her. He'd kneel by the tub and wash her, giving her sips of wine, sometimes tipping the glass too much so the wine ran down her chin into the bath water. He wouldn't let her use her hands to wipe it off; he licked it off her face.

One night, after his hands had washed her, massaged her under the water, after his fingers had slipped inside her for only a moment – just long enough to make her cry out when he withdrew them – he left and came back with a scarf. He blindfolded her, plunged his hands into the water again, between her legs. Warm water seeped inside her, along with his fingers. Her body started sliding down; she felt water just below her ears but she didn't care. His other arm reached around and held her under her breasts, keeping her from drowning so he could keep driving her mad. One hand pinched her nipples while, under the water, the other hand made her scream out. The sound echoed around her, bounced off the tiles. He left his fingers inside her while her breathing evened out and then he whispered, "Stand up – I'll help you. I don't want you to see yet."

Still blindfolded, she felt the towel being wrapped around her, rubbed over her skin, gently in some places, rougher in others. Her hair had been pinned up. He undid it and she could hear him picking the hairbrush up off the sink. He started at her hairline – long strokes over her head and down her back – but he didn't stop at the ends of her hair. The bristles scraped over the small of her back, her buttocks, not hard enough to scratch the skin, but hard enough to make her shiver. And to wonder. It was the teasing side of pain, but he could go further; even though he hadn't, she knew he could. She reached back, dug her fingernails into his side, through his shirt. She could go further, too.

He slept with her that night, and sometime past midnight she woke up curled against his back, her mouth touching his spine. She wasn't completely awake – was still drifting – so it was as if she heard her own voice from a distance. She said it softly, her lips parted over one of his vertebrae. She said it like a breath – more air than voice. She said, "I love you," and felt something stir in his body when she did.

"I love you," he said, in just as small a voice.

She wasn't even sure he was awake, wasn't really sure she was. And in the morning, she wasn't sure either of them had meant it. Neither one said anything about it – probably never would, she guessed.

Sometimes, sitting on the set, when she was supposed to be concentrating on the actors' wardrobes, she thought about that one tiny moment, wedged between sleep and waking. Maybe the truth is told in moments like that, or maybe it only seems like the truth. There were too many other times when her feelings for Anthony didn't seem like love at all.

She was distracted by her concern over Belinda as well. The preliminary hearing was in a couple of weeks; there would almost certainly be a trial, and Sara wasn't sure how resilient Belinda would be.

On the set, Sara was friendly to Randy, even though she was probably the only woman not interested in seducing him. As these things usually go, that made her the one he was interested in. Her fascination was really with Hannibal – in an anthropological, psychoanalytical sort of way. Randy had a wheelchair for Hannibal to sit in when he wasn't shooting a scene and he'd push him around in it, letting the animal visit with different people. He explained to Sara that walking upright wasn't natural for Hannibal, and the wheelchair was a way to let him conserve his energy and still be sociable. More and more, Sara found herself mesmerized by Hannibal. His hands were always gentle and curious when they touched her face or her arm, and his eyes appeared to hold centuries of wisdom. She did consider that Randy might misinterpret her interest in the orangutan as a budding attraction for him, but that concern wasn't enough to tear her away from this animal whom she was starting to like more than most people.

The mood on the set had become juvenile and high-schoolish, largely because of Hannibal's presence. There were typewritten notices posted in the makeup trailer, the wardrobe trailer, and by the coffee stand, warning any women who were having their periods to stay away from Hannibal. Everyone on the set began to regress to ninth-grade behavior. Each day there were at least one or two women who would giggle and run away whenever Randy and Hannibal approached. They'd wave from a safe distance and say things like, "I'll come talk to you in a few days." The crew would snicker and blush and whisper things to each other. Sara thought it was ridiculous, although she wasn't having her period yet, so she could afford to think whatever she wanted. She was sure, though, that when the time came she would act with more maturity.

"What exactly would happen if a woman in her period came near Hannibal?" she asked Randy one day, as two of the female extras hurried past them.

"He'd get excited, he'd want her – badly, probably – and then I could conceivably get hurt trying to get him under control. He'd suddenly look at me as a male rival."

"What does he look at you as now?"

"His authority figure," Randy said. "And the person with an unlimited supply of bananas."

"So bananas are his favorite?" Sara had always wondered if that was just a cliché, if there were certain members of the ape family who wouldn't be caught dead eating a banana.

"He likes them a lot. But he likes Milk Duds better."

On this day, the director was cranky because the sky was overcast. He couldn't tell if it was fog or actual rain clouds, and he never trusted the weather reports. He was trying to move quickly and was impatient with everyone. "Time is money!" he kept saying – as if anyone doubted that.

It was not a good day for anyone to have visitors on the set, and Sara was regretting that she had told Anthony where they were shooting. He'd said he might come by, but now she was trying to will him away. She knew if she called him and told him to stay away, it would guarantee that he'd show up, so she was putting her faith in the energy of willpower.

But faith and willpower were not Sara's strong suits. As the crew was setting up a shot and Sara was sitting beside Hannibal in his wheelchair, holding his hand, she noticed out of the corner of her eye a dark blue Mercedes pull into the parking lot. "Shit," she said under her breath. Hannibal glanced at her as if he knew the implications of the word, and Randy stopped brushing the orangutan's hair and said, "What? What's wrong?"

"Oh, nothing. My boyfriend just drove into the parking lot."

"That's bad?" Randy asked.

"Well, it's just not the best day for him to come." Have a positive outlook, Sara told herself. It's not like Anthony doesn't understand tension on a set.

What happened next seemed to happen in split-second timing, but time is often not what it seems. Anthony's shape grew larger as he walked toward them across the sand, throwing no shadow behind him because of the dull, muted day. Sara had turned in her chair and was watching him, which prompted Hannibal to imitate her; he adjusted his large body and looked in the same direction. Other than menstruating women, Hannibal had another quirk – there were certain men he didn't like. It was an instantaneous, primal sort of thing, one that had to be respected, because he certainly wasn't going to be talked out of it. There were two crew members who had to avoid him completely. Hannibal had actually bared his teeth at one, and had thrown a cup of milk at another. No one understood why; he just seemed to be an orangutan with strong opinions.

Anthony was about ten yards away from them when Sara felt something rumble through her fingers – those that were entwined with Hannibal's. She looked at the orangutan, saw his lips curled back and his eyes locked in rage. Randy was standing up with his back to them because the prop girl had come over to ask a question, but to Sara it seemed like he was a mile away.

"Uh, Randy," she said, not as loudly as she wanted to.

Just as Randy turned around, Sara noticed that one of the women who had frantically run away from Hannibal earlier was walking over to Anthony, either because she knew him or because she recognized him – at that point it didn't matter. Hannibal was up out of his wheelchair, moving on all fours, right toward Anthony; he was back in the jungle, there was a threatening male in his territory, the scent of a possible mate, and he was going to have none of this walking-on-two-legs shit. Sara couldn't believe how fast he was moving.

Anthony stopped dead, the girl who had intercepted Anthony screamed and took off toward the parking lot, and Randy took off after Hannibal, pulling a whistle out of his pocket that Sara had never seen him use before. About two feet from Hannibal, he blew it and the high, piercing noise made the orangutan stop and put a hand up to cover his ear – a small, childlike gesture that didn't fit with the angry, aggressive jungle animal he'd been just seconds before. Anthony was frozen in place. It was only then, in that limbo moment between total chaos and restored calm, that Sara noticed Anthony staring directly into Hannibal's eyes, and she wondered if he had been doing that the whole time. Hadn't she read somewhere that direct eye contact with a wild animal was potentially dangerous?

Randy led Hannibal away – back to the van, Sara assumed, where there was a mattress and bedding for Hannibal's frequent naps.

As Anthony came up to Sara he said, "I guess that was pretty close, huh?" And he had a look in his eyes that she had seen before. It was the rush of having slithered along danger's edge and having lived to tell about it.

"This wasn't a good day to visit," she said. "I guess I should have called you."

"Yeah, it does seem to be a bad day for gorillas." Anthony leaned down and kissed her on the forehead.

"Orangutan. Hannibal is an orangutan."

"Oh, and I see you're on a first-name basis."

"The reason I didn't call you," Sara said, giving in to her irritation, "is that you would have come anyway. In fact, that would have ensured that you'd come."

"What are you angry at me for?" Anthony asked calmly. "It's not like I asked the orangutan to attack me."

"I'm angry because you seem to bring drama with you wherever you go. Is anything ever calm around you, or do you just have this magical ability to stir things up and leave everything in chaos?"

"Everything? As in what, Sara? What do I leave in chaos?" She hated it when he sounded this calm.

"My life, for starters."

Just then, Randy came back with the director, who was now in a worse mood than before. Their conversation had apparently been going on for several minutes, but broke off when Anthony extended his hand to Randy and said, "Thanks, man. You probably saved my life." Without missing a beat, he then offered his hand to the director. "Anthony Cole – nice to meet you."

"I know who you are," the director said, flustered enough to momentarily forget some of his anger.

"I'll be out of here in just a minute," Anthony told him. "I certainly didn't mean to disrupt things. I know how that can be."

The guy should run for office, Sara thought.

"Well, it's always unpredictable working with animals," the director said and then looked behind him for someone to yell at, suddenly remembering that time was money and he was supposed to be pissed off because, after all, a few bucks had just been spent while nothing happened. "Come on, let's get going!" he shouted. "What am I doing here, a remake of *King Kong*? Someone go up to the parking lot and find Fay Wray, if she hasn't stolen a car and driven home already!"

When the director walked away, Anthony turned to Randy again. "Listen, I really owe you. Why don't you have dinner with me and Sara tonight?"

Sara tried to conceal her astonishment; she didn't even know *she* was having dinner with him.

"Well, I have to take Hannibal home first – out to the valley, but I can meet you. Just tell me where." Randy sounded tentative, and Sara didn't blame him.

"Great. Sara, why don't you make a reservation at that Italian restaurant we went to last week – the one in Santa Monica?"

"Why – is your car phone broken?" she asked icily. She was even more irritated now. There was something in the way this was evolving that hinted of hidden motives. And along with that, Anthony's tone seemed patronizing, which never failed to set her off.

"Fine – I'll be happy to call," Anthony said, still in that patronizing mode. "See you tonight, Randy. Sara can give you directions. Let's say eight-thirty, okay? I'll pick you up at home, Sara."

He had heated himself in one of the chairs, and leapt up with the abruptness of someone who'd just remembered an important appointment. "Later," he said, tossing the word over his shoulder. Sara watched as he left a trail of footprints in the deep white sand. He could have been anyone right then – just a man on the beach leaving footprints like everyone else. But he wasn't like everyone else; he was the one who kept crashing into her thoughts, making her doubt her own perceptions, the one whose whispers guided her into deep tunnels that only felt like home when she was bound and blindfolded and made his prisoner

Maybe it was the lighting in the restaurant – subdued and dreamy – or the wine after not eating much all day, but Sara felt she was floating. She watched Anthony and Randy conversing with the cautious enthusiasm of people who don't know each other but feel as though they do, and she drifted in and out of the conversation, more involved with studying the movement of their hands, the flash of white teeth as one or the other smiled into the candlelight. She looked around the restaurant; she was definitly sitting with the two most attractive men in the place and that realization tugged at the corners of her mouth and gave her what she knew must be a mysterious, secretive smile.

They had cappuccino and chocolate cake; the tastes mingled together delicately in Sara's mouth, prompting her to say a silent thank-you to God for having been brilliant enough to install tastebuds in people's mouths.

"This has been a great evening," Anthony said. "I don't want it to end yet. Sara, your house is close – maybe we should all go back there for a while."

Sara glanced at her watch – past ten. But it was Friday; they didn't have to work the next day. "Sure, I guess so," she said. She tried to read Anthony's motives, knowing him well enough to suspect something. There were always layers to everything he did. The more she peeled them away, the more intricate things became. But the wine had made it impossible for her to figure out anything as puzzling as Anthony's mind tonight.

When they arrived at Sara's house, Anthony immediately turned on the heater, switched off the bright lamp she'd left on and turned on a softer one. He was moving around the house as though he lived there.

"I still can't get over how you saved my life today," he said to Randy, sitting on the couch and motioning for Randy to sit in the armchair across from him. "You know what the theory is, don't you? That's a bond for life."

"I don't know if it was quite like that," Randy answered. "You might be exaggerating the seriousness a little. Hannibal's pretty well trained, and he's very smart. He might have just been trying to scare you."

"Yeah, well – he did that, all right. Come here, Sara."

When she started to sit beside him on the couch, Anthony grabbed her waist and pulled her into his lap. He buried his face in her neck and his hands massaged the small of her back, working their way up to her shoulder blades. Her eyes met Randy's and something about the way he held her gaze made her wonder if something had been decided over dinner while she was lost in her own thoughts.

"So, what do you think, Sara?" Anthony asked, his voice muffled by her hair.

"About what?"

"Oh, come on. What do you think the three of us are doing here?"

She kept looking at Randy and still he hadn't averted his eyes. Then she felt it coming over her – the conquest. Anthony's conquest. The same feeling she got when she looked at a woman she knew Anthony would be attracted to. Continents shifted inside her; Sara was moved out of the way and Anthony was in control of her perceptions.

So now, with the house, and the light, and even the heater adjusted to Anthony's liking, she saw the night through his eyes. There was no place where his vision ended and hers began. There was just one long, continuous view, taking them both toward whatever he wanted.

"Okay," she said, already knowing.

He lifted her off his lap, stood up and took her by the hand. Pink lamplight spilled into the hallway from the bedroom (Anthony had made her change the light bulb weeks earlier) and Randy's footsteps echoed theirs with a certainty that should have surprised Sara but didn't.

She'd dressed for Anthony that night – black lace garter belt with no underpants and sheer black stockings. He'd discovered it earlier, between the salad and the entrée when he put his hand under the table and rested it on her knee. She'd slid his hand up, over the top of her stocking, over the bare skin of her upper thigh, and then she'd parted her legs just enough. Randy was talking about retiring Hannibal sometime next year, letting him breed . . . and she leaned forward in her chair so Anthony's finger slid in even deeper.

Randy had seemed so much more innocent then – just a few hours earlier – unaware of how the night would end. But now he looked different to her, peeling off his shirt, sitting on the end of her bed to take off his shoes. His eyes looked different now, too – more like Anthony's, something lurking behind them, something that made her look twice, wonder about it, consider checking his ID.

She turned back to Anthony and began unsnapping one of her garters. "No," he said, grabbing her wrist. "Leave them on." He had undressed her up to that point, leaving her in stockings and garter belt, and she was forbidden to take up where he left off. He stood in front of her and she unbuttoned his shirt – a system of silent commands that she no longer questioned. But she was caught by Randy's reflection in the mirror – naked now, stretched out on her bed, watching them.

"Do you like Randy's body?" Anthony asked, following the trail of her thoughts with bloodhound accuracy.

"Uh-huh."

"Get on top of him."

The buttons of Anthony's shirt felt cold against her back as he pushed her toward the bed. She looked in the mirror again when she had climbed on top of Randy – one body, naked in the soft pink light, held down by a woman who had shopped at Victoria's Secret and was wearing her purchases, and one man fully dressed, guiding their actions.

"Fuck him, Sara," came Anthony's voice from behind her, winging over her shoulder and into her ear.

She looked down at Randy and there was an instant of confusion; she thought she was looking down at Anthony, right into his eyes. But it couldn't be. These eyes were blue – Randy's eyes. Maybe Anthony was playing behind them the way he played behind hers; maybe he conquered everyone he came in contact with. Randy gasped a little when she took him inside her; she closed her eyes and contracted her muscles around his cock, making him gasp again. She concentrated on the movement of their bodies –

a dance with two rhythms, melting into one – and the feeling of floating returned. She was buoyant, weightless, the lamplight like syrup around her, and time was falling away in pieces. Hands on her hips, but not just Randy's. Four hands held her and she opened her eyes, saw Anthony in the mirror, naked now too, straddling Randy's legs behind her, his cock hard against her buttocks. His hands slid up from her hips to her breasts, and Randy moaned beneath them, said, "Wait," in a whisper that almost got lost.

In a movement so sudden it shattered the air around them, Anthony pulled her up; the mattress moved a little as her weight on it lessened. "Get off and lie on your stomach," he said.

She obeyed, but left one hand on Randy's arm, feeling her breath still tethered to his – a thread not yet broken. Anthony pushed her thighs apart with his knees, pulled her body back so she was half-kneeling, and when he plunged into her, he was rougher than Randy had been. Sounds came out of her throat – low, guttural, fuck-me sounds. She was face down in the pillow, still feeling weightless, when Randy moved beside her. She wasn't sure what he was doing and she didn't want to look at him – she wasn't sure why – but in a moment he'd moved up to the top of the bed. She felt his thighs framing her head and his hands under her chin, gently lifting it until his cock was at her mouth; willingly, she took it.

She was divided in two – an earth separated by an equator, with Anthony setting fire to one region and Randy presiding softly over the other, stroking her head, gently moaning when she circled him with her tongue.

When Anthony came, it was in angry, violent thrusts –

anger because she hadn't come yet despite his commands. He liked to watch her, liked to pull back and study her face while she was in the throes of orgasm. It was one of the only predictable things in their lovemaking. This time, though, she'd ignored him when he'd whispered, "Come for me, Sara," her attention shifting back and forth across her body's geography, from one climate to another.

Startling her again, Anthony grabbed a handful of her hair and pulled her head back sharply, forcing her mouth to abandon Randy. "Come on, Randy," Anthony said. "You fuck her. Make her come. She looks beautiful when she comes, don't you, Sara?"

"I don't know – do I?" she answered, rolling over and lying on her back.

Randy was on top of her, inside her, eyes locked on hers, asking questions she tried to answer. "Don't worry, it's just a game. A control game," she tried to make her own eyes say. But sometimes she wasn't sure how much of a game it was; sometimes it felt too serious. When her body trembled and her throat arched, she wasn't sure whose orgasm it was. Maybe that belonged to Anthony now, too. Maybe she came for Anthony, lying beside her and Randy – watching them, pulling the strings. She wondered what would have happened if she'd been alone with Randy; she'd never know. That was part of the game, too – all the unknowns she and Anthony had stockpiled. Bargaining chips. But when the stakes grew higher, a weapons stockpile that neither of them took lightly.

The three of them lay in a confused tangle, still breathing harder than normal, six legs, six arms wound together with no self-consciousness about who was touching who.

Sara's left leg was on top of the pile; she could see a run in her black stocking, starting at the knee and traveling down toward her toes. Anthony and Randy both had their eyes closed, and Sara knew if she closed hers, she'd drift toward sleep. Not a bad idea, actually – it must be late. She let herself float again, this time in the darkness behind her eyelids.

It might have been the first fragment of a dream – the sound of her front door opening and closing. But she wasn't really sleeping yet. And it might have been the sensation of another breath in the room – an instinct that the air had parted to accommodate another presence. Whatever it was, her eyes snapped open, she turned her head sharply toward the bedroom door and saw Belinda framed there, staring at them.

"Oh God. Get off! Let me get up! Belinda, wait!" Sara shouted, because by the time she'd unwound herself from the pile of limbs, Belinda had turned and fled.

She grabbed her robe, managed to get it on as she raced through the living room, and almost slipped on the front steps, not exactly accustomed to running in nylons and nothing else.

Belinda was unlocking her car door, but stopped when she saw Sara.

"Belinda, please don't leave like this."

"You shouldn't leave your door unlocked. Anyone could have walked in." Sara couldn't tell if it was the way Belinda's face was tilted toward the street lamp that made her eyes shine like that, or if tears were pooling in them. She'd dyed her hair again – it was white-blond down to the roots.

"But anyone didn't walk in," Sara said. "You did. I didn't mean to leave the door unlocked, but . . . Look, I don't know what to say. I feel like so much has happened that we haven't talked about and now this is one more thing. I don't know how I got into this kind of stuff with Anthony. It's . . . I've never had a relationship like this before and I know I haven't talked to you about it. . . ." She suddenly felt exposed and foolish, standing in the street with her bathrobe pulled tightly over black fuck-with-it-on lingerie.

"Was Anthony the reason for that night with us?" Belinda asked.

Sara knew they might always refer to it that way – as "that night" – a night that shuddered away from definition, the way they had shuddered away from each other.

"I don't know," Sara said truthfully. "Sometimes I think, ever since I met him, he's been the force behind everything."

Belinda took a step closer, put her arms around Sara, and pulled her in. They stood like that for what seemed several minutes, the scent of sex between them – the only reminder, right then, of two men Belinda didn't know and Sara might or might not know, depending on how honest she was being with herself. Then Belinda pulled back just enough to look at Sara. Their bodies were still welded together, but a thin stream of night air whispered between their faces. Their mouths were so close that Sara could taste peppermint on her friend's breath. But the narrow distance separating them belonged to Belinda this time; it would take so little to cross it, but maybe it would take everything.

Belinda drew her breath in quickly and turned her face away. "Good night," she said quietly, and Sara didn't stop her from getting in her car and driving away.

She didn't notice, until she reached the front door, that

she had walked down the sidewalk and up the path with her fingertips touching her lips. As if she had been kissed, and was trying to understand it, or pretend that it had really happened.

Eighteen

Sara

MORE AND MORE, Sara found herself wondering if California had a monopoly on fickleness – on fleeting, quicksilver alliances that, like tumbleweeds, had no root systems and thus blew away whenever the wind rose. Not that she thought other places were immune to this behavior, but it did seem like a real California thing. And, not coincidentally, it also seemed to fit perfectly with California's weather. There was no predictable rotation of seasons, no security of knowing that the trees would turn in autumn, drop their leaves in winter, bloom in spring. She thought of New England, where no matter what surprises tumble out of life, there are certain things one can depend on. Storm windows, for example – they are put up in winter, taken down in spring. And the first snow; it may or may not come in time for Christmas, but it will come, and children press their noses against cold windows watching for the first flakes. Maybe in places like that, where seasons turn and the earth responds, people are steadier with each other; their alliances have more weight, more substance.

It was mid-October, and already, through much of

September, it had rained buckets. But in California, winter comes when it damn well pleases, no matter what the calendar says. And then, in true fickleness, it goes away.

For the last week of shooting on *Love Perils* the sky was cloudless and smoggy; heat rippled over L.A.'s freeways and the sun smoldered in brown haze. They were the kind of days some cynical person would photograph, make into postcards, and send out with this admonition: "Think twice before visiting."

Actually, the weather was behaving like a man, Sara thought, as she sat sulking in the sun, waiting for the next wardrobe change. And Randy was definitely behaving like a man, which of course wasn't wholly inappropriate. Part of his charm, however, had been his openness, his lack of guile. In New Age lingo, he'd seemed to be in touch with his feminine side. Now, he behaved as though he'd taken a crash course in machismo – some weekend seminar structured around the premise that manliness was next to godliness. She thought of that song from *My Fair Lady* in which Higgins sings, "Why can't a woman be more like a man?" Why in bloody hell would she want to be? To be ruled by a penis? To stand idly by while the penis stamps the passport of anyone inquisitive enough to stray beyond the safe borders of their native land?

It wasn't that Randy had turned into some flinty-eyed border guard; it was just that he'd changed toward her. He was acting like they'd never touched, never tasted each other, as if they hadn't offered up the most intimate hollows of their bodies for exploration. There is a look that many people who have been intimate get when they glance at each other. For others, there is nothing. The thread is either there, intact, joining them, or the space between them is blank. There is no middle ground; it's one extreme or the other.

Randy kept cutting Sara off with his eyes. A quick snip-of-the-scissors look, a look that reminded her of when she was a child and her mother had to take off a Band-Aid. "We'll do it fast so it won't hurt," her mother would say. But it was a lie. The quick-rip left a patch of fire on her skin. Pain is always pain.

For a few days, she had to avoid Hannibal because of her period. She knew then how Indian women must have felt, banished to the Moon Lodge every month. But even when Hannibal was resting in the van, Randy avoided her. When her exile ended, and it was safe to resume contact with Hannibal, she decided to tackle Randy's studied indifference head on.

They were shooting on Melrose Avenue, bringing traffic to a crawl because every passerby had to slow down and stare. She found Randy and Hannibal sitting under the awning of a store front, watching the cars.

"Mind if I sit with you?" she said.

"No, go ahead." Randy glanced at her and then resumed his study of the traffic situation.

She took Hannibal's hand and the orangutan widened his mouth and lifted his upper lip in what, she now knew, was his way of smiling. At least *he* was glad to see her.

"Randy, we have to talk," she said after a few seconds.

"Is there anything to say?"

"I think there's a lot to say. That's why you keep running away from me. Look, I didn't know what was going to happen the other night. Things just seem to spin out into strange directions with Anthony. I have a hard time saying no to him – sometimes he makes me forget the word. But you were a willing participant. And now you're acting like you're mad at me, as if I forced you into something, and I don't really think that's fair."

"No, that's not it – I mean, I don't think you forced me." He took Hannibal's other hand, and it occurred to Sara that they were using the animal almost as a conduit. They were talking through him; unable to reach out to each other, they put him in between. For his part, Hannibal looked from Randy to Sara, as if he were following a tennis match.

"I feel like I got sucked into something and I don't know how," Randy said. "I've never done anything like that before. I don't know if I ever even thought about it. I'm pretty straight, really, but suddenly there I was – in something that felt out of control in a way."

"Anthony has a way of throwing control out the window," Sara told him.

Randy looked at her and for the first time since that night, defenses were down and they were just two slightly confused people, holding onto an orangutan's hands. A bridge over troubled humanity.

"Randy," Sara said, "Belinda is my best friend and I never told her about the things I've gotten into with Anthony. I still haven't talked to her about it – but now she's seen some of it for herself. What I'm saying is, you stepped into an exclusive club the other night. Normally, there are only two members."

"You mean there's never been anyone else included – like I was?" Randy's eyes were narrow, aiming right at her.

"Well, there was someone, one other time. But it was different."

"A man?"

"No – a woman. Actually, a girl. Chronologically, she was above jail-bait age, but emotionally I'm not so sure. Anyway, she's not important. What I'm trying to get you to understand is that you became part of something that I haven't even talked to my best friend about. We can't become strangers now – we're not strangers. There are certain experiences that link people together, and I'm afraid the other night was one of them."

"It scared me," Randy said softly. "When I was driving home afterward, I didn't know who the guy was who had done that. It was like I had become someone else for a few hours. It sounds weird, but it was like I was under a spell."

"It doesn't sound weird. Not with Anthony."

He studied Sara for a minute and then said, "Does Anthony scare you?"

"Yes," she answered.

"Then why are you with him?"

"Because I'm addicted to him. And because I believe I can survive it."

After the final day of shooting, there was a wrap party at a small restaurant in Hollywood. Because the production company had rented the whole restaurant for the night, Hannibal was allowed to come. But he spent the whole evening eating tortilla chips; apparently, he wasn't in a gregarious mood. Sara came alone. She hadn't even mentioned it to Anthony – for a handful of reasons.

Bolstered by two glasses of wine – more than she could handle gracefully – Sara waited for a moment when Randy wasn't engaged in conversation and, when she saw an opening, placed herself squarely in front of him.

"So," she said. "Are we going to exchange numbers, promise to call and then never follow up, exchange numbers and actually keep in touch, or shake hands, utter some hackneyed, Hallmark-card farewell, and walk away without looking back?"

"Jesus, did you just say all of that in one breath?" Randy asked. He beamed his smile at her – a beacon through the fog of one glass too many.

"Yeah – wine expands my lung capacity."

"Sara," Randy said, turning serious, "I don't think we should keep in touch. I'm still uncomfortable about what happened. I wouldn't know how to think of you – how to define you if you were in my life."

"Wait a minute – people have to come with definitions or they can't be in your life? Is that like never leaving the supermarket with a can that doesn't have a label on it?"

"You know what I mean."

"Yeah, I guess so," she admitted reluctantly. "So this is it, huh? The last supper? We'll see each other's names on movie credits and think, 'Ah yes, the name rings a bell." '

Even through the wine, she could tell Randy was starting to feel sorry for her, which was not at all what she wanted. She started to speak, but he cut her off. "Sara, don't make this more difficult than it has to be, okay? Don't do this to yourself."

"Actually, I was trying to do it to you, but my aim was off," she said gently, acknowledging defeat, pulling back into herself, deciding that the clock had struck midnight and she'd better leave before her Volvo turned into a pumpkin. Or before she did.

Whales swim through vast oceans, calling to each other across hundreds of watery miles. A whale, longing for contact with another of its kind, sends out a signal – a low, resonant sound that asks another whale to answer, to come closer, to give it the companionship it craves.

For a few hours, Randy had joined Sara in a corner of her world that usually felt lonely – occupied only by her and Anthony. For those few hours, he had been a kindred spirit, another of her kind, captured as she had been by the mystery of Anthony's power. She could imagine, in the future, sending out a signal – one note, played on her soul as though it were a tuning fork. The sound would roll across vast distances, asking for a companion, asking for Randy, since he'd been one once. And she could imagine hearing nothing in response. Only silent, empty distance.

She drove west, toward her own neighborhood, her eye on the speedometer and on every car, every stop sign, every light. The wine hammered in her head; she didn't trust herself behind the wheel. She had one of those epiphanous moments when life is reduced to utter simplicity – an of-course-that's-it moment. She saw, with sudden clarity, the link between all living things. Whale, ape, or human – the calls go out across miles, asking only to be heard, asking only for an answer. Sometimes there is one; more often, there isn't.

Whoever doesn't answer has the last word. Along Sunset Boulevard, Sara stopped at a yellow light and waited obediently through the red. A woman, apparently homeless, was sitting on a bus bench, her shopping cart beside her. Four teenagers in a jeep behind Sara were yelling into the window of the Honda beside them. Against the wall of the Roxy, a man was strumming an out-of-tune guitar, doing his best to mutilate an Eric Clapton song ("Bell Bottom Blues," but only a Clapton aficionado would recognize it – it sounded more like "Bell on a Noose"). People cruising the streets, cruising the night, waiting to see who would get the last word, knowing the odds were against them.

Philippe's preliminary hearing was set for a Monday morning, just three days after Sara finished work on the movie, so she had those few days to devote to Belinda. Mark had tried a couple of times to prepare Sara for what he said was going to be "one of the more newsworthy trials."

"Is this the word at the lawyers' lunch counter?" she'd asked.

"It's just logic, Sara. Look at the following the guy has. He's like a cult leader. So, Belinda will be called as a witness, but that's the only time she'll be allowed in the courtroom. I just want to make sure you know that."

She'd been relatively calm until that point; the word "witness" went right to Sara's anger. "Witness? She's the victim," she had reminded her brother. "What the hell kind of justice system do we have if a rape victim is called a witness? She didn't witness a crime – she *was* the crime."

"Legally, it's the state of California against Philippe. If Belinda wants to file a civil suit later, it'll be her against him. But right now, it's the state's case."

"It sucks," Sara said. "No wonder this country's screwed up. I hope I never serve on a jury."

"I don't think you have to worry about that," Mark had told her.

Neither Sara nor Belinda had received any more threatening phone calls, which was mostly where the lull came from. And the mail had contained only the usual bills, catalogs, and the occasional Auto Club magazine which seemed to arrive even though it was never requested.

The deputy district attorney who was prosecuting Philippe was a woman in her mid-forties, who, Mark had told them, handled a lot of rape cases. "You're lucky," he said. "If you'd gotten someone less experienced, in a high-profile case like this . . . well, I'm not saying it would be disastrous, but I'd be worried. Iris Hensley is a tough attorney."

Belinda didn't seem worried at all, which probably should have worried Sara, but she was so anxious for things to go their way that, mentally, she smoothed out the rough seas ahead and saw only calm, clear water and an easy sail to a guilty verdict.

Sara told Belinda she'd pick her up at eight-thirty Monday morning and go to the hearing with her. She arrived at Belinda's house about ten minutes early, just in time to watch Belinda remove most of the makeup she'd put on.

"I have to look conservative," Belinda explained, rubbing Vaseline over her eyes until they were ringed with a sticky smudge of black mascara. "I don't know what I was thinking of, putting all this stuff on. Just a little lipstick, I think. Not this red color, though." She took a deep breath and sighed audibly. "Looking conservative is not easy for me."

"I don't really think it's easy for anyone," Sara said, plopping down on the couch to await the transformation. "Even for conservatives. That's why they always look so uptight. Can you imagine the stress involved with choosing a wardrobe that Pat Buchanan would approve of? I mean, how would you even know where to shop?"

A few minutes later, Belinda emerged from the bathroom, her hair straight and soft around her face – no gel, no spikes, just a boyish, innocent-looking haircut. Her face was scrubbed and un-made-up except for pale lipstick, and she was wearing a plum-colored suit that she'd bought at Ann Taylor for the express purpose of looking appropriate in court.

"Sara," Belinda said, putting her wallet into her purse, "where does the quote 'Vengeance is mine . . . sayeth the Lord' come from? The Old or New Testament?"

"I don't know. Probably the Old. Didn't the Lord get a lot nicer in the New Testament? Why do you want to know this?"

Belinda rummaged through the clutter on the dining room table and then handed Sara a folded piece of pink stationery. The biblical quote was typed on it, neatly spaced in the center of the page, with no other message.

"When did you get this?" Sara sniffed the paper for telltale signs of perfume.

"It was outside my door early this morning. I guess someone left it there in the middle of the night." Belinda kept combing her fingers through her hair, either from nervousness or from unfamiliarity with her courtroom hairstyle.

"We'd better go," Sara said, dropping the pale pink paper on the coffee table.

The traffic heading toward downtown wasn't as bad as Sara had expected, but she marveled that anyone could battle it out on the freeways at this hour five days a week. At some point along the Santa Monica Freeway, Belinda said, "So, you don't know where in the Bible that quote is from, huh?"

"What difference does it make? It was a threat – I don't care where it came from."

"It's just that Philippe uses a lot of biblical references. I always felt kind of ignorant – like I should know where the stuff comes from." She was picking nervously at the buckle on her purse.

"Belinda, my biblical knowledge can be summed up this way. In the Old Testament, everyone seemed to be into sheep. There was a real shepherd craze going on, unless of course you were royalty – they didn't have any pets. Then in the New Testament, they got into donkeys and everyone rode around waving palm leaves. I never have figured out what the appeal of palm leaves was."

Belinda laughed and Sara was struck by how long it had been since she'd heard the sound of her laughter. "That analysis really doesn't help, Sara," she said, giggling again.

"I know. I studied V-8 engines instead of the Bible."

Sara could see the county courthouse looming up ahead – one of those L.A. landmarks she recognized but had never actually visited. It was, after all, a landmark to which one hoped never to be summoned. "Belinda," she said, "Mark warned me that there might be some press here. I mean, it is a high-profile case. I just don't want you to be surprised."

"I guess I expected that," Belinda said vaguely. "I've tried not to think about it."

After paying the parking attendant twelve dollars, they walked through the main entrance of the courthouse, and through the metal detectors, all of this accomplished without attracting any attention. Sara thought maybe Mark had overreacted. There wasn't anyone around who looked like a reporter, and she didn't see a single camera. They got into the elevator and pushed the button for the ninth floor.

At nine, the doors opened on pandemonium. The hallway was jammed with reporters, illuminated by camera lights and annoyingly loud with voices competing to be heard. Belinda grabbed Sara's hand – like a young girl suddenly, afraid of the playground bullies. They edged out of the elevator, were blinded by the lights turning on them, and through the chaos Sara noticed a blond woman shoving her way toward them. This has to be Iris Hensley, she thought; as the woman called out, "Belinda, come on," Belinda's hand left Sara's and it was almost like she was swallowed by the crowd.

There was a crescendo of voices to her left, almost drowning out the relentless hammering of reporters' questions. From the chorus, Sara caught words like "Judas" and "unbeliever" and the phrase "crucifying Christ." She turned, and on the outskirts of the media mob a group of people – mostly women – were pointing at her, and in the direction Belinda had gone. They would shout out something and then, at intervals, look toward heaven (or the ceiling, if one happened to be an unbeliever). Sara first noticed it on one raised hand; then she realized they all had them – tiny crosses drawn on their palms in dark red ink. Sara was struggling past people, trying to catch up to Belinda, who had been stalled near the door of the courtroom. She heard Iris Hensley say, "Get the hell out of the way!" and then a hand from behind dug into Sara's elbow. She turned and found herself looking into the blazing eyes of a woman who hissed, "The flock will tear you to pieces for this crucifixion."

"Fuck off," Sara said, and jerked her elbow away. There was blood on the sleeve of her white blouse – blood in the vague shape of a cross. The crosses on their palms weren't drawn, as she had thought; they were carved. For a second, she felt sorry for the woman – for all of them, so hypnotized by Philippe they were carving their flesh for him. "What's wrong with you?" Sara said. "The man's a rapist."

"The man's a savior!" the woman shouted back.

Sara plunged through the crowd again, her moment of sympathy gone. She finally made it to the heavy wooden door. When she opened it and slid into the courtroom, she felt like breathing a sigh of relief, but she was confronted by a basic law of nature: escape is an illusion, and closing a door behind you doesn't mean you're safe. The first person she noticed was Philippe – poised, dripping with self-control, turning slightly to see who had walked in, and when he saw Sara, smiling in a way that made her shiver. Belinda was sitting in the row directly behind Iris Hensley and had saved Sara a spot beside her, but before Sara could edge her way there, the courtroom was ordered to stand as the judge entered. A tall, striking black woman came in, and Sara took it as an encouraging sign that this woman would be presiding over the case. Somehow, she didn't think Philippe could work his magic on her.

She got to her seat with a minimum of "excuse me's" and as soon as she sat down Belinda whispered, "The two back rows are all followers of Philippe's."

"Oh, that explains the scorch marks on my back," Sara whispered in return.

She looked again at Philippe, knowing as soon as she did that it was a mistake. She felt his magnetism – the strange ability he had to seize the air between him and another person and turn it into a force field. Even though he hadn't looked back at her, Sara felt herself being reeled in. He was leaning in toward his attorney – an impeccably dressed man with prematurely gray hair – and Sara had to wrench her eyes away. In the background of her awareness, she heard the case being announced – the state of California against Philippe. Even in court, he didn't have a last name, which meant he had probably changed it legally.

Belinda was sitting stoically, her eyes straight ahead, focused on nothing, it seemed; Sara tried to read what was going on behind them. She guessed that Belinda was probably feeling inconsequential. The state of California against Philippe – the whole state? By comparison, anyone would feel small – a little toe on the foot of some giant. "The witness" – just there in the courtroom to help out the state. A small blond girl with a style all her own, in grown-up clothes which were definitely not her style, waiting to put her hand on the Bible and tell the truth about how Philippe rammed himself into her, leaving his come in her. Of course, his come was divine, so she shouldn't have minded. But how he slammed his divine fist into her face?

Sara could tell that Belinda had already looked at Philippe, probably while Sara was battling her way through journalists and the carved-palm disciples. It was the way Belinda was deliberately not looking at him now that revealed she already had. When her name was called and she stood to walk to the stand, her spine straightened even more, vertebrae locking into place, forming a defense line against the enemy before her.

The D.A. questioned her first, beginning with a question as wide as a football field: "Tell us what happened on the night in question."

Belinda told the story with all the pieces in chronological order. Sara had learned the events in small slivers that had come out over weeks, like pieces of shrapnel working their way to the surface. But Belinda had organized them in her mind, was putting them all in order and – even more impressive – was keeping her emotions just under the surface – visible, but not disruptive. It was the first time that Sara had really allowed herself to think that Belinda could handle everything – the pressure of a trial, the attempts to discredit her. Sara knew from talking to Mark that the preliminary hearing was just that – preliminary, not the real thing, a tease really. Philippe's attorney wasn't going to haul out all his artillery. But it was a chance for Belinda to prove that she could take the stand, recite the events, and not fall apart. A dress rehearsal – and so far, she was pulling it off.

Iris Hensley didn't press for details; she let Belinda's story stand, apparently satisfied with the fact that it sounded credible. Then Philippe's attorney stood up. Sara hadn't really looked at him before – just a glance – but she hadn't scrutinized him. Now she did, and a wave of nervousness rose in her stomach. The guy was attractive in a smooth, Las Vegas sort of way. And in a Belinda sort of way, which terrified Sara. If they had seen him at a restaurant, Belinda would have found an excuse to walk by his table. He probably had a gold chain around his neck, Sara thought, hidden beneath his five-hundred-dollar Bijan shirt. She looked at his hands and noticed a chunky gold ring with a dark stone set in it. It was on his wedding-ring finger, but it didn't look like a wedding ring. That's good – keep them guessing. He probably gets laid a lot that way, Sara decided.

"Ms. Perry," he said, gliding over to the stand – moving in close so Belinda could smell his cologne. A man like that would almost certainly wear cologne. Eternity for Men, Sara guessed – just to prove how sensitive he is. He stood in front of Belinda for a long moment, letting his image sink in, his cologne fill her head. Shit, Sara thought, this guy's really dangerous. "Rape is a terrible, violent crime, isn't it? We all know this," he said. A bedroom voice, of course.

Belinda nodded and said a faint "Yes."

"But I'm a little confused here. Maybe you could help me out with some of the details."

Belinda nodded again and Sara wanted to scream, "Stop that! He's fucking with your head!" But Belinda had had her head fucked with by men like him for years. They didn't have a recovery group for that yet – an Asshole Addict Rehab.

"Now, isn't it true that, before the night in question, you spent some time with my client – private time, hours in fact, in which you confided in him, asked for his help, his guidance? In fact, isn't it true that you shared confidences with him – things you had never told anyone before?"

"Yes," Belinda said.

"Well, is it fair, then, to characterize your relationship with my client as a very friendly, close one?"

"Yes."

"And you invited him to your home on a previous occasion for a small dinner party, correct?" His voice was well tuned and perfectly modulated. Even Sara was getting hypnotized by it.

"Yes, but there were other people there. We weren't alone," Belinda answered. Her voice, by contrast, was getting feeble.

"I understand, Ms. Perry. I'm just trying to understand the history of your relationship. As I told you, I'm a little confused. Now, on the night in question, you invited him over to your house, correct?"

"No – I mean, yes, but it was his idea. He called me and asked to come over."

"I see, but you said yes."

"I – well, yes, I said that was okay."

"Fine. And you made an effort to look nice, to light candles and establish an inviting atmosphere in your home, is this right?"

"Yes," Belinda said, lowering her eyes. Oh, great, Sara thought – guilt rears its ugly head.

"Thank you, Ms. Perry. I think that clears up some of the confusion for me," he said. "That's all."

Belinda looked bewildered; her eyes met Sara's – wide and questioning. Shell-shocked, actually, and Sara didn't blame her. She was out of her league with this man; she was always out of her league with men like him, yet she kept dating them. She'd date this guy if the situation were different. The judge called a fifteen-minute recess, and Sara took Belinda's arm and led her out of the courtroom. The hallway was still packed with people; tiny red crosses, carved into palms, waved in front of them. Sara noticed the Emergency Room doctor who had treated Belinda; Belinda noticed him, too.

"What's he doing here?" she asked Sara.

"He's probably the next witness. We have to go home, Belinda – you're not allowed to hear anyone else's testimony."

She was talking to her like a child – she knew that – but Belinda looked confused, dazed, and very childlike. Sara held her hand and led toward the elevator.

When they got to the parking lot, with the brown heat of downtown Los Angeles pressing down on them, Belinda asked in a small voice, "So, what do you think?"

Sara took a deep breath. Playing for time, breathing for time, hoping the right words would come to her. "I think you'll have to be very careful. Philippe's lawyer is good.

He's smooth, he's attractive, and . . . what I really think, Belinda, is that you should put tape over your eyes and not look at him." So much for diplomacy, but she was angry – not at Belinda, but at whatever force in the universe had put together this cast of characters.

"See, this is what I mean. He's out to get you. And he's good at it. Look, you've dated men like him, you've been fucked over by men like him. Just keep remembering that, okay?"

They got lost trying to get to the freeway; Sara always lost her sense of direction when she was downtown. Belinda was quiet, staring mutely out the window at the confusing maze of one-way streets. Finally she said, "It'll be okay."

And Sara wanted desperately to believe her. Something about the tone of Belinda's voice, though, made her want to ask more questions. But she wasn't sure what the questions were. Just then, she noticed a green freeway sign directing them to the Santa Monica Freeway.

"Oh, great," Sara said. "Finally. We're not lost anymore. We're on our way home – out of the senseless murder district and into cleaner air."

She hoped it was an omen – the sign pointing to home, just as Belinda announced that she'd be fine. But Sara knew that omens are tricky things. People always think they see them, recognize them, and too often they're only seeing the mirror-image of their own wishes.

Nineteen

Belinda

BELINDA'S REMEDY for depression had always been to wash her hair. For whatever reasons, the act of shampooing seemed to dispel some of the dark clouds that hung over her. If too many still remained, she'd dye her hair, which was why its color had changed so often over the years. For Belinda, depression had been a nagging problem, but it had never been this bad before. Even after the birth of her child, and the loss of her child (the two acts were permanently linked in Belinda's mind), there were days that felt lighter, days that gave her a glimpse of what the end of grief could feel like. But there had been no relief lately. The depression just stretched on – a long, sad road to more of the same.

The sky was just getting dark. It had become Belinda's favorite time of day – nightfall – because she could close the curtains and pretend there was no world outside. She never lit candles anymore only lamps. Memories ignited with candle flames – ugly memories – and she didn't think the flames had any right to dance around so merrily. Wasn't that what they were doing that night? She was being raped by candlelight. She'd been meaning to throw them all out – little wax traitors laced with sweet scents.

She'd already washed her hair twice, but a few clouds still huddled around her shoulder blades and her stomach felt knotted and tense.

Sara had wanted to stay this afternoon when they came back from the courthouse, but Belinda didn't want company. She almost never wanted company these days. After she dried her hair, she went through her address book and crossed out the names of all the people she didn't want in her life anymore. There were a lot of them. A few were Philippe's followers who had given her their numbers when they were trying to organize a weekly meditation group. Maybe they went ahead and formed the group. She pictured them meditating about her – about her defection, her betrayal. She crossed out Philippe's name and number too, except his number was encoded into her brain cells. And now that she'd put a thick line of black ink through it, the number kept running through her mind, like a commercial jingle, heard once and replayed involuntarily, repeated a thousand times in the brain.

Iris called just as Belinda reached the W's in her address book. She said that the preliminary hearing had gone as she had hoped. There would be a trial in five weeks. The judge ruled that Philippe would be "held to answer."

"Held to answer," Belinda repeated, feeling the moisture from her breath collect on the mouthpiece of the phone. "It sounds like such an innocuous phrase."

"Lawyer talk," Iris said. "Anyway, you were great today. Convincing without being maudlin. I was very pleased. So, we'll talk in the next couple of days."

The whole thing was becoming surreal – the news cameras, the courtroom, the review of her testimony as if she were an actor about to open on Broadway. The world according to network sound bites. She was trapped in it now.

She took a bottle of Stoli out of the freezer and poured some into a water glass. One reason she kept it in the freezer – other than the fact that die-hard vodka drinkers did it – was that she didn't want Sara to see it. She'd been drinking too much lately; she knew it. But there didn't seem to be a reason to stop. And she barely felt the effect of the alcohol, which was probably some kind of warning sign – a body too numb to know it was being poisoned. At least she hadn't started drinking during the day. It was the nights that got bad, the nights that found her standing in the kitchen, pouring too much vodka into too big a glass.

Last night, the phone rang just before midnight, and only half awake, she answered it. There was only breathing on the other end, but instead of hanging up she lay there in the dark, listening to it. She was sure it was Philippe, but did she know the sound of his breathing that well? Could the sound of one person's breathing be that recognizable? Is it like fingerprints – no two breaths are the same?

There were other nights when she heard the sound of footsteps outside. Or thought she did. They were soft, menacing, barely louder than her own heartbeat – the sounds of a child's nightmare. When she went out to the store one night, a car that was parked near the front gate suddenly blinded her with high-beam headlights and she stood frozen in place, a bright ache spreading out behind her eyes. While she was in the market, she kept feeling like she was being watched, and on the way home every pair of headlights in her rearview mirror seemed too close, too determined. That night she felt the vodka, but instead of chilling her, it seemed to burn into her brain.

Tonight, she lit only one small lamp, and she sat where its light couldn't find her; the glow from the porch light slipped past the edges of the curtains just enough for her to see how much vodka was left in her glass. Her second glass. She thought about the dream she had had a few nights earlier. Philippe was making love to her – not raping her, but making slow, tender love. She woke up with his name caught in her throat; she woke up wanting to return to the dream, and when she was unable to, she cried for the first time in weeks. He'd entered her dreams before – several times – and she wondered if he did it deliberately. She wondered if he had that much power; either answer had its downside.

Once, a friend told her about a psychic who was supposedly very accurate, especially about the future. Belinda was going to visit her, but then her friend said, "And she'll come into your dreams for about a week after you see her." Belinda never went. The thought of having her dreams invaded terrified her.

She was about to get up for more vodka when there was a knock on the door. Maybe Sara . . . but Sara would follow the knock with "It's me," or something like that.

"Who is it?" Belinda called out, knowing her tone read more like "Go away!" A crotchety old lady, swigging vodka behind closed curtains, shooing away visitors – the image was much too close for comfort.

"It's Mark."

Belinda hid her glass in the bookcase and opened the door. She'd never noticed before how much Mark and Sara looked alike. Sara was a dark female version of her brother – same prominent, angled cheekbones, the same wide mouth and slightly pouty lower lip.

"Hi, Mark – this is a surprise. Come in."

He still walked with a pronounced limp and the scar on his face, which wasn't that noticeable under the porch light, turned into a defining feature when Belinda switched on another lamp.

"I'm sorry to barge in," Mark said. "I didn't have your number – I just remembered where you live from coming by with Sara a while back. She doesn't know about me coming over here. I wanted to talk to you about something, and I thought I'd do it on my own."

"Okay. Come sit down. You want something to drink?"

"No, I'm fine – thanks." Mark sat on the couch and Belinda tried not to think about the last time a man was in her house, on her couch, taking up space in this room. She sat beside Mark, wondering if this was the way she had sat beside Philippe; that part was hard to remember.

"Belinda, what I wanted to talk to you about is probably going to sound really unpleasant right now, given the fact that you still have to go through the criminal trial. But I'd really like you to consider filing a civil suit against this guy, no matter how the criminal trial turns out."

"Civil suit?" Belinda was trying to focus her mind.

"Even if he's found guilty and is in jail, you can sue him for damages. Not only are you entitled to them, but it's another way to disempower him, to keep him entangled in legal matters. The point is to discredit him as much as you can, and not let anyone forget what he did and what he's about."

"What if he's not found guilty?" Belinda asked.

"Then that's even more reason to file a civil suit. Look, Belinda – I'll represent you on contingency. You won't have to pay me anything unless we win. I know this isn't something you want to go through and I'd be the last person to tell you it'll be easy. It won't be. But I really feel that you should consider it."

"Why are you doing this, Mark? Are you telling me the truth – that Sara didn't ask you to come over here?" She realized, as she heard herself, that it was almost impossible to believe that anyone was telling the truth anymore.

"It was completely my idea. I'm doing it because I think Philippe is someone very dangerous. He has a certain power, a dark power. The evening news showed the frenzy outside the courtroom today – Belinda, people are carving up their flesh for him. What's next? Grape Kool-Aid? I'd like to see him brought down. I hate people like him, and I'll admit I would love to be responsible for helping to destroy him. Look, there are no sure wins in the judicial system. He *should* be found guilty, but –"

"What if I'm found guilty?" Belinda said, cutting him off.

"What are you talking about? You were raped."

"Sometimes I'm not sure what my feelings were toward him. I don't know why I still have dreams about him, or even how long I've been having them. Maybe I got what I deserved. Maybe it was my punishment for having expectations and fantasies."

Mark slid closer to her on the couch and took her shoulders. It felt to her like he was trying to hold her together between his hands – keep her from splitting down the middle. She didn't know her cracks were so visible.

"You told him no – right?" Mark's face was just inches from hers.

"Yes, but –"

"But nothing. You said no; he didn't stop – that's rape. I understand how you feel, Belinda, really –"

"No, you don't. People think they understand but they

can't understand. There's no way they can even come close."

Mark frowned and his brow creased the same way Sara's did when too many thoughts collided. "What about the counselor from the Treatment Center? Are you still talking to her? She can help you through this – that's what she's there for."

Belinda shook her head. "The thing is, I don't want to explain this to people who have no way of relating to it, but I don't really want to be around people who *can* relate." She paused and thought about what she'd just said, about the message lurking beneath the words. "I guess I just don't want to be around people at all."

Mark dropped his hands from her shoulders and stood up, shifting his weight from one leg to the other, carefully introducing the still injured one to its function.

"I'm sorry, Mark," Belinda said softly.

"It's okay. I don't want to make your life more difficult. But at some point, I wish you'd think about it – the civil suit, I mean. It's not only for your sake. There might be other women in the future, unless he's really stopped and revealed to be the bastard that he is."

"I know. Thanks – I'll think about it."

When she let him out the door, she wanted to ask him if he saw anything strange outside her house – someone sitting in a car or lingering too long on the sidewalk. But she didn't; she wasn't even sure about her own observations anymore. She didn't know if she'd witnessed omens of danger or painted danger signs over clear air. Maybe the footsteps outside her window were the sounds of her own fear, stalking her, coming for her – with no face, no voice, just the sound of footfalls in the dark. And her biggest fear was the one she couldn't tell anyone about –

the fear that she deserved all of this. The pain, the punishment, the long nights when she wished she could cry.

It was as if Fate had stepped in to prove her father right. "A bad girl," he called her, again and again after she got pregnant . . . and we all know what happens to them. The last words out of her father's mouth indicted her, sealed her future as surely as a gypsy curse. He died at home in his own bed, the way he wanted, with the cancer charging through his body like an unbeatable army. They all knew death was close. Her mother, glassy-eyed and numb, sat quietly weeping and Belinda looked down at her father's pale, drained face and said, "I love you." Because underneath everything she really did, and because she might never get to say it to him again. His raspy, bone-dry voice whispered back, "You disappointed me. How can you call that love?"

And then he died. A scarlet letter formed on Belinda's soul – hers forever. A parting gift. He might as well have inscribed the words on a locket, handed it to her, and said, "Never take it off." As if she had a choice.

At two o'clock in the morning, Belinda sat in a patch of moonlight on a splintered bench at Lincoln Park in Santa Monica. There were people in sleeping bags less than two yards from her, along with one man who sat upright, wide awake and guarding the contents of his shopping cart. It wasn't the most dangerous park to visit at night, but it was miles away from safe. During the day, it might be a park Belinda would visit to watch children on the swings. She would bring her fantasies, her memories, her hope for a clue to what her child might have looked like. But she didn't bring any of that with her tonight. She was sitting in the eerie quiet, weighted down with questions no one could answer and an armload of guilt. She was prosecuting Philippe for rape, but something inside her felt that rape was her just punishment for stumbling so many times in her life. Her father, if he were alive, would probably call it her "just deserts." According to her father, many people got their "just deserts" in the form of terrible misfortune – usually people he didn't like.

She knew she could get raped again, coming here at night. Or she could be beaten to a pulp – a nauseatingly accurate description, she thought, since pulp was what she'd look like afterward. She was here to tempt Fate, to walk right toward it. She was asking for it, whatever form "it" might take. Maybe if all the bad things that were slated to happen to her happened quickly, the rest of her life would be smooth and free of crisis. Maybe. But she had been sitting on the bench for half an hour and all that had happened so far was that the man in the nearest sleeping bag had stopped snoring.

She turned to see the man with the shopping cart walking her way, leaving his possessions behind. Maybe he'll attack me, she thought, slice me with the flash of a silver blade. Then her blood would be her penance, more of her "just deserts."

Instead, he sat down beside her. He was old – into his seventies, Belinda guessed, but maybe he'd been aged by life on the streets. Shocks of gray, greasy hair stuck out from a blue knit ski cap.

"Do you know why they couldn't pull the sword out of the stone?" he asked. "Why only Arthur could do it?"

"No, I guess I don't. My knowledge of Arthurian legend is a bit limited."

"Because all they could see was the stone. They gave the stone all the power. They didn't consider that the sword might have some, too. And if you don't see power, it's not there. They were slaves to the stone."

"Uh-huh." There it is, she thought – that line between genius and insanity. The guy probably used to teach literature and now he lives in the shadow of a shopping cart and knows where all the best garbage cans are.

Belinda stood up, said, "Good night – I have to go," as if she were ducking out of a cocktail party, and left a ten-dollar bill on the bench.

She saw them as soon as she arrived home and got out of her car. They were standing in front of the gate like sentries – three of them, moving toward her, looking like apparitions in the filmy predawn air. They had been waiting for her, and she understood then that she'd been waiting for them. As they got closer she saw exactly who it was – Kenneth, Astrid, and Michelle – names she crossed out in her address book just hours before. She didn't slow down or stop; she slid past them as effortlessly as a ghost, knowing they'd follow her, resigned to whatever fate they'd brought with them. All three had crosses carved in the center of their foreheads, between their eyebrows. As she passed them, Belinda's hand inadvertently came up and touched her own forehead. Strange how naked it suddenly felt.

"The seal of God is on our foreheads," Kenneth said.

"And what's on yours? Blood. Philippe's blood. The blood of the Lamb." Michelle's voice lapped over the end of Kenneth's sentence.

Once inside, they closed around her in the dim, one-bulb light of the living room. If there was a temptation to resist, Belinda couldn't dredge it up. Everything inside her felt molten and sticky. She deserved the punishment they brought.

"Sit down, Belinda," Astrid said, with an authority that was unusual for her.

Belinda lowered herself into the armchair – one of her garage-sale finds. The roses on the aging fabric glared up at her.

They kept their circle tight around her; they had closed ranks. Kenneth sat in a corner of the couch and two chairs were pulled up in front of Belinda's.

"You've been led astray," Michelle said. "The Bible talks about this – wars on earth, wars arising in heaven."

"Michael and his angels fighting against the dragon," Astrid added. "We're here on the side of the angels. Philippe is on this earth to lead the angels. You've sided with the dragon."

"The beast," Michelle continued. "The beast of Revelations – with a mouth uttering haughty and blasphemous words, blasphemies against God and those who dwell in heaven,"

"Philippe's not God," Belinda said weakly.

"If anyone slays with the sword, with the sword must he be slain," Kenneth said, raising his voice as though a congregation had gathered to hear him. "The Bible tells us this." He pulled a small Bible out of his pocket and held it up. "Your accusation is a sword."

When they moved in closer, tightening the circle, when hands pinned her arms, Belinda saw for a moment her blood spilling over the red roses on the chair. But the image dissolved; her blood still chugged along in her veins, safe for the moment. Michelle took a pen out of her pocket, and with one hand grasping Belinda's hair and tilting her head back, she wrote something on her forehead. It didn't feel like a cross was being drawn there; they weren't recruiting her. They were exiling her. Belinda was pulled up and pushed into the bedroom, placed in front of the full-length mirror, and then the overhead light was switched on. In the center of her forehead, Michelle had written: 666.

Kenneth opened his Bible to a marked page and read: " 'If anyone worships the beast and its image and receives a mark on his forehead or on his hand, he also shall drink the wine of God's wrath, poured unmixed into the cup of his anger and he shall be tormented with fire and brimstone in the presence of the holy angels and in the presence of the Lamb. And the smoke of their torment goes up forever and ever and they have no rest, day or night, these worshipers of the beast and its image and whoever receives the mark of its name.' "

The three of them backed up suddenly, releasing Belinda, and she crumpled to the floor. She heard them leave, walking in unison so their steps sounded like the steps of a single person. And only after they had closed the door behind them did she raise her head and look into the mirror again. A pale face stared back at her, with the black numbers inked into her forehead.

She tried to stand, but couldn't, so she crawled to the bed and pulled herself up, scrambling under the covers for safety. Any minute, the lightning bolts might come, she thought, the wrath of God might be unleashed on her; only the covers pulled over her head would keep her safe. Children knew this; adults always forgot. Her teeth felt muddy and the ink would leave smudges on her sheets, but the bathroom was too far away and her legs weren't working.

Maybe in the morning, God would move on to some other sinner and it would be safe to crawl out from under the covers. But she knew He'd be back. She had a price on her head, the sign of the beast between her eyes. And if her father never forgave her, she couldn't expect God to.

Twenty

Sara

SARA GAVE in more willingly now to the scarf over her eyes – folded twice, so no light could seep in. It used to scare her – the plunge into darkness, into blindness, the heightening of her other senses. But now she gave in to the confusion of not knowing what part of Anthony's body was touching her. He would play across her skin so lightly, it could be his fingers or his cock – she couldn't tell at first. Trapped behind her blindfold, she was at his mercy. He'd let her know only what he wanted her to know, and not until he felt like it. He only had full command over her when she was blindfolded; even with her wrists and ankles bound, if she could see she still had some control. But in total darkness, with only the nerve endings in her skin to tell her what was happening, she was his slave.

It had taken a while. At first, she resisted – tensed her muscles, and tried to see his shape through the silk. But he ignored her protests, and now after months, she allowed herself to be stroked and teased and carried along blindly. She'd gotten used to it, knew the symptoms – how time would collapse, and how the shivering in her body would get so intense she'd have to cry just so she could handle it. But she surrendered to all of it, became a true slave.

Toward the end of each session, he would untie her. Each time the last thing he took off was the scarf from her eyes. It was always in this order: ankles first, then wrists, then the blindfold. There were things that Anthony was meticulous about, and untying Sara in a particular manner was one of them. He was like that with his house, too; he didn't want anything moved around, even an envelope. He didn't like cup rings left on the furniture; he had several sets of coasters and insisted on people using them. It was why they had started to go to Sara's house more than his – they always fought at his house. Sara always seemed to do something to upset the orderliness of his ultramasculine environment. The last time they were there, she called him an anal-compulsive jerk and he fired back by calling her an aggressive bitch. So it worked out better if they ended up at Sara's. It was better for Anthony's furniture and better for their relationship.

She blinked at the sudden flood of light into her retinas, even though the light was dim. Her skin was still warm and damp, and she stared at Anthony's back as he turned away from her, scarves and silk ties crumpled in his hand. He stood up and walked to the dresser; there was now a special drawer for them.

"You know," Sara said, her voice just above a whisper, "if you didn't have such a good body, I probably never would have gone to bed with you." She was watching the movement of muscle in his thighs and buttocks as he bent over, closed the drawer, and straightened again.

He came back to the bed and lay down beside her. "Yes you would have."

"No, I thought you were kind of full of yourself. But

you had this athlete's body – I checked you out. I could tell even through your clothes. It's always been a difficult thing for me to resist."

Anthony's fingers traced a pattern on her face, around her eyes as if he were drawing another blindfold onto her. But she saw everything now – the pink light splintered in his eyes, the way shadows pooled just beneath his jaw.

"Are you telling me you wanted me just for my body?" he asked, kissing her mouth softly. A feather kiss.

"Mm . . . not exactly. I'm just saying it might have been the deciding factor."

"Not my scintillating intellect and sharp wit?"

"Well, let me put it this way – if I met some guy with a great intellect who was terribly witty, and he had rolls of baby fat on him, buck teeth, and bad skin, I might want to talk to him on the phone, but I certainly wouldn't want to see him with his clothes off."

"You're a snob, Sara – did you know that?" Anthony's eyes were crinkled at the corners. It was one of the ways he had of smiling, one of the ways she liked.

"I am absolutely a snob, and proud of it."

The phone was an unwelcome intrusion, and when Sara reached for the receiver, Anthony grabbed her wrist. "Don't answer it."

"I have to," she said. "It's late. No one would call this late if it weren't important."

She wondered when she said "hello" if her voice had that I-just-got-laid sound to it.

"Sara, it's Mark. Sorry to call so late, but I . . . Are you okay?"

"Yeah, why?"

"I don't know. You just sounded funny when you answered. Listen, I'm at Mother and Dad's house. I know it's the middle of the night but I think you should come over here."

Sara sat up and almost pulled the phone off the night stand. She felt the blood drain from her head. This is how it happens – a phone call in the middle of the night. "What's wrong? What happened?"

"They're fine," Mark said quickly. "They're both fine. It's not . . . you know, not what you just thought. But some strange things happened out here tonight. I've called the police. But I think it has to do with the rape trial, and maybe you should come over for a little while."

"I'll be there as fast as I can."

"Sara, listen to me. No one is hurt. I don't want you driving like a maniac, okay?"

Since his accident, Mark hadn't even rolled through a stop sign. He drove a Toyota Land Cruiser now and stayed in the right lane on the freeway. His Porsche days were over.

"What happened?" Anthony said when she hung up and went to the closet. She pulled out a pair of jeans and a sweater and tossed them onto the bed.

"I'm not sure. Mark's at our parents' house. They're okay, but something happened there."

"I'll go with you."

She didn't argue, but it went through her mind that Mark hadn't met Anthony yet and her parents hadn't even heard about him. She was going to arrive in the middle of the night, in the midst of an emergency, with a man no one had been introduced to yet. But she couldn't think of that now. She didn't want to drive out to the valley alone, and besides, Anthony had a faster car.

Two police cars were parked outside her parents' house when they arrived.

"That window's broken," Anthony said as they walked up the path.

Sara followed his eyes to the living-room window. There was a jagged hole the size of a football, but she doubted that it had been made by a football. The front door was ajar, but as she started to push it open, Sara stopped as if she had hit a wall of glass. The welcome mat on the front step was red with blood. She looked at the bottom of one of her shoes; the white sole was stained red. She couldn't speak and she was too frightened to move. Maybe Mark had lied to her just so she'd keep it together until she got here.

Mark must have heard them because the door opened and he said, "Sara, come in. I know how it looks, but Mother and Dad are fine. They're not hurt." Then he noticed Anthony. "Oh, hi – I'm Mark. I'm Sara's brother."

"Anthony Cole."

"Right – nice to meet you."

Sara had recovered enough to catch the look her brother threw her – a knowing, oh-that's-what-you-were-doing look.

Claire and Roger Norton were sitting on the couch, close together, holding hands. They looked small and frightened, the way elderly people often do when life startles them, comes at them with more force than they can handle. Three policemen were there, and one of them was holding a brick with a note attached to it by rubber band.

"I know how you feel," he was saying. "This note isn't really a threat, though. We can file a report of vandalism, but there was no overt threat made against you."

"Mark, what the hell happened?" Sara whispered. Her parents hadn't even noticed her arrival.

Mark motioned her and Anthony into the dining room.

"They were sitting in there watching television," he said, "and they thought they heard a cat screeching. Mother went to the front door and before she could open it, a brick came through the window. It had a note on it – some kind of religious message, I think, but I'm not exactly sure – that's what it sounds like. Anyway, Dad told her to stay put, he opened the door, thinking he might get a look at whoever it was, and there was a cat with a knife in it on the door mat. That was the blood you stepped in."

"Jesus," Anthony said. "Their cat?"

Mark shook his head. "Mother thinks it belonged to one of the neighbors. It didn't have a collar on, though. The police put it in a plastic bag and they're going to take it to Animal Control so it can be disposed of. They really are doing everything they can. I think they feel bad that they can't do anything else."

Sara looked into the living room and saw the cops getting ready to leave. "I want to see that note," she said, and left Mark and Anthony standing by the dining-room table, where Thanksgiving dinners had been served in happier times, where grace had been said, and where Sara had done her homework in the afternoons.

"Sara, I didn't know you were here," her mother said when she walked into the living room.

"I know – you were busy when I came in. Can I see that for a minute?" she asked the cop who was the designated brick-bearer. He looked so young, she suddenly felt old.

The note was typed on a small piece of white paper.

" 'If you will not awake,' " Sara read aloud, " 'I will

come like a thief and you will not know at what hour I will come upon you.' "

She handed it back to the policeman. "How can you say that isn't a threat?"

"It's not a specific threat," he told her. "I know it doesn't seem fair, but that's the way we have to handle it."

"It's from Revelations," Anthony said, coming up behind Sara.

"How'd you know that?" Sara asked.

"I took a class in college on the New Testament."

Sara stared at him, cataloging one more surprise – Bible study? Maybe his father coerced him into it.

Mark moved in and said, "Good night, thank you," to the police, and Claire and Roger Norton stayed huddled together on the couch – the oldest and the youngest people in the room.

There was a moment of awkward silence after the police left, broken finally when Roger Norton said to Anthony, "Hello – we haven't met." He released his wife's hand, stood up and crossed the room to the only stranger there.

"I'm sorry – Dad, Mother, this is Anthony Cole," Sara said, stumbling over the words, and deliberately not defining exactly who Anthony was. Friend? Boyfriend? Man who ties me up? She figured that a cordial introduction and the fact that he was standing in her parents' living room at one o'clock in the morning was quite enough.

Anthony shook her father's hand. "It's terrible that you and your wife had to go through this," he said, and Sara could see her father warming to him.

"The world didn't used to be like this," Roger Norton said wistfully. "Used to be you could leave your door unlocked and if something came through the window it was one of the neighborhood kids throwing a baseball too hard. We used to know all the neighbors by name. Now we know a few, but people keep to themselves more. They get those alarm systems and things, and they're suspicious of everyone. . . ."

Sara knew where this was going – the orange groves that had been paved over and the traffic that was never this loud. She went over to the couch and sat down beside her mother.

"You okay, Ma?"

"Oh, I guess so. Thank you for driving all the way out here, dear."

Claire Norton seemed to get narrower every time Sara saw her, as if she were turning into a thin line.

"Maybe they won't be back," Sara said, taking her mother's hand. "I think this has to do with the trial and the fact that I'm Belinda's friend. These people she got involved with . . . well, I just think they wanted to scare you and they might think they've done enough now, at least to you."

"They certainly succeeded in scaring us. I keep thinking about that poor cat, though." She shook her head sadly. "I suppose tomorrow I should go around to some of the neighbors and find out who it belonged to."

"Mother, I don't know if that's the best idea," Sara said. "If he were my animal, I don't think I'd want that to be my final image of him. Maybe it's better that they're spared that."

"Maybe you're right." Her mother glanced across the room at Anthony, who was still listening politely to Roger Norton's history lesson on how the San Fernando Valley used to look. "He seems like a nice young man," she said.

"Uh – yes, he's an interesting person. Can I make you a cup of tea or something?" She'd have offered to prepare a five-course meal right then if it would get her mother off the subject of Anthony.

"No, you don't need to, dear. I should go make up Mark's bed. He said he'd stay here tonight."

Mark walked them out to the car, past the bloodstain and the broken glass, and Sara noticed how all three of them averted their eyes.

"Hey, nice Mercedes," Mark said. "A 280 SE – I haven't seen one of them in a long time."

"Yeah, it's my pride and joy," Anthony told him, running his hand along the door, stroking it as he would a woman's thigh.

Sara hugged her brother goodnight. "It's nice of you to stay with them tonight. You can't seem to get away from those Lone Ranger bed sheets, huh?"

"Well, they are habit-forming, but they're safer than drugs. Drive safely."

As they pulled away, Sara looked back at Mark standing in the driveway waving at them. For a moment, he was thirteen and she was ten, being driven off to summer camp the only year their parents could afford it. He'd stood there just like that, smiling and waving, and she had watched him through the rear windshield until he was just a speck in the distance. She was struck by how much a family changes and how much it stays the same and how, after a while, it's hard to tell the difference.

"It might rain," Anthony said. "I can't see the stars."

Sara turned around in the seat and fastened her seat belt. "Thanks for coming out here with me tonight."

"I liked meeting your parents and your brother. You're

lucky, Sara – I never had a home that felt like that – with that much love in it."

"Yeah, I know." She stretched her arm across the seat back, put her hand on Anthony's neck and played with his hair, lifting it up with her fingers and letting it drop. "Don't ever cut your hair."

"Okay. Don't ever get your tits done."

Sara laughed. "What made you think of that?"

"I don't know – I was just negotiating. Long hair for breasts *au naturel*. I like your breasts – they're perfect. And they're real."

"Will you stay with me tonight?" she said, massaging the tendons in the back of his neck.

"Sure. On the couch or in the bed with you?"

"On the kitchen floor."

There was something so young about the way he slept beside her that night, bending against her, his forehead pressed lightly on her shoulder, that it reminded Sara of an apology. But he'd really done nothing to warrant an apology, if that's what his body was telling her; she'd played too. Everything he'd done to her, she'd gone along with – reluctantly on some things, like the blindfold, but she hadn't said no. She wanted to study Anthony's face like a painter would – for the essence under the skin – but she'd have to move to do that and she didn't want to wake him.

Sometime during the night he turned so his back was to her and she turned with him, holding him around his waist, pressing her breasts into his back. She didn't know how long they stayed like that; she drifted in and out of sleep. She thought she heard rain, but it was soft and intermittent. She thought she felt Anthony wake up at one point, but she fell into deep sleep and wasn't aware if there was a body next to her or not. When she woke up again, it was to the sound of rain, the smell of a fire, and cold sheets where Anthony had been. The light coming through the window was dull; the clock said six-thirty, but the sky looked like it hadn't caught up.

She put on her robe, which hadn't had a belt on it for months, and went out to the living room. He was wrapped in the extra blanket she kept in the closet, lying on his back in front of the fireplace. She stretched out on the floor beside him.

"Couldn't sleep?" she said.

"No. I felt like sitting by a fire. You don't mind, do you?"

She nudged closer and unwrapped the blanket. Closing her eyes, she let her mouth mark a trail along the pulse in his neck, down his chest, over each nipple. Anthony took her hand and put it on his cock, but she wasn't going to be rushed. Her mouth had its own timing, and it continued slowly, lazily, making patterns along his ribs, biting him lightly sometimes, making him wait. The closer she got to where he wanted her mouth to be, the more she slowed down, until finally he pushed her head and forced her mouth open with his cock. His hands covered her ears and it sounded like the ocean in a sea shell until she realized it was the sound of her own breathing.

"Oh God, Sara," he whispered, trying to make her go faster. But it was early and she had only one gear – slow.

He gave her control for a few minutes, but when he said her name again it had a different sound to it. She stopped, put her hand where her mouth had been and slid up his body until her face was buried in his neck. "What do you want?" she asked. It was often a risky question.

"Wait here for a minute," he said, and stood up.

She heard him go into the bathroom, heard the toilet flush and the sound of running water; then his footsteps going into the bedroom, and the sound of the dresser drawer opening and closing. He came back with a brightly colored bundle of scarves and sashes in his hand. A silk bouquet.

"Turn over on your back," he said, kneeling down. "And slide closer to the stereo."

He took one ankle, wrapped a red scarf around it and looped it around the leg of the cabinet that held her stereo. He pulled her legs wide apart and bound the other ankle to the leg of the coffee table, dressing that one in blue. He straddled her, pulled her arms over her head, holding her wrists together with one hand while wrapping a sash around them with the other – her bathrobe sash, purloined for just this purpose.

She knew, when he reached back and got a white silk scarf, that this was one of the times she would be blindfolded. It wasn't always like that, but lately it was. He didn't cover her eyes, though – not yet, anyway. He lifted her head slightly, brushed the silk across her mouth and wrapped it around her head, silencing her. White silence. She started to say no but she was too late.

"Trust me, Sara," he whispered. "Remember? You have to trust me."

She knew her eyes had fear in them, and that he saw it, just before he covered them with a black scarf. She thought she'd become his slave before, thought she had surrendered completely, but she was wrong. She'd still had a voice then. Now she had nothing, except the trust he asked her to have; and terror was nipping at its heels.

One of his hands was on her waist. He was kissing her left breast; she felt the edges of his teeth on her nipple, and she searched wildly in the mute darkness for his other hand, went over her body inch by inch for any sensation she might have missed. Where was it? What was he doing? Before, she had been able to ask. Usually, he wouldn't answer, but the sound of her own voice had made her feel safer.

Finally, he put his other hand on her right breast, pinching her nipple hard enough that a sound escaped from her throat, but it was muffled by the scarf. The crackling of the fire sounded louder, and rain was tapping on the metal gutters along the edges of the roof. He moved down her body as smoothly as water and she could feel his cock, hard against her thigh. Then nothing.

He was gone, except she didn't hear footsteps. He had to still be there. She concentrated until she heard his breathing . . . and another sound . . . something being moved on the coffee table. The next sound was unmistakable – a struck match. She waited – forever, it seemed – and then the temperature between her legs changed, got warmer. He'd lit a candle and was holding it between her legs; she could smell the wax and the faint scent of vanilla. She pictured the candle in his hands, created a paint-by-numbers image over the black backdrop that was her sightlessness. But the image was only of his hands cupping the candle. She didn't know what he was doing or what he was thinking of doing, and her imagination bloomed like a mushroom cloud, strongly suggesting destruction.

"Trust me, Sara." He didn't say it this time; he wasn't saying anything. But she heard it – an echo of all the times he'd said it before. She repeated it to herself, wordlessly, imprisoned in her white silence.

His fingers began tracing her, drawing tiny wet circles,

and then deeper, wetter ones – probing her, exploring – with the candle lighting his way. He hadn't moved the flame closer, but now her own heat combined with the candle's and it seemed like half the moon was melting and taking her body with it. She thought she might never have been opened and exposed this much. Her breath was getting faster – sharp bursts of air hitting against the silk gag. He was making her come with his finger, and she was balanced between fighting it and giving in. Anger was somewhere in there – percolating up through the fear and the heat and the ultimate decision to surrender. She was angry that he wasn't going to fuck her; he was keeping his body away from hers, except for his hand.

The heat won out over everything else. She trembled against the restraints, squeezed her eyes shut behind the blindfold, rode on the dark waves of what he was doing to her.

His fingers and the heat from the candle retreated, and her body calmed down, waited again for whatever was going to come next. He surprised her and took the blindfold off fist. She met his eyes for only a second, lowering hers to see if he was still hard – it seemed an important thing to know right then. He was. He stared down at her for a few seconds; maybe he was deciding about the gag, deciding if he ever wanted to hear her voice again. But then he lifted her head and unwound it.

"Why didn't you fuck me?" she said hoarsely. Her throat was dry.

And then with a suddenness that surprised her, her eyes filled up with tears and her face crumbled. He knelt over her to untie her wrists and she turned, trying to take him in her mouth, but she was crying too hard now to do anything else. Calmly, he moved down to one ankle, undid it, and went to the other. Only when she was free did he acknowledge her tears. He lay down on top of her, propped himself on his elbows, and wiped her face gently with both hands. She thought of windshield wipers.

"Why are you crying, Sara?"

"You didn't want to make love to me. You just wanted to scare me," she sobbed.

"Do you think because it was just my hand that I wasn't making love to you?" Anthony said, putting his mouth to her ear, filling her head with whispers.

"I don't know." She felt silly then, groping for some kind of logic.

"Fear's part of it. It's part of what you're learning about yourself. When it comes to these kinds of games, you're still in kindergarten. Stop fighting it."

"And you're in graduate school, aren't you?" Sara asked. "You've done this a lot, haven't you, Anthony?" They'd never really talked about it. She'd assumed, but hadn't asked.

"I've done it enough to know what I'm doing." He reached over and picked up the white scarf. "Do you want to blindfold me, Sara? Do you want to tie me up right now? You can do whatever you want to me then – it'll be your game."

She shook her head no.

"See – it's scary both ways. You still don't know which side of the game you like better – controlling things or giving in. But you're going to learn the same things about yourself either way, and that's what you wanted or we wouldn't be here. I've told you before – it's why we met, it's why we're together. You were looking for this without even knowing it."

Sara looked down at her body. Two small blue bruises

decorated one of her breasts. Teeth marks. The bruises he left were getting more intimate; they were left in more secret places now. And these were just the ones she could see.

Twenty One

Sara

SHE HAD an hour before Anthony was to pick her up. He'd told her only that they were going to a small dinner party at someone's house – just a few people, friends of his. That was as detailed as the information got. It would be the first time he'd introduced her to any of his friends. In the months they'd been together, she had met a few business associates and actors he was working with, but not his friends.

Their relationship might as well have begun on a deserted island; it seemed to grow in isolation, outside the boundaries of their normal lives. It left them with only each other to feed off – most of the time, anyway. Allison had been an exception; so had Randy. But they were just visitors – their time was limited from the beginning. Tonight marked a change, and Sara was trying to not be nervous about it.

Anthony had stopped by unexpectedly earlier in the afternoon. Sara had been unloading groceries and the front door was open. She must have been preoccupied because she didn't hear his footsteps until he was behind her, standing at the doorway to the kitchen.

"Jesus, you scared the hell out of me," she said, wheeling around.

"Sorry, the door was open. I got you a present," he said, and handed her a small bag from Victoria's Secret. "I want you to wear these tonight, okay?"

She unwrapped the tissue paper and took out a pair of black nylons with a wide band of lace at the tops, concealing the rubber strip that would hold them to her thighs.

"Moving away from garters, are we?" Sara asked. She felt her cheeks redden; it always seemed to happen when he told her how to dress, and he was telling her more often these days.

He pulled her hair back and kissed her neck. "I don't need to tell you what else to wear – or not wear – do I?"

"No."

"See you later."

"Thanks for the present," Sara called after him.

The stockings lay on the bed as Sara went through her closet looking for the perfect thing to wear, willing herself to think as Anthony would. She finally settled on a black silk dress – sleeveless, but with a jacket that could go over it. It was ankle length, with a slit up the side. She held it up and stood in front of the mirror, seeing how high the slit was, trying to determine if she could dress as Anthony wanted, only stockings underneath, without getting arrested for indecent exposure. She decided that, as long as she was careful when she crossed her legs, it would be all right.

She took almost a full hour getting ready – an incredible

amount of time where Sara was concerned. Her indulgence in primping usually topped out at fifteen minutes. She slid the dress over her head, feeling the silk glide over her black push-up bra, then over bare skin and nylons. She was getting used to slipping a dress over naked skin, walking into restaurants and feeling the air-conditioning between her legs, shivering across her belly. Anthony had been stripping her down – for months now. But not just her clothes. He'd taken sandpaper to the places inside her that she'd spent years lacquering – so many coats of it – but he'd been relentless, sanding them down until she was bare as raw wood. Sometimes now she would stand in front of the mirror naked, looking at her body as if it were a constantly evolving piece of sculpture. And she'd wonder at the rest of her nakedness – all the new, raw places that felt strangely docile.

She studied herself now and frowned at her reflection. She'd lost weight. The waistband of the dress was so loose, it wasn't even at her waist. She went back to the closet and rummaged around for a belt.

Sara had been having trouble eating lately. Everything tasted funny to her and her stomach didn't seem to want to receive food. She knew the reason; it had to do with the phone calls she was still getting. It was a man's voice now, telling her she wouldn't be spared, she had befriended Judas, and God's wrath would be visited upon her. She hadn't told anyone about these calls. Anthony had been with her a couple of times when the calls had come, but each time she'd said it was a wrong number. Her parents hadn't had any other problems, and she was trying to convince herself that as long as they were left in peace, she could handle whatever came her way. Her stomach didn't quite agree.

Belinda hadn't said anything, but Sara suspected that she was also still getting phone calls or letters, or both. She was looking thin and drawn as well. But in a couple of weeks, it would be over one way or another, Sara hoped.

When she opened the door for Anthony, he took a longer look at her than he usually did. Then he stepped inside the house and kissed her cautiously, in deference to the lipstick she hardly ever wore, but had made a point of applying tonight. His hands ran smoothly over her hips, checking. "Good girl," he said.

When they left her house, he drove to Sunset Boulevard and turned toward the ocean. It occurred to Sara that he could be going to his own house. Maybe Anthony had tricked her – mistrust suddenly reared its ugly head.

"Where do your friends live?" she asked.

"Pacific Palisades – right along the bluffs. From the second floor there's a view of the ocean. It's really beautiful – you'll like it."

"You sound like a real estate agent."

"Yeah? Well, it's not for sale. Sorry. Anyway, it's Joey Pagano's house that we're going to. You've heard of him, right? He's produced two of my films. We've known each other for a long time. His girlfriend, who sometimes lives there and sometimes doesn't – depending on whether or not they're speaking – will probably be there tonight. Her name's Christine. And Stephen Sadler and his wife – great actor. I've been hoping to work with him at some point."

Sara's brain had stalled at the mention of Joey Pagano's name; she only half-heard what Anthony said after that. Pagano was a producer with questionable connections, and a trail of rumors and warnings that dragged behind him like chains. "You don't want to cross him"and "He has friends who can take care of anything" were some of the often repeated comments about him.

"What dangerous company you keep," Sara said softly, just as their car turned in at a large metal gate. If Anthony heard her, he chose to pretend that he hadn't.

The house itself was concealed by the gate, which was solid and imposing, and by a line of trees planted along the fence. Anthony pushed the button and a woman's voice responded: "Yes?"

"It's Anthony Cole."

Without further comment, a buzzer sounded and the gate moved slowly, dramatically revealing a two-story white mansion at the end of a long driveway. Willow trees bent in toward the front door, framing it gracefully, and blooming azaleas and rose bushes were everywhere. Landscaping by Monet, Sara thought.

The door was opened by a maid who said, "Good evening, Mr. Cole," and nodded toward the living room. Sara could hear a murmur of voices but she was more interested for the moment in the wide, curved staircase that looked as though it had been built for Scarlett O'Hara to float down; the paintings, ornately framed and individually lit; and the oriental rug that probably cost more than her entire house. Actually, half of Sara's house would have fit neatly into the foyer. Anthony took her arm and led her toward the voices.

They stepped down into a sunken living room with soft lights and long leather sofas arranged around a huge stone fireplace. Four silhouettes turned toward the sound of their footsteps.

"Anthony – great to see you." Joey Pagano sprang from the couch and came to them.

Sara had only seen photographs of the man and was a

little surprised that the top of his head barely reached her shoulder. His bodyguards must love him, she thought – they can just carry him around piggyback when things get dicey. His shirt was unbuttoned to reveal a braided gold chain around his neck. He and Anthony hugged for several seconds before Anthony seemed to remember that Sara was standing beside him, and introduced her.

Joey Pagano shook her hand with both of his, but his face gave off less warmth than his hands. His mouth was thin and straight, and there was something about his eyes that reminded Sara of a bird pecking for food. He motioned the two of them toward the sofas where the other three guests no longer looked like silhouettes.

"Anthony, you know everyone. Sara, this is Stephen and Veronique Sadler, and Christine Drake." Christine, whom Sara assumed was Joey's girlfriend, was no taller than he was. Her blond hair was pulled into a tight ponytail. She walked past Sara with a quick "Hi," hugged Anthony, and said, "Hello, darling," in a voice that had more height than she did. It was the way her hand rested on Anthony's hip that made Sara wonder who besides Joey had been her boyfriend. She took note of Christine's ruffled shirt and bell-bottoms – a fashion trend that she was not happy to see revived.

She recognized Stephen Sadler from his movie roles, but at the moment was unable to recall any of them specifically. His wife was one of those women with a regal bearing and a haughtiness that was simultaneously intimidating and mesmerizing. Veronique – what a perfect name for her, Sara thought. Women like that only need one name. She could, Sara was certain, make her presence felt in any situation without ever uttering a word. She was exotic-looking – jet-black hair, cut short, a full mouth, and wide, almond-shaped eyes. She was wearing a black velvet Donna Karan bodysuit and black boots. The only jewelry she wore was a diamond wedding ring and gold hoop earrings.

They sat in a semicircle sipping champagne, and Sara let the conversation swirl around her without trying to participate. She felt as though she were on a first date, as though she didn't know Anthony and needed to hold back, check him out. And there was something about the familiarity between the other five people that seemed vaguely threatening to her. There was a history here that went beyond work, and Hollywood, and industry talk, and Sara couldn't put her finger on what it was.

The maid drifted in on silent feet, the way maids always do in houses like this, actually waiting for someone to notice her presence before saying that dinner was served. The industry talk continued at the dinner table – stories about Anthony and Joey being on location in Greece, opinions on current films. Everything felt subdued and elegant. The place settings were perfect and expensive, and the maid circled the table with a silver platter of salmon and rice, garnished with vegetables. But Sara couldn't shake the feeling that another dialogue was taking place under the surface – one that everyone could hear except her. She was careful to take only small sips of wine; she noticed that a second maid would appear out of nowhere to refill glasses as soon as any of them got a little low.

"Anthony tells me you're a costume designer," Joey said, his eyes darting around the table and lighting on Sara.

"Yes – mostly for TV movies at the moment."

"Well, I'll have to keep you in mind. I have a couple of things coming up."

Great, Sara thought – the Mafia payroll. Or at least the

mailing list. “Thanks,” she said politely. “I can always use work.”

“Isn’t it sort of frustrating, doing what you do?” Christine asked her. “All that shopping, and you can’t take any of it home for yourself?”

“Well, fortunately a lot of what I buy I wouldn’t want to take home,” Sara said evenly. She couldn’t help thinking that Christine’s outfit would definitely be one she’d be glad to leave on the set. The hint of dislike that Sara had felt for this woman upon meeting her had grown into a large tumor that was metastasizing rapidly.

“Well, if you ever need suggestions on where to shop, I’d be happy to help you,” Christine said. “Unfortunately for Joey, shopping is something I do a lot of.”

“Thank you, but I’ve been a costume designer for quite a while now. I usually know where to go.”

“Anthony and Joey were furious at me when we were on location in Europe. I had to buy extra luggage for all the clothes I bought. So, where are you from originally, Sara?” Christine’s tone was getting sweeter, in a murderous sort of way.

“I grew up in the valley.”

Christine turned to Veronique and said something in French. They both laughed and Sara felt like leaping across the table and strangling both of them.

“Have you and Anthony known each other long?” Veronique asked. Her voice was deep and throaty, and every syllable was soaked in French.

“About five months or so, isn’t it?” Anthony said, answering for Sara. He put his hand on her thigh under the table, but slid it up only to the lace top of her stocking. “Sara’s not sure yet if we’re compatible,” he added, and then withdrew his hand.

Christine laughed and said, "Well, you can be rather elusive, darling. How well have you gotten to know our Anthony, Sara? Has he remained a mystery man or has he let you in on all his secrets?"

"Stop it, Christine," Anthony said sharply.

She turned to him with a look of blond indignation. "Well, she is part of the family now, isn't she?"

"I said stop it."

"Let the games begin," Joey said softly – so softly that Sara wondered if anyone else heard him. His thin mouth was turned into a slight smile and his eyes were resting on Christine.

Stephen cleared his throat nervously. "I hope we're not going to have a *Who's Afraid of Virginia Woolf?* evening," he said.

Sara looked at Christine and made her voice even and cool. "Anthony's secrets are being parceled out gradually. I'm filing them alphabetically." She fought the temptation to ask Christine if she was one of them, and if she should file her under Q for "quick fuck."

There was too much simmering under the surface of this carefully orchestrated evening. Sara's stomach tightened and she took a large swallow of wine, hoping that would untangle her intestines. She looked around the table for an ally and decided that, should she need one, Stephen was the only one who might qualify. But she wasn't even sure of that; his nervous glances at Veronique made it perfectly clear who had control of the relationship.

Joey pushed his chair back. "Should we wait a bit for dessert and coffee? Anthony hasn't seen the latest addition to the house, and of course, Sara needs a full tour."

Christine smiled sweetly at her sometime boyfriend.

"Why don't you take Anthony and Sara, dear – the three of us will stay here and chat."

Sara followed the two men, watching Anthony from behind, trying to remind herself that he was her lover. Tonight, he felt more like a stranger. It was the way he'd been avoiding her eyes, the way he had fingered her under the table but had made a point of not touching her. Her mind raced, as she tried to figure out what was going on. What alliances past or present were at work? And exactly what secrets was Christine referring to?

The upstairs was just as tastefully decorated as the rest of the house, but Sara was starting to get the feeling that nothing here was chosen for personal reasons. It had an *Architectural Digest* feeling to it – an impersonal, I-hired-the-best-decorator ambience. Joey led them into the master bedroom where the bed faced an enormous television screen and French doors opened onto a small balcony. Sara walked outside and stared out at the dark ocean, dotted with the reflection of stars; a quarter moon lay on its side in the night sky. For just a moment, standing on the balcony in the clear air, she thought she might have been exaggerating everything. Maybe she was being overly sensitive; maybe she had only needed some fresh air and a little breathing space.

Anthony broke the spell, coming up behind her but not touching her. He stood a couple of feet away, the distance between them a harsh statement. Something's not right, it told her.

"Great view, huh?" Anthony said, speaking more to the view than to Sara.

"Uh-huh."

"Come on – Joey wants to show us something downstairs."

"Really, and what might that be? Bluebeard's chamber?"

"Lighten up, Sara."

She hated comments like that. Once when she was fifteen and Mark was teaching her to drive a stick shift, she got frustrated at her own ineptitude, cursed one of her own mistakes, and Mark said, "Just lighten up. Relax, would you?" She slugged him in the ribs so hard he was bruised for a week. People usually tell you to lighten up when you have a damn good reason not to, Sara figured, and they shouldn't be allowed to get away with it.

Joey was taking them into the basement. Bluebeard's room, red with the blood of his past wives, did not seem all that unlikely. Their footsteps sounded hollow on the wooden stairs. At the bottom was a wire cage containing enough wine to give half of Paris a slight buzz. He led them past that and Sara saw that the basement was huge. It was unusual for a California house even to have a basement, much less one with a ten-foot ceiling.

They stopped in front of a closed door, and as Joey reached for the knob, Sara noticed the conspiratorial look he threw at Anthony. She considered turning on her heel and walking back toward the wooden stairs; there would be comfort in the sound of her own footsteps striking out on their own. But instead, she heard her footsteps follow theirs – across the threshold into a room that instantaneously turned red when Joey flicked on the light. Red recessed lighting, deep red walls – velvet, Sara realized, after staring at them for a second – and a display of things she'd heard about but had never seen for herself.

"Remember how I talked a while back about building a dungeon in my home?" Joey was saying to Anthony. "You probably didn't think I'd do it, huh?"

She'd moved ahead of them; their voices fell away behind her as she ventured further into the red, windowless room. Dungeon – a new language – but a lot was new to her. On the wall ahead of her was a large wooden X, about eight feet tall, with rings and leather cuffs at the top and the bottom. She envisioned Anthony on it, his arms and legs tethered to the wood, stretched into the shape of the frame. Hooks were mounted on the wall beside it, with various things dangling from them – several paddles and whips, two pairs of handcuffs, some silver clamps Sara assumed had to be nipple clamps, although she'd never seen any before. In the center of the room was a bed – not a bed in the usual sense, but a padded leather cot, probably four-by-eight, she guessed, with three pairs of rings along the sides. Sara saw herself on it, but didn't want to, and chased the image away. In one corner, a short metal bar was hanging horizontally from the ceiling; it looked like a trapeze bar, but the leather cuffs attached to it with thick wire cable made its purpose clear. The cable was attached to a wheel mounted on the wall. It looked like a winch, and just below the top bar, mounted on the floor, was another. Only instead of leather cuffs, there were metal ones, with locks; a large metal ring was in the center of this bar. Sara squatted down on her heels and touched the cold metal.

"What's this ring for?" she asked.

Anthony and Joey laughed softly.

"For tying down certain appendages," Joey said.

She went over to the opposite corner of the room, where something shiny had caught her eye. It was a dagger – an ornate military one with a carved handle and a clear red marble set in it. The blade was about three inches long. In a pile beside it were a couple of thin ropes and some long pieces of twine. The dagger made her think of pirates; the red floor still made her see a lake of blood. She didn't ask any more questions.

Anthony's voice caught up with her, asked her something, but all she heard was her name.

"What?" she said, and turned around to see only him there. Joey had left them. It was quiet and strange in this place he had taken her to for reasons that he still hadn't made entirely clear. She stared at the walls, thought about Bluebeard again, and the tiny gold key to the secret chamber no one was supposed to enter.

"I said, are you intrigued?" Anthony moved closer, stood just inches from her, but made no move to touch her. The air felt thick and dead between them, the way air often does in soundproofed rooms – eating sound, biting off the resonance of voices.

"I don't know. Maybe." Sara's voice plopped down in the space between them. She walked over to the wall and surveyed it like a careful shopper, determined to make just the right choice. Then she took down one of the whips. It was not one of the most vicious-looking ones; it was smaller, almost as if it had been designed with some kind of Victorian sensibility. A lady's whip, Sara thought, and almost laughed. She was still smiling a little when she turned back around to Anthony and she knew her expression froze him in place. She could sense his fear; immediately, she claimed it as a prize, wedged it between her legs where it heated up and leaked moisture. Her steps over to him were slow and deliberate.

"Intrigued, Anthony?"

He didn't answer. He just watched. It was a waiting game, and for the moment it was her game.

She circled around behind him and drew her arm back.

The whip sliced through the red air and she snapped her wrist at just the right instant to make it crack against the back of his thighs. His muscles flinched, but nothing else moved. Even his arms hung straight at his sides, his hands unclenched. But she didn't believe him; he was a good actor. When she drew her arm back again, Sara aimed higher, hit his buttocks, and he bent a little at the waist – but only slightly. She moved in, leaned into his back, and put her hand between his legs.

"Spread your legs."

He did, and she could feel fear course through him. She could read his thoughts. He was afraid she was going to come up with the whip, snap it right between his legs. As she stepped back again, she considered it, but she was more enticed by the idea of keeping him off guard, letting him experience some of what she had felt during the evening.

Her arm drew back and she thought, "Right across your ass again, Anthony, like a disobedient child." Thought it but didn't say it, and then aimed too low. The whip cracked across the back of his left knee. His spine straightened quickly and he turned to face her.

"Let's change places," he said, "since you're feeling so brave now. We're in a roomful of toys here – what's your preference?"

He walked over to her and took the whip from her hand. "I think we've done whips enough for now. How about the table, Sara? Or the wall – don't you think you'd look good on the wall? You couldn't possibly be afraid of that, could you?"

She stared hard at him, trying to emit fire from her eyes. But Anthony had the fire now. She thought of Prometheus, who stole fire from the gods and for his crime was bound in chains. Was that what she had done? Stolen a power that wasn't hers and now, as punishment, she would have to submit to tethers and restraints?

"Come on, Sara, where's your spirit of adventure?" Anthony said, taunting her. "This is your first time in a dungeon. Don't you want to experience all it has to offer? It's just the two of us here."

She walked slowly over to the X frame on the wall, turned, pressed her back into its center, and spread her arms and legs, imitating its design. Without hesitating, Anthony came over and strapped her ankles and wrists to the wood. He didn't move back at first, but covered her body with his, raising his hands to hers as if he too were bound there. Then his hands dropped, found the skirt of her dress and pulled it up. She didn't want to give in; she wanted to defy him, but she was already wet. His fear had done that to her. The now familiar marriage of anger and anticipation was defining her reactions.

He kissed her, played with her tongue, took her lower lip between his teeth and pulled on it; she felt a bruise forming. She commanded her eyes to stay open, but they rebelled against her and closed. A moan rose up in her throat, but she swallowed it before it could become sound. She heard his zipper and in a second he was inside her, knowing just how to move to make her come, knowing just how close she was. She was about to give in completely – her will was slipping – when he pulled out and her eyes snapped open. Two shapes were in front of her, and the smell of perfume filled the air around her.

Sara blinked and tried to process what her eyes were seeing. Veronique was pushing Anthony aside – black velvet and the unmistakable scent of Obsession. But it wasn't only her; the other three had come in also. They were standing by the door, watching.

She looked around wildly for Anthony. He was standing to her left, zipping up his pants and smiling at her. Don't cry, she told herself as soon as her eyes started burning. Part of her couldn't believe he was letting this happen, but part of her knew this writing had always been on the wall – one of those walls she had refused to look at. This wasn't their own private game anymore – it had turned into a sporting event. The audience was studying her, waiting for her to break. She could swear that Christine was smiling, but it was hard to tell – Sara's eyes were starting to blur. Don't cry, she told herself again.

Veronique went down on her knees. Sara thought of the alley, of another stranger, and she wished she were back there. Anything but this. Anything but being pinned to the wall, on display. Veronique's tongue found everything it was looking for, while Anthony stared at his captured prey, on loan for the moment to a black-haired Frenchwoman whose mouth was acquainting itself with Sara's taste.

The other three started moving closer. Were they going to take turns with her or was the game just to make her fall apart under the weight of their presence?

She tried not to feel what Veronique was doing; she tried to go numb, but as Joey moved closer to her with Christine and Stephen just behind him, Veronique's tongue moved faster. So did Sara's breathing, although she desperately wanted to slow it down. Stephen was staring at his wife, on her knees with her head between Sara's legs. So much for an ally, Sara thought – he looked as if he'd seen this before.

Suddenly her memory took her out of her red prison, backward through time, to the orange grove where her ten-year-old body was pinned to the ground by Tommy and Lane, while Jerome stood over her, trying to get up his nerve and his penis. It was the two boys watching her that had made something inside her feel it was crumbling into dust. It was how she felt now – pinned again, this time to the wall, watched by an even larger audience.

Veronique rose from her knees, wiped her mouth with the back of her hand. The diamond glinted at Sara; it was mocking her, too.

"So, what should we do with her?" she asked the others, as she stepped away from Sara.

Sara closed her eyes. It didn't matter that her dress was still on – she felt naked. She might as well be tied to a post in some village square, her flesh and her fear exposed to throngs of strangers. There weren't throngs here, but there were strangers, especially Anthony. Or maybe she just wished he were a stranger – then there would be no betrayal. The ultimate humiliation was that she had trusted him to know where her boundaries were and to honor them.

Veronique went to the wall and ran her fingers over a couple of the paddles, caressing them. Then she took down a whip. Joey smiled and nodded. Sara hoped they'd whip her, hurt her. Pain would be less humiliating than pleasure. Pain was simpler – they could hurt her, break her skin, draw blood. But if they made her come . . .

But Veronique didn't stand back from her as she would have to in order to whip her. She pressed her body into Sara's, drove her tongue into her mouth, and Sara could taste herself on Veronique's lips. Then her lips slid across Sara's cheek to her ear.

"Have you ever been fucked with a whip?" she whispered, and Sara felt the handle of the whip go inside her.

Veronique pulled back just enough to look at her victim

with all the haughtiness she'd spent years mastering. Her dark eyes were heavy-lidded and cold, the kind of eyes that squint above cigarette smoke and dare people to come closer.

Sara was lightheaded and short of breath. She knew if she looked at Anthony she'd pass out – the trusted palace guard who had turned her over to the enemy. He was the enemy himself, had been all along. So she looked at Veronique instead – at her full mouth, the veins in her long white neck. She hated it that the handle of the whip felt good, hated her body for receiving it so willingly and for moving in rhythm with it. The dagger glinted at her from the corner.

The handle was pulled out sharply, suddenly, and before she could stop herself Sara gasped. Veronique took a few steps back, and Sara thought, "Now – now she'll whip me." She felt a surge of relief, waited for the heat between her legs to subside. But her tormentor moved in again – not as close, but too close to whip her. She held the whip between Sara's legs and flicked her wrist sharply, expertly. The leather snapped against her, the aim perfect, and wet, and designed to make her come whether she wanted to or not. Veronique's rhythm was as steady as a metronome; all the eyes watching her ran down her body like rivers of hot oil. She couldn't fight anymore. Her body was going to betray her, lose the war – an unconditional surrender. She screamed when she came – from the release, but also from the hatred she felt for all of them, particularly Anthony.

He untied her wrists first, then her ankles. Seeing him bent down before her, with her hands now freed, she thought of hitting him, choking him. But more than anything, she wanted to get out of there. It was hard to steady herself at first. She had to stand there for a moment in front of the X, like a painting that had stepped out of its frame. And then she focused her eyes on the door and walked out, looking at no one.

She found her jacket and purse in the living room, picked them up and walked calmly out the front door and down the driveway. It was false calmness, but the illusion was vital right then. She'd forgotten about the gate, though. What if it didn't open and she had to go back to the house? Fuck it, she thought – I'll climb the damn fence before I'll do that. But when she got closer, she heard a clanking sound and the gate slid back.

She charted her course – over to Sunset Boulevard, to the nearest pay phone where she could call a cab. It wasn't that long a walk, except that she was wearing heels. The street was faintly lit – an upscale residential neighborhood with well-tended yards and two-car garages. Lights shone from windows, and in a few houses smoke curled up from chimneys. She thought of families around dinner tables, or in living rooms watching television. Normal lives – but now that seemed like a veneer to her. It might be the biggest lie of all, Maybe there are always secrets lurking underneath – rooms you don't tell the kids about, adventures you don't tell your partner about, fantasies played out in soundproofed dungeons. Medieval language for modern-day games.

Headlights were coming up behind her, and even though she could tell by the sound of the engine that they belonged to a Mercedes, she was hoping it wasn't Anthony. But the car slowed down and his voice bounced across the sidewalk.

"Sara – please wait. Look, we have to talk. Sara! Goddamn it, just stop for a minute."

And she did. Her muscles were still trembling and too much blood was pumping through her heart, but she had made a deliberate effort to walk calmly out of the house, and she was buying into her own illusion. Anthony pulled over, turned off the ignition and the headlights, and got out of the car.

"Look, I know it was intense –" he began.

"Fuck you, Anthony," she said, cutting him off. "Don't you dare patronize me. It was one thing playing these games in private, but you never intended to leave it at that, did you? You were always leading up to this, because what really turns you on is to be able to break someone. But you know what? You didn't break me. You succeeded in humiliating me – congratulations – but I'll survive. What are you going to do, Anthony – keep combing the city for new victims?"

"Sara, it's not like that. Look, maybe you weren't ready for what happened tonight. It's just another game. I know what you're going through – let me help you deal with it."

"Thank you very much, but that's sort of like Mike Tyson offering to guide someone through an acid trip. I think the risks would outweigh the benefits. You went too far, Anthony. I'm not hypnotized by you anymore. I look at you now and all I see is another asshole who went to charm school."

She brushed past him and headed for the lights of Sunset. "Sara, please don't do this. I'm sorry," he called after her.

"You're not sorry – assholes don't get sorry! They're not programmed for it!"

The taxi would take her home along familiar streets, past stores and landmarks she'd seen a thousand times. She would walk through her front door and everything in her house would be just as she had left it. But everything in her life had been rearranged. She was going to be stumbling over unfamiliar obstacles for a long time.

She might never look at men the same way, or women for that matter. She would always wonder now where their secret lives were. What locked doors kept them safe? What toys were locked in there? What colors were the rooms?

She had once been so certain that she knew men, had them wired. But Anthony had taken her back to the orange grove and shown her how much she didn't know. He'd taken her back to the ten-year-old girl who found herself knocked to the ground, surprised by boys she thought she knew. But he hadn't just taken her back, he'd left her there. Even the night felt the same – a warm breeze, a dome of stars. She had thought that with Anthony she was learning how to trust. Just as she used to think she was learning to outrun the boys she played with every afternoon. Now she didn't feel she could outrun anyone, and trust might always look like a wild card. If she'd only looked up Anthony's sleeve . . .

Twenty Two

Sara

FOR THE second night since she'd left Anthony standing on the sidewalk with her anger ringing in his ears, Sara couldn't sleep. She lay in bed feeling minutes tick by like judgments. It was almost eleven. She knew sleep would keep running away from her; it had vanished from West L.A., fled to another county, where people in nice, safe relationships curled up under down comforters behind gingham-curtained windows. Her eyes blinked against the darkness and her mind kept replaying the scene – the awful scalding of humiliation when they left her no choice but to surrender. Five people whom she now hated watched her come. Their eyes were like putty – sticking to her, cementing her to the wall more securely than the leather cuffs.

Her rage at Anthony was white hot and getting hotter. What's beyond white, she wondered, on the heat scale? But then what did it matter? She wanted him to suffer, no matter what color his suffering came in.

There was only one thing she wanted more and that was to feel close to Belinda again, feel her floating along the same wind currents, bumping into her occasionally when the winds shifted. Lately, it felt as though they inhabited different skies. Sex had come between them, Anthony had come between them, and rape – that was there too. But they'd had a friendship, Sara reasoned – a strong one. And friendship, if it's real, can survive anything, overcome any obstacles, right? Maybe. Only one way to find out, she decided, as she got out of bed and dressed in the dark. She wouldn't call first – Belinda might say no. That was one word Sara didn't want to hear, partly because it was the word she hadn't been able to say to Anthony. Just the sound of it would open up the wound of her failure and rub salt in it. The soundtrack of the past five months had been a virtual chant of "yes" and "trust me, Sara" – the latter spoken so many times by Anthony that it settled into Sara's brain and started to sound like her own voice.

Belinda's house was dark. Sara knocked and waited for the sound of footsteps on the other side of the door before saying, "It's me."

Belinda opened the door wearing the blue antique kimono Sara had given her two Christmases ago. "Sara, are you okay? It's really late."

"Yeah, I know. I really needed –" She didn't finish the sentence because her throat clenched and tears welled up in her eyes. Sara wasn't sure, anyway, what the ending of the sentence was. What did she need? Just to be there? Was that going to be enough?

Belinda took her hand and pulled her inside, locking the door behind her. Without saying anything, she led Sara through the house into the bedroom. Before climbing into bed, she switched off the small bedside lamp and Sara watched as the kimono slipped off her, her body a pale shape pausing among the shadows for a moment before crawling under the blanket.

"Come on – get in," Belinda said.

Sara stood back from the bed, feeling awkward and shy. Things were moving slowly, like a dream, but she wasn't sure whose dream was playing. She kicked off her sandals, stripped off her jeans, but left her T-shirt on. When she got into bed beside Belinda, she left a distance between them; they were close enough to feel each other's body heat, but far enough away to be chaste. Two girls at a slumber party.

"What happened?" Belinda asked after several minutes. "You were crying. Is it Anthony?"

"It *was* Anthony," Sara said. "I left him." She rolled on her side so that she was closer to Belinda. She thought her T-shirt was brushing against Belinda's bare skin, but she wasn't sure. "We'd gotten into some pretty serious stuff, bondage, all that – we'd been doing it for a while, but –"

"He tied you up?"

"Well, yeah, but I tied him up too. It was something we played with privately. I can't really explain it, but I was definitely into it. Except the night before last, he went too far. He tied me up in front of other people, let a stranger humiliate me. He put me on display, in front of five people I didn't know. Between us, in private, it was a game. But the other night wasn't. The night you walked into my house, when we were with Randy, that was a different game."

Belinda slid closer, and Sara put her arm across her waist, delicately – like a question. Belinda's answer was to turn on her side and slide one leg between Sara's. "I was jealous," she said softly.

"Of Randy?" Sara asked. She didn't know if she was frightened or relieved. She thought maybe she'd suspected it, when she and Belinda had stood out on the sidewalk that night. But she couldn't be sure.

Belinda's arm imitated Sara's – wrapped around her waist and rested below her rib cage. "Yes – of Randy," she said.

"Belinda, I'm sorry. I'm sorry I've kept so much from you."

"We've both kept secrets from each other." Belinda's voice was whispery and wide as an echo. Sara tightened her grip, afraid suddenly she might fly away, or dissolve into the air.

"I was so taken in by Philippe," Belinda continued. "I guess, in a way, I was his prisoner. Except it didn't feel like a prison – it felt like freedom – from all the things I didn't want in my life anymore, all the sadnesses. And then the rape made me feel like I'd been such a fool. And these people hate me, Sara. They blame me, they think I'm the traitor." She moved down a little in the bed and rested her head on Sara's shoulder.

Sara didn't want to move, but there was something wrong with being half dressed while Belinda was naked. She didn't want anything to separate them, even thin cotton. She sat up and pulled her T-shirt off, over her head. When she lay back down, Belinda let her head fall against Sara's shoulder again and circled her waist with her arm.

"Belinda," Sara said. "All those people who follow Philippe are prisoners too – they just don't know it. You didn't know it for a while either. It's just another kind of bondage, you know? I didn't see it before, but you and I have been going through the same thing. It's just that I've been playing it out sexually, and –"

"And I sold my soul?" Belinda asked, her tone harsh.

Sara moved her arm from Belinda's waist to her face, cradling it in her palm, as if she were expecting tears to fall and wanted to catch them when they did. "No, that's not what I meant. You didn't sell your soul. Your soul's fine. He raped your body."

"Sometimes I'm not so sure," Belinda said – Sara could feel the sound waves in her hand. "If it's all about bondage, then where does it stop? How do you know where the boundaries are until they've been crossed? And then it's too late. Look what happened to you – was that any different really than being raped? It *was* a rape of sorts, wasn't it? You felt safe with Anthony. You tied each other up and played your games in private. You thought it would stop there, that it would never go outside the boundaries of your own private world. But it did – he had different ideas about where the boundaries were. Well, I thought I was safe with Philippe. I let him into my life in ways I hadn't ever let anyone in – even you. I trusted him. I thought we had something special, private – sacred, actually. But now I have people leering at me like those strangers leered at you. You know, I always thought you were so much stronger than me. I wanted to be like you. I was always going for the wrong kind of man, trusting the wrong guy. I thought, with Philippe, I'd finally done something right. I thought he'd help me change, be more like you. But the whole time, you were becoming more like me."

It wasn't Belinda's tears Sara should have been prepared to catch; it was her own. They came without warning, the way her tears always did.

"Don't cry," Belinda said gently. "We'll both be all right."

She pulled Sara in then, as if she were a magnet, rolling

over on her back and putting Sara under her arm. Sara's face was close to her breast. "I guess I shouldn't tell you not to cry," she said after a few seconds. "If you need to, then you should."

Moments went by in silence, with Sara's tears dripping onto Belinda's skin, until they finally just stopped on their own – the way they always did.

"You know what Anthony told me at the beginning?" she said, moving her face only a little along Belinda's skin. "It was when we were just starting to get into bondage games. He said it's all about surrender, whether you're the one being tied up or the one doing it. It's not about control – that's an illusion – it's about surrender. Both sides of the game are alike. Well, you know what else is alike? Being tough and being vulnerable. You thought I was protected because I was tough – so did I. But all it meant was, someone like Anthony had to use different tactics. Dangerous people can find their way in whether you're vulnerable or well defended."

"I can't get him out of my head, Sara," Belinda whispered. "I'm so scared. It's like he set up residence inside me and he won't leave."

It seemed like such a small movement of her head – just a tilt of the neck – and Sara's mouth was on Belinda's. It was probably more than that – more movement, more adjusting of each of their bodies – but it didn't seem like that. Sara rolled all the way over so that Belinda was underneath her; she felt so tiny and frail, Sara was afraid her weight would hurt her. But Belinda breathed easily beneath her, returning her kisses and wrapping one leg around Sara's body. There was something different about the way their mouths were meeting; it wasn't sex, or at least it wasn't like sex Sara had ever experienced before.

There wasn't that raw edge; there was no ravenous hunger. Something deeper was going on. Sara tried to turn off her mind, stop thinking, but she couldn't. She kept wondering if this was about intimacy, not sex, and if those two things could ever coexist. Maybe it always came down to a choice.

Belinda's breasts were against Sara's, their bodies were welded together, skin to skin, but wound to wound was how Sara thought of it. They were tending to each other's injuries. She moved down to Belinda's breasts and heard her moan a little under the pressure of her mouth. She thought of moving down further, of tasting her, making her come. But it seemed inappropriate. That wouldn't take care of any wounds; it might even open up some recent ones. She returned to Belinda's mouth and they both shifted around at the same time so they were lying on their sides. Belinda's hand slipped between Sara's legs, but changed course and moved up to the small of her back.

Their kisses grew lighter and finally stopped, but their bodies stayed pressed together. Sara thought for the first time in two days and nights that she might be able to sleep, but she felt in Belinda's body the residue of too many sleepless nights. There was a papery thinness to her skin, a tiredness in her muscles.

"Have you been sleeping?" Sara asked after what seemed like a long time. A moth was flapping against the window shade.

"Not really. I take a lot of hot baths. That seems to help me relax and then I can sleep a little. What about you?"

"I haven't gotten much sleep the last couple of nights."

"Let's take a bath," Belinda said, sliding out of bed and

walking across the creaks in the wood floor to the bathroom.

Sara watched her go, and listened to the sound of a struck match, saw the glow of candlelight spill out of the doorway, and then there was the sound of running water.

She stayed in bed for a few minutes, sliding her leg across the sheets to where it was cold and no bodies had left their warmth behind. The pillows smelled faintly of coconut. It all felt new to her, as if she had never been in Belinda's bed before.

When she went into the bathroom, Belinda was just turning off the faucets and stepping into the tub. Steam rose up from the water into the candlelight. Sara got into the tub and sat at the opposite end, facing Belinda. Their legs arranged themselves as if they did this every night.

"Sometimes I wonder if I'll ever be able to be with a man again," Belinda said. Her face was shiny with beads of sweat and her hair was limp.

"I know – me, too. At least that's how I feel at the moment. But we should probably be careful about using the word 'never.' "

"Sara, I had a baby once. A long time ago. I was sixteen."

"What?"

"My father wouldn't let me keep him. I wanted to. He wouldn't consider an abortion, either. He made me have the baby and then they took him away in the delivery room. They never told me what happened after that. No one would say who adopted him or where he lived."

"Him?"

"Well, that's what I think. They never said if it was a boy or a girl."

Sara didn't know what to say. She knew how painful

this confession was. She looked at Belinda through the steam and the orange flickering light and saw her younger, raw from the pain of childbirth, reaching for her baby as it was being taken away from her forever. Someone probably used the phrase "for your own good."

"My father never forgave me for getting pregnant," Belinda said. "I guess I never forgave myself, for any of it. I thought that Philippe – " Her voice broke off. She slapped the water with the flat of her hand and a shower of droplets splashed against the white tiles and trickled down. Sara watched them. In the candlelight, they looked like orange tears, she thought.

"Belinda, you were only sixteen. There wasn't anything you could have done. You can't blame yourself for your baby being taken away. Your father was more powerful than you."

Belinda smiled, but it was a sad smile. "Yeah – just like Philippe was more powerful than me, and Anthony was more powerful than you. When does it change?"

"I don't know. Maybe now."

Both of them slept that night, lying close to each other, touching as lightly as butterflies. Once during the night, Sara was jolted out of the sleep she desperately needed; her dream woke her. In it, she saw Belinda pregnant, but the fetus was growing outside her body. Tiny, webbed-finger hands were clutching to her belly, and milky eyes looked out at a world they weren't supposed to be seeing yet. It was horrifying, although in the dream, Belinda didn't seem to mind.

Sara lay awake for a long time after that, getting up the

nerve to go back to sleep again. She reached over and touched Belinda's stomach, reassuring herself that it had just been a dream, reassuring herself that Belinda hadn't flown away on the dark breeze of a night that still didn't seem real.

Twenty Three

Belinda

BELINDA KNEW what to expect when she got to the courthouse – people who hated her, had names for her, who had distinguished themselves as the Chosen Ones by carving crosses into their foreheads and palms. And the press, shouting questions that collided and became indistinguishable; flashbulbs that blinded her, left bright circles of light on her retinas.

She was in the backseat of Mark's Land Cruiser; he and Sara were in the front. Sara twisted around so she could hold Belinda's hand. Mark glanced at them and Belinda read the questions going through his mind, but he had the grace to keep them to himself. Anyway, she thought, it's not as if she and Sara were lovers. Or were they? They hadn't defined what happened, either because they didn't want to, or weren't able to.

Belinda was wearing an off-white suit one size too big for her. Iris had advised her what to wear. "White, or even a pale beige, will register innocence to the jury," she said. "And I want you to get it at least one size larger than what you usually wear. That way, you'll look frail." Belinda didn't argue. She wanted Philippe to be found guilty, but more than that, she just wanted all of this to end. She hadn't talked to Mark again about his offer to represent her in a civil suit, and he didn't bring it up. One thing at a time, she decided. One day at a time – wasn't that how recovering alcoholics dealt with their addiction? She had become addicted, she knew that – to Philippe and all she had thought he was offering her. She craved the sound of his voice.

Recently, on several nights, the phone had rung, and she'd picked it up each time, wondering if she should. Through the receiver she'd hear a tape of Philippe's voice. She even knew the title of the lectures that the anonymous caller was playing; she'd heard all of his tapes so many times, she practically had them memorized. She knew she should hang up immediately, but the sound of his voice lured her; she was the junkie and the timbre of his voice was heroin. She'd have opened her veins for him. But then she remembered – she had opened her veins for him. Her veins and everything else.

Each night, with each phone call, it was the same: the tug of war between addiction and withdrawal, and then the power surge of memory. In the end, she'd hang up the phone, but it was always a delayed reaction.

"Belinda," Mark said, glancing in the rearview mirror, "Philippe's attorney is very smooth, and very sneaky. Harrison McKee is not someone to take lightly. I just want you to remember that when you're on the stand."

Sara laughed. "Harrison? His first name is Harrison? Sounds like he was named after a town."

"You're thinking of Harrisburg, Sara," Mark told her. "Three Mile Island?"

"Yeah, well – the confusion is understandable. At the preliminary hearing, he reminded me of a nuclear meltdown, only he was just getting started."

Walking into the courtroom, Sara and Mark put Belinda between them – like bodyguards, there to protect her from harm. But she couldn't help thinking that they were too late. She'd already been pulled down by the pack; it had been feeding off her for months. She still wondered if Philippe and his followers truly were in league with God. If that was the case, then she was just the lone sinner, stranded out in the desert, waiting for the vultures to finish her off. But she didn't say any of this to Sara and Mark.

The hallway outside the courtroom was even more crowded than it was at the preliminary hearing. Iris's assistant, a nervous young man whose name Belinda could never remember, was waiting for her at the elevator.

"They're just finishing up opening statements," he said. "Any minute, we'll be able to go in. In the meantime, try to ignore all of this, if you can."

Lights were turned on her and questions bounced around her. The man pulled her through the crowd, separating her from Sara and Mark, and underneath the machine-gun fire of questions, she could hear chants of "Judas." Finally – although it was probably only minutes – the bailiff called her in and she walked into the courtroom where there was only one camera and the reporters had note pads instead of microphones.

As she walked to the stand, Belinda tried to remember when she last ate. She felt dizzy and flushed; sweat was running down her sides. She had thought about fixing some food last night but couldn't recall whether she actually had. After she was sworn in, and sat down, she felt a little more connected to her surroundings. She had been here before; she could handle it again, she told herself. As Iris stood up and began walking toward her, Belinda let her eyes drift over to Philippe. She felt his power immediately – something being sucked out of her. She knew she had to tear her eyes away from his, but it was difficult; his eyes were like the sound of his voice – a junkie's dream. She imagined air bubbles in her veins, traveling toward her heart where air bubbles don't belong.

"Ms. Perry," Iris said firmly. Belinda's thoughts were scattering, and Iris knew it. "I'd like you to tell us what happened on the night of September twenty-first. What were you doing between six and six-thirty of that evening?"

"I was taking a shower," Belinda answered. I have to pay attention, she warned herself. Don't look at Philippe. Don't look at the back rows and the eyes that hate me.

"And then what happened?"

"The phone rang. It was Philippe, asking me if he could come over. He said he'd been thinking about me all day."

That gave her the thread to the story.

She'd recited it so many times, but the beginning was always hard. Once she got his words – the cadence of his voice – in her mind, she could do it.

This time, though, she faltered midway through. Up until now, she'd described their conversation, as they sat on her couch, as one that dealt with the pressures of Philippe's work and the people who opposed his teachings. Through everything, she had kept the secret of his marriage. Since she'd never even heard a rumor about it, she believed that she was the only one who knew. But this time, when she got to that part of the story, something happened. Things around her started to slow down and vibrate with noise. The camera that was recording the proceedings for the evening news sounded louder; the reporters taking notes looked like they were moving underwater. She could hear their pens scratching across the pages of their note pads.

"He told me he has a wife who he can't divorce, but who he never sees or talks about," she blurted out. The noise level rose in the courtroom – a crescendo of voices – until the judge slammed down the gavel. "I can clear this courtroom, and I will if there's another disruption," she said.

Iris Hensley stared at Belinda with an expression that could have been anger or just surprise. Belinda couldn't tell. "Go on, please, Ms. Perry."

"He said his wife is ill with multiple sclerosis, so he doesn't feel he should divorce her. But he keeps her a secret and sends her money. He said he was confiding this to me because he felt so connected to me."

It was at that moment that she dared to look at Philippe again. He was listening to his lawyer; they were leaning into each other, but he was staring at Belinda. She thought of her skin being peeled off, huge sheets of it. She thought of human lampshades and the red, bloody flesh left behind, still glued to the bones as if it didn't know yet that it had no skin. It was how she felt and the image was coming from Philippe's eyes. She fought back, continued the story, back now on familiar ground. She concentrated on Iris's face and on putting all the pieces in order. . . . "Yes, I told him to stop. Yes, he hit me, tied me up, raped me. I said no again, but he hit me again, and then I didn't say anything."

Iris went to her desk, got a large, blown-up photograph and put it on the board so the whole courtroom could view it. "I'd like to mark this as Exhibit One, Your Honor," she said.

She warned Belinda about this, but still it was a shock. Her own face, magnified so that it was huge – the blood on her lip, the blue swelling on her cheek, and eyes that looked flat, dead. Belinda stared at the photograph and wanted to throw something over it – a coat or a blanket. It looked too naked, too exposed.

"This cut on your lip," Iris was saying – Belinda was fighting to pay attention – "was from the defendant's fist, is that your testimony?"

"Yes, he slugged me."

"And the bruise under your eye?"

"He told me to be quiet. I didn't know I was making noise. But he hit me with his fist, and then I tried to stay quiet so he wouldn't hit me again."

"Ms. Perry, you went to the Rape Treatment Center at Santa Monica Hospital just hours after the defendant left your house, is that right?"

"Yes," Belinda said.

"Yet you didn't file a police report until the following day. Why was that?"

"I wasn't sure I had the strength to . . . I didn't know if I could go through all of this."

As Iris Hensley sat down, Belinda started to get up.

"Excuse me, Ms. Perry – I have some questions for you, too," Philippe's attorney said, and she blushed as she sat back down. She'd let her mind scatter again.

McKee took her picture down from the board before walking over to the stand – close, as he had last time. She caught his scent – some kind of cologne or aftershave that smelled expensive. Everything about him was manicured and silken.

"Ms. Perry, my client had been to your house before, hadn't he? By invitation?"

"Yes."

"You'd arranged a dinner party, is that right?"

"Yes, but there were –"

"Just yes or no will do." Harrison McKee paused and

smiled at her. Belinda remembered what Sara said about him before. She was right. This man was Belinda's type – the blueprint for destruction she always went for. She even knew what he drank: red wine with dinner, cognac after. "This dinner party took place after some other private meetings you'd had, is that right?" he continued.

"Yes."

"Several, in fact."

"Yes." Belinda felt the weight of the jury's eyes. They were judging her, and she had to remind herself that she wasn't the one on trial.

"Isn't it fair to say that you were quite infatuated with my client?" McKee asked.

"Objection," Iris said. "This is a trial about rape, not infatuation."

McKee's velvet smile brushed across Belinda on its way to the judge. "What we're trying to find out here, your honor, is if a rape occurred at all, or if it was consensual sex."

"I'll allow it," the judge said. "I'd like to hear the answer."

Belinda tried to sound calm; she felt like he was taking her into dangerous territory. "I don't think I – I mean, no. I wasn't infatuated. I thought of Philippe as my teacher. He was helping me, counseling me."

She dropped her eyes and stared down at her hands. She knew she shouldn't have; but she couldn't help it. And when she looked up again, McKee was in front of her, holding her green velvet dress.

"Mark this as Exhibit A, Your Honor?"

The judge nodded and said yes.

"Is this what you were wearing on the night in question, Ms. Perry?" he asked.

"Yes," Belinda answered.

"And what else were you wearing?" he asked her.

Her voice felt like a thorn stuck in her throat. "Nothing," she said softly.

"I'm sorry – I couldn't hear you. Could you repeat the answer?"

"Nothing," Belinda said, a little more loudly.

"No underwear? No pantyhose? Not even a bra?"

"No."

"Well, was everything in the laundry or is this how you always entertain men at your home? It seems a rather suggestive way of dressing to meet with your teacher. Or maybe this is your usual state of dress. I assume you are wearing underwear now, so is it just at night –"

"Objection!" Iris called out, slapping her hand on the table as she stood up. "Badgering doesn't even begin to describe it."

The judge narrowed her eyes at McKee. "Sustained. You know better, counselor."

Harrison McKee backed up and held the dress away from him, by the shoulders, as if he were a salesman showing it to a shopper.

"The rip along the side here," he said, as he scooped up the dress and held up the damaged part of the fabric.

"You claim this ripped when you were being assaulted, correct?"

"Yes."

"Ms. Perry, this is an old dress, isn't it? An antique? The velvet is thin and seems extremely fragile. I would imagine a dress like this could rip just from putting it on in a hurry, or from sitting down the wrong way."

Belinda was picking at the cuticle of her thumb, holding it away from her suit in case it bled. "I don't know," she said. Her face felt hot.

"At what point exactly did the dress rip?" McKee was close to her again.

"I don't know."

"You have no recollection of when it ripped, yet you're asking the jury to believe that my client ripped this off you during a vicious assault? You're not even sure whether it was intact when you answered the door, are you?"

Belinda opened her mouth to answer, but before words came out, Iris objected.

The judge hesitated for a minute before saying, "I'm going to sustain it. I think you've made your point, Mr. McKee."

He turned his back on Belinda, and for a moment she thought he was done. But he was just putting the dress down.

"It's your testimony that my client bound your wrists to the headboard, correct?" He moved in on her again; once more she smelled his cologne.

"Yes."

"Some people like this kind of rough sex, Ms. Perry. Are you sure you didn't make your preference clear during the intimate discussion the two of you had while sitting on your couch?"

"It's not my preference," Belinda said. "And that's not what we were talking about."

"The cut on your lip could have come from biting down on it, couldn't it?"

"He hit me."

"I know that was your testimony, Ms. Perry, but people have been known to bite their lip, especially during rough sex. They even get bruised sometimes."

Belinda felt her eyes stinging. Harrison McKee knew he could make her cry. He's just like so many others, she thought. "That's not how it happened," she answered defiantly.

"Ms. Perry, you did, in some of your earlier private meetings with my client, discuss past lovers, past intimate relationships, did you not?"

"Yes."

She saw herself in Philippe's office, with its dim, filtered light and its thermostat-controlled climate.

"In fact, you talked about past liaisons in detail, didn't you?"

"I guess so, yes."

"And didn't you tell him about how some of your lovers were very angry, hostile men, but you stayed with them anyway, continued to take unkind treatment?"

"But it wasn't –"

"Just yes or no, Ms. Perry."

"I'm not sure. I might have." She couldn't remember whom she told him about. It was like acid had been spilled across her memory. Some of it had been eaten away.

"When you were sitting on the couch," McKee asked, "who initiated physical contact?"

"I just touched his hand."

"But before that, my client didn't touch you at all, is that correct? I mean, before you reached over and took his hand?"

"No, I guess not."

"Thank you, Ms. Perry. That will be all."

When they got back to her house, Belinda let Mark and Sara stay for a while, fixed tea, and tried to believe them when they told her that she did well on the stand. "You were as precise as anyone could be under the circumstances," Mark said. "That guy's good. Did you notice that he never objected once when the D.A. was questioning you? He just sits back and then moves in for the kill. I don't think that stuff about the dress is going to fly, though. It was a long shot. I mean, most people wouldn't be able to pinpoint exactly when their clothes got ripped during a rape."

Sara brushed the hair off Belinda's forehead. "You know, that asshole Philippe had twice as many people there this time than he did at the preliminary hearing. What's he doing – mailing out pen knives with instruction cards? Join the masses – carve a crucifix on your body and come to the courthouse."

After about forty minutes, Belinda said, "I'm tired. I need to take a nap." What she really wanted was to be alone. She wanted to look in the mirror and see if the sign of the beast was still visible on her forehead.

When Sara hugged her good-bye, she said, "Belinda, you never told me about Philippe's wife. That was kind of a shock, to put it mildly."

"I never told anyone – until today."

After they left, she stared at her face in the mirror for a long time. At moments, it looked familiar to her, but then a stranger would move in, take over, look back at her as if through a window.

She didn't bother to take off her suit. She kicked off her shoes, peeled the blankets back from the bed, and lay down. The coolness of the sheets made her think of the surface of a lake. She imagined herself drifting, floating on top of glassy water like a leaf. Weightless.

It was almost dark when she woke up. Without turning on any lights, she walked through the house and opened the front door. She wasn't sure if they had knocked, or if she just happened to wake up right when they arrived. It didn't matter anyway – she'd been expecting them. The crosses on their foreheads had become scars; the scabs had healed, but the marks were deep enough to be permanent.

"Let us in, Belinda," Kenneth said.

Astrid and Michelle stood behind him, watching Belinda with narrowed eyes. She moved aside, let them pass, hypnotized by them, and then followed them into the living room. The moon was shedding white light onto the floor – enough to see by, but it reminded her of ghosts – eerie and transient.

"Lie down on the floor," Astrid told Belinda.

With the movements of a sleepwalker, she did, keeping her eyes open to their faces above her. They were on their knees, leaning over her like petals of a flower, closing up for the night.

"We warned you," Kenneth said. "We told you what you were doing to your soul. How are you going to endure the weight of your blasphemy? You've saturated yourself with evil. A savior was brought to you and you tried to crucify him. It's a blessing that your child was taken from you."

"What?" Belinda said in a hoarse whisper. How did they know? Philippe must have told them – another betrayal, but maybe it was just more of what she deserved.

"A child conceived in sin," Kenneth added.

Her three visitors didn't know it, and Belinda didn't tell them, but there was a fourth person with them. Not a person, actually, but a spirit. He was hiding there, trapped in the shaft of moonlight. Belinda could see him, see her father alternately shaking his head sadly and nodding in agreement – the sadness was for her sins; the agreement was for her punishment. She thought of her bed sheets and how they felt like the surface of water. She was light enough to float there, just hours ago. But she must have been mistaken. Maybe she'd been sinking all along and hadn't known it.

"Philippe told us there would be those in our midst who would turn against us," Astrid said. Her voice was brittle, as though she'd aged decades in days. "It turned out to be you. Even though he tried to help you, opened his heart to you, you sold him to those who want to see his work destroyed."

"Just like Judas," Michelle added.

"How will you live with yourself? The days will be so dark."

Belinda couldn't tell anymore who was talking. The room was darker and their voices were all starting to sound the same. She was being pushed under the surface, heavy as a stone. Didn't Philippe do that to her once, when he made her dive down into the deepest waters of her memory? She wanted to be weightless again, but they were telling her she never would be – sinners are heavy people; they leave footprints wherever they go. Belinda thought of mud – a soft river bottom where all heavy objects ended up if they fell into the water. It was probably better along the river bottom – smooth, no footprints.

Suddenly, she realized it was quiet around her – dead quiet. They were gone. She got up, found her car keys, and walked out the front door without closing it behind her. The street was silent. They had disappeared as if they were phantoms. But she knew they weren't.

She drove down Wilshire Boulevard, through Santa Monica to the bluffs, and then turned right. The ramp took her down to the Coast Highway and the smell of the sea. With the ocean on her left, she drove north to Topanga Canyon and turned inland. The canyon was dark and the air seemed colder along the winding road that hugged the mountain and took her higher, closer to the stars. Her car complained, but she stepped down harder on the gas as the road got steeper.

Midway up, just around a sharp curve, she saw the turnout she was looking for – a place where people could pull over if they had trouble, or if they wanted to look at the view. Gravel crunched under the tires when she pulled over. She got out of the car, left the keys in the ignition, and stood looking out at the canyon. A deep ravine yawned like a black hole below her; somewhere down there the creek snaked along, flowing quickly now after all the rain they'd had. The moon dangled above her, making her off-shade suit glow pure white.

Her skirt caught on the guard rail as she climbed over it, but came loose after only a second. She let her hand steady her, hold her in place, and she felt her body's weight, made heavier by her sins.

When her hand let go, it was as if the air claimed her. For an instant, she was caught on a wind current, or at least that was the way it seemed to her. Then she picked up speed. The moon chased her down, which didn't surprise her. It probably thought she belonged to it – a splinter that broke off. A girl in white who would be much lighter once her flight was over, once she hit the bottom.

Twenty Four

Sara

SARA WOKE with the feeling that some part of her sleep had been disturbed, either in dreams or in one of the restless spaces in between. It was still early – the sky barely light – but she couldn't go back to sleep. Her mind kept trying to grab onto the thread of something – something vague and shadowy that hovered just out of reach.

She got up, fixed coffee, brought the paper in, but couldn't bring herself to read about yesterday's court proceedings. It was a front-page story; Belinda's picture, alongside one of Philippe, stared up at her. She folded the paper in half and told herself she'd get to it later.

She wasn't sure why she turned on the television. It wasn't something she normally did. Maybe she just needed some sound in the house, something to keep her company – voices and silly commercial jingles that told her the whole world was happy. She was brushing her teeth when she heard it.

"A man driving home last night, up Topanga Canyon Boulevard, was too late to stop what appeared to be a suicide. He came around the curve just as an unidentified woman was climbing over the guard rail."

Sara ran out of the bathroom and stood in front of the television with her toothbrush still in her mouth.

"We have a camera crew on the scene where rescue workers have brought up the body from the rocks below. No identification will be released until next of kin are notified. According to the witness, the woman left her car, climbed over this guard rail . . ."

That was when the camera showed the car. A yellow VW bug. The toothbrush fell out of Sara's mouth. "Jesus God – no," she said, although the words barely got out, her throat was so constricted. She didn't hear the rest of the news story. She dialed Belinda's number, saying to herself, "Answer, Belinda. Please answer. Please be there."

But the phone just kept ringing – no answer. Even the answering machine didn't pick up. She might have unplugged the phone, Sara thought, desperate to come up with alternatives to what she feared the most. Panic was strangling her; it felt like a snake wrapping itself around her body, squeezing out every bit of strength.

She threw on some clothes, grabbed her purse, and told herself that when she got to Belinda's, she'd find her asleep with the phone unplugged and the answering machine turned off deliberately. Her VW would be right there on the street, right where she usually parked it. After all, there had to be more than one yellow VW bug in Los Angeles.

She told herself all of this and more, chanting it like a mantra as she drove into Westwood, trying to ignore the chilly arms that wouldn't release her, wouldn't even let her get enough oxygen. Her prayers became more fervent when she turned onto Belinda's street, and then fear welled up again. Her car wasn't there.

Sara tried to run down the path to the rear guest house, but her legs felt so heavy, a fast walk was all she could manage. She wanted the scent of jasmine incense to be drifting out of the house, and the sound of Paul Simon or U2. When she saw the door standing open, Sara stopped, too afraid to move closer. There was no smell of incense or morning coffee, no sound of life at all. Only silence hobbled out to greet her, like some squatter who had moved in during the night.

Finally she got her feet to move. The house was cold, or maybe it was just that Sara's blood was getting thinner by the minute. Soon it would be water. Belinda's purse was on the dining room table. Sara opened it and found everything there but her car keys. Her wallet had money in it, credit cards, a few receipts stuck in one of the pockets. She walked into the bedroom and saw the blankets stripped back, the pillows wrinkled as if someone had clutched them tightly. She didn't know why, but she looked in the closet. Nothing looked different; it was a mess, as usual. In the kitchen, she found an almost empty refrigerator, and two bottles of Stoli in the freezer. An open box of Saltines was on the counter. It looked like Belinda had been living on crackers and vodka. No wonder she kept shooing Sara out of her house.

Footsteps were coming down the path. Sara ran to the front door and said, "Belinda?" just as Mark came around the corner of the front house. "Mark, what are you doing here?"

Without saying anything, Mark hugged her and then she knew. She'd known all along, really, ever since she woke up that morning. But it was too horrible a reality to just accept without a fight.

"Are you sure?" Sara asked, still trying to fight it.

"Yes. I called someone I know at the police department. I told him I was her attorney. Her mother was notified.

She went down to the morgue a little while ago and identified the body. She lives in L.A. – not that far from here. Somehow that surprised me. Did Belinda ever see her mother or talk about her?"

Sara shook her head. "Oh God, Mark, I can't cry. All I feel is rage. They did this to her. That bastard – he broke her."

Mark held her tighter. "I know," he said. "I think we should get out of here now. I'll stay with you as long as you want. I don't think you should be alone."

"Yeah – okay." She turned around and closed Belinda's door. It seemed irreverent to leave it open.

Mark stayed with Sara for most of the day. There were moments when a few tears escaped, but they had trouble getting past Sara's anger. She knew grief would take a long time to surface.

Court had already been called into session by the time Belinda's name was released on the news. It was Philippe's day to testify. The jury wasn't supposed to listen to the news or read the papers, but even if they didn't know that Belinda was dead, Sara guessed that Philippe probably did.

She needed to do something – for Belinda, for herself, for all the pain that Belinda hadn't been able to live with. What did she say that night – when does it change? And Sara had answered, "Maybe now." But she would have to do something – things don't change on their own. By late afternoon, she had made a decision.

"Mark, you don't have to hang around anymore. I'll be okay," she said, gathering up all the coffee cups they'd left around the house. They'd both had too much coffee and not enough food.

"Are you sure?" Mark looked at her suspiciously. He knew her too well.

"I'm sure. I think I need some time alone."

On his way out the door he said, "I'm going to call you later and make sure you're all right."

After he left, Sara went and stood by the phone, staring at it. After several minutes she dialed Anthony's number. She wasn't sure what she'd do if his machine picked up. She didn't want to leave a message.

"Yes?" he said after the first ring. It was his business voice, his this-is-the-fiftieth-call-today voice.

"Hi, it's Sara."

She anticipated the change in his tone even before she heard it. "Sara, how are you? I heard about Belinda on the radio. I didn't know if I should call you or – I mean, I was going to, but after a few – God, it's so terrible. You must really be going through hell. Are you holding up okay?"

He was stammering. Good, Sara thought. He's nervous. "Anthony, I want to see you," she said, her own voice amazingly calm. "I guess I realized, with what happened to Belinda, that I really need you – especially now."

"Sure, I'll come over," he told her.

"No. I think I'd feel better meeting you someplace." She paused. "Actually, what I want to do is meet you at Joey's. I want to go back there – retrace our steps, I guess." She was forcing herself to sound soft and sincere – an engraved invitation with a flowered border. "You were right," she continued, "I reacted too quickly. I guess it was all just too much. But I don't want it to end like that."

Anthony hesitated. She could sense him thinking and

was afraid he was going to say no. She didn't know what she'd do then – she didn't have a back up plan.

"Are you sure that it's a good idea to do that now?" he asked finally. "I mean, I don't want it to end like that either. I don't want it to end at all. But this is a rough time for you. Wouldn't you rather – "

"I want to go back there," she interrupted. "I think that's where you and I need to be to work this out. I can meet you tonight. Do you think Joey will let us?"

"Probably . . . Okay, I'll meet you there at eight. If there's a problem on Joey's end, I'll call you back. Sara –"

"Yes?"

"I really have missed you."

"I'll see you at eight."

The evening news showed a portion of Philippe's trial testimony earlier that day. After he had invoked the Fifth Amendment over twenty times, his composure cracked, making a guilty verdict somewhat inevitable. The jury saw glimpses of a madman. "I know what people need better than they do," he said, looking from the jury to the courtroom camera, his face red, angry, perspiration on his forehead. "Every one of you should turn yourselves over to me if you want to be saved. But so few of you have the courage."

Sara watched his performance with no emotion. So, he'd be found guilty, go to jail, probably appeal, lose the appeal, and serve some more time in jail. So what? Belinda's dead, she thought – that's all that matters, and that can't be undone.

She took a shower, put on a pair of loose black slacks and a green silk blouse. She deliberately didn't put on a bra or underpants, but this time it wasn't for Anthony's benefit. She didn't want anything binding her.

She knew when the phone rang a little after seven that it was Mark. Throughout the day, friends who had known both her and Belinda had called, but on TV the news had just ended... .

"Did you see the news?" Mark asked when she answered the phone.

"Uh-huh. I'm surprised his attorney didn't kill him right there in the courtroom."

"He probably wanted to," Mark said. "So, what are you doing now? Do you want me to come over there? Bring you some dinner?"

"No – actually, I'm going out."

"Where? Sara, I don't like the way you sound. Where are you going?"

"Back to the orchard," she said softly.

"Excuse me?"

"You heard me. Mark, don't worry, okay? I'm not going to do anything illegal. But I am going to settle a score, and this time you can't help me."

Anthony's car was in the driveway when she got to Joey's. The maid answered the door, ushered her in, and Joey and Anthony walked out of the living room into the foyer. Anthony's expression was tender and expectant. He kissed her lightly on the cheek and said, "How are you?" as if he really wanted to know.

"I'm doing okay," she answered. "Considering."

She shook Joey's hand and said, "Thanks for letting us come over. I got freaked out the other night and I knew for Anthony and me to work this out, we had to go back in there together – try to make it turn out differently this time."

Such a pretty liar I've become, she thought, looking at Joey with gratitude she didn't feel, seducing him away from what she knew he'd assumed. He'd been counting on joining them. In your dreams, she said to herself. He caught on and with only a hint of disappointment, said, "Sure – well, you two go on."

Sara could sense Christine's absence from the house. Either another fight or a shopping trip, she figured, but then, she didn't really care.

Apparently seeing it as good hospitality, Joey had unlocked the door to the dungeon for them and turned on the lights. Sara took a deep breath when she crossed the threshold into the red world she'd run away from not that long ago. She hadn't planned every detail of what was to happen; she'd left room for inspiration. Anthony closed the door and she turned around to face him.

"Come here," she said, and watched expectation glimmer in his eyes.

She put her arms around his neck and kissed him. His mouth was so familiar, but she closed her eyes and thought of Belinda's mouth.

He pulled away and stared at her. She could see, in his glasses, the reflection of her own eyes. "I really did miss you," he said. "I'm glad you called, especially right now. I mean, I know this has got to be a really painful time for you."

Sara unbuttoned his shirt. She'd always liked him in a white shirt, but now she couldn't wait to get it off him. She tugged at the buttons on his Levi's, but before she could finish, Anthony walked over to the leather bed, sat down and took off his shoes and socks. Then he stood up, peeled off his Levi's, and tossed them into the corner, near the metal contraption that could stretch a person to an uncomfortable extent. That was when Sara knew exactly what she was going to do. He stood before her naked, expectant, but what he didn't know was, the tables had turned. It was payback time.

She walked over to him slowly and stood just inches away. She reached up gently and took off his glasses, putting them on the leather bed where he could retrieve them later. Anthony put his arms around her waist, kissed her again, and she let him – still keeping her secrets to herself, still playing out her deception. His hands checked her out through the fabric of her clothes; she knew what he was thinking – that she had dressed for him. But then he thought everything was for him – Narcissus at the pond, seeing only his own reflection.

"Take off your clothes," he whispered.

"Not yet. Come over here."

She took his hand and led him to the corner where the steel bar hung from the ceiling, shining in the soft red light. The leather cuffs dangled just above his head, but she turned the handle on the wall and lowered them until they were level with his shoulders. She looked down at his body. He was almost hard, but she wanted more. She lifted his arms gently, put his wrists in the cuffs and buckled them in. But she didn't turn the handle yet. His elbows were bent, his hands clasped in front of him; it almost looked like he was praying. She kissed him again, played with his tongue, ran her fingernails down over his nipples, scraping them, pinching them – hurting him just enough to turn him on. Her right hand grasped his cock; she was so attuned to his body, her hand knew just how he liked it. It was the rhythm of their brief history together – her hand on his cock, or her mouth, or the movement of their bodies together. It seemed like an old dance now. She stopped just when she knew he wanted her to go faster.

"Sara, I want to see your body," Anthony said. "Take off —"

"Not yet," she told him again.

She began turning the wheel, tightening the cable that was attached to the leather cuffs. His hands rose slowly. When his arms were straight above his head and his feet were still planted firmly on the floor, she turned the wheel once more, forcing him onto his toes. That was when she saw the first flicker of doubt on his face, but he composed himself, looked at her again as if he trusted her completely. She knelt in front of him, licked his cock, taking it in her mouth for a moment, but only long enough to confuse him. Her teeth grazed the tender skin around the tip, leaving red marks there – something to remember her by. Then she put the metal cuffs around his ankles and locked them in, slipping the key into the pocket of her slacks. She stood up again, directly in front of him, and looked into his eyes. There it was, she saw it – the beginning of fear.

"How do you feel, Anthony?"

"Loosen my arms, Sara. You pulled them too tight." His voice sounded strained, but he was still forcing himself to be calm. "You've never done this before. You're not doing it right – it's too tight."

"Oh well, let me loosen it, then," she said. But she didn't. Instead, she grabbed the handle and tightened the cable some more. She watched his shoulders stretch up painfully. The muscles on his arms resisted and he arched his neck back and screamed.

"Sara – don't do this, please!"

Ignoring his pain – or pretending to – she walked slowly to the opposite side of the room where the pieces of twine and rope were piled in the corner along with the jewel-handled dagger. Pirate's treasure.

There is an art to revenge – she knew that. It was a lesson she'd learned years ago; her hand had learned it when the soft bones of Jerome's face broke beneath its force. Revenge requires seduction and an aim that's cold, perfect. After that day in the orchard she'd sworn she'd never choose that method again, and in a way she was being true to that vow. This was not a matter of choice; it was the only way to free herself from Anthony. It was what he would do if he had to. Once again, she felt him guiding her movements – his bones, her muscles; his blood transfused into hers.

She picked up the dagger and a piece of twine, and returned, stopping in front of him.

He looked at the dagger and then at her. Pain was etched across his forehead and his eyes pleaded with her. "Sara, I know you're angry. But you don't know what you're doing."

She dropped the dagger on the floor near his shackled feet. "Actually, Anthony," she told him, as she wrapped the twine three times around his cock before knotting it, "I know exactly what I'm doing."

She pulled his cock down and attached the other end of the twine to the metal ring between his feet. When she stood up again, he was crying.

"Does it hurt?" she asked.

He nodded yes. He was breaking – slowly – a monarch who had suddenly become a prisoner.

She saw his pain, ached along with some of it, but wouldn't permit it to alter the course she'd chosen. They were sequestered there, the two of them – teacher and student – and the student was proving how thorough her education had been.

"You didn't count on this, did you, Anthony? What's

that saying – when the student is ready the teacher is there? Or is it the other way around? You did teach me, but I'm a fast learner. Now it's my turn to teach you. Here's the lesson: You shouldn't ask someone to trust you, seduce them into trusting you, and then turn on them. You humiliated me, Anthony. You stood me up against the wall and opened fire. Humiliation wasn't part of what you taught me; it wasn't supposed to be part of the game. But it always was a part of your plan, wasn't it, Anthony? So, now you're paying the price for that. Did you really think there wouldn't be any consequences?"

"Sara, please." He was practically yelling now, but it didn't matter. The sound would be absorbed by fiberglass and red velvet. He strained against the cuffs holding his wrists and his feet, but it did no good.

She had expected all the fear to belong to him, but when she bent down and picked up the dagger, fear rose up in her, too. She turned away for a moment, trying to stem the tide. Regaining control, she forced her eyes to remain hard, cold, and she tightened her grip on the dagger to stop her hand from shaking.

"Jesus, don't," Anthony said. His voice cracked.

"What's wrong, Anthony?" she said. "This game is one you know about – fear – but not from the helpless side of it, right? I'm in control of the game now."

But even as she said it, she wasn't sure. Her control was slipping. Anger was mixed in with her fear, turning everything into one huge dangerous wave.

She stood a few inches from him and traced the tip of the dagger along the muscles of his chest, up along the collarbone and across the hollow of his throat. She dropped it down to his cock, wrapped in twine and tied down. She lifted his balls up with the dull edge of the blade. The shaking in her hand was getting worse. Belinda's face swam through her mind and she thought, for a quick second, that she smelled coconut lotion. But it couldn't be. She was here with Anthony – alone in this red chamber – and Belinda was gone. She ran the tip of the dagger around his nipples in wide circles. A low moan escaped from him; he was pleading but he was too exhausted to be any louder. He was crying again, and if he weren't stretched so tight, he would probably be trembling. Belinda wouldn't leave; Sara saw her face, saw her falling through the long night and crashing against the rocks, ending up as red as the floor that Anthony's toes were barely touching.

This was too dangerous – she knew it. She'd waded in too far. Hadn't there been times when she'd held Anthony, stroked his face, wondered if she loved him? The images were dull – fogged up by her rage. She had him strung up – helpless and hurting. She had a knife in her hand, and all that anger inside her. This is how killers are born, she thought. The temptation to do serious damage wins out; an arm pulls back, lunges forward, and lives are changed forever.

She didn't mean to – or maybe she did – but suddenly the knife blade wasn't teasing anymore. It cut an inch-long gash above Anthony's left breast – not that deep, really, but blood oozed from it. He gasped, cried out, and then Sara felt something warm on her foot. He was so scared he'd peed. She stepped back, but it was her own fear that sent her reeling away from him, over to the wall where her arm drew back, and with a strength that shocked her, plunged the dagger into red velvet. The wall bled fiberglass where she'd stabbed it.

"Goddamn you!" she screamed, turning back around to

face him, leaving the dagger in the wall. "Did you think you could just go on fucking up people's lives and never have it turned back on you? I hate you for what you did to me! And I hate you for what happened to Belinda!" Her throat hurt from screaming like that.

"I didn't kill Belinda," Anthony sobbed.

"Yes, you did – you and every man like you – every man who lives off other people's pain. You're all the same. You may have different names, but it doesn't matter. After a while, you all have the same face."

Sobs were racking his body; it looked as though he was trying to say something, but no words could get out. Sara stared at him, and saw the faint shadow of a seven-year-old boy, weeping confused tears at the torture of being forced to kneel in prayer while his father towered over him naked, with an erection he neither touched nor used on his son. Was it sex or punishment? And what were the prayers supposed to be for? The child didn't know, and the man didn't either. But Anthony had spent years making everyone pay – especially women. They'd been paying for his mother's sin of sliding past the open doorway with blind eyes. Looking at him now, Sara almost unlocked his feet, almost let him down. Lesson completed – you're free to go. But she didn't. She had her own anger and she felt entitled to it, no matter how many other emotions were laced through it. To release him would be to grant him amnesty, and she didn't feel that generous. His bondage was her freedom – at least for the moment.

"You know what I really hate you for?" she said, clenching her teeth against the rush of anger and tears, and other things she couldn't even define. "Even to free myself from you, I had to become like you. Years ago, I swore I'd never again resort to revenge. But with you I didn't have a choice. You never gave me any choice, Anthony."

She turned slowly and walked out, leaving the door open and Anthony hanging there. His arms were probably numb, stretched above his head so long, and a thin trickle of blood was making its way down over his heart.

Joey must have heard her footsteps; he was waiting for her in the foyer. His eyes widened when he saw her face – her expression must have looked frightening – and he opened his mouth to say something. But she walked past him and opened the front door. Her other hand fingered the tiny key in her pocket. Turning to him, she took it out and held it up.

"You might want to unlock his feet and let him down," she said. "He's probably very uncomfortable." But instead of handing him the key, she threw it past the willow tree into a deep bed of flowers. "And don't worry about the blood – it's a shallow wound."

Her tires screeched down the driveway and she barely waited for the electric gate to open before stepping down hard on the gas and speeding away. The night smelled like roses; her mouth tasted like salt. The onslaught of tears had begun and she knew it wouldn't end soon. So this is what grief feels like, she thought, wiping her eyes with the back of her hand so she could see the road ahead of her. It's the softer side of rage, the underbelly – pale and vulnerable and full of tears.

She drove down the hill in the vague direction of home, but she didn't want to go home yet. Along the coast, fog rested like a blanket, white and forgiving. She pulled into one of the beach parking lots, locked her car doors, and sat staring out at the surf. She thought about losing her virginity when she was seventeen – how she'd hoped it would be a life-changing event. It wasn't then, but this time it was. Because that was really what Anthony had done – he had taken her virginity, imprinted her, schooled her in the dark eroticism of surrender. But he had schooled her in other things, too – fear, humiliation, and ultimately betrayal. None of it would go away easily. Its calligraphy was written on her soul.

When Sara finally drove home and climbed into bed, it was only a formality – she knew she wouldn't sleep. She thought about the memories that pile up during a life. There were those she wanted to breathe life into and those she wanted to bury. But she knew that burying memories is hard, if not impossible. The best she could do would be to lay them in a shallow grave where any rough season could scrape by and expose them again. She closed her eyes and pictured Belinda – how little like a memory she seemed. It was strange to think she couldn't just dial her phone number and talk to her.

Hours had gone by – almost the entire night. It was the blue hour just before dawn, the hour when ghosts are most likely to come, if they come at all. Sara was still wide awake.

"I told you it would change, Belinda," she whispered. "If you'd just waited. Everything would have been different. Why did this have to happen to you?"

She got up and walked to the window, let the curtains float around her, brush her skin. She thought – but it had to be a trick of the light, a mirage of that blue time of day – she thought she saw a black BMW with the headlights turned off driving slowly past her house.

$9\frac{1}{2}$ WEEKS

Elizabeth McNeill

A woman. A man. Nothing – but nothing – else mattered.

The first time we were in bed together he held my hands pinned down above my head. I liked it.

The second time he picked my scarf up off the floor, smiled and said, 'Would you let me blindfold you?'

The third time I heard my voice, disembodied above the bed, pleading with him to continue.

I was beginning to fall in love . . .

$9\frac{1}{2}$ WEEKS is the story of a love affair like no other: a crazy, obsessive relationship that burned through two lives like a branding iron through flesh. To read it is to undergo a truly disturbing – and erotic – experience . . .

THE AFTERNOONS OF A WOMAN OF LEISURE

Elizabeth Bennett

Joanna has everything a woman could desire: as the young, beautiful wife of a wealthy financier, her days are her own to spend at leisure – but her nights are solitary. Her older husband sleeps alone, and Joanna increasingly seeks a sense of fulfilment, some trace of danger and excitement to satisfy her.

Several chance encounters shock Joanna into action. She becomes involved with the mysterious 'O', a woman whose clients and employees experiment with pleasure, pain and 'issues of control'. Joanna's experiences with 'O' are exciting, but also dangerous. Identities are revealed, alliances shifted and plots undertaken. Joanna begins to gather secrets and to lay the foundation of her terrible revenge: graphic, erotic and ultimately murderous.

SCRUPLES

Judith Krantz

SCRUPLES . . .
A temple of high fashion where the rich and the super-chic could sip champagne, browse, gossip – and buy the most beautiful clothes in the world.

SCRUPLES . . .
The dreamchild of the fabled Billy Ikehorn, whose ruthless search for fulfilment would lead her from lover to lover before she met the one man who could match her ambition and her passion.